The Final Fifty: Escape the Poison
Emma Ellis

Copyright © 2023 by Emma Ellis

All rights reserved.

No portion of this book may be reproduced in any form without written permission from the publisher or author, except as permitted by U.S. copyright law.

Cover by Miblart

Prologue

The Tunnels

How can it be, in a bid to save my family, to rid them of the destruction of the Raft and the strangling grip of the Centre, that all I have found is tyranny?

I wrote a book once, detailing my life and the decisions I made. An attempt to justify my part in the regime that governed us, perhaps. Or maybe I wrote it as an educational tool, to inform people of the depths of the deception they were living under. To explain how my world crumbled, and how we found solace here.

Now I find it hard to remember my reasons for writing it. It seems like a lifetime has passed since then. The final pages of that book would seem so untrue now, full of misleading confidence and empty promises, though that's nothing the people of the Raft weren't used to. Coming from me, especially. My words were as polluted as the Raft. Fiction portrayed as fact. I left that book behind in a moment of optimism.

Optimism. Such a big word, and as lost as the Raft now.

This was meant to be a stronger place. Rock solid. The foundations of the planet carved so beautifully, yet with such brutal force. That contradiction should have been a warning. Nothing beautiful can come from such filth. Was I naive to not have seen this coming? Rock can be broken, chipped away, eroded by mere wind. In reality, it's as brittle as our bones.

This is not just my story now, but hers too. Survival is something we are all lumbered with. The monotony of on and on, the cyclical way life comes back to gnaw and mock and remind you of every mistake you've ever made. The sheer task of existence weighs us down, her more than most.

I'm tired. Of division, of us and them, of holding our differences together with the glue of lies. I'm bored of it. Let my anger be released, let it blossom in a way hope once did. For somehow, reader, we are here again. At that rocky precipice. Only this time, I don't know if I have the strength to climb.

Perhaps my friend will instead.

Chapter 1

The Raft

I stumbled away from the edge, tripping over rubble and crevices, heaving myself back to standing and looking down at swollen feet. When did they start looking like that? Grey and cracked like gnarled old pavement. Oversized, bloodied, and bruised. Shoes long gone, cast away with everything else that made me feel human.

My catch was lost, slipped from my hands and fallen among the cracks. I scrabbled on my knees, fumbling for anything that was not gravel and tarmac, looking for the welcoming softness of flesh. I found the fish with its half-eaten side still dripping. Its open mouth looked sad, little pointed teeth frowning at me. Too late for emotions now.

My last packaged food had run out the day before, scavenged from half-collapsed apartment blocks and the dregs of old food stores. Was it the day before, or maybe the day before that? It was too hard to tell in the smog. Too hard to know anything. I had lost track of the days long before. It hurt to count them. I'd been alone too long.

The fish would have to do. It was better than starving, anyway. I took another bite and chewed. Not so bad, not really. I'd had worse.

I sat and waited for it to kick in, for the sharp edges to become fuzzy, and for colours to pierce the grey. But the relief didn't come. Not these days. All I had was pain and guilt. Were the pharmaceuticals and narcotics less concentrated in the fish now, perhaps? I hadn't bothered with a testing kit for a while. Hadn't even seen one.

My stomach growled, a beach ball over emaciated hips. One fish wasn't enough and sobriety wasn't easy to endure. More. That would fix it. More.

Finding more was a simple task. They came up for air, gasping at the barrier between my world and theirs. What sad little lives they had. Born half-dead, their own world discarding them, kicking them out, alive yet lifeless.

Sounds familiar.

They were slow, high on their own pollutants, probably. I lay down at the broken concrete and reached over, grabbing the biggest creature I could manage, squeezing it hard as it tried to slither free.

The concrete dipped and started to break up as I crawled away. Slowly. No point being quick. Death was proving to be too slow, anyway. It loitered in the shadows, a lethargic presence refusing to show itself. I'd cheated it for too long.

I'm here! Come and take me!

I licked my fingers clean, lips smacking against the last tendrils of flesh. My hands still looked grimy, sludge embedded under my fingernails, the sea coating me completely. How was I not dead yet?

Hurry up, death. I've been waiting for months.

The movement inside me reminded me why, banging against my insides like I was a door being forced open. My fight for life could not end just yet. I needed to stay away from the edge for a little longer.

I'll try, little one. I'll try.

The fish kicked in and the air began to spin around me, hazy wisps of smog becoming hazier, the sharp edges of my mind no longer jagged but smooth and slippery. I could glide from one thought to the next. The world looked like a bad picture of itself, an impression. What were those pictures called again, the ones that don't look like anything? Paintings. That was it. The world looked like a painting. With a grin, I picked scales from between my teeth and stood. The concrete buckled and broke away, right up to my toes. I crunched them into balls. There was nothing but air underneath. I could jump in, let the slurry take me, the waves sucking the last of my breath away.

There had been frequent moments of clarity over recent months, but this was not one of them. I had been here before, countless times, with this longing for the dark. The smog wasn't thick enough, it still allowed me to see. The fish wasn't strong enough, I could still remember. I ate more, as quickly as I could, sucking at bones, a rancid burp to finish. A softness closed in.

That's better. I'm ready now.

But then, that voice came. The voice I longed for licked at my ears. A whisper in the wind.

You have to try. Promise me.

A new longing replaced the old. I wouldn't jump. Not yet.

I backed away, each heavy, swollen footstep reminding me of the promise I had made. It was always there in my mind, behind the curtain of fish guts and regret. There was a point to this hell. Purgatory was not without purpose.

In my daze, I felt his hand holding mine, for a while at least. Even in the heat, it felt cold.

I'll join you soon, my love.

I had a dream that day. A dream, but not a dream. I was awake but not awake. A man called to me. This one didn't come with the threats or sharp knives I was used to. He had a voice of kindness. The state of me was usually enough to make the looters and muggers recoil and run away. But this man stayed.

How long had it been since I'd known kindness? The passage of time was evident only in my cramps, my skin stretching daily to remind me of it. When I was lost in my fugue state, gravity reminded me, counting the weeks in ways I could not. All the things that I had forgotten but not forgotten, masked by the guise of delirium and denial. Perhaps it had been merely days, and this man was one of many. But nonetheless, there he was, imaginary or not. Calling to me, unfamiliar, wary.

I carried on walking. I had no business with him. Why should he give a shit about me anyway?

'Come with me, dearie.'

I lifted my head to look at him, unbalancing myself as I did so and staggering backwards. He caught me and I shook him free. I didn't need any more men saving me.

'Take this, please,' the man said and handed me a packet. 'Come with me. Let me help you.'

He grabbed my arm, and I shook myself free again.

'Here, take the whole box. There's some juice in there too. You need the vitamins.'

Vitamins. They used to matter. Not now though. Nothing mattered now.

That familiar voice again, carrying on the wind, making my heart jump and then sink. *You're all that matters now. Please live. Please.*

I took the box.

'I'll come find you tomorrow to see how you are,' the man said. 'You should look for food within the fence. There's more in the apartments there. And stay away from the edge. You could come back with me, if you like? Maybe you'll think about it? There's a nice apartment next to where I live with my wife. We can look after you. You need help, in your condition.'

The fog whipped up. The smog obscured his silhouette, leaving me alone in the darkness. That made me feel better. I sat down and drank the juice he'd given me, then went for a piss. I was always pissing those days. Annoying. It was getting near impossible to stand from a squat. My legs didn't want to behave. *Who cares?* Useless legs would make me drown nice and quickly. When the time came, I'd sink like a stone.

I slept, somehow. The roaring waves woke me, along with the rough concrete digging into my bones. I couldn't tell if it was day or night; the smog was so thick. I felt hot, too hot. Perhaps the sea would be cool. The waves were thrashing at the concrete, closer than the day before, or had I just sleepwalked closer to the edge? They were calling me, reaching out for me to join them. I got up to walk over, just a look. I was not risking death that day. I'd stay sober.

Yeah, right. I'd been telling myself that for months.

But I would. I had food, lots of it in the box beside me. The oblong box looked like it once contained shoes and was now filled with little packets and open wrappers. Where had it come from? I struggled to think. Some kind man, some angel, perhaps? He was here, then went that way, maybe. Down that street where the buildings still stood and most of the glass was unbroken. Or maybe the other way, with the collapsed buildings, the development that was never finished, the cracked road that was soon to give way. How was I meant to know? The part of my brain that knew directions and landscapes had long gone to sleep.

What's the point?

I picked up the box and found it heavy, its corners cutting into my forearms. I must have been getting weaker.

I opened a packet and ate. It was dry, like eating dust, and too sweet. The juice was sour, but I needed the fluids. Fish were salty, so it was complimentary, maybe? The idea didn't repulse me like it would have before, in that other life, when other food was abundant. I stared at the fish, goading me, tempting me.

No. Not today.

He came back. Later that day, or in the night, or the next. I couldn't be sure. The air was like tar, the stringy smog sticking to my face. Mostly it was dark, but sometimes there was a light, a sporadic hint of sun or moon, streetlights flaring momentarily before flickering off. Just to taunt me. It was mainly black, as welcoming as death.

But he was there. Walking in the near-darkness, his torch cutting through the grey as he waded through the oil-like air. I stood and watched as he got closer, waiting to see more than just his shadow. He didn't look like an angel, though he looked clean. Cleaner than me, anyway.

'Come on, dearie. Let me take care of you.'

I followed silently behind. I was so tired, everything hurt. More fish would help. The thought made me stop after a few steps.

'No, dearie. Come on. No more of that now.'

Chills crept over me, my skin prickling. I wanted to be clean, to scrub this filth off of me. My stomach was in knots. I needed a shit, and to be sick too. I stayed still, waiting for the nausea to pass. The man came back to me and put his arm around me.

'We'll take it slower. You're doing well. We have to walk, I'm afraid. There's no Autocars around the Perimeter. Not that they get much power these days anyway.'

His skin was on my skin, his warmth on my cold, the touch soothing my chills. When was the last time I had spoken to another person? When had I last felt another's warmth?

The last hand I'd touched had been stiff and lifeless.

'Not far now. June will be happy with this haul. Got a lot in my box today. She'll moan, though, for sure. It's just her way. You get used to her.'

I fidgeted as I walked, holding my stomach as if it was going to fall off.

'Yeah,' he muttered, talking more to himself, glancing down at my waist. 'June is going to be mad at me.'

The streetlights flickered on just as we passed a fence. I didn't recognise anything around me. It had been so long since I'd dared venture away from the edge, where everything I had known had disappeared. Where I felt his hand turn cold.

The buildings weren't clean like the ones I remembered. The smog had smeared itself over the whole of the Raft now. Nothing shone anymore.

'Just a few more streets, dearie. Not far.'

My stomach growled, and I looked in his box. Packets of food, with labels from a lifetime ago. When there was life, when food was everywhere. That signature so familiar. The Selbourne Range, it said, like that made it taste better. Anything will do when you're starving. The fish was filling; it sated my hunger. Sometimes it took the pain away. Now I was emptier than ever.

The streetlights went off again, but ahead a beam sliced through the dark.

'That's June. She's waiting for us.'

Her torch light shone straight at me; all I could see was the yellow glare.

A voice came from the direction of the light. 'Oh, for Raft's sake, Danny. What trash are you bringing home?'

'I couldn't leave her, June. Look at the state of her.'

'Exactly my point.'

'She needs help.'

'She's a long way past help. What the fuck are we going to do with her in this condition?'

'She could have a wash and a meal, at least.'

'Eurgh, she stinks of fish. Some fucking fish junkie in my house? No.'

'She can stay in the apartment next door. She's in a bad way. Not long to go, by the looks of her.'

'We're all in a bad way, Danny. You going to give her our food?'

'I got a good haul today.'

'Well, she can have some of yours, then. Fucking fish junkie. Don't waste water on her. She can sponge herself down, if she even knows how.'

'She can hear you, June.'

'Can she? She looks half-dead. No point wasting anything on a corpse.'

'Have a heart.'

'Fuck you and your heart. You want to starve for this girl, that's up to you. I'll keep my food, thanks.'

My head hurt. Their voices were like metal on concrete. Holding my hands to my ears, my eyes started streaming. I just wanted the noise to stop. I wanted it all to stop. I wanted to stop.

'It's okay, dearie. Let me show you to your room.'

The place smelled clean, almost like the old days. Danny nudged me up the stairs.

'There, there. Take it easy,' he said behind me, his box of food rattling with each step, torch lighting my way, June's tuts and stamping feet taking his softness away.

I was too weak to climb and had to crawl on my hands leaving grimy patches on the floor.

'And who's going to clean that?'

'Just be quiet, June.'

He sat me in an apartment as the electric buzzed back on. It was the brightest light I had known in ages. The apartment had fine, clean furniture. It was strange to be indoors. There was no wind, and I couldn't hear the sea. The silence felt thick and dusty.

'There's a bath through here. Ignore June, there's hot water, and you can use it. We don't know how long the taps will have water for, that's all. There are loads of clothes in the wardrobes. The bed is made. Whoever lived here left plenty of stuff behind.

You go right ahead and make yourself at home. I'll leave some food here, and I'll be just next door. Knock if you need me. Get some rest.'

He walked away and shut the door to the apartment. The sound of his footsteps on the stairs disappeared with him. I was inside a well-made Centre property with thick walls. Silence. In my old Perimeter place, I would have been able to hear the neighbours breathe in the next apartment.

I was left in muted peace, in the void between what had happened and what was to come. In the emptiness, without the constant wind, my eyes stopped watering for the first time since I could remember. The clarity of the room was dazzling. Brightly coloured furniture, decorative objects laid out on the table.

I went into the bathroom, raw and blistered feet against the plush rug, so soft it made me unsteady, like it would give way. In the mirror, a woman's face and body lingered. Mine, I assumed. But it looked nothing like me. My old self was long gone, replaced by this troll. Matted hair stuck to my head; dark eyes framed by a grimy face. Deep lines entrenched with dirt. I removed my clothes. My body had fared no better; a ramshackle mixture of bones and swelling. A punctured, half-inflated tyre. I stood under the shower, felt the pressure of the water on my chafed skin, until the water at my feet ran clear.

I slept. I don't know how long for. When I woke there was more food next to me. VitaBiscuits mostly, some IsoJuice. I ate everything I could until the nausea came, and I shivered under the blankets and slept some more.

When I woke, I ran a bath. I submerged myself in the water, looking up at distorted images of the ceiling decorations, the safe space dissolving into a blur. Old scary movies would show victims being held down by some villain, squirming and fighting as their attacker kept them under. Perhaps someone would do that to me. I would just lie there, let them take control, let them take the task off my hands.

I came up gasping, my lungs forcing me afloat.

Just a little longer. I could fight just a little more.

A tune buried in the back of my mind resurfaced, and I wanted to hum it. A part of my mind that remembered what it was to feel close to someone, to be loved. To belong.

Then my body was ripped in half.

I bit down on a towel as pain coursed through me in burning waves. More pain than I had ever known.

I should have brought some more fish.

I spent the night with my head buried in a pillow as fluids spilled out of me. Then something more solid, bit by bit. Pain cut through my mind fog. Joy brought lucidity, a long-lost clarity. It brought to life what was dead in me. It lit up the dark. Her cries reminded me that the purgatory had a purpose, and that purpose was now in my arms.

Chapter 2

The Tunnels

Thirty boxes. *Microbes*, nowhere near enough. Thirty boxes for one whole day, and it wasn't even decent produce. Months we'd been at it, and thirty boxes of mediocre mush was the most we'd managed in a day. It was a pittance. A poor quality, barely palatable pittance. We used to make a thousand times that on the Raft, where we had well-fed experts and equipment we'd developed for years. Where I had complete records of research, not to mention well-trained, expert staff. Who'd have thought I'd actually miss them! My lunch ration was still sitting on the side, pretending to be food. My stomach growled but silenced itself as soon as I looked at that plate.

No. I wasn't hungry enough for that yet.

I slammed a fist on the table, the other I banged against my head. What was I missing? What was I forgetting? How had I left such a gap in my research? We were meant to be prepared.

It was the panic we had left in; my head was a mess back then. It was not much better now, if I was being honest with myself. If I could figure it out, if I had a decent meal, maybe then I could think.

Hungry faces were everywhere. Expectant, ravenous, aware of my failure. I was a walking broken promise. It was not a famine, not yet, but the thought haunted me. I looked mournfully at the pile and stuck the final labels on as Clementine arrived to record the stock.

'How many is that?' She gestured to the pile of boxes.

'Thirty. Only thirty.'

'Well, it's better than none. Perhaps if the lab staff ate their rations, their brains would work better, and efficiency would be improved?'

'I'm fine.'

'You're not, though, are you? The factory staff aren't either, some of them at least. You need to eat, Sav. It *is* food.'

It wasn't; it was filth. 'I need proper food. This lab and factory need to work.'

'Set an example. You can't be mad at the engineers when they're famished. If they saw you eat our food, maybe they'd trust it.'

'Just a few more days. We'll sort the factory soon.'

She hugged me, which I didn't return. I was fine.

'You're getting there.'

'Your faith is appreciated, but undeserved.'

'I believe in you,' she said with a smile that seemed genuine. Often I couldn't tell with Clementine. In the last few months, she'd been promoted to head treasurer in the Council, and she took that job more seriously than anything. My poor performance seemed to have let her down. 'It's late,' she said. 'Tomorrow is a new day. Go home. Take some food to Grace and Ethan.'

I looked at the floor. 'You know I can't do that.'

'I won't tell anyone.'

I lifted my hand to my cheek, the bruise still tender and swollen. 'It's not worth the risk, Clem.'

She left, her soft footsteps gliding across the rocks. Unhurried. She was a Subterranean native and had no reason to hide, unlike me. She had the freedom to go home when she saw fit.

'I'll see you tomorrow,' she said, her now distant voice finding its way back to me easily, bouncing along the rock walls of the tunnel. The lab's section of the Tunnels was an echo chamber. The clamour outside congregated here more than anywhere else. It was like constant tinnitus. I'd put a request in for some noise-cancelling headphones, but the miners needed them more. Everyone else needed everything more than me. For now, I had to put up with it, but it was the least of my worries.

The whirring machines in the corner spat out useless chunks of slop as I started to clear up. A Council guard would be here soon to check we weren't stealing, to watch me squirm as they scrutinised the produce. The pile of boxes in the corner would say more than my words. My flushed face would give my shame away.

I went over the plans again, for the millionth time. What had we missed? Something vital. Something in starch synthesis that I couldn't remember how to replicate. One part of the machinery that wasn't up to scratch. The correct coding for the 4D printer, perhaps. We had the vitamins, at least. The injectable that Amalyn had pioneered had been dished out, but bulk food was missing. No fibre, no minerals, calcium was non-existent. And so much of the food we did produce had no substrate to bind the minerals to. All we had was unpalatable liquid. No macronutrients, after months of trying. I felt like the fraud so many in the Tunnels were beginning to see me as.

I eyed the satellite phone sitting on my desk. It had been in the lab since we'd arrived. The number was on all the paperwork we sent out with the proof of the Centre Elite ripping off the Tunnels' food supplies. In case anyone left behind on the Raft could call. In case anyone was still alive. Its silence was a daily reminder that so many had perished. There was likely no one left. The last solarplane from the Raft had arrived months earlier. Those onboard had heard about the rescue mission through word of mouth. We never even checked the satellite images anymore. There was no point in looking at what didn't want to be saved. What couldn't be saved.

'Professor.' Kevin strode over to my desk, his mop of red hair dazzling under the lab lights. 'The latest synth roast potatoes have turned out much better. I think they're really good now.'

He handed me a sample. I put a spoonful in my mouth. It tasted like dust in mush.

'Oh, Kevin, no. That's awful.'

'I think it's okay.'

'Trust me, it's not. Have you tested it? The fibre content will be zilch. Grind the lot down and make it into soup. We'll try again tomorrow.'

His smile fell. 'But –'

'No "buts," Kevin. It's no good.'

He shuffled away, dragging his feet like an insolent child. I swear the Council suggested he worked there just to wind me up. The man had the intelligence of the filth they farmed and broke more equipment than he cleaned. Most of his time was spent asking me the same questions he had asked a thousand times already. I'd hoped he'd at least keep the lab orderly, but the man couldn't tell a beaker from a conical flask. 'Glass is glass,' he'd say.

My computer pinged. Mabel and Marcus's message alert tone was as whiny as they always had been. The Mars lab was going much better than mine, much to my annoyance. Perfect, in fact. They'd had all the equipment ready, though. That was my excuse. Plus staff with a refined palate. How was I meant to achieve anything when the population was used to eating filth?

Mabel asked pointless questions like always, seeking reassurances that weren't needed.

'That all sounds fine, Mabel. Carry on,' I typed.

My replies were as short as ever. They didn't need to bother me at all. Their lab could function without me. But they had a brief: new food-flavour demands for a new planet. No expense spared. Mars wanted sweetness and spices, exotic flavours that were long obsolete here on earth. They wanted new textures and more calcium. The Mars Press was saying that we were developing similar sensations, even though we weren't. Food that made people thinner. Food that cured diseases and stopped ageing. I didn't bother reading the bogus articles anymore. I had enough on my mind without concerning myself with their rubber-stamped crap.

I'd asked Mabel and Marcus to send me details and plans for the factory equipment, but they had none. The factory had been set up almost a year before, machines made by people who had no access to Mars. It was flown there and plugged in, that was all. Everyone who had made the kit was probably at the bottom of the sea by now. Certainly they were not in the Tunnels, anyway. The Centre never thought to take the plans in case there was a problem at their end. As short-sighted as ever.

Mabel and Marcus knew which buttons to press, that was all. Useless.

'Professor Selbourne.'

Harvey Jones entered the lab, wearing the same smock and sandals as we all did, plodding along with the bowed stance typical of a Subterranean. I tried my best to avoid looking at the scars across his face and body. His entire skin was as rough as the mines, one of his eyes white and opaque.

'I wanted to know if I can count on your support for my campaign?' he said, getting straight to business.

'You're assuming someone has nominated you?'

'Naturally. And I can't imagine anyone will run against me. This Interim Council is hardly up to standard.'

'That's not really how fair elections work, Harvey.'

'What I mean is, I'm the most favourable choice. I was never a Select suck-up, as my scars show.'

'Your bravery is commendable, of course.' I remembered the day he was forced out into the desert for daring to speak against the Select. He'd shown more loyalty to his people than I ever had.

'I should warn you that I mean to cut ties with Mars,' he said. 'The Select can rot, along with the Centre who caused you and your people so much anguish.'

I shook my head. I'd heard all this before. 'That was never the deal, Harvey. And the help flows both ways. The lab there –'

'The lab there is working well,' he interrupted, 'and this one isn't. Have you considered that they are not being truthful?'

'I'd know if they weren't. But that's not the point. The Select and the Centre might be evil. We are not.'

I'm not, is what I meant. The cries from the whippings in the mines told me the truth about the morality of some of the Subs. My own bruises did, too.

He scrunched up his nose. 'Vengeful is not the same as evil.'

The heavy steps of Council guards approached the lab. They were the only ones who wore trousers instead of floor-length smocks, shoes with thick soles instead of our flappy sandals. The Subs with the straightest backs and the hardiest bones were chosen to be guards. No one could outrun them. Two of them now hovered in the doorway before eyeing the measly pile of boxes.

'Is that it?' said one.

'Afraid so.'

He stepped closer, his face inches from mine, hand over the baton that hung from his belt. 'Some think you're making loads of food and keeping it for yourselves and the other invaders.'

'Shut it, Juan,' Harvey said. 'You and your lot need to start showing some respect to the Rafters. They're here to help.'

'Help? Or bleed us dry?' the other guard said.

I looked at the floor. 'I'll figure out the kinks soon. We're trying very hard.'

'The only reason you're here is so you can make decent food for everyone. This is barely enough to feed the Council,' Juan spat.

'As I said, we're trying.'

He leant in closer, his breath hot on my face. 'Try harder.'

'All right, that's enough. I mean it, leave her alone.' Harvey elbowed his way between me and the guards. His chivalry felt like a show, a vote-winner.

With a grunt, the guards left.

'Thanks, Harvey,' I said when their footsteps had receded. 'But he's right. We're meant to be able to make food. I need to stay in contact with Mars, just in case they can help.'

My promise to the Prime Minister still rang in my head, as did her promise to seek revenge if I backed out of the deal. If Marcus and Mabel couldn't get in touch with me, would they tell the Centre Elite? Would something bad happen to my son? I couldn't take that chance.

'You'll figure this out. I have every faith in you and the other Raft refugees. You'll prove your worth, I'm sure. It'll be a pledge of my campaign to be your voice.'

'Thank you for stopping by, Harvey. All candidates will be announced shortly, I understand?'

'This evening. I think I can hear the news bike now.'

Rusty bike components screeched through the echoing chamber, and a bicycle rolled up outside the lab doors. The rider thrust leaflets into our hands. A glossy one for Harvey, a scrappy one written in English for me. Harvey's face went red.

I read mine. Harvey's name was at the top of the list followed by three others. 'Marco Paradiso, who's that?'

'Nobody. A joke nomination.'

'Juliette St Clair.'

'Again, no one.'

'And Isaac Selbourne.'

He coughed and shifted his weight from one foot to the other. 'Well, I think that confirms that I will be the best candidate, don't you think so?'

***

After a sixteen-hour stint in the lab, I arrived home to our room, housing our beds and some seats around a small table, with a single-ring stove in the corner. The communal bathroom was down the hall. But we had the whole city to explore, I reminded Grace when she'd sulked after we were downsized, though exploring the city wasn't something she had taken much advantage of. Her school was close by down the corridor, and that was usually as far as she ventured. She had twelve children in total. 'Handfuls,' as she described them, with a smile. None as good or as bright as Ethan, of course.

'Mummy!' He greeted me as I walked in. 'Pierre is here to play.'

'Glad to hear it.'

The floor was covered with drawings. Recycled tree carcass paper was quite the norm in the Tunnels, and Ethan got through piles of the stuff. That was the one bit of filth I'd come to accept without flinching. Around the piles of paper were his toys, little trip hazards of building blocks and toy diggers. The smell of warm muck was coming from the stove.

'Hey,' said Grace. 'Dinner is almost ready.'

However much she minced it and disguised it, I couldn't get past the smell. I still hadn't touched it since we had arrived. She put her arm around me.

'Christ, Sav, you're even thinner than you were yesterday. You need to eat.'

'I'm fine. We'll crack the factory issue soon.'

'You'll never figure it out if you don't eat. Lab samples aren't enough. If I can stomach the native food, you can too.'

Like I needed more nagging.

I huffed and sat on a hard chair, kicked off my flimsy sandals. My feet were sore from standing all day, the footwear giving no arch support at all. I placed them on the cool rocks, the throbbing abating slightly. 'I'm still so cross. We missed one bit of information, and I can't replicate it. Just one bloody bit of equipment. Two, really. One for the lab and one for the factory.'

'Don't be so hard on yourself. You're still making food.'

I had to be hard on myself. People were relying on me. Ethan and his friend were playing at full volume, trashing each other's blocks, making monsters out of the diggers. Ethan played heartily but looked pale and hadn't grown much since we'd arrived. His calorie count was low. He ate the filth, but rations were meagre. What filth food had been harvested before our arrival had to feed more people, and Rafters were at the back of the queue. Ethan's friend Pierre had normal childhood podge around his arms. Pierre, I knew that name. Celia's nephew, the family of a Council officer. He clearly had plenty to eat back home.

'So, the clinic called,' Grace said. There was no joy in her voice.

'And?'

Tears sprang to her eyes. 'Nope. It's not going to happen.'

'I'm sorry.'

'They don't want any more of us Raft people, they say. Plus, well, I'm too old, it turns out.'

'You look as beautiful as the day we met,' I said, and I meant it. She still glowed.

'Shame my ovaries don't.'

'Technology might improve.'

She linked her arm in mine, her bones on my bones. 'It's fine. We have Ethan. I mean, I'd still love another. I'd have a dozen if it were possible. But Ethan is enough.'

I hid my relief. Another mouth to feed would be a stretch. I didn't have the energy and doubted she did.

I kissed her cheek. 'You have too much love to give.'

She went to stir the food, her oversized smock failing to disguise her waif-like figure. I wasn't the only one getting thinner.

'You see the candidates?' she asked. 'Was it you who nominated Isaac?'

'Me? No, God. I'll leave the politics to them. I'm not even sure Rafters are allowed to nominate.'

'Don't call us that. The Subs use that word, and not in a nice way.'

'Sorry. Just a habit.'

Grace ushered Pierre out the door to go home for his dinner with only the slightest protest from Ethan. She spooned slop into a bowl and handed it to Ethan, who skipped round the room with it, not sitting still for a moment. He had no concept of conserving calories.

Grace held out a bowl, and I shook my head. She didn't argue. We'd been having this debate for months. At work I ate what we had left from the Raft, which was hardly anything. Scraps. But we were making it last. I could make do for the time being.

'It's not surprising someone nominated him,' I said, to cover the sound of them chewing filth. 'He has a lot of friends, influence.'

'Controversial choice, though, I hear. Since he was so friendly with the Select, he never had to do surface time.'

'Listen to you with all the gossip!' I laughed, and Grace rolled her eyes at me.

'The other mums were talking.'

The Select were long gone, but their memory remained. The mental scars were as deep as the physical ones. Isaac had chosen to see their positives rather than the negatives. He'd done what was needed to survive. He'd kissed ass and sucked up, keeping himself and Clementine alive and well. No shame in that. No judgement. It was something I could relate to.

'I doubt he wants it anyway,' I said. 'No one seriously wants to go against Harvey.'

'You've been spending too much time in the lab,' Grace said. 'And careful what you say in front of people, even kids. The walls have ears around here.'

Chapter 3

The Tunnels

'Congratulations,' I said to Isaac as he arrived at the lab the next morning. He came by my workplace most mornings. 'To say hello,' is what he always said. To be first in line for any samples is what I believed.

He was beaming, his grin reaching from ear to ear. He looked so much like our father when he smiled, his prominent forehead lifting, his square jaw. His hair had grown back since the Select had left and he now also had the same untameable frizz as me and our father.

'I've got a lot of ideas. I really think I can do this,' he said.

I'd half-expected him to rebuff the nomination. He always seemed so stressed even in his current role of Council tunnel planner, and running for the top job would be a massive burden, but he glowed with excitement. The prospect of power agreed with him.

'Well, we've been muddling along with the Interim Council. A bit of leadership is needed,' I said. 'Perhaps a new leader will make this place a bit fairer, as we were promised.'

'How is it unfair? We dug these tunnels years ago. It's only right the new arrivals do their bit.'

'The corporal punishments, I mean.'

Isaac waved away my suggestion. 'Such punishments are scant, and only used when necessary. The Council drew up recommendations and rules. It was a group decision.'

'If the rules allow people to be beaten, Isaac, then the rules are nonsense.'

'The rules are why my nomination is such a good thing. If you don't define the rules, the rules define you. Look what happened to dad. He was a government advisor once but had a pitiful voice. He didn't agree with them, and was out.'

I frowned. I didn't need reminding. 'Well, maybe make some rules that protect Rafters instead of having them beaten.'

'The Subterraneans were subjected to the same and worse when the Select were here. You Rafters have had it easy for too long.'

Easy? I bit my tongue.

'And at least we have rules here to stop sexual misconduct,' he said. 'Coming from the Raft, that must be a breath of fresh air.'

'It is. That much is appreciated.' I certainly didn't miss Greg's wandering eyes. The thought still made me shudder.

'Harvey thinks he's guaranteed,' Isaac laughed.

'He is popular,' I said, as I turned to the lab equipment. I didn't care for gossip.

'He's too bitter, though. He doesn't understand that the Select did good things.'

'You can hardly blame him. He has more scars than anyone.'

'Well, he never did learn to shut his mouth.'

Isaac walked over to the testing station and picked at some samples. His back had become so much straighter. The Council were first in line for lab food, though we had argued endlessly for the miners to receive the most. Their calorie requirement was much higher as they dug the tunnels and mined the rock used for making furniture. Such pleas fell on deaf ears among the Council and their families. Their satisfied stomachs weren't going to relinquish that privilege. Isaac's expanding waistline protruded from his smock, convex where we were concave.

'Mr Selbourne!' Kevin appeared from nowhere. He had a knack for it. 'Have you tried some of this mixture? I think we're making progress.'

We? Pretty much all Kevin did was get in the way and gorge on substandard scraps.

'Glad to hear it, Kevin,' Isaac said, taking a little pot off him. 'I hope you're pulling your weight around here? Making your mum proud?'

'I really think so.' He thrust his chest out and grinned.

'Why don't you go have a clean-up of the factory, Kevin,' I said. 'There's some spillage from the third mixer, I believe.'

He ran off like an excited child, his spindly physique so indicative of the Subs. Sometimes I felt like I was addressing one of Ethan's school friends. Isaac waved at him. Mocking him, I thought. His smile gave that impression, anyway.

'We'll be able to put you and your family in a bigger home soon,' Isaac said now we were alone again. 'The digging is ahead of schedule, thanks to the motivating tactics of the Council.'

'Motivating tactics' meant beating and whipping my fellow Rafters. Each rock was mined with blood.

'There's no need to rush,' I said. 'We're fine. Everyone just needs some rest.'

'Imagine if you were still on the Raft. You'd be resting at the bottom of the sea.'

'Harsh, Isaac.' I scowled at his cold candour. My friends had suffered that fate, and my heart still ached for them.

He shrugged in response, and spat out some roast potato mix. 'Kevin is actually pleased with this mush? I suspect one of your Rafter staff is withholding vital information.'

'And what purpose would that serve?' I asked, with all the bitterness I could muster. 'They're a lot more useful than Kevin. Can't you put him somewhere else?'

'Not really. You've worked with the guy. You know he's good for nothing. Too weedy for the mines, too thick for much else.'

'The food labs should employ the brightest minds,' I said. We had the pick of the crop on the Raft. In the Tunnels, they were offloading their rejects.

'Well, when it is a functioning lab, maybe you will.' His smugness made me grind my teeth. 'Kevin's mother is important in the Council, so she needs her son to be useful.'

'We all need Kevin to be useful.'

'Anyway,' Isaac continued, 'it's good for you to have a Sub here among you. Someone who comes from a country of decency. Who knows what the Raft cultural mind dictates? Such an odd place you lot called home. Hardly somewhere of honesty and integrity.'

I clenched my fists. 'The Perimeter was a place of survival. The Centre was the home of lies and dishonesty.'

'Yet you yourself, little sister, admit to pedalling their message for your own gain.' He shook his head and tutted. 'You understand, we have to be careful here in the Tunnels. We were promised so much by you, and you have delivered so little. You've made me quite the laughingstock at the Council. You and all the other Rafters are a drain on our resources, not the big contributors I'd promised you'd be. There are so many of you all.'

'There are less than a thousand. So many others never made it.'

'Well, it's more than we can cope with, considering our current food supplies. Your people really damaged our protein sources, if you remember?'

'The *Centre* damaged your protein sources, which we alerted you to at the first opportunity. The Centre are not *my* people,' I said through my teeth.

Isaac saw us all, the Perimeter and the Centre, as one. The sea was the border in his eyes, not that fence.

'And our culture never condoned whipping and beating,' I said. 'You hated the Select for doing that, but you continue with it.'

'Our motivational methods have worked for decades. We all learnt that way.' He walked around the lab, scrutinising the equipment, running his hand over surfaces and inspecting for dust. 'Once the new accommodations are built, and the food is up and running, the pressure will be off. I promise you that.' He picked some of the mix from his teeth and helped himself to a bottle of IsoJuice, or what was meant to be IsoJuice. It was still much too sour and thick compared to what I had made before. The warmth of the brother I had found almost a year earlier had long gone. My failures had eroded that kindness. This man that remained was more alien to me by the day. 'And anyway, the new laws will be written up by the new leader. I'm sure there will be some room for Rafter's rights.'

His eyes had blackened over the previous year. The Select that pinned him down had gone, and so he elevated himself and soared higher than I had ever imagined.

'Harvey is promising equality,' I said.

'As am I, once the Rafters have earned their place. As I said, we all had to earn our place to prove our usefulness. Do you want us to continue the labour of the undead? We allowed the frail and elderly to retire, so someone has to do that work.'

'It's not the work, Isaac.' My voice sounded more desperate than I intended. He did not appreciate weakness. 'People want to help. They want to earn their keep. Just ask them to ease off the punishments, okay?'

He eyed my bruise. 'They shouldn't have hurt you like that. You are important, and my sister. I have explained that to them.'

'But the rest, too. We've come from hell on the Raft to help build a community here.'

'Fine, fine.' He raised his hands defensively. 'I'll bring it up at the next committee meeting and make it part of my manifesto pledge. No corporal punishment, or at least stricter criteria for using it.'

'Thanks. And I will figure the lab out, I promise. We're getting close.'

After he left, I went for my allocated walk time, although I could not take too much exercise since my calorie intake was so low. It was calculated that I could walk for twenty minutes, twice a day, on top of my commute. I had no idea who'd calculated such a figure. I was still losing weight, but that was okay. The people in the mines needed the food and the calories more. I'd promised them so much more.

Out of the lab and down a short tunnel, I came to a mezzanine overlooking a chamber. It was not one of the biggest chambers, just a congregation area, but it was still impressive. Subs were cleaning below, their long, scraggy frames doubled over. A lifetime without calcium and vitamin D had made them arched and weak. Isaac was right, everyone had suffered.

The sound of cries echoed from a nearby tunnel, and I followed them to see what Isaac had told me he would stop. That message hadn't reached the guards just yet. Where the tunnel ended, people were using machines and manual equipment to bore their way through, creating new quarters for the residents. I could smell the dust mingled with blood from some distance away. The light sensors at the sides winked at me as I made my way through the tunnel, flickering and struggling. The power wasn't holding out well down here.

The workers looked emaciated. All of them were from the Raft, and all Perimeter, clearly. Where once their skin had rashes from the salt and smog, now it was scarred. In the mines, they all looked the same, with masked faces orange from the dust and dirt of the rock.

I had brought a few packets of substandard biscuits with me to give them some fuel. It wasn't much, but it was all they were allocated. They must have been eating the filth food, too. They'd have been dead otherwise. Most of them I had greeted when they'd first arrived, their faces full of hope, seeing foreign lands for the first time. I remembered that feeling, the awe and wonderment of the Tunnels. My fellow countryfolk had made their escape, trusted me when I told them that a greater place awaited. Their adventure had just begun, I said. I'd promised them freedom, fairness, a fresh start. They'd seen none of that. Since we'd arrived, we'd been pushed into tiny homes in a separate Raft wing of the Tunnels, cramped in together with no room for our stuff. Not that we'd brought any, anyway. Privacy was as rationed as our food.

After I'd handed out one box of biscuits, I reached for the second and straightened up too quickly, my head starting to swim. I leant against the freshly mined wall, cold and rough. A few deep breaths of dust and body odour and I was okay again, and I carried on handing out snacks. Among the workers, I spotted a face I hadn't seen since moving to the Tunnels. It was one I hadn't expected – or wanted – to see ever again. His hives had cleared and been replaced with smudges of dirt and dust, but those saggy lips and toothless mouth were unmistakable. *Peter?*

He looked my way as if my eyes had spoken to him. He clocked my gaze and walked over. I noticed his limp, his slanted shoulders, bloodied welts blotting his smock. He had clearly not escaped the guards' punishments.

'Well, well. Selbourne.'

'The Centre didn't want you on Mars, then?' Of course they didn't. No amount of fancy words could make up for his appearance and lack of Centre blood.

'It was my choice, actually.'

I nodded. *Yeah, right.*

'My daughter, my wife. They crossed the bridged before the anchors blew. I'd never have the chance to see them again if I didn't come here.'

'Before *you* blew them up, you mean?'

He clicked his tongue. 'Any of the Subs here enquiring about me? My daughter would be thirty-two years old now. My wife, Julia, sixty-four. Italian, though she had family in Toulouse.'

'No, doesn't ring a bell.' I found it hard to believe Peter gave a toss about anything besides power and his bank balance. Was he a spy for Mars? They said they'd have the means to punish me if I didn't keep up my end of the deal. Was Peter here to check on me? The dust on his shirt and bruises up his arms made me think not. Snitches get treated well. Lars certainly did when he was spying for the Elite back on the Raft. Peter was as lowly as the rest of us.

'Well, if you wouldn't mind asking around. For an old friend.'

Friend? I almost laughed at the word. I decided to ignore his request, audacious as it was of him to think I owed him a favour. 'I'm surprised you're here. Bit grubby and rough for the likes of you,' I said.

His eyebrows raised slightly as if to say, *And what are you going to do about it?*

'I'll bet no one here knows who you are,' I said.

He looked pathetic and shrugged. Maybe I had been wrong and there was a hint of shame in him? No. No chance. Just busted, that was all. Regretful, maybe. Robbed of his power and influence, here he was as good as an Alternate. I bit my lip as it dawned on me, knowing that feeling all too well. 'I won't say anything,' I said.

'Say what? You're as guilty as me.' He smiled that sickly sweet smile, loose lips lifting into a sneer.

I handed him a packet of biscuits and turned away. 'Nice to see you again, Peter.'

Chapter 4

The Raft

'You're not giving her that much.'

'It's only a tiny bit, June. She needs it.'

'She can eat more fish if she's hungry. She's not having my share. Bloody freeloader. She didn't collect any of this. Handouts. Pity food, that's all this is.'

'I found three more boxes this week. We can spare some.'

'It's time you woke up, Danny. We can survive until the food and water run out, and then we can either slit our wrists or starve to death. There's nothing left here. No Raft, no planet, nothing. Everyone fucked off and went to Mars. The rest are all in the sea.'

'Some went to the Mainland.'

Doors slammed shut, feet stomped up and down. With the front door to the apartment open, the sound carried.

'If you believe those rumours, you're more of a bloody fool than I thought. By feeding that woman, you're just making our deaths come quicker. You can keep trying to log on to that damned computer and sending emails and whatever, but there's no one out there coming to save us. No one. The quantum cables aren't working, I told you that. Just use that stupid head of yours. Who's going to reply? They're hardly going to fly back from Mars to pick us up and take us with them. She's vermin, like us.'

June's voice came through clear as day, Danny's softer and harder to hear. I shook my head to shut them out. My ears had popped overnight, my brain fog cleared. Everything sounded loud and imposing. There was a crispness to every syllable.

I got up and shut the door. The breeze that came from having it open was negligible, anyway. I got back onto the bed, fat pillows supporting my back, more luxury than I even knew existed. Besides the pile of bloodied sheets in the corner of the room, the place was clean and tidy, with just a little surface dust from its abandonment, and a tide line in the bath from my soak. I'd found a nightgown in the drawers, all fancy lacework and frills. Useless, non-functional additions crafted by someone who had more than plenty. I couldn't take in what I was seeing, the garishness of the furniture, the misplaced affection. Someone had cared for this stuff more than they had cared for the land beneath their feet. How had an apartment been so meticulously preserved when the world outside was sinking?

With the noise of June and Danny's row shut out, my ears were for her and her alone. Her lips making sucking noises and gurgles. Sounds of brand-new innocence, of life and hope. I fed her and she guzzled greedily with a strong latch. By some miracle, she seemed healthy.

My coarse hand stroked her delicate cheek; a juxtaposition of what life promises with what it takes away. My fingers were crisscrossed with blue-black lines, the dirt ingrained, part of me, burying into every crease and digging new ones. I'd never be able to clean it away. Each blemish was like a tattoo reminding me of when I'd crawled out of that hole, every pile of rubble I'd climbed over. That's why Perimeter's skin ages so quickly. We always blamed the salt and smog, but really, we were hollowed out by loss and grief. Each line was etched from pain.

She deserves better.

I'd wrapped her in fine blankets, a little bundle of newness. Her deep-blue eyes bore into mine.

I know you, little one. I can be strong for you.

This day had been coming for so long. Somewhere deep inside, I'd known this. I just never thought I'd survive to see it through. My grief had been suffocating. It had rid me of any remembrance of love. Screams haunted me, hands gripping before falling away, the sound of rocks landing against lifeless bodies. Dull thuds before the crash. A warm body turning cold. Hope had withered away; my swollen belly was a dead weight. But now ... *Now!*

The front door opened, and footsteps approached. I didn't look up, but I heard Danny's gasp, followed by, 'June! Get in here!'

'What the hell do you want now?' she sighed when she came into the room. 'Oh, great. The baby's arrived. As if we don't have enough mouths to feed. Now there's one more.'

'Oh, June, just look.' His voice came closer. 'A baby.'

'Hardly a big surprise, Danny.'

'Ignore her,' he said, clearly to me. 'Congratulations, dearie. Is it a boy or a girl?'

'A girl,' I croaked. When did my voice get so hoarse? It had been such a long time since I'd spoken to anyone.

'She speaks!' June said, raising her arms to the ceiling. 'Praise the Raft, she has a tongue. Perhaps we'll even know her name soon!'

'June, why don't you line that drawer with towels and blankets? Make a nice crib for the baby.' June tutted and dragged her feet, muttering to herself the whole time. 'You had her all by yourself, dearie? Are you feeling okay?'

'I feel fine, thanks. Tired, that's all.' I looked at him then, the first time I'd really paid attention to his appearance. He was obviously Perimeter, him and June. Before they'd moved their lives within the Centre fence, anyway. He had familiar deep lines across his skin, dark circles surrounding tired eyes that lifted when he smiled. Thin hair peppered with grey. His face bore a kindness that matched the benevolence of his actions.

'Is she strong? Healthy?'

'She seems okay. She's so tiny, I'm not sure if she's too small? My friend had a baby a few years ago, and she seems smaller than he was. I don't know.'

'Well, she's simply gorgeous. We always wanted children. Never made the list, though.'

'Yeah, only Centre and their suck-ups ever got fertility treatment,' June said, coming back over to the bed. I felt her gaze scrutinise me like an icy chill. Her face was actually less stern than her voice suggested. Her animosity must be a new thing, I thought. She was probably pretty once.

'This little one was conceived through love and nothing more,' I said.

'Bollocks,' said June. She had a big voice for someone so small.

I shrugged. 'Believe what you will.'

Drawers screeched open and slammed shut as June continued to fashion a crib. I watched her fold blankets and towels with precision and care. Her face was failing to maintain its bitterness as she searched for pinks and yellows with frills. I smiled.

'Are there any Autocars around?' I asked. 'I need to go and collect some stuff.'

'You should rest,' Danny said. 'I can go foraging for you. What do you need? Nappies? Baby clothes?'

'Yes, all that. But there's somewhere specific I need to go.'

'Most of the Perimeter is in the sea, dearie.'

'I know, but this place won't be, I think. Can you help me? I don't think I can walk all the way.'

'I'll try and find a working Autocar, one with enough charge. There are still some around the Centre. Just can't call them, you have to find them. Some still work a bit, Raft knows how.'

'Thanks.'

'Well, I'm not babysitting while you two are off searching for scraps,' June said as she walked away.

Danny left me some biscuits which I devoured, then, after another feed, I watched the baby fall asleep and lay her down in the crib June had put together. I searched the house for sanitary supplies, moving slowly, my body protesting, ransacking drawer after drawer. Every time I thought I'd looked in all the cupboards and drawers, I found a few more, housing discarded clothes, trinkets, utensils, mostly stuff that was a waste of material and looked brand new. Such finery deemed unworthy of taking to Mars. I doubted they'd have been limited on their luggage space. How overflowing with useless crap these drawers must have been! Not that it was important. What mattered now was sanitary supplies, and after some searching, I found a mediocre amount, but I figured it was enough to keep me decent enough for a short trip out. I made a papoose out of some ornate scarves and fastened the baby to me. *Baby.* She'd need a name at some point. A name is forever, though. And at that moment, I felt like forever was tempting fate. What was left of the Raft didn't have forever.

The baby nuzzled in close, and I made my way down the stairs, gripping her with one hand and the banister with the other. My body felt like jelly, and every step made the area between my legs throb with a deep pain. But there was no time to waste. She had to survive. Now I'd looked into those eyes, felt her little hand grasp my fingers, everything had changed. I couldn't wander and wallow anymore. I couldn't rely on fish to blow away my grief. I needed to be clearheaded.

'You shouldn't walk so soon, dearie. You need to rest,' Danny said as he ran to meet me at the apartment door. I covered the baby's head loosely with a blanket, shielding her from the worst of the smog. He'd found an Autocar that now sat idling at the curb.

'Have you any luggage bags?' I shouted over the noise of the wind. Less than twenty-four hours inside and I'd already forgotten what it could get like out there. 'Also, something to break into a building with. An axe or a crowbar.'

Danny came back with a suitcase. Whichever Centre resident lived there before had clearly been on a holiday or two. I imagined visiting friends at the other end of the Centre, taking an Autocar all the way there, no expense spared. That wouldn't even have been their best bag – they would have taken that to Mars with them.

Just as the Autocar was about to pull away with myself and Danny inside, June ran over and shuffled in, her tiny backside barely making a dent in the space. 'Just to see what a waste of time this trip is,' she explained.

I nodded.

Danny squeezed her knee, and she looked away from him, glancing at the baby for a moment. 'Total waste of time,' she said again.

I gave my handprint to the Autocar which greeted me, yet I had no idea how it would take payment. It wouldn't, most likely. Were there even connections to the banks anymore? I'd obviously spent no money in months. After I inputted the address and the Autocar pulled away, seemingly unconcerned with the state of the Raft or the reliability of payment. I breathed a sigh of relief and relaxed a little.

The drive was almost an hour and the smog only got thicker. By the time the Autocar stopped, the pollution was dripping down the windows like oil. For the brief spells, I had a view of the world outside. All I saw were derelict buildings. No people, not a soul. Could it be that there was no one left? Had they all succumbed to the sea? A lump caught in my throat at the thought. Surely some had made it to the Mainland. I shut my eyes and hoped.

The Autocar stopped and June scoffed as we alighted in front of the building, its low-rise height likely a stark contrast to her own old dwelling. She looked older than she sounded; her stunted physique a trait of those who had tried so hard to walk forwards as the Raft spun the wrong way. A counterbalance of existence. My heart ached for her, for the love she would never know. For it was a love I never knew existed until hours earlier. June was without desire and purpose. There wasn't much left for her but scorn. She eyed the building up and down, then did the same to me, making conclusions that were undeserved, yet understandable. My new lines and grime weren't enough to convince her of my upbringing. She had judged and judged wrongly. I ignored her glare.

Danny found a bit of loose tarmac and smashed the window to get in. There hadn't been any loose tarmac here before. The ground must have been breaking up. No looters had made it to this street, to my relief, so everything I needed would still be there. The lift wasn't working, so I hobbled up the steps with Danny supporting me by the elbow.

'I'll carry the baby,' June said.

'It's fine. She's sleeping. I can manage.'

'Well, don't say I didn't try to help.'

The electric was on, just, the hallway lights flickering. Danny got out a crowbar and, after a few minutes and so much force I worried his arm would snap, he broke the door enough to open it. When it swung open, I hesitated for a moment.

'You okay, dearie?'

'I'm fine.'

I took a deep breath while I stood outside the home my baby would never know. A future that would never be. Just stuff. Possessions, that's all that was inside. Things I could live without. Mementos that held more sadness than joy. The memories came with me wherever I went. This was a building, that was all. Physical. What I missed was something deeper than that. I took another breath and walked in.

The place didn't smell familiar. It was musty, unused, empty, though perhaps we had brought that in with us. On the living-room floor were discarded glasses. Boxes that had never been unpacked, now covered in dust. Isn't dust mostly skin cells? Some of him was still here, in the dust and the fingerprints on the glasses. A hoodie slung over a chair, a bathrobe on a door hook. I ran my hand over the material briefly, touching one of the last things he had, then moved away. I didn't come for those. There was just one thing I really needed. It was still there, on the desk where we had left it. *We.*

'What is that thing?' Danny asked as I picked it up.

'A phone.'

'Phones aren't working anymore.'

'Told you this would be a waste of time,' said June.

'This one will work,' I said, finding the handwritten number still taped to the side of the phone. 'It has to.'

The battery meter showed it still had seventy-five per cent. I dialled the number, and it rang while my heart sat in my throat. The tinny sound repeated, again and again, until it clicked off. *Microbes!* I dialled again, fist clenched, biting the inside of my cheek, eyes closed, muttering a silent prayer.

Please pick up. Please.

My heart didn't dare to beat. And then ...

'Hello?' A word so welcoming to me. Her voice, far away yet clear as a bell, tinged with surprise.

I took a moment to answer, disbelief stifling my tongue. She was there.

'Hi, Sav? It's me. It's Amalyn.'

Chapter 5

The Tunnels

That phone had not rung once since we'd arrived, so when it did, I didn't acknowledge it at first. It was just another noise adding to the din. It was the light that alerted me, the red flash in my peripheral vision. I paused for a moment, blinking, disbelieving. Then it clicked off. Had I just seen that? Had it actually rung? I rubbed my eyes, sceptical of my own senses. Then it rang again, and this time I ran to it, hurling myself over the lab, sending some beakers flying.

It couldn't be. It just couldn't. Someone left on the Raft!

'Hello?'

Silence and static. Was there anyone there? Then: 'Hi, Sav? It's me. It's Amalyn.'

The world stood still for a moment.

It couldn't be!

'Ams … It can't be. But you –'

'I know. Oh god, Sav, I know!'

Tears were streaming, I couldn't find my words. *She's alive!*

'My parents?'

'They're here, Ams. They're alive.'

In a brief pause I heard her sigh of relief. 'This signal won't last, remember?' she said quickly. 'Can you get us? There are people still here, there's not much land left, hardly any food.'

'Ams, oh my god. I mean ... you're alive! It's been so long since the last plane, I don't know. Archie ...?'

'He didn't make it. I'm sorry. So sorry. The baby did though. She was born yesterday.'

I held my hand to my mouth, my heart caught in my throat. Reality hit me like a rock. Ams really was alive, and she needed me. *She.* A baby girl. 'Oh my. Ams, I don't know what to say.'

'Can you help us?'

The static on the line got louder, and I shouted over it. 'The airports are gone. I need to figure this out. It's not been great here. The lab isn't working. I'm missing some information.'

'Really? I have Archie's computer here. I can try to get it working and send it all over.'

'That would be great, thank you. I can't believe it's you. There should be food back at my old place. Check the hallway cupboard. I'll do what I can, you know I will. I'll call you tomorrow.'

And then the line went dead.

My whole body shook. Had I really just heard her voice? She sounded older, her voice harsher. The smog must be closing in. The baby, she'd had the baby. A little girl. But Archie. *Archie.*

No time to mourn, no time for emotion. She had a baby. She was alive and more people from the Raft wanted to come. That was all that was important now. I ran out of the lab and down the corridor to the Subs' quarters and the Council office. I ran until I found it, weak legs propelled by adrenaline, likely taking me well over my calorie count for the day. Sod that, I could count calories later. As my head started to spin, I arrived at the glass-walled room with a long table down the centre, blinds open, serious faces. Harvey, Isaac, Giao and others were sitting there when I burst in.

'Isaac!'

'Savannah, this is quite inappropriate,' said Giao.

I held my hand to my chest, leaning on the door for support. 'Amalyn is alive. Isaac, you remember her? She just called on the satellite phone. There are still people who want to come. On the Raft. We have to help.' I gasped for air, catching my breath.

'The legendary Amalyn?' Harvey stood up. 'The one who designed the injectable vitamin formula?'

'That's her. And I reckon she'll know what we're missing in the lab. She was brilliant.'

'Such a great mind, still alive. And one who has blessed us all with such an infusion. We must do whatever it takes,' Harvey said. I straightened up and a wave of joy washed over me.

'Well, this is something that needs Council discussion, obviously,' Giao said. The blandness of his voice dampened my excitement.

'What's there to discuss?' I asked. 'She has a baby!'

'We need to discuss the fact that we are overrun with Rafters,' he said. 'The new accommodation tunnel is not complete, and we do not have enough food. Not to mention the Raft airports are gone. How would we collect them?' He held up a finger for each point and seemed disappointed not to have thought of more.

'We could drop off some food from a plane until we figure out what to do. Isaac, don't you agree?'

Isaac sat silently, looking at the floor.

'Did you not hear me?' Giao said, louder, his facial tic suddenly more prominent. 'We don't have enough food for our own citizens, let alone spare to likely lose in some reckless fly-by.'

His words knocked the wind out of me more than my run had. I had no breath to protest.

'We will discuss it,' Giao said. 'Now get back to work. Your role here is to make food, not tell the Council what to do.'

Giao had been at the helm since the Select left, taking over the position that Lady Monet had left vacant. One Council member was allocated for each member of the Select to mimic their hierarchy until a leader had been elected and could employ their own staff. This Interim Council was supposed to be balanced and neutral. That neutrality was meant to apply to the

Raft refugees as well, but in reality they seemed as neutral as the Minister of Impartiality had back on the Raft.

Deflated, I left feeling smaller than ever. Weak legs carried me back to the lab, but I couldn't work. How was I supposed to concentrate? I plodded around the lab, grinding my teeth. I shouldn't have done that; my molars were feeling too soft, but I was seething, hot rage pumping through me, my body shaky and unsteady. Why had Isaac just sat there mute? Amalyn had helped us so much and she deserved our help in return.

Giao, with his prudish face and tic, never missed an opportunity to remind me that the lab wasn't good enough, to tell the miners that they hadn't dug enough, that we took up too much space. I could never tell if it was the stress of his job or the love of giving orders that made him like that. He had the pressure of the Tunnels weighing down on him, he frequently said. The only time he seemed to tame his tic was when he was giving orders. It was a relief no one had nominated him for the democratic leadership position. By the amount he had aged over the past few months, I suspected he would be pleased to step down. Amalyn and the rest of the Rafters would be his last command, his last chance to assert his brief spell of authority. His last chance to utilise the control he had over the Council guards. Her future was in the hands of the Tunnel's final dictator before democracy could take over.

I kicked the wall. *Microbes!*

As humankind perseveres, the only thing that is preserved is power. And the power-hungry were forever ravenous.

I wasted time at the lab, fiddling with some equipment and rearranging some files. Trying to look busy instead of just staring at the satellite phone, willing it to ring again. Kevin flapped some papers in front of me, Chris and Ester stood with him, braced for my response. More substandard results.

'Go check the factory, all of you,' I said. I needed space, not hassle.

I couldn't call back yet. Who knew how much power her phone had? Did she have a charger? I couldn't be sure. When I spoke to Amalyn, it would be to tell her good news. It had to be. I leant on the desk for a while, took some deep breaths and tried to let it sink in. Amalyn was alive, and she had a baby. *Archie's baby*.

Tears fell, both happy and sad ones. I had grieved so much for my friends. Now I was feeling Archie's loss all over again. He'd tell me to cheer up, calm down. He'd put the kettle on and help me figure it out. But he wasn't here. I felt my insides hollow, my lungs struggling to draw breath. My palms were sweaty as the room went out of focus. I was too hungry to be so emotional. Sat on the floor, propped up against a desk, I tried to calm down. To think of the good news. One hurdle at a time.

Amalyn really might have known what we had been missing, or she could resend all the files. It seemed unbelievable that anything still worked over there. The grainy satellite photos showed there was hardly anything left of the Raft. It had been so long. Where had she been all this time?

As I was about to leave later that evening, Isaac came cycling over to the lab. He sauntered in, his posture casual, relaxed.

'It's been voted on,' he said. 'Your Raft acquaintances are welcome. In a year. By then we should have more accommodation, and hopefully you will have solved the food crisis.'

My stomach knotted, and the room closed in. 'You said you can take as many as was needed. You told me that when we came here!'

'That was before we were burdened with so many of you. Before we learned this lab could not produce enough food. A year should give us time to prepare.' There was a flatness to his voice. Rehearsed, impersonal.

'They don't have a year.' I wiped a tear from my eye. I wanted to seem strong and resolute in front of him. Instead, I was feeble. Too tired, too hungry. The confidence and poise I'd once had on the Raft had been buried in the Tunnels, deeper than the rest of me. Until I figured out the lab and started making enough food, I yielded no more influence than the silkworms.

'Listen,' Isaac said, coldly. 'If we have enough food *before* that, then maybe we can reassess.'

'There are other cities,' I pleaded some more. 'Bordeaux, for example.'

'They have even less tunnel space than us and no manpower to mine more. And they don't have a food lab, although a working lab seems like a pipe dream at the moment.' He scrunched his nose when he said this, like the lab smelled as bad as the filth food.

'But the Rafters can help mine more tunnels. And Amalyn can help with the lab.'

'She can give assistance on the phone or email, can she not? And when we have stockpiles, we will do a food drop. Collecting them though, is impossible. The Raft's airports are long gone. We simply don't have the resources to finance such a mission.'

'No, there must be a way.' The desperation in my voice made me feel smaller than ever.

'The engineers have it as one of their projects. If they come up with a cost-effective solution, I'll let you know. In the meantime, they'll have to fend for themselves for a year.'

And with that, he left.

I had never felt so insubstantial, even when up against the Centre Elite. Where was my brother who was so encouraging all those months earlier? He had been so welcoming back then, yet that side of him had since disappeared.

Cynicism ate away at me. Archie had always taught me to doubt those in power, and now I had to cast that doubt over my own brother. It made me bite my nails and tug on my hair. The words 'cost effective' played over and over in my head, like the Raft refugees were somehow a drain. Nonsense. What price could be put on a life? We were all doing our bit, being useful. And if the reports were to be believed, the Sub-grown filth food was on the up, the shortages were ending, the filth food succeeding where the lab was failing. Not being able to go and collect Amalyn was one thing, but implying there was no room was absurd. These were ideas propagated by rumours, not facts. We'd squash in, we'd make it work until the new accommodation had been built.

I rubbed my temples and groaned. I had to help Amalyn.

There must be a way. There must!

My stomach cramped, and my knees buckled. I'd left her. She'd been buried under rubble at the edge, and I'd left her. I'd thought she was dead. If only I'd stayed, I could have helped. She would be here now. I'd left her then, and I was abandoning her now. No. I couldn't. There had to be something I could do.

A few moments later, Harvey came into the lab. His face was flushed, purple and sweaty, making his scars look like thick veins.

'I tried, I really did. They just don't care enough, the Council. They don't see the Raft people as refugees. Scroungers, one even called them.'

'Thanks for trying, Harvey. We'll figure something out.'

'I'm going to make this a pledge on my campaign. To do whatever it takes to rescue any Raft people. All of you are useful here. So much work has been done since you all arrived. Of course, it's not perfect yet, but it's a damn sight better than leaving you all there to die. We all fled from somewhere, once. I think the Council have short memories.'

Using the Raft as a political bargaining chip was hardly what I had in mind, but some support was better than none. 'When are the elections?'

'In three weeks. I'll be vocal on this matter throughout my campaign. You have my word. As soon as I'm in charge, I'll formulate a plan.' His eyes were glinting, a little sparkle of ambition igniting them. Inspired by other's peril. Typical politician. I couldn't help think that if Harvey was batting for the Raft refugees, Isaac would be opposed. They were each playing their hand, that was all. Pitting themselves against each other rather than working together, a game of tug of war with the Raft refuges as the rope.

I swallowed my discomfort and thanked him before he left. Whatever his motivation, he was still on my side. I had to keep that at the forefront of my mind, rather than my disdain for politics.

Three weeks. *If* he was elected, a plan could commence. No, that was too long. Amalyn needed rescuing right away. Could their food last even that long? It was baffling that they had survived that long without the labs and factories. Could Mars have some spare food to send them? I briefly pondered asking Marcus and Mabel, but quickly thought better of it. The flight time was too long, anyway. The best I could hope for was getting the lab up and running and sending food.

After another day of failing to make enough food, I left for home, walking slowly with the weight of my worries with a brick lodged in my gut. The miners were also done for the day, their unwashed scent filling the space, wafting around the eternal breeze that circulated in the Tunnels. The design based on the termite system kept the air flowing, but I bet that termites smelled better than sweaty humans.

I made it out of the corridor onto the mezzanine floor, where the air smelled fresher and the dappled light was easier on the eyes. I walked to the balcony edge and looked out over the central chamber. The scale of it was still awe-inspiring. A dusky orange light came through the porthole windows as the last of the autumn sun peeked through. The breeze kept the temperature constant even at night. I took a deep breath of cool, musty air. There were no MindSpas in the Tunnels yet. We were encouraged to spend time in the library or gallery if we needed that sort of therapy. I hadn't braved those, the concept too alien, too *Alternate*. Taking a moment to breathe, listen to the clinks of mining axes, and observe the light changing from natural to artificial was the best I could do.

'Sav!' Sara came running over, face flushed with excitement. She seemed so much taller since the time when she first showed me round the Tunnels. She stood straighter, her skin glowing. The vitamin injectable had made her a picture of health and rid her of a lifetime of buckling bones and weak muscles. Her hair had grown back silky smooth, and she looked striking. 'Oh my god, I heard the news. Amalyn is alive?'

'That's right, but there's no way to get her.'

'They'll figure something out. Giao and the Council are overly practical, but they're not evil. They want to help.'

Some miners walked past us, or should I say hobbled, their legs swollen and bruised from beatings. Sara's claim seemed absurd. Evil was everywhere.

'She has a baby, Sara. A day-old baby.'

'It really is wonderful news. I'll work on the Council, I promise. At the next meeting I'll plead your case.'

'That didn't help much with the last problem. Some Rafters are saying there are still spiders in their rooms.'

'They're just spiders,' Sara said, rolling her eyes. 'There's really not much we can do. We're not sterilising the streets like the Raft did.'

I wished they would. I'd seen an ant a few days earlier, just crawling around like it was normal.

'If a Raft representative was able to attend Council meetings, I think that would really help,' I said, for the hundredth time. 'I know you're sticking up for us, but it would be good if the actual Raft people could be heard.'

'I know. Some of the candidates are talking about that for the election. It's just the language barrier. We don't always use English.'

'All the more reason to get Amalyn here. She speaks French and Spanish.'

'I'll do my best. Giao is sympathetic. He really wants to help.'

The same Giao who had told me 'No chance' just a couple of hours earlier? Her optimism was lost on me.

'And Isaac,' she continued, 'he knows how much Amalyn has done for us. He doesn't want any more Rafters to die.' Her voice was like sand blowing over sand. However hopeless everything felt, the sound of it was soothing.

'Just words, Sara. I think that we're alone in this.'

Down in the chamber below, chants had started up and were getting louder. A campaign parade was marching through. It was Harvey with a crowd of a couple of hundred, mostly Rafters, a few Subs. No Council members with the Subs. They were easily distinguishable. Rafters were short, rough-skinned, and withered. Council members stood mostly upright, freshly swollen from the meagre food we made, while regular Subs were long, like the weeds they grew. Stretched, reaching up for the light, hunched and weak.

'Refugees welcome!' they were chanting, over and over. Harvey was standing on a table, raising his arms in time with the chants, fist pumping the air. He held his chin high, reminding me of a Centre.

'See,' said Sara. 'You're not alone.'

'Perhaps not,' I said. The chants were loud. So many people felt a passion for the cause. In Harvey, though, I saw someone impassioned by hate. I saw not someone who cared, but someone who wanted to win.

Chapter 6

The Raft

'Was that really the Mainland?' Danny asked as I hung up, his eyes as wide as the computer monitor.

'It was. A city in the south of France.'

'Well, I'll be. You hear that June? Another country.'

'What I heard was a load of nonsense,' June said through pursed lips. 'And now all I can hear is the sea getting closer.'

'She's right, dearie,' Danny said to me. 'We can't hang around too long. The coast is only a couple of streets away.'

I licked my lips, the familiar taste of salt confirming just that. *Microbes!* How had I not realised? The Raft's erosion had sped up. The sea was now close to our old apartment, and so much of the Perimeter had been lost that the smog blanketed all the remaining land. How many people had been lost along with it? I shuddered to think. Wandering the coast for so long, dodging the cracks, hiding in the shadows, I never noticed the extent of the erosion, or how few people I had seen.

We'd made plans to save so many people, Archie, Savannah and me. A lifetime ago. In the lab, collecting all the documents we needed, we'd decided to get word out and escort as many as possible to safety. We were supposed to give them all a chance. Instead, I had wallowed in grief and denial, awaiting death and yet escaping it. Had any of them made it to safety? Had millions perished? I could have done so much more. I had failed.

I remembered so little of the months since then. Lost in grief, I'd paid no attention to the there and then. My mind only replayed those final days over and over again.

Ams, go, please. Save yourself and the baby.

I can't, Archie, I'm not going to leave you.

His blood trickling, thick and warm, his hand gripping mine. I held him close, felt every heartbeat, every breath. He took so long to die. For days we were stuck under there as he held on, suffering for too long. His body fought, convulsed, and rasped, groaned and bled out until he finally let go. His head wound made him delirious, making him forget where he was, the darkness adding to the delusion. At least his body was numb; the chunk of concrete crushing his spine took the pain away. I hoped so, at least. When he could speak, he expressed only worry about me. His final utterances were only for my safety, trying to make me leave.

You have to survive, Ams.

I can't without you.

Please, save yourself. Go.

No. I'll never leave you alone. I can't live without you.

I should have promised him more, let him die with some hope for his baby. He died thinking that I'd given up, that we would die too. I should have reassured him. I should have told him more times that I loved him. I should have run when he lifted me over the edge. There was so much I should have done, so many decisions that had gnawed at me, doused me with a pain like I'd never known. But it was too late. The fish had taken the edge off the agony for long enough, and now I had to do what he had asked, what I should have assured him I would do. It was too late to tell him, but still I whispered it anyway.

I'll try, Archie, I'll try.

I squeezed my eyes shut, forcing the thoughts from my mind. There was just one life I needed to save now. She was all that mattered. There must be a way off the Raft somehow. I needed satellite images to find out what remained of it.

I grasped the table as my knees went slack, then a second later realised that it wasn't me that was giving way. The building was swaying, just slightly, a few degrees maybe. A rumble then emerged and grew louder.

June folded her arms and tapped her foot, impatient to get away from the edge.

'I'll be quick,' I said. 'I just need to grab a few things.'

I went to the bedroom first and collected some of his T-shirts. They were not the highest priority, but my heart was guiding me. I'd forgotten how hideous they were. I laughed as I inspected them, found one with a tick on the front and 'just do it' written underneath. He'd loved that one.

I went back to the living room and his computer, which was turned off, the power this far away from the Centre too unreliable to keep it going. I started unplugging it all and packing it down.

'We have a computer at our place,' Danny said.

'Not like this one.'

'I have the same one. I worked in IT.'

'Yours won't have the right access. This has all the instructions for the lab. All the satellite access and plans for the solarplanes –'

'Solarplanes?' said June. 'Satellites? I knew she was one of them. It's obvious now she's had a wash. Her complexion is far too good. The Centre left her behind. Even they didn't want her.'

I ignored her as the baby strapped to me woke. I rubbed her back. 'There, there. There's hope, little one.' *Please don't be afraid. Mummy's got you.*

She had his wonky mouth, the little point to his ears. She was all that was left of him. I held her tight. I had no idea love could feel like this. What a horrible world I had brought such a perfect being into. She was too innocent for this. He should have been there, too. He should have been able to hold her, to love her this much. He gave his life to save us, shielding us from the rubble.

'Have you named her yet?' Danny asked, and stroked her hand. She gripped his finger.

'Not yet.'

June rolled her eyes at Danny making kissy noises at the baby. 'You worked for the government, I assume? Only the most corrupt people qualify for fertility treatment.'

'June!'

'It's okay, Danny,' I said. 'I wasn't lying. She was conceived naturally.'

'Bollocks.'

'I'd think the same if I were you, but it's true,' I said. 'My little miracle. And I'm your best chance of surviving, both of you.' I glared at June, who looked away. 'I'm also knackered and sore, so stop being such a bitch for a moment.'

After a click of her tongue, she shut up, and Danny helped me load the computer and all the other paraphernalia on the desk into the suitcase. In the bedroom, I grabbed my old overnight bag, and we filled that too. I went to the kitchen and found a packet of spaghetti and some bottles of smoothie that would probably be spoiled by now, but were worth taking in case.

Another rumble shook the apartment. No time to look for anything else. I turned to leave after one last glance at the home that was so briefly ours, a last glimpse at the happiness we could have shared.

'We really need to go, dearie.'

'I know.'

We left the apartment and bundled back into the Autocar, the sound of crashing waves edging closer.

'One more stop! Please, it's really close to the fence. Sav said there should be tons of food at hers, if it's not been looted.'

Savannah's apartment was still standing. No surprise there, it hadn't been built for paupers, just a stone's throw from the Centre fence. It used to be clear skies around there, but the smog stayed as thick as in the rest of the Perimeter. If it weren't for the Autocar telling us we'd arrived, I wouldn't have recognised it.

I sat for a moment, looking up and imagining climbing those three storeys. There was no chance the lift would be working, and I could walk easier without the extra weight of the baby. Swaddled in blankets and just waking up, I opted to leave the baby with June, as it meant a quicker getaway for her in case the land started to give. My arms ached as soon as they were empty and June made a face like it was the worst thing she'd ever been asked to do, especially since the baby started screaming. But she held her tight, supported her head, instincts taking over. I saw the twinkle in her eyes as she rocked and tried to pacify her.

Again, Danny smashed windows and forced open doors. Inside, the deserted apartment was still cluttered with photo frames and Ethan's toys. They'd clearly packed hardly anything. I grabbed a few photos. Sav would like them, including one of Archie and Sav, another with the entire team in the lab on the Selbourne Range release day.

'Jackpot!' Danny called from the kitchen. He'd found hordes of food, enough to see us through for weeks. All the best, most nutritious food we had made at BioLabs.

'Check in the hallway cupboard. I'll bet there's more.'

'More wine, certainly.'

I laughed. 'Sounds about right. Let's take all we can carry.'

I grabbed what I could and loaded our bags. A pile of paperwork on the table caught my eye. A thick wodge, bound together, *The Poison Maker* written on the front. There was no time to read it now, so I packed that too.

Back at the Autocar, June handed me a still-crying baby and scowled, then loudly whispered to Danny. 'I knew she was posh. Having friends who lived somewhere like this!'

The power was out when we got back, though mercifully it came back on after a few minutes. I fed the baby and put her down to sleep in the drawer-cum-crib that June had made. My chest felt cold in her absence, my arms too light, hollow. I resisted the urge to pick her up again. I had too much to do.

Danny set to work assembling the computer. The way he instinctively knew which cables went where showed that he was clearly a computer engineer.

'All that for a bloody computer,' June said as she sat on the sofa and put her feet up on the coffee table.

'Have you forgotten the conversation on the phone?' said Danny. 'She was talking to another country, June. Another country. Imagine that!'

'I can't. That's my point. The rest of the world is on fire or flooded. We've all seen the images. And now this Centre snitch is trying to tell us there are people out there who give a shit about us? Pull the other one. It's all nonsense. Stupid rumours made up by stupid people.'

I ignored her and carried on plugging in cables with Danny. She could moan all she wanted. This would work, I knew it would. It had to.

'Just think,' Danny said to her, working up a sweat arranging cables under the desk. 'We heard people had gone to the Mainland. We heard the stories of the planes.'

'Stories, exactly. Just stories. It was bollocks then, and it's bollocks now.' She waved her hand at him as if batting him away. 'Turn some of those lights off, for Raft's sake. Who knows how much power we have?'

Danny got up to turn them off.

'I've been there,' I said as I took Danny's seat. 'To the Mainland. The cities are underground, in tunnels.'

June laughed. 'Well, we can humour this crazy lady if you like, Danny. But I'll bet a week's worth of SyntheSpaghetti that she's just another nutcase.'

The monitor lit up and I held my breath. 'Here we go.'

The startup screen hesitated, a swirling circle but nothing more for a time.

Come on, Archie. This has to work.

I could feel him with me, see his little twitch of excitement, his face engrossed in the screen. His login name came up emblazoned across the monitor. *Rey.A.* Short for Archibald Reynolds. The baby stirred, and I went to her, humming to soothe her until she nodded off again.

Sleep little Reya, sleep for now.

And that was it. The computer froze.

'I did say it was a waste of time,' said June. 'The quantum cables are buggered. Danny has been trying to get his computer working for months. But he won't listen to me, even though routing the quantum cables was literally my job.'

I shook my head. 'There must be a way to fix it.'

June shrugged. 'Probably. The cables broke with the Raft. It'd be easy in the Perimeter as most of the cables were exposed. Here they're dug into the bloody concrete. Got a digger in that apartment of yours, have you? A pneumatic drill, maybe?'

'We don't need to get the whole Raft reconnected. Just one computer,' I said. 'If this was your job, you must know of a hub somewhere? Some backup?'

June folded her arms and looked away.

'For Christ's sake, June,' Danny said, his wrinkled forehead getting even more creased. 'This could be a genuine opportunity. What have you got to lose by helping the girl?'

June was startled by Danny's tone and looked at me. Her face softened, just slightly. 'Fine. There's a hub near the Parliament buildings. They have their own network, separate from the rest of the Raft. The other cables breaking won't have affected it.'

'Fuck's sake, June. All this time, we could have had a computer working,' Danny said. I swear I saw steam coming out of his ears.

'What was the point? Who were you going to email? Me?'

Danny rolled his eyes and started to repack Archie's computer. 'Twenty-five years we've been married,' he muttered, almost to himself. 'Twenty-five bloody years.'

Chapter 7

The Tunnels

The echoes in the Tunnels were louder than ever. A constant wave of chatter and emotions reverberated off the walls as I walked home. Campaign leaflets filled my hands and pledges filled my ears. Commuters agreed or disagreed with the campaigners. Plenty of others like me kept their heads down. I flicked through the leaflets when I had some space, the photos on the front showing the candidates smiling broadly, thumbs up, shaking hands with people. I couldn't help but see the falseness in it, the pretence for the sake of power. Posing, filtered, artificial expressions. Deliberately blurred angles and accentuated highlights. Overly polished and puppets for their PR team. Unrecognisable, all of them. Ambition was a charade for dishonesty. Elections on the Raft were less of a democracy and more of a showcase of narcissism, a who's who of the Centre Elite. As I made my way through the Tunnels that night, it felt less like the cohesive community I had visited months earlier, and more a facade for those who craved control.

Marco Paradiso's leaflet was insisting that aboveground was habitable now and we should start getting used to the outside air again. His leaflets littered the floor more than the rest, thrown away as quickly as they had been taken. No one was stupid enough to believe that idea. It wasn't just Harvey who bore the scars from the unrelenting sun.

Juliette St Clair seemed to promise nothing more than upping the wattage of power to each home, with no suggestion of how she would actually do it. But it was a popular idea, judging from the sounds of approval people made when they read her leaflet.

Harvey's main headline was for Rafter's rights, and as I crossed a balcony, this most divisive of topics was on the lips of everyone walking past. The different languages and accents made it impossible to tell what they were saying, though the heated exchanges and gesticulations made it clear that Harvey's campaign had hit a nerve.

Sara and Clementine were having a drink in a seating area as I walked past, and they called me over. They were sitting on rock-carved chairs furnished with a cushion each at a round table, with a shelf off to the side housing a kettle and some cups. It was one of the many areas where people were encouraged to socialise. The level of interaction in the Tunnels still felt alien to me. Socialising at random times, just for the sake of it. It seemed disorganised in its spontaneity. I sat with them and politely took a sip of the drink they handed me. It tasted like ash. How old were they both now? I struggled to think. Early thirties? They both looked half as old as I did when I was their age. They'd never had to put up with all the salt and smog that we did. Even their vitamin-deprived years in the Tunnels hadn't been as harsh on their skin as the Raft was on ours.

'Harvey is upsetting people with his Rafter's rights pledge,' said Clementine. Her hair had grown so much since I arrived, and now fell past her ears in dark, silky waves. She hadn't inherited the Selbourne frizz that Isaac and I shared. 'The financials just don't add up. As much as we don't want anyone left behind on the Raft, it's not that simple.'

'I don't see the issue,' I said. 'It's not like loads more people are going to come. There's hardly anyone left out there.'

'I feel like we opened a floodgate when we said Rafters could come.' I must have shown my hurt in my face, because Clementine quickly took my hands in hers. 'Not you, Sav, obviously. You're family. It's just the Tunnels weren't ready for such an influx. It's been quite an adjustment. Balancing the books is hard.'

'Once Sav gets the food lab going, everything will be fine.' Sara smiled at me, as supportive as ever.

'Oh, I know, I have every faith in you, Sav, and I'm sure Amalyn will be a great help. But there is so much animosity here against the Rafters since they poisoned our food supplies.'

I clenched my jaw. However hard I tried, I couldn't shake the reputation the Centre had left us with.

'Dad has some great ideas,' Clementine said. 'He's publishing his campaign leaflet this evening. I think he's in with a shot. He's ambitious, and more likeable than Harvey. Our first democratic leader should look the part, at least. Harvey and his scars, well ... he's hardly a pin-up.'

Sara scowled. 'Clem!'

'What? I'm just saying what everyone thinks. Have you seen his leaflet? They've tried to blur them out, but they obviously can't hide them.' She dug one out of her pocket and laid it out on the table. 'It looks so fake, don't you think, Sav?'

'I think he's probably not used to posing for photographs.'

Clementine leant back in her chair and tucked her hair behind her ear. 'Anyway, Dad is determined to get costs under control if he's elected, with my help as head treasurer, of course. That'll make life easier for everyone.'

'Yeah, we haven't really recovered since the Select changed the currency and banked so much for themselves,' said Sara.

'They'd still be here if it wasn't for the new currency,' said Clementine. 'If you don't like the Select, despite all they did for us, then you should feel pleased about that, at least.'

Sara shook her head. 'I feel a bit of unity is what the Tunnels need. That's what caused all the problems on the Raft, with my own family. I'd hate to see the Tunnels go the same way.'

'Me too,' I said, determined to get a word in. Talking about the cost of human life was making me angry.

'I guess,' said Clementine, sounding a little bored now. She quickly changed the subject. 'Hey, how are Grace and Ethan doing?'

'Okay. You should stop by, both of you. It's been a while.'

Home was calling me and I got up to leave, saying goodbye to Sara and Clementine. Long days in the lab meant so little time with Grace and Ethan. I couldn't remember when I'd last had a day off.

Grace used to get upset if I didn't spend any time with her. These days, she seemed to welcome our time apart, which made me want to be with her all the more, to prove my worthiness and reclaim her affections. Perhaps she just understood the pressure I was under, or perhaps she was just happy in my absence. That idea made my heart ache, the thought that she no longer needed me making my chest cave in. I had always been the rock she leant against. To pick her up and reassure her. Now she needed no such words. There was no animosity at home, just little affection. She wasn't lost in the dark place like she had been before. She had a vivacity she had lacked on the Raft, as if life in the Tunnels fulfilled her in ways the grey Raft never could. Maybe that was it. Face-to-face teaching, plus Ethan, was all she needed. I was a sideshow.

I upped my pace, ignoring my unsteady legs. Grace may not have missed me, but that didn't mean I didn't miss her. The busyness of the Tunnels had not abated during my short sit-down with Clementine and Sara, and even more news bikes were doing the rounds, adding to the throng. Isaac's leaflets were out, and I grabbed one and read it through. Despite his attitude towards the Raft refugees lately, some part of me still thought — or hoped — he'd make some promise to look after us and whoever else might come along. Instead, the picture of him on the front showed him with broad shoulders in a stern, authoritative pose. The text promised mandatory calorie tracking in a bid to shrink rations to cope with the 'Rafter influx,' and expanding the native food due to the current 'Rafter failure.' He'd actually said that! I scrunched the leaflet into a ball, cursed, and threw it on the floor. He was playing the other side of Harvey's coin, and as I neared home, the divisions between residents sounded more impassioned than ever.

I arrived on edge, tense, my shoulders tight. I had lived in a divided world once before, and felt it coming again. If this carried on, we could be pushed to the fringes of civilisation. As I walked into our home, it hit me how much we had given up on the Raft. Our nice apartment, my successful career, though it was stupid to feel any sort of regret. The Raft had been falling apart. But how could I convince Grace that it had not been a mistake to turn down Mars when the society in the Tunnels seemed to be crumbling like the Raft concrete?

Grace hadn't yet seen Isaac's leaflets when I got home, only Harvey's, so was in a better mood than me, until she started cooking at least. The induction kept failing again, losing heat and turning itself off. She cursed and slammed the pot down.

'Ethan's at his friend's house,' she said, not looking at me as I came in and sat down. 'He should be home soon. This bloody thing never works as it should. They don't allocate us enough power for a single bloody stove.'

'Maybe it's faulty? Let maintenance know?'

'I told them weeks ago, no one ever comes. This food is bad enough without having to eat it cold.'

'I like it cold, mummy,' Ethan said as he walked in. He had pen marks all over his face and his smock was on backwards.

'You have fun with Pierre?' Grace asked. She beamed at the sight of him.

'Matteo was there, too. He has more toy trucks than me.'

'It's nice that he lets you play with them,' I said.

'Pierre had most of them. He only let me play with the little one.'

'Damn, this thing won't heat up at all now,' Grace said, taking her frustrations out on the stove's dial.

I went over and nudged her out of the way. 'Let me have a look.'

'No, just leave it. We can eat it cold. Did you see that Juliette St Clair is promising more power for every home?'

'I did, yeah.'

'Oh, I'm sorry, I shouldn't be going on about that.' She rubbed my back, robotically. There was no warmth in her touch. 'Any more news on Amalyn? It's so great she's alive, just a miracle, her and the baby.'

'What baby?' asked Ethan.

'Shh,' Grace said. 'Grownups are talking.'

She dolloped lukewarm slop into bowls as I shook my head. 'I'll have the lab working soon, I know it.'

'I miss IcyCrema,' Ethan said.

'I know, sweetie,' said Grace. 'Eat your dinner.'

'I've had no news since I messaged you earlier,' I said to Grace. 'It's so wonderful. I'm just terrified for her. How awful it must be on the Raft.'

Grace nodded and sat down. 'Do you think she could stop by our old place to grab some things? Clothes, mainly. We brought so little with us, and these smocks are just awful. I have some cosmetics there, too. I'd love my face cream.'

'Grace! Seriously?'

'Well, if she's there anyway.'

'I think she has other priorities, like surviving and looking after her baby.'

'What baby?' Ethan banged his spoon on the table.

'Ethan, be quiet,' said Grace. She turned to me again. 'I know she has other priorities. It's just you never warned me how limited the supplies here would be. Especially face cream. I don't think anyone even uses it.'

'There's no UV to worry about, no wind or salty air.'

'Just rock dust and filth food,' she said, smoothing out her forehead with her hands. 'I'll bet the Select had face creams.'

'I should think you're right.'

'Pierre's mum has face cream,' Ethan said. 'I saw it in their bathroom.' He was pushing his food around his bowl.

'Is that right?' Grace leant in closer to him. 'What did it look like?'

'I thought I had to be quiet. Grownups are talking,' he said, mocking Grace.

'Cheeky boy,' I smiled.

'Perhaps Ams can bring us some wine?' Grace said to me. 'I'm sure there are some bottles still at our place.'

'I think the Raft survivors should have dibs on whatever food and drink is left.'

She huffed and ate a little of her food, staring at nothing. 'I wonder what she's been doing all this time? She should have called months ago, before the airports all crumbled away. Silly to leave it so long, really. She could have been one of the first here.'

I got up from the table and went to work on my computer. 'I'm sure we'll find out soon enough.'

Chapter 8

The Raft

We got back in the Autocar with no time to waste, a sense of urgency rushing through me. The salty air was a wake-up call. My old apartment was never so close to the edge. We didn't have a moment to lose. The sooner we were off the Raft, the better. My haste was lost on June, however, whose sulking overrode her instinct to hurry. She dragged her feet down the stairs. Her tatty shoes looked like they'd fall apart if she scuffed them anymore. The cupboards at her place were no doubt full of fancy clothes the previous occupier had left behind, but she wanted none of it. She was loyal to the Perimeter, and even the sight of Centre clothes made her screw up her face with even more bitterness than usual.

As we drove more central, the buildings got grander, despite their coating of soot. Hard angles gave way to curves, while functionality gained futile details and lavish additions. But it was all tarnished, just the same. However fancy they made the buildings, it was all turning to shit. The haze was kicking up and blocked our view. The autonomous sensors on the Autocar seemed unaffected, though, and we arrived at the Parliament building. I recognised it from all the photos and film footage of the Centre. Its orb shape, once golden, was now a blackened oval. The plinth where the great bell stood had eroded and looked ready to collapse. Even such meticulous structures don't last forever without care. The moat that surrounded it was thick like the sea, a dark soup of muck.

'It's a small building next to this one. I can't remember which side,' June said as the vehicle stopped. She lowered the Autocar window for a clearer view, letting the smog in. I draped a blanket loosely over Reya's face. Her little lungs were too tiny for such dirty air.

'That one, over there.' June pointed into the murk, and I squinted to see what she was looking at.

'I'll carry the bag,' Danny said.

We got out and wheezed and coughed our way the thirty metres or so to the building as I rearranged Reya's blanket to make sure her face was protected. She gave a little cough and carried on sleeping.

The data centre looked like a doll's house next to the Parliament building, so tiny and simple, easily overlooked. Danny seemed exhausted as he wrenched the crowbar at the windowless door for several minutes. Perspiration dripped down his reddening face and grime collected in the lines around his eyes as they scrunched with effort, giving him a primal, savage look.

When we managed to get inside, all the equipment was off. The room was stifling and leaving the door open only served to let the smog in. I tried the power switch. The lights turned on and the room buzzed into life, the air con in the roof started humming and spluttering, smelling damp and swirling the smog.

I closed my eyes for a moment and imagined what Archie would be doing if he were here. He'd smile that wonky smile and have us up and running in an instant, I knew. Instead, I had a reluctant June, a telecoms engineer, and Danny, whose IT skills had him designing the coding for online grocery shopping. Hardly the dream team I was used to. Still, they knew a hell of a lot more than me.

June rummaged around the room and collected some cables, and the two of them went about connecting the various parts they needed as I reassembled the computer as best I knew how. By some mercy, the power held out.

'The hub has its own power feed as well, its own SolaArbs and battery bank,' June said, 'plus back up. Fool proof. Until this bit of land sinks, anyway.'

Which meant the Centre had deliberately turned it off when they jumped ship. They didn't even think to leave it on for those of us striving to survive. But I tried to let my anger go. We were here now. This had to work.

When it was all plugged in and assembled, we stood back and waited. The screen turned dark blue, the little spinning circle in the middle. I had my back to the screen and looked up at the

ceiling, praying to I don't know who. I just couldn't look. Then
...

'Something's loading on the screen now,' Danny said.

I turned around, feeling lightheaded, and steadied myself and hobbled to the computer. The wallpaper photo was of us, Archie and me, a selfie we had taken in a bar years earlier, a lifetime before, him kissing my cheek, my smile as genuine as a smile could be.

'That the baby's dad?'

'Yeah.' I blinked and wiped my eye. Danny said nothing more. We'd all lost someone – many, most likely. He put his hand on my shoulder and I swallowed back more tears. There was warmth in that gesture, a sympathetic hand, one that understood the pain I was feeling. I had no words to say how much such a small act meant to me. I wasn't alone anymore.

I clicked on a few files, mimicking what I had seen Archie do countless times before. Eventually I found it – the hack for the satellites, our current position and trajectory. The wasteland that was the Raft was there in plain view. As I searched some more, I found the files containing the proof that Archie had put together: our blackmail to the Centre, communications with the Mainland, Harold's video accusing the Centre of hunting him down. Then the food-shipping information, Solarplanes Progressives' flight plans, BioLabs' recipes and factory instructions. Everything.

I sat down, took a deep breath, and leant back. 'See?'

'June, you should see this.'

'Meh,' June said as she looked over Danny's shoulder, then stayed quiet for some time as she flicked through the files. 'So people live like filth on the Mainland, crawling around in the dirt in caves and tunnels. I think I'll take my chances on the Raft, thanks.'

'The Tunnels are huge,' I said. 'Grander than you can imagine.'

'Filth is filth,' she said, standing up straighter. 'And what's the point, anyway? They're hardly going to bother picking us up. What are they going to do? Send the Cavalry? You're dreaming, sweetheart.'

I searched the satellite images again. The smog was thick, too thick to see any detail, but the outline was clear enough. Hardly any of the Raft was left. It looked less than a quarter of the size it had been, maybe even less. Just a jagged oval bobbing around in the rancid sea. Archie's old flat, my parent's place, the lab, the bars – all of it fish food. The airport was gone too, as Sav had said, along with the solarplanes. The Centre and a few miles circling it was all that hadn't crumbled away. In one section, the sea was right up to the fence. The SolAir and ArbAir fields inside the fence were still hanging on, protected by the Centre border, but with the smog it was no wonder the power was patchy. The fence was holding strong, though, no doubt the Centre had given it extra fortifications. All the rest was gone. As elated as I had felt to speak to Sav, with this information, it all seemed impossible. Without an airport, without planes, we were stuck.

'What did I tell you?' said June. 'Total waste of time.'

It couldn't be. This couldn't be it. There had to be a way, I was sure. We were so close to the Mainland. I zoomed out of the satellite image. France was right there, just a few miles away. There was no way I was giving up that easily. I just needed some sleep, some time to think.

I sent the files Sav needed, the recipes and plans for all the lab equipment. At least that was something useful. Danny repacked the computer and all the cabling. I thought we should just leave it there, but we didn't know what looters were still around. June huffed and tutted as she coiled up cables with less care than I would show SynthoSpaghetti. As we made our way back to the apartments, a pit formed in my stomach, a fear that I hadn't known before. I didn't give a shit about the Raft or sinking along with it, but Archie's baby girl had to survive.

My whole body ached as I walked up the stairs to the apartment, hopelessness combining with exhaustion. I shivered when I was hot, sweated when I was cold. Reya cried, as restless as me, and I walked her around the room, jigging her up and down, rocking her a little, encouraging her to sleep. But her cries became full-blown screams. I sat as she cried some more, her little lungs belting out their fear. How could I console my baby and tell her everything was going to be all right when everything was screwed? She could read my mind, feel my emotions, I was sure. I couldn't smile enough to fool her. Barely a day old and I sensed she was already wiser than me.

I stood too quickly, and the area between my legs stung and throbbed. My physical pain made Reya cry all the louder, however hard I tried to ignore it. I hadn't yet dared to look down there. What would be the point? No doctors or hospitals. In any case, a tidy snatch was hardly important. My womanhood had served its purpose. If only the pain would ease.

After a few more circles of the living room, Reya calmed. She nuzzled into me, and I kissed her head. Her serenity, however temporary, gave me a sense of determination. I sat at the table and gazed into her eyes before they closed in a dozy, innocent sleep. I wondered if she had any inkling about the hellhole she had been born into. It wasn't fair. She deserved so much more. A worthy world and a worthy mother. She had neither.

I lay her down in her drawer and fetched myself a glass of water. Bed wasn't calling me, sleepiness eluded me. As exhausted as my body was, my mind was awake with worry. Bed was empty, unwelcoming, fraught with desires that would not be satisfied. Bed was loneliness. So instead, I sat up and missed him all the more.

On the table was the rest of the stuff I had gathered that day, the thick wodge of bound-together paper, *The Poison Maker* written on the front, among it. I had totally forgotten about it. I picked it up and started to read.

This book is not meant to justify my actions. Far from it…

My body was begging me to sleep, but I read on, eyes widening where they should be closing, heart racing when it should be slowing. Sav had written down everything from those years.

References to Archie that made my tears come freely. The time when I first met Sav, the dumb-ass interns wetting themselves and crying every five minutes. I'd found them equally as annoying as her. I made myself a cup of weak MimikTea and continued to read about her job for the Press, Peter Melrose and the Minister of Impartiality.

Oh my god, Sav!

The deal she made, the Centre's ownership of Ethan. Then part two of the book, *The Invisible Kick*, where the Centre's malice really came into its own. The Prime Minister's threat to Ethan. The bloody explosives at the edge! We were just the Centre's great experiment. All their evil was there, written down in black and white. All this time, Sav knew who the Poison Maker was. She actually consented to their lies and learned how the big businesses buy their way into the National Press, Bio-Labs included. Sav knew about it all and allowed it to continue. But it was for her wife and son. Her baby boy. How Grace had suffered, how desperate she had been. I looked over at Reya sleeping in the crib, and the hollow feeling I had battled for so long was filled with love for her. No wonder Sav never said anything. Before, a lifetime ago, before I'd had Reya, I might not have understood. But now, now!

Fair play, Sav.

When I was finished, I tried to sleep but couldn't. Sav's words were turning over and over in my mind. The Centre, the fucking Centre! They killed him. They blew up the edge of the Raft and ended his life years before it should. His daughter will never know her father because of them and their sick ways. My anger quelled my own guilt.

I reassembled Archie's computer and scanned copies of every page, fingers slamming on the keys as I clicked and figured out the software. Rage simmered through me, shaking every muscle. Anger at the Centre for taking Archie from me. For what they made my friend do, how they held her life to ransom, how they brainwashed the entire Perimeter.

I shrank the pages so I could fit twice the amount on the limited paper I had found, and I printed copies of the book. Then I bound them with a hole in the corners and some cable ties I found in a kitchen drawer of knick-knacks. Sav's story would be read. If I found anyone, surely this memoir would help convince them. Everyone knew Savannah. The Selbourne Range had made her a household name. Everyone read her words in the National Press. For years those words had been twisted to suit the Centre. Now her most honest account would straighten things out, if, as she said, there was anyone left to read it.

Chapter 9

The Tunnels

I couldn't sleep that night. Worrying about Amalyn and her baby, worrying about all the Rafters' futures in the Tunnels, what shape our lives would take after the election. I couldn't rid myself of the feeling that I had misled people somehow. The life I had promised was turning into another prison. There was no alternative, I reminded myself as I tossed and turned. For most people, anyway. The Raft was disintegrating. The Tunnels were better than death. Still, I fretted.

After I had turned over many times and could fluff my pillow no more, I got up and left our room, saving Grace and Ethan any knock-on effect of my sleeplessness. I needed the breeze of the Tunnels to take away my worries and hot flushes. I looked back at Grace before I left. She always slept so well; it was like a gift. However discontent she was while awake, when asleep she appeared serene. She slept on the edge of the bed these days, as far from me as she could, wedged up against the wall rather than feel the touch of my skin. It was hard to be affectionate when we all lived in just the one room. I'd justified the chasm between us this way since we arrived. Things would improve, I told myself. Everything would surely improve.

I paced the mezzanine for a while before walking down a tunnel, letting my fingertips brush the rough walls, digging my nails into the carved details. We'd been there for a few months, but the ornateness still amazed me. Things were painstakingly crafted for reasons far exceeding functionality. There seemed little point in the effort.

With everyone asleep, the echoing of the corridors had abated. Only my own footsteps sounded back at me, accentuating my temporary seclusion. The repeating engraving over the walls of the tree and eye design was looking at me, and only me. There was an eeriness in the stillness. The air felt thicker, a swamp of silence. I revelled in the peace. When it was quiet, I heard nothing but truth. As soon as people spoke, the air filled with crap.

My previous methods of relaxing were lost to me now. No MindSpa, no food to gorge on. I missed wine, if I was being really honest. I'd barely had a drop of booze since I arrived. The Tunnels made some spirit alcohol that I'd braved once, and it had taken a layer from the roof of my mouth. It aids digestion; they claimed. I suspected the filth food needed all the help it could get in that regard. Maybe when I got the factory working, I could start making synth grape powder and brew my own wine, or figure out what goes into beer. It couldn't be that hard. That'd certainly make me and the Rafters a bit more popular around there. In the larders, they grew marijuana, a narcotic made of filth from decades before. The Subs said it aids sleep. It also made you hungry, and being hungrier when there was nothing to eat but the muck currently on the menu did not appeal.

So I was left to pacing, wandering the halls, my mind bouncing from pointless thought to pointless thought. Procrastinating the processing of my burdens. I should have been productive in sorting my head out, written a list, thought about the factory rather than moping in the resounding silence. I paced back and forth, hoping my stress levels would ease from the bit of alone time.

The main adaption I was struggling with was the general lack of peace. I had no time to myself, ever, except for the odd late-night pacing. The Tunnels were always busy. They sounded hectic, the constant commotion rattling my bones. Work was over-staffed, and home was cramped. There was no place or time where I could just breathe and not think about bumping into someone or them coming to talk to me. There was no time, except in the dead of night.

Sensor lights flicked on as I walked, giving the otherwise dark tunnels an ethereal glow. I felt a little empowered that they were coming on just for me. I smirked. Wasting power and wasting calories. Imagine if the Council guards saw me! Perhaps I would claim I was sleepwalking.

Campaign leaflets littered the floor. No one had swept them up yet. It seemed careless to make them on material that could be discarded so easily. They should have digital screens here, like on the Raft.

No. That's a stupid idea.

I didn't miss the constant mind bombardment, the inescapable onslaught of information and propaganda. At least here I could walk on the discarded leaflets, wiping my shoes on the drivel.

I stood still for a moment, the echo of my footsteps sounding down the tunnel long after I had stopped pacing. There was another tapping sound.

Microbes! That's someone else's footsteps.

I couldn't very well run off without looking like I was up to no good, so, my tranquillity lost, I waited for the passer-by to come. I leant against the banister as the footsteps drew closer. Had the Council guards started doing night patrols? I didn't have long to ponder this as, just then, someone spoke.

'Professor Selbourne?'

If I wasn't feeling tense enough already, his voice made the muscles in my neck tense. 'Giao. Didn't take you for an insomniac.'

He stopped and leant against the banister a few feet from me, staring into the void below. 'Haven't slept well in a few months now.'

'The pressure getting to you?'

'Something like that.' He breathed out. 'It's good to walk in peace sometimes. I like the Tunnels best when they're quiet like this. I can think.'

'I know what you mean.'

His hair looked greyer than the day before, his tired face more lined. He half-smiled and continued to stare into the void.

'Well, when the elections are over, you can enjoy your retirement.' I didn't mean that to sound as snide as it did. Giao was not at pensionable age – he was younger than Isaac, even – but his time as leader was coming to an end, which was a thought he should have been relishing.

'I suspect I'll have more time to myself soon enough.' There was a sadness in his voice, an emptiness around him. Even his tic was absent. I supposed I had interrupted his peace as much as he had mine. 'You were perhaps the person I least expected to see. Don't you have a wife?'

'I do. I was restless, didn't want to disturb her.' He nodded, slowly. 'And you?' I asked, realising I knew so little about Giao outside of his Council duties. 'No special someone at home?'

'My partner, Blane, is on Mars.'

'Oh. That must be tough.'

'It's only temporary. He's the Select's personal assistant. He went to help them settle in. Once they're comfortable in the new society there, he'll come back.'

'I hope he does.'

We stumbled into a lingering silence for a moment, just enjoying the peace and calm. So different from the usual racket.

Standing next to Giao then, he didn't seem like the ogre he could be at Council meetings. He seemed tired, that's all. Tired and lonely.

'I know I can seem harsh sometimes,' he said, as if reading my mind. 'But you have to understand, I was appointed interim Council leader to provide some continuity after the Select. We're in a transitional period here. Citizens are worried about food, power, finances. As much as I sympathise with the refugees, the citizens of the Tunnels must come first. These Tunnels must prove to be a success in the absence of the Select. We must prove we can rule ourselves effectively, whatever the cost.'

I thought about this for a moment. 'I don't see that allowing refugees to perish is a great benchmark for success.'

'Perhaps not. But I have my brief and my priorities. Who knows what the next few weeks will bring,' he said as he stood straighter. 'I'll leave you to your thoughts. Good night, Professor.'

The soft scuffle of his steps disappeared down the tunnel and, after a few minutes, I started to relax again. The Council members always made my limbs stiff and teeth clench. I knew what power did to people. However much power anyone has, they use it all. It makes people manipulative. Giao's other agenda was clear to me now. To mimic the Select, to rule as they did, to please his partner and the Select on Mars. Those people on another planet had more influence than those just a few miles away.

I stretched my neck and shoulders and made to leave, thinking that I should at least attempt to get some sleep. As I walked away, I spotted one of Isaac's campaign leaflets and noticed something I hadn't seen before. I bent to pick one up and look closer. In the background behind Isaac, full of self-worth and poise, was Giao, like Isaac's shadow. Giao was endorsing Isaac's campaign. I shivered.

Backing Isaac would surely sway opinion in favour of the Select mindset and against Rafters. This was not the neutral stance he was meant to be taking. His endorsement gave Isaac a stamp of legitimacy. I rubbed my temples and dropped the leaflet.

I made my way back to bed, no more ready to sleep, my mind more buzzed than ever. I slipped into bed beside Grace. She didn't stir. I lay there and I stared into the blackness, wondering. Giao had his reasons. Continuity, he said. To keep things as they were until the elections. To please the Select and for Blane's safe return was most likely what he meant.

Who was I to judge him for putting one person's wellbeing above a nation's? I had made that same deal with the Centre Elite years ago. Still, the thought made me toss and turn. A leader with an ulterior motive. I knew a thing or two about that.

Chapter 10

The Raft

Reya woke screaming, a desperate cry, pleading for something she couldn't get from my milk. As much as I'd tried to eat food besides fish, it was impossible to avoid. All the fish and toxins I'd ingested over the previous months were leaving her tiny body; was she craving it now?

I tried to feed her, but she screamed more, her needs clawing at me for the comfort I could not provide. Her cheeks were flushed. She felt warm against my chilled skin and looked at me with helpless eyes. I could not console her.

It wasn't only Reya's crying that stopped me from sleeping, but remorse as well. The anger only abated my guilt for a short time. That hollow pit inside me wouldn't let me forget my mistakes. The blackness was calling me from beyond this room, another darkness I yearned for. When I closed my eyes, I shivered and sweated. I had created a life, carried her in my poisoned body, birthed a daughter into a doomed world. How could I have been so cruel? I should have stayed with Archie, waited for the waves to take me, ended things before her suffering could be measured in cries. Now Reya had a right to live that I could not guarantee. My child, my miracle baby girl, was a day old, and I was already unworthy of her love. One more life I was responsible for destroying.

She cried for Archie, too. I was sure of it. The father she would never know. He was so level-headed. He'd have known how to soothe her. As I cradled her and kissed her head, her shrill cries increased.

I lay her back in the drawer and a voice inside me told me to shut it, to shut her away and silence her screams. My head rang like a bell, echoes of her pain rattling inside me. Just a bit of quiet, a long enough to sleep. That's all I needed. A dark drawer would be more comforting to her than I was. Mothers aren't meant to be cruel. They're meant to provide safe homes and bright futures. Her father was dead because of me. We could have been off the Raft now if it wasn't for me. Everyone was dead because of me. I couldn't pick her up, I couldn't shower her with love, I wasn't capable of it nor was I deserving of receiving it. She ought to have better. Archie's memory deserved better.

I opened the window and let the smog in. A gale blew and carried with it the smell of salt and slurry, reminding me of my months at the edge, of my last moments with him. Sitting on the bed, I hugged my knees. Tears streamed down my face and my skin prickled. I shuddered in the hot air. I wanted the wind to be louder, to take her cries and screams with it, to blow away her longing for whatever I couldn't give her.

I got up and stood at the window, leaning forward and sticking my head out. Where was Archie's body now? Still in the rubble, somewhere at the bottom of the sea. Perhaps devoured by fish, picking at his bones. My eating fish was like eating part of him as well.

I breathed in the salt. I wanted to drown in it and join him in the sea, to let all my fears wash away, to fill my panicked lungs with silt and sludge. He was calling me from the dark, his embrace reaching for me. I promised I'd never leave him, but I did. There was a trail of broken promises and failures all around me. I was meant to save so many lives, but I couldn't save Archie. Now I couldn't save his daughter.

Go, Ams. Save yourself.

What was the point when all I wanted was to be with him?

I leant out further, sucking the smog in deep, choking as it scoured my throat. My skin itched and sweat collected everywhere. I pulled myself up and sat on the window ledge, putting one leg out, then the other. His arms were closer with every extra inch I leant out. I winced from the pressure between my legs, felt myself rip again. He could take the pain away. I'd feel him soon. I'd be in his arms again soon.

'What the hell are you doing?'

Danny's hand grabbed at my nightgown and pulled me in. The din of the room swarmed around me, coming back into focus, Reya's screams ricocheting off the walls. June was there, picking Reya up while her screams grew louder.

'Have you gone deaf?'

'I couldn't ... she wouldn't settle. I don't know how.'

'Shut that bloody window. The smog has even made it to our place.'

Danny shut the window, the roar of the wind disappearing and leaving the room feeling empty, a vacuum. 'There, there, dearie. It's okay,' he spoke to me softly, as if I were the baby. 'It's a learning curve.'

'She wants Archie. What if she needs fish, too?'

June leant in close, her nose inches from mine. 'Fucking junkie.'

Collapsing to my knees, I held my head in my hands. 'I had to, I couldn't find enough food. Please. I don't know what to do. I can't look after her. She won't stop crying. I'm so tired. Just so tired.'

'It's okay, June is being mean. Here.' Danny lifted me gently by my arm and led me to the bathroom. 'Why don't you get cleaned up? We'll look after Reya tonight, and you just get some rest.'

'Fucking babysitters. Great,' June said, as she left with Reya.

'No, please don't take her away!' I shouted.

'We'll be right next door. We're not going anywhere,' Danny said. 'You need some sleep, and you'll feel right as rain in the morning.'

They left, Reya's cries diminishing. The room was bright and the lights too imposing. The quietness Reya left behind was too much. My heart raced. Would she be okay? She should be here with me. Next door felt like a million miles away.

An emptiness came over me. Who was I? A bereaved woman. A failed mother. A murderer. My jaw hurt. I went to the bathroom and brushed my teeth, spitting out blood. Putting my hand in I felt a loose incisor. I pulled, and it came out with ease, causing less pain than was satisfying. I looked in the mirror and made my face into a grin. At least no one would ever want to perv on me again. The gap in my mouth now substantiated my position as the edge-dwelling junkie June thought I was. I stood under a hot shower, feeling as unclean as I had in the months before scavenging at the Raft's edge. The water couldn't wash everything away. I was as polluted as the sea.

When I crawled into bed, it was cold and too soft, the mattress and blankets forgiving in a way I didn't deserve. I should have had a bed of nails or hot coals. Despite the stuffiness in the room, there was a chill. A hardness where soft arms should have been. I stroked the vacant sheets, blinked away tears, spoke his name over and over, before my body gave in to sleep.

**

Sleep brought some relief from physical pain for a few hours, but my dreams were filled by him. I woke crying several times in the night, reaching for him, his absence ripping my heart in two every time. It gets easier, Danny had said. There was no way it could get any harder. I was broken into a million pieces.

I cried myself to sleep again. Woke again and cried myself to sleep once more.

When morning came, my puffy eyes burned, but I felt fresher, slightly. My heart skipped a beat when I remembered she wasn't there, my arms cramped with emptiness as I ran to the apartment next door.

'Reya!'

'It's fine, dearie. She's fine.' Danny and June were both seated at their table. Danny was holding Reya over his shoulder, rubbing her back. 'I found some formula on my last forage. She's had some of that.'

'Good afternoon. Sleeping in till lunchtime a habit for you, is it?' June's scorn was deserved. I blushed with shame. A voice in my head repeated, *bad mother, bad mother, bad mother.*

'Shut it, June,' Danny said. 'She needed the rest.'

I took Reya from Danny. She looked at me like she knew me already. Had she missed me? Did she ache for me as I did for her?

'Hey there, mummy missed you.' I felt her forehead, looked in her mouth. She seemed calm, well, alert. Her eyes followed mine, aware, coordinated. 'She been okay?' I asked. *Have I harmed my daughter?* Is what I meant.

'She settled eventually, and slept right through till seven,' Danny said.

'Thank you so much. I just felt so helpless. I still do. We're stuck. Her life is over before it's even begun.'

'Oh, come on, we'll figure the food thing out,' Danny said, and handed me a cup of weak MimikTea. 'You said you used to make food, right? So maybe we can do that. And this part of the Raft inside the fence will last for ages yet. Maybe the Mainland will drop some food off. We've lasted this long. I'm not giving up yet.'

His optimism was refreshing. Holding Reya, the cramps in my arms went away, but a shadow still encased us. The sweet and musty smell of MimikTea always brightened Archie's moods. I shifted Reya to my other side so I could have a sip.

'What's that mark on your arm?' June asked.

'My tattoo? It's the symbol for the Golden Fifty. Some old friends, that's all.'

'Well, some of your old friends clearly like to graffiti perfectly nice buildings. Seen that symbol sprayed on a block where I was foraging this morning. Marking their turf, I reckon. Fucking gangs.'

The mouthful of hot tea burned in my throat. 'Wait, you saw this symbol? Are you sure?'

'I ain't tripping on fish like you are, sweetheart.'

I sat down, my knees weak as it dawned on me, almost dropping my cup. I held my forearm to my chest, feeling their closeness in my heart. 'That means there must be some other people alive!'

'Oh great, more nonsense from the batshit crazy junkie.'

'June!' Danny said. 'Can't you see she's having a tough time?'

'She's full of crap. There are no people left, Danny. Not besides this stray.' She grimaced. 'When's the last time you saw someone?'

'It's been a while, it's true,' he said. 'But that's not to say there isn't anyone else.'

'Want to share out the food more, do you?'

'There might be people who can help.'

'They can help us starve.'

The sound of their debate receded from me, becoming like waves hitting the coast, a slurry of words with no meaning. All I could think was that there were people alive here, some Golden Fifties still hanging on. The symbol was proof. It meant hope. There were friends here, somewhere. I brushed my hair away from Reya's face and kissed her. 'They're alive, little one. There are some left.'

'We should be careful. If there is anyone here, they'll be pretty desperate. People do stupid things when they're desperate,' Danny said.

'Yeah, like taking in strays they can't feed.' June narrowed her eyes at me.

'Had a knife pulled on me a few months back. Nothing recently, though,' Danny said. 'If there is anyone here, they're keeping to themselves.'

'There must be some people left,' I said. 'They're just hiding. They're scared. I need to find them.' I yawned and shifted uncomfortably in my seat. It had only been a couple of days, I reminded myself. Full recovery would take time.

'You should rest, dearie.'

'I've had enough sleep, thanks.' I hoped the redness of my eyes wasn't too obvious. 'There's no time to rest. I need to figure this out. I have to get Reya to the Mainland.'

'Oh, for Raft's sake,' June said, throwing her arms in the air. 'If she wants to exhaust herself over some goddamn fantasy, then don't stop her. It's one less mouth to feed.'

'You've got milk, have you? Enough formula?' Danny said, raising his voice now. 'If she dies, how are we going to feed the baby?'

'We're not, obviously.'

He gasped. 'You're better than that, June.'

I left their apartment; they could argue without me. I needed space to think. Reya was dozing. I should have caught up on some sleep too, but my mind was in turmoil.

There must be some Golden Fifty left.

Sav and her family had made it, and my parents had gone with them. There was so much good news, but one massive hurdle to overcome. How to get off the damned Raft.

Danny's convictions alternated between there being no one left and the streets being unsafe due to unsavoury people. Neither could be one hundred per cent true, I concluded, but what was certain was that inaction was not an option.

I made up my mind. There was one option. However risky it was, I had to try. Archie had an e-pad that connected to satellites, which I had found in the apartment. I carefully took the monitor and hard drive out of the suitcase and there it was, Archie's old e-pad. Relieved, I sat down and turned it on. By sheer luck, the battery was almost full. I clicked on the satellite images and saw the weather-beaten blob of the Raft, still right next to France. We'd not moved much since before. Or maybe we had drifted miles and returned. How would I know? I zoomed in and searched the coast, every inch of shoreline. My jaw dropped when I found them. Boats. Still clinging to the edge, a bit of dock remaining on what was currently the east coast. I knew then I had to get a boat, and soon. Who knew how much longer that bit of dock would last? If the Raft spun around in the sea, that would make the journey so much longer. It was like France was protecting us, that bit of coast, anyway. Keeping us close and shielding us from the worst of the erosion.

I reached for the satellite phone and dialled.

Chapter 11

The Tunnels

Amalyn had sent the email with all the missing information we needed. It had everything, including instructions for the bulk production of fibre, and my recipes with the key stage I had been missing. I kicked myself for not having it all in the first place. There were thousands of steps in such complex processes that I had honed over the years, and I had been so careful before we left. But in the panic at the end, I had missed something. We were supposed to have an extra day to prepare. Archie and Amalyn were meant to help me check everything was complete. But it didn't matter now. I had what I needed to make the lab efficient and get the food on a par with what we used to make.

I made a test batch, allowing the gorgeous taste of perfectly synthesised roast potatoes, fluffy and moist, to melt in my mouth. They were as heavenly as I remembered, more so, since

I hadn't eaten anything decent in so long. I turned the fans up to stop the smell spreading, then saved the information and hid it away in a password-protected file. For the moment, I wanted to be the only one who knew, until I'd had the chance to speak to the Council.

With a full stomach, my head was the clearest it had been in months. I rinsed my mouth out and wiped my face, not leaving a crumb to give me away, and I walked down the corridor to the Council offices. I wasn't going to wait for Sara to appeal to the Council. My Raft voice needed to be heard.

The Council officers were sitting round the table, leafing through paperwork, seemingly doing nothing besides designing campaign posters. Celia, Kevin's mother, was sitting next to Isaac, leaning into him and hanging off his every word. My entrance went unnoticed. I stood in the doorway a moment, a speck of dust to them.

'I've spoken with Amalyn,' I said to the room. 'All the information I need is with her on hard copies. The Internet on the Raft is down. There is no way for her to send it to me. The satellite phone certainly isn't good enough to convey such complex information. We need to go and get it. But once I have that, the lab will be functioning and efficient, I promise you.'

Giao put his paperwork down and paused a moment. 'Fine,' he said, smiling but not smiling. He took a sip of his filth tea. Its steam fogged his glasses.

'Really?' His response surprised me. 'Well then, when do we go?'

'We don't. No one does. They're welcome here to live, work and contribute. But they have to make their own way here. Their airports have gone, we have no boats, and I won't risk any of our people.'

'We can get boats,' Harvey said, leaning forward on his elbows. 'We could speak to Bordeaux. They certainly used to have boats. They still have docks, I'm sure. We could wait for a weather window –'

'No,' said Giao, loudly, cutting Harvey off. 'Even if they do still have boats, who has sailed recently? No one. It's too dangerous. Storms are frequent and the Raft could be anywhere.'

'Actually, the Raft is close at the moment,' I said, 'just off the west coast of France.'

'If we can help, we should,' said Harvey.

'I'm still in charge,' said Giao. 'Perhaps in the unlikely event of getting elected to this position, you can then decide to lead our people on a suicide mission.'

I looked at my brother. He was silent, and pointedly not looking my way. 'Isaac, back me up. You know Amalyn, how much she did for us –'

'What she did was send a load of Rafters here with no way to feed them,' Isaac said, staring at his clasped hands on the table. 'Hardly the hero you make her out to be. Perhaps if she and yourself had been organised enough at the start and brought all your information with you, we wouldn't be in this mess.'

Celia's face was almost as red as her hair, and she rolled her eyes every time the Rafters were mentioned.

'Well, those Rafters will remember your callousness in the next elections,' said Harvey.

'Rafters will not be getting a vote, obviously,' Giao said.

'Why the hell not?' said Harvey. 'They live here. They should have a say.'

'They haven't *earned* a say,' said Isaac with venom, Celia nodding along with him. 'They use our medicines, eat our food, gorge on our power, take up our space, and for what? It was their government that robbed us of our synth food, remember? *Their* government, who *they* elected.'

'Elections on the Raft were a farce, and you know it,' I said, my voice loud.

'There are some people from the Centre living among us,' said Giao. 'Their people robbed us blind. They stole our food and took it to Mars. Or have you forgotten? And you want to give them a vote? No. That would be ridiculous. They gave up that liberty when they associated with such people.'

At least he was differentiating between Perimeter and Centre. That was something. I walked up to the table, close to Giao and Isaac. 'You say that like we had a choice. We were cordoned off by the fence. We had no choice.'

'I'm sure there was a lot more you could have done,' said Giao. Isaac smiled at that.

'Giao, seriously. These people are digging tunnels, working in our factories. They deserve a say,' Harvey said.

'It's in the laws that you all signed.'

'Nonsense.'

'Read the small print. You must be a resident in the Tunnels for ten years before you are eligible to vote.'

'Ten years!' Harvey and I exclaimed together.

'Again, Harvey, if you are elected to run this country, you can do what you like. In the meantime, we must stick to the laws that the Council wrote and signed. And we signed the laws preventing mob rule.'

Mob rule! I clenched my fists so hard my nails cut into my skin.

'Bullshit,' said Harvey. 'Those rules were made when we were under the dictatorship that was the Select. We're a democracy now.'

'Not yet, we aren't,' said Isaac. 'The running of these Tunnels was handed over to the Council by the Select. Nothing else has changed. The elections haven't happened yet.'

'There'll be an uprising. Riots!'

'That's what the porthole doors are for, isn't it?' said Isaac.

'No!' Harvey's hand instinctively shot up to his scars. 'We said never again. That was what the Select did.'

'The Rafters get whipped and beaten,' I said to Isaac. 'Are you following the example of the Select?'

'We were all subject to such discipline when we built the Tunnels. Are you saying the Rafters should get preferential treatment?' Isaac asked.

'No, I'm saying that perhaps you should learn lessons from the past instead of repeating the same mistakes.'

'Letting Rafters in has proven to be a mistake so far,' said Isaac. 'Perhaps we should learn from that.'

I stared at him, my mouth hanging open. My own brother saying our arrival had been a mistake.

Harvey got up from his seat. 'For god's sake, they're refugees. What the hell is wrong with you?'

'Perhaps I'm just hungry, like so many of us.'

He didn't look hungry. His face was fuller than when I had first come to the Tunnels.

'Giao,' I pleaded, 'you must understand how important it is for Amalyn to get here.'

'I do, and I hope she makes it. I really do. But we currently have no means to collect her. I'm sorry.'

Isaac smirked, revelling in the diatribe. He looked like less of a big brother and more like a bully. Giao backing Isaac made Harvey's campaign look like a sideshow. But what was his motive? It was no great surprise that he was concerned about the effect of the Rafters, but he didn't seem to be as anti-Rafter as Isaac. And he wanted out of power, or so he claimed. Why throw his weight behind a candidate?

There was no point in me staying in that room. Their bitterness was so entrenched. And it was my fault. My rage was at myself as much as them. If the factory had worked from the start, us Rafters would have been their saviours, not scroungers. Had hiding the truth from them about the information on the lab been the best play? As I paced the corridor, I decided that it had been. Withholding the food, saying that Amalyn would bring the information with her, was my best hand. They agreed she could come, at least. If she didn't make it, well, I could just say I figured it out myself.

But she would make it, she and her baby. She'd find a way.

My anger wouldn't dissipate. How could my own brother be so cruel? He had been the one encouraging us to come, and now he had forsaken us. A hint of power and he had turned into everything I hated about the Centre, the Select, anyone who put their own agenda and desire for control above ordinary people. He was playing politics, angering Harvey to create division, I was sure of it. He couldn't believe those things he said, not my brother.

I trudged back to the lab. All that awaited me there was a farce, killing time to make it look like I still didn't know what I was doing. My job had always been to feed people, now I was to trying not to. I held that knowledge as ransom for my friend's survival. The clean slate of honesty the Tunnels presented months earlier now seemed as dirty as the Raft.

I heard the miners picking at the rock in the new wing they were digging. Even from that distance, I could smell their perspiration and hear their pain. Their misery echoed in the tunnels. My full stomach knotted with guilt. They should have food now; this was so unfair to them. Perhaps if I made a little more, increased production by a couple of boxes, that could help. But how to do that without letting the other factory staff know? Chris, Betsie and Esther, the lab staff, were Rafters, and had worked at BioLabs. They'd understand and keep it under wraps, I was sure. But Kevin would be harder to convince, yet also easier to fool. The BioLabs employees' experience was minimal, but they'd had a lot more than Kevin.

Sara was waiting for me when I arrived, slouching over a desk as if she wanted a nap. It wasn't just the Rafters who looked overworked, I noted. As head of human resources, she seemed to be everyone's assistant, and she was too polite ever to say no to a request. She seemed to spend all her time running errands and delivering bad news. Then I remembered I hadn't prepared my weekly progress report for her.

'Sara, I'm sorry. Can I give you the report tomorrow?' I logged in and saw our lack of progress in the spreadsheets, with only double-digit numbers where there should be triple-digit.

'Sure, it's not due till then, anyway.'

'Oh.' I stopped reading. 'Then why are you here? Sorry, I didn't mean for that to sound as rude as it did.'

'I've been listening to Harvey and Isaac debate all morning. I've forgotten what polite sounds like. I wanted to say again how pleased I am about your friend.'

'Thanks.' I saw that her face was drawn. She looked at the floor. 'How are you?' I asked.

'I'm fine. I was wondering if you know the names of the Rafters who have already arrived?'

'There's a thousand of them. I don't know all their names.'

'Perhaps I could see the register of the Rafters? I know Clem is in charge of it, but was wondering if you had a copy, since you welcomed most of them here.'

I frowned. 'It's supposed to be confidential. Did Isaac or Harvey put you up to this?'

'No, it's for me.'

'Is there someone you're looking for?'

'I don't know, really. Maybe. I thought I saw someone I knew. Probably my mistake, though. It's been such a long time since I saw him. Years since I was on the Raft. It wasn't even the Raft then.' She played with her sleeves.

'The Council have the lists. But names are only disclosed if you make a submission to the register and you are matched to someone on their contact list. You'll have to speak to the Council. I'm sure Clementine will help.'

'I know. I didn't want to bother anyone else with this, really.'

Yet she was here, bothering me, being cagey, testing my patience. 'I wish I could help, Sara. What's the name of the person you're thinking of? I could ask around?'

'No, it's fine, really. Don't worry about it. I'll submit my name on the register with the Council. I should do things the proper way.'

I started scanning the spreadsheets again, thinking I might as well practise looking busy. But Sara didn't leave, and stayed slouched against the desk, eyes darting from one corner of the floor to another. She reminded me of the interns back at Bio-Labs on their first day.

'Is there something else I can help you with?'

'The Council have asked me to pass on a message ...'

'I was there ten minutes ago. They're still getting you to do their dirty work, then?'

'They said it would be for the best if the Rafters here didn't know that others might be coming. Best to keep it quiet for now.'

'The Council, or Giao and Isaac specifically?' The bitterness in my voice wasn't meant for Sara. I regretted it and bit my lip. She didn't need negativity from me as well as the Council.

'It appears to be a Council decision. They're worried about the way it looks, with the elections coming.'

'They want me to lie?'

'No, just keep it to yourself. For now.'

'Well, I told Grace yesterday, she's probably spoken to other parents. I've no idea how many people know.'

'Maybe just don't say anymore. They don't want to give false hope.'

I sighed and turned my attention to the spreadsheets once more. *Hope.* The deadliest of things. But sure, why not? I was good at lying.

Sara finally left after that, and I could get on with figuring out how to make the equipment marginally more functional without giving anything away. I looked at the satellite phone sitting next to my computer, longing to hear Amalyn's voice. A brief call with as much static as words wouldn't scratch that itch. I wanted a glass of wine and a sofa to catch up, to chat for hours, to laugh like we used to. To grieve. And to meet her baby. I went down memory lane for a while, and my attention was snapped back by the sound of the phone ringing, as if it had been listening in on my thoughts.

'Ams?'

'Sav, hey, did you get my email?'

'I did. You've saved the lab! But listen, the airports are gone. We don't know how to get to you.'

'I know. I've seen the satellite images. It's all gone, Sav.'

'They say when we have enough, we can do a food drop. But there's no way to come and get you. There are elections soon, and some candidates are more sympathetic. If Harvey gets elected –'

'I can't rely on that. I'm not sitting tight for weeks to wait and see.' She was speaking quickly, sounding almost frantic. Through the crackly line, it was difficult to make out every word. 'We're close now, really close to the west coast of France, and the time of year is good. There'll be storms soon. We could miss our window. Without the airports, it's impossible for you, but we're not far.'

'But without an airport –'

'I'll get a boat.'

'What? Ams, no, that's crazy. You have a newborn.' She couldn't be serious!

'We won't survive here for long. We can't wait. Reya deserves a chance.'

'Reya?'

'That's what I've called her. After Archie. Archibald Reynolds. She has his ears, and his wonky mouth.'

'Oh, Ams.' My eyes were streaming. She sounded so strong and resolute. I was a mess.

'Don't, Sav. No tears. No pity. You thought we hadn't made it, so no guilt either. I can do this. I know I can. I'm going to find as many people as I can and get a boat. There are some Golden Fifties left, I know it. We can sail as close to Toulouse as possible. If you could send me the details for the tunnel entrance closest to the west coast, I can get there.'

'Of course, I'll send coordinates. It's near Bordeaux, I think.'

'Okay, I'll get there. Whatever it takes. I'm coming.'

And then the line cut out.

She sounded older, sure, but she was the same Amalyn. I remembered her, the woman who would not be told. Stubborn, determined, reckless. Bad-ass.

Chapter 12

The Raft

Bordeaux. That didn't sound too far. I zoomed in on the map and found it. It was so close I felt like I could reach out and touch it. I needed to check the boats were intact, plan a route, and find people to help.

Reya settled much better that night and I even managed a few hours myself. First thing the following morning, I left for the docks to check on the boats. I covered Reya with some face cream I found in the bathroom cabinet. Then I made a tent out of blankets, tying it round my neck to shield her from the worst of the elements. June and Danny weren't up yet, by the sounds of it. I padded down the hall and stairs, still with wobbly legs and in pain. The Autocar was where we'd left it, still accepted my payment and, despite the sky being almost completely clouded, had enough solar power to run. I counted off these small miracles and dreaded the time when my luck would run out.

I followed the route to the docks on the e-pad, keeping its brightness down to conserve the battery, then set the Autocar to idle when I arrived. A concrete wall lined the coast that was too high for me to see over. The e-pad told me I was in the right spot, but I had to check. Any convenient way to get up to the platform had long gone, and just a few metal loops remained of a ladder. With the e-pad in its case slung over my shoulder, I tightened the papoose scarves and climbed. Up on the platform were concrete posts and crumbling concrete. I trod carefully, testing each step before committing my weight. It felt sturdy enough.

There were two boats bobbing away alongside the dock. Huge Centre fishing trawlers, the decks still laden with nets, the smell of rotten fish still hanging in the air. There was no branding on the side, as no pharmaceutical company actually wanted to be associated with fishing. I wondered if the Centre residents knew where some of their medications had come from. They probably ignored it, like everything else that happened outside the fence. Burying their heads in the dirt as usual.

With the e-pad, I took pictures of the boats, trying to ascertain the makes and models. Zooming in, I checked the hulls, or what I could of them. There were no obvious holes from what I could see. They were still floating so they couldn't be in too bad a condition. I didn't dare climb aboard, not without help. It was quite a leap from the dock to the boat and they moved erratically in the wind, huge beastly things that I did not know how to control. I could find a manual, I hoped, but to actually drive one of them? Out to sea, the water looked like thick soup, so viscous a boat would capsize in it rather than float. A task that seemed so doable a few moments earlier had suddenly got a lot harder.

I climbed down again, gingerly on weak legs, the pain still unrelenting. As I got to the last step, I stumbled and fell to my knees, gravel cutting my skin, grazing the skin of my palms. Reya let out a cough, but she was secure against me and safe. I started to cry, sobbing with self-pity, shame, and desperation. As my cries got louder, Reya joined in, screaming her own sadness out. I stayed kneeling, hopeless and helpless. When my crying eased, I clenched my fists and yanked my hair. A gust whipped up and brought with it the smell of rotten fish and rank sea, reminding me of Archie's resting place. That boat could take us far away from here, away from the Raft, away from him. From those arms that would never hold me again. Instead of escaping, I imagined us slipping under, giving in to the dark. The hollow feeling returned with a thud.

I screamed. Not just with my throat, but with every part of me. I screamed as if every cell in my body would burst. I slammed my fists into the gravel until my knuckles bled. When the despair left me, anger rose, heat welling up as every muscle tensed. I was so fucking angry. With myself, with him, with this fucking place. With the impossibility of it all. I couldn't even climb down a ladder without falling. Pain ripped through me still. I was useless. I screamed some more, and when my lungs deflated, I looked beneath the tent of blankets. Her teary eyes peered up at me, her cries muted now, little gasps of exhaustion. *Come on, mum,* I felt her say. *Pull yourself together.*

Standing up, I steadied myself then walked along the concrete wall until it ended and just the edge remained. A short cliff gave way to the sea below. I glanced down, squinting through the haze and fog, and could see several fish gasping for air at the surface. I felt the familiar desire, but Reya's muted sobs reminded me why I mustn't, why I needed a clear head. She wanted feeding. She needed clean milk, not something contaminated.

I promise, Archie. I'll try.

From where the concrete wall was no more, I could lean over and see other boats, just shadows in the mist. I took a few more photos, hoping that I'd be able to find instructions for working them, then walked away from the edge.

When I got back, the Autocar was still ticking over. Just as I was about to climb in, the wind carried another sound. A voice. It was high, sweet, with the smallest of giggles. A child? Reya was grizzling a bit, but not laughing; she was too young for that. I checked the Autocar charge, and it had enough battery for now. I walked back along the coast, towards where the voice had come from.

The wind kicked up gravel, scattering it noisily across the ground, and when it calmed there it was again, the dainty laugh, childish sounds. If I had eaten a fish, I'd have assumed it was some hallucination, but I was sober. I walked for a couple of minutes in the dense smog until I saw a shape ahead of me. A woman holding a child by the hand, zigzagging over the cracks and holes. I recognised that gait. It was someone with no fear of the edge, needing to see what was in the sea, the child staggering and scurrying along beside her. I held my breath, thinking for a moment I had imagined them as the smog grew thicker and enveloped them. Then it cleared a little and there they were again, sooty stick figures on the edge.

'Hello?' I called out, stepping closer. I watched their hands for the glint of metal, a weapon, but they were empty. 'Hello, do you need help?' The shapes froze. 'I'm not going to hurt you. I can help.'

I remembered when Danny had found me, how distrusting I had been, yet how I followed, desperate to find some comfort.

'I have food.' I inched closer. They didn't back away. The girl hid behind the woman, peeking at me, wild curious eyes checking me out. Her cheeks were hollow, her legs like matchsticks. 'Are you hungry?' I rummaged in my bag and found a packet of VitaBiscuits. The tiny figure broke free of the handgrip and ran towards me, then stopped abruptly a couple of paces away. 'I'm not going to hurt you,' I said again. I gasped at how filthy she was, dust and grime covering her. Her dress was thick with treacly smog, as was her hair. I couldn't tell what colour either was meant to be. I knelt down. 'It's all right. Here.' I handed her the packet, which she snatched and tore the packaging off. 'Who's that? Your mum?'

She shook her head, stuffing a biscuit into her mouth.

'My name's Amalyn. What's yours?'

She carried on chewing, pondering the question for a moment. 'Cora.' Her voice was a sweet little whisper.

'Nice to meet you, Cora. Who's the person with you?'

'Just a lady who stays with me.' Crumbs of biscuits fell from the gaps in her bottom teeth, big ones starting to grow through.

'Well, how about I take you both back to my place and get you cleaned up and fed? Would you like that?'

Her big eyes looked at me longingly, yet her forehead strained with worry.

'What's your friend's name?'

'Tilly.'

'Okay, let's go speak to Tilly.' Reya gave a little snivel under the blanket that was covering her. Cora looked taken aback at the sound. 'It's okay, that's my baby, Reya. You want to see her?'

Cora nodded, and I lifted the blanket a bit.

'She's so tiny,' Cora said.

'Come on, let's speak to Tilly.'

Tilly was still frozen to the spot on bowed legs, her eyes glazed and unfocussed. She looked dirtier than Cora. Her clothes were ripped, and across her right forearm, a symbol was visible through the dirt. That symbol I knew so well, the one that meant she was a friend.

'Tilly?'

She didn't respond, her mind stuck elsewhere. I could smell the fish on her.

'Tilly?' I lifted my sleeve. 'Look. I'm Golden Fifty, like you.'

She blinked, some recognition there, somewhere.

'Let's get you cleaned up and fed.'

Cora took her hand, but Tilly hesitated. I opened my bag, then lifted the blanket to show her. No weapons, just a baby. Her eyes focussed for a second, though recognition seemed a long way off. Bloodstains mingled with the grubbiness on her clothes. She had a raw-looking wound on her arm that seemed to have been made by a knife, along with bruises around her neck. I had escaped the worst of the looters and robbers while I was alone. Tilly clearly had not.

I started walking, and they followed me. We got to the Autocar and the three of us squished in. I tried not to look at them with pity, Tilly's lost face and little starving Cora. They didn't want pity. They had survived where so many hadn't. Tilly was stronger than she knew.

After a few minutes in the Autocar, Reya coughed, still sleeping and dreaming. Tilly's eyes suddenly snapped into the here and now.

'A baby?' she mouthed, the quietest of rasps, like she'd been screaming for weeks and no one had heard.

I lifted the blanket. Cora's eyes lit up again. Tilly, though, looked at me and recoiled as she blinked over and over, disbelieving, trying to understand what she was seeing.

'Centre?' she asked with a wheeze.

I didn't answer, just shook my head. She looked in no state for a debate. The Autocar arrived at the apartment block, and despite her wariness, Tilly followed me upstairs with Cora running ahead. I hoped Danny and June wouldn't be in. No such luck.

'Oh, for fuck's sake. Now the stray is bringing in strays.'

'She's just a kid, June,' I said. 'I couldn't leave her.'

'That one's no kid.' She narrowed her eyes at Tilly. 'Danny, seen what this hussy has done?'

Danny appeared in the doorway. His kind smile didn't waver at all. 'I found some extra biscuits today. I'll bring some over,' he said, disappearing into his apartment.

I showed the bathroom to Tilly and Cora, ran the bath, gave them fresh clothes and towels, and fluffed up the pillows in the spare rooms. While the bath was filling, I showed them the shower, helped them undress and bundled them in there, the water turning black as it collected underneath them. Was I ever this dirty? Worse, probably. After shampooing, Cora's hair was pale blonde instead of black, while Tilly's was dark and grey, bouncing with curls. The bath was full, and I helped them get in, the tub easily big enough for two. Cora delighted in the bubbles as Tilly remained silent, distant. She wasn't present yet.

In the living room, I looked through my photos of the fishing boats, making notes of all the details I could see, including the model numbers written on the side. All ready to research instructions when I got back online. I had two more people to get to the Mainland now. It didn't look like they were going to be much help, but I had two more souls to save.

Somehow.

Chapter 13

The Tunnels

Amalyn's call had emboldened me. If she could be that brave, so could I. Well, maybe not as brave as that, but I could do more than just put up with being treated like shit. A bit of authority from me would be just what the Council needed to see sense. I once commanded respect, took delight in quivering bottom lips and shaking hands as I inspected and scrutinised. What was I here in the Tunnels? Some flimsy joke of a scientist with a crew of inept slackers, with a useless lab, unclean, disordered and unfunctional. Walking around the factory, I found spillages that hadn't been cleaned up, glassware in the wrong place, spreadsheets with gaps. How the hell were we supposed to get this lab up and running when the staff were so lax?

Ester and Betsie sat in the corner, doing nothing in particular.

'Lazing around, are we?'

'Not really sure what to do, Professor,' Betsie said with a shrug. 'The factory just doesn't work.'

I had a few ideas. 'Clean up the mess, fill in the logs, try another batch with an adjusted spin rate. There is literally tons you could be doing instead of sitting around. And where the hell is Chris?'

'Went for lunch, I think.'

'It's only eleven thirty. Who said he could go?'

Blank faces stared back at me.

'Get to work. Now!'

'Yes, Professor,' they replied, and stood weakly. They looked thin and unsteady. I felt bad for a moment. But only a moment, mind. They could eat their filth rations if they were that malnourished.

Acting like my old self for a moment left me feeling liberated. My skin prickled, buzzing in the same way the lights in the lab flickered. Screw trying to be nice and amicable. That had never produced results before and was unlikely to work now. I needed more resources, more materials, and some staff who were a lot more useful than Kevin. Speaking of Kevin, where was he?

After a quick lap of the factory, I found him leaning over the side of a vat with a spoon.

'Kevin, what the hell are you doing?'

'Cleaning the equipment,' he said, with starch powder smeared across his cheeks.

'You're eating raw materials. What the hell, Kevin, that's disgusting. Not to mention a contamination issue.'

'I'm not.'

'You've got a spoon in your hand, and your face is a mess.'

He wiped his face on his sleeve, smearing the dusty gloop across his cheeks. 'I just thought maybe I could figure out what was wrong if I tasted it at every stage.'

'Your job is not to figure out what is wrong, Kevin. You have no knowledge of the processes and have never even tasted the end result of most products. It's your job to clean up the mess and put things away. Now fix this.'

I rubbed my temples, trying to massage the stress away. Kevin's actions hadn't caused any problems. He couldn't make things worse, but the lack of discipline was maddening. I had been too soft, and he was too useless. I went for a walk, just to get some space and walk off some steam. Perhaps I would see Giao and I could insist he send me staff who understood basic lab etiquette.

'That's beyond your daily calorie allowance, Selbourne,' a Council guard shouted after me as I passed him.

'Excuse me?'

'You're exercising too much. It wastes calories.' He was slouched against a wall, clearly conserving all he could.

'I cannot quantify my day like that. I have things to do.'

'Get a bike, pedalling is more efficient. Or walk more slowly.'

I shoved my hands in my pockets and clenched my fists, then relaxed them. Even that probably burned an extra calorie. I recognised the guard. I'd seen him with his little girl, who was in Grace's class. He seemed like a pleasant man when he dropped her off at school. How much a uniform and bit of authority had added to his demeanour.

'If we had your famous food, no one would need to count calories,' he said with a sneer.

'You have my lab's injectable vitamin. How's that working out for you? Your kid is in my wife's class. Nice healthy kid, tall for her age. You're welcome, by the way.'

Screw walking slowly. I marched off, my sandals flopping against the floor, my jaw grinding down what was left of my molars.

I walked from one chamber to the next with no destination in mind, just to let off some steam. I flapped my smock, fanning myself, encouraging my sweat to dry. The air circulation wasn't enough to cool me down. Hot flushes and anger were a stifling combination.

The chamber below began to fill with the sound of meal ration preparations. My eyes watered from the smell of liquid mud. Any grumbling in my stomach ceased and wound into a knot. My portion would be waiting in the lab for me when I got back. All the more reason to walk around some more.

Amalyn had to get there soon, then I could show that the lab works properly. That would fix everything. I would be revered once again. The Selbourne Range would be appreciated for the genius it was. But until then – eurgh.

Also taking a stroll across the mezzanine were Clementine and Sara. Clementine looked taller than ever, holding herself high. If her chin had been up a few degrees more, she'd almost have the posture of a Centre. Not the bulk, and not the gaudy teeth, but the way she carried herself oozed that same confidence.

'Sav, what are you doing out and about? You look pale. Let's have a seat.' Clementine's tone sounded more disgusted than caring.

'I just needed some air.'

She led me over to some benches that lined the edge of the wall, carved from the rock and with no cushions to soften them. My bony backside protested as I wriggled to get comfortable.

'You know, you have to watch your calorie wastage,' Clementine said.

I scowled a response. 'You're quoting from Isaac's manifesto. He's not been elected yet.'

'Not yet, but he will be.' Her smile widened, eyes glinting.

I had no patience for such whimsical crap. 'Is Giao in the office? I want to speak to him about Kevin. He's so useless I just can't have him in the lab any longer. Or I need some able staff to counteract his uselessness, at least.'

'He's on a call to Mars at the moment,' said Clementine.

'Mars?'

'Yeah,' she laughed. 'It's ridiculous. There's a delay of a few minutes, so a short conversation takes ages. He really wants to talk to him, though.'

'Who?'

'Blane,' Sara said. 'His man on Mars.'

'Giao reckons he'll come back once things are calmer here,' said Clementine, gesturing around like she was in the middle of a riot.

'It's hardly raucous,' I said.

'Anyway,' Clementine said, 'he just needs to destress. He's got a lot of responsibility. I think he's looking forward to when the elections are over, and he can step back. That's why he's throwing his weight behind dad's campaign. Backing the one who offers the most stability going forward, the one leading the polls and with a clear route to victory.'

'Harvey might win,' Sara said. 'His campaign is going well.'

Clementine smirked. 'I think you like him for more than just his campaign pledges.'

'Clem!'

'Oh, come on, Sav, have you not realised? I'm not judging, Sara. You should go for it, if that's what you really want. All we've done our whole lives is dig, study and work. No harm in enjoying ourselves a little now. It's about time, don't you think?'

Sara's face was ablaze. 'Nothing is going on between Harvey and me, and even if it were, he's got a good heart and really cares about people.'

Clementine rolled her eyes and leant back against the rock. 'With a face like that, he needs a good heart.'

I noticed then the unnatural way her smock hung off her shoulders. She'd padded the shoulders out. I looked down at her feet and noticed the extra lift sewn into her sandal. She was giving herself more height and artificially filling herself out.

Making herself look more formidable? Healthier? She stroked her hair in a way I had seen the Select do. Clementine's dark waves were lovely, but didn't have the Select's level of shine or their length. The way she caressed them, though, it seemed she thought they did.

I blinked away the thought. She was just enjoying feeling healthier. And gossiping. No harm in that. Clem was family. She wasn't turning into that sort, like the Centre or the Select. It was just a bit of gossip, that was all.

'So, what sort of fun are you having then, Clem?' Sara asked, giving her a nudge.

Clementine's face went redder than Sara's.

'Anyway,' I said before she could answer. I wasn't going to waste time listening to idle chit-chat. 'Everyone is moaning about the food. I feel like they've forgotten that the injectable us Rafters brought with us is making them healthier.'

'People have short memories, Sav,' Sara said, with sympathy in her eyes.

'An injectable just isn't as exciting as food, though, is it?' said Clementine. 'It's the food people were looking forward to.'

'Still, the injectable is clearly showing its benefits,' I said as I eyed her hair.

Clementine stopped stroking her hair and tucked it behind her ear. 'Lots of people aren't even bothering to get their monthly injection. The Rafters are hardly a good advert for it. They have worse skin than us.'

'We had much worse air on the Raft. The wind, salt and smog were a lot to bear.'

'Well, some people are worried the injectable will make them look like a grubby Rafter.'

Grubby Rafter! I winced at the phrase. She sounded like she hated us, like she saw herself as superior. We were all so similar, yet it was our differences that people noticed.

'Anyway,' she continued, 'I guess we'll see if the food helps, if they ever get to have any. The thirty boxes a day doesn't really go very far. Most people don't even get a bite.'

'The Council could step back and let others take it,' I suggested.

'We need to set an example. Show people there's nothing to fear from Rafter food.'

Fear? From refugees who ran from a country that was crumbling beneath their feet? Fearful of people who were deserted and left to die by an oppressive government that did nothing but think of itself and its Elite followers? I swallowed my anger as best I could. What gave Clementine, or anyone, the right to judge us? We were just trying to survive. Perhaps that's what they feared – our resolve.

I said my goodbyes and left. Clearly, more confidence and brazenness on my part was not going to be enough to make people see us differently. I walked quickly to the sound of tuts from disapproving Subs I passed. If they wanted me to watch my calories, perhaps they shouldn't get my blood boiling. But my limbs did feel heavy. Maybe I really had wasted too many calories, or maybe it was the hurt from Clementine's words draining me. She was so welcoming before. That was a long time ago, though, when I arrived full of promise and ambition. Clementine was a little girl when she came here, and the Tunnels were in their infancy. Now she had grown up, she'd forgotten what it was to be an outsider.

I tried over and over to justify the conversation in my head. The Tunnels weren't that old. Anyone over thirty was likely born aboveground and arrived here fleeing some awful climate or government. We were all the same, the Subs and the Rafters, only the Rafters were the last to join the clique. We looked different – shorter, weather-beaten, eroded by our hardships. The few Centre that were there stood out like giants. To some, they were something to aspire to, I assumed, from Clementine's artificial additions.

I walked past the mining tunnel and lingered for a moment, watching Perimeter and Centre working together. I recognised one of them, grafting, lifting rocks with comparative ease next to his Perimeter colleagues. It was Jerome, the Solarplanes Progressives employee who made the evacuations possible. He was Centre, and he saw through all the crap the Elite had spoon-fed him his whole life. And now here he was, working with people who had lived on the other side of that fence. To me, it was proof that cohesion was possible.

He looked up and waved, revealing the Golden Fifty tattoo on his forearm. The symbol of the collective who believed in travel and seeing the world. A common dream of people living worlds apart. I waved back and smiled, and made a mental note to drop some more food round to the miners later.

After that conversation with Sara and Clementine, I had no will or strength left to speak to Giao. Not that I wanted to walk in on a conversation between him and his boyfriend, anyway. I made my way back to the lab, more moans about wasting calories from the Council guards following me down the halls.

Screw them.

Chapter 14

The Raft

I needed instructions for the boats, and for that I needed the Internet, to search the Centre's systems. Which meant I had to ask for Danny and June's help again. June wasn't that bad, not really. Just bitter and angry. We'd all felt like that. What she needed was a little kindness, a dash of hope.

Cora was sitting up in bed, big eyes just taking in the room around her. I didn't think she'd had much of a nap yet; she looked far too alert. She was cuddling her knees and flinched as I poked my head round the door.

'Sleep okay?'

She nodded.

'I'm going to make some food. You want to help?'

She nodded again and jumped out of bed, pausing a moment as her toes scrunched on the fluffy rug. I wondered if she'd ever known such softness. She probably didn't remember how it felt to be comfortable.

Clean and scrubbed, Tilly sat at the table. She had looked like she needed sleep but when I showed her the bedroom she had backed away. Not ready to be alone in the strange place yet. All the time while Cora slept, Tilly's eyes went to the floor. When Cora was awake, Tilly watched her every move with eyes framed by blue-black circles, like she feared for her.

'She ate the fish,' said Cora. 'We never found enough other food, so Tilly ate the fish and gave me the proper food.'

Tears came to my eyes. No child should know such guilt. Tilly didn't look up. The only colour in her cheeks seemed to come from shame, but to me, she looked like a hero. She'd somehow managed to keep Cora alive.

I made a simple stew with SynthoSpaghetti, RealioVeg chunks and some protein pieces. Cora passed the ingredients and helped me to stir. I rummaged through a box of stuff we'd taken from Sav's place and chose the best bottle of wine. It actually looked like a decent meal, something we would have had before they left.

With their hair dried and tied back, faces scrubbed and fresh clothes, Tilly and Cora looked quite presentable. Tilly alternated between shivering and sweating. She had a jumper that she put on and removed continually, which looked like an arduous task each time. As tiredness took her over completely, I walked her to the bedroom.

'Stay in bed as long as you need,' I said. 'I'll leave you some food on the stove. You can help yourself when you wake up.'

She didn't reply, only nodded slightly and climbed onto the bed fully clothed. She needed to get the fish out of her system, no doubt. I left her a cup of weak Noffee, some VitaBiscuits and a glass of water.

I checked on Reya, fast asleep in her drawer. Leaving the apartment door open so I could hear if she woke up, Cora and I went over to Danny and June's, armed with hot stew and chilled wine, hoping the smell of the food would soften June a little.

'Hello?' I knocked and went in. 'We've brought you dinner.'

June was sitting at the living-room table. She narrowed her eyes at me. 'Why?'

'Just being neighbourly,' I said, as I placed the pot in front of her.

'Bollocks. What do you really want?' Her voice was cold, it's chill sharpening the edge of every syllable, though I could see that it was fighting with her hunger.

'Well, I was hoping you would give me a hand over at the hub again tomorrow morning? I need to use the Internet.'

'What's this, then? A bribe?'

'If you like.'

She sniffed. 'The junkie had any?'

'I've saved her some. She's sleeping.'

'Waste of food on someone like her.'

'I'll see you in the morning, then?'

She didn't respond for a moment, then got up and went to the cupboard. 'The kid had any? She should eat some. I'll get her a bowl.'

June washed her hands and set four places at the table while Cora and I hovered in the space.

'Sit down, will you? It's rude to just stand there like that.'

Cora ran her hands over the tablecloth, her fingers tangling in the lacework. After collecting Reya, I sat next to her and Cora gave me the biggest smile, showing me all the gaps where her baby teeth had fallen out.

Danny arrived, arms shaking under the weight of the box he was carrying. He dumped it on the floor with a heavy thud. 'Smells great in here! I found a few more bits, too. We have quite a stockpile.'

'That's handy, since there's so many of us now,' June said, but without her usual sharpness. Cora smiled at her, and June poked her tongue out. She ladled the food into the bowls, and I sat back and watched as Cora gobbled it all down, licking her bowl clean at the end and finishing off with a loud burp and a giggle.

The wine was decent, the sort of bottle we'd save for a special occasion. I had a small glass, while June and Danny polished off the bottle. By the time they were finished, I thought I even saw June smile, a proper smile, her frown lines morphing into happy ones.

Cora jumped off her seat and onto my lap and wrapped her arms around my neck, her head on my shoulder.

My eyes were welling up. 'Hey, what's this for?' I hugged her back, her hair tickling my nose.

She shrugged, then went to Danny and June and did the same. June's expression melted into joy. Any anger left in her at that moment withered away and was trampled by simple happiness. Danny's grin was wider than I'd ever seen. Then Cora sat back in her chair without a word, like her act of kindness was as innate as breathing. She yawned and stretched out her arms.

'Come on, young lady,' I said. 'Time for bed.'

***

Reya cried half the night. It's normal, I kept telling myself as I held her, feeding her, rocking her, speaking to her in soft murmurs. She's healthy. This is just what babies do. I wanted to sing to her but couldn't recall a song. We used to have music once, didn't we? That seemed like so long before, another life, another world, when the joviality of music was normal. Even in the bleakness of the grey Raft, we had music. Now all I had was grief, and a forgotten song. My own cries were silent, hushed tears from my broken heart.

I fed and changed Reya, and just when she had settled, Cora woke screaming from a nightmare, sweating and shaking. When I asked what it was about, she shook her head and was tight-lipped. I got into bed with her, stroked her hair as she fell back asleep. She was so young to have watched her world crumble away. Too young to know such loss.

The next day, Cora and Reya both woke early, seemingly unaffected by their fitful nights. When Cora got up, she came into my room, confused, like she'd forgotten where she was.

'Morning, young lady,' I said as I rubbed the sleep from my eyes.

'We're indoors.'

'That's right. You're safe here.'

She bit her lip, considering this for a moment. 'Safe' was an alien word to her.

As soon as Reya grumbled herself awake, I got her up, and we went to the hub, with some eye-rolling from June, but with Cora sat next to her, not nearly as much as usual. I left Tilly sleeping. When I went to check on her, she was fast asleep, but she'd eaten her biscuits and drunk half of her drink. I left some more, with a note on the table to say we'd be back soon.

'What you want the Internet for, anyway?' June said when we got in the Autocar. 'More fairy tales?'

'Look,' I handed her and Danny the e-pad with photos. 'See the boats? I need to find instructions on the Centre's systems on how to work them. I've never been on a boat. Don't suppose either of you have?'

'Do we look like that sort?' said June.

I shrugged. 'Anyway, they're on the east coast. It's not far from there to France. If I can get to Bordeaux, that's the nearest entry point for the Tunnels.'

'You hearing this, Danny? Boats. Tunnels. Crazy.'

Cora squeezed my hand and smiled. Her still-soft skin soothed the hardest parts of me. 'An adventure,' she said.

'It will be.'

We alighted the Autocar by the Parliament buildings and set to work organising the computer. The hub's power and Internet were working, so I read Sav's instructions about the Tunnels' entry point and found the instructions I needed for the boats. All the Centre files were organised and labelled, and easy to navigate. The ease in finding the instructions gave me hope, though a quick glance over them made me doubt again. It wasn't like I had forever to learn them. We had to leave soon, really soon. Who knew how long the Raft would be in such an ideal place for the journey, and winter storm season was approaching. We didn't have long.

With the meagre amount of paper I could find, I printed what I could of the manuals and images of the coast, and took screenshots as well.

When I got back to the apartment and read through the instructions again, it became very clear that I'd need help. It was complex, way beyond my understanding. I was a biochemist, not a marine engineer. Danny had a look through and was mildly better at understanding the technicals, but still not confident. The Centre's boats were just too high-tech, relying on presets that were more complex than coding an entire lab. Plus, there was weather, tides, understanding the sea. If Archie had been there ... I hit myself on the head. Archie was not there. Such thoughts had no point.

Just reading the manual simply would not be safe. Safer than staying on the Raft, maybe, but still almost certain death.

But some people knew how to use boats. Some Golden Fifty certainly did. Fishing had once been their job on the Raft, before the Centre demolished the docks to build their own. The Perimeter boats were older designs, sure, the Perimeter fishing boats were not to Centre standard, but they'd have an idea. I tried asking Tilly if there were others, but she was silent, still recovering.

I left Cora with June and Danny and went for a walk. There were some Golden Fifty out there, somewhere. I could feel it in my bones.

'Be careful, dearie,' said Danny. 'It's not safe out. People are desperate.'

'Exactly. People are desperate. And I can give them some hope.'

I saw confusion on their faces. They didn't understand. They couldn't fathom how it felt to let so many people down. I was supposed to have got so many of them off the Raft and I'd failed. If there was a chance of getting some of those left, anyone, to safety, I had to take it. I just needed to find someone who could pilot a boat.

I remembered the cuts on Tilly's arms and the knives I'd seen in people's hands months earlier. Surely a message of hope was all they'd need. So, torch in hand, its batteries good for a couple of hours, I searched. But the torch was useless – smog was still smog, even when lit up. Walking was painful. Fatigue sapped my energy – I needed iron and calories, enough to sustain me and Reya. I was running on empty and I knew it, but I could worry about that later. I'd find more baby formula if need be. It seemed unlikely that all of it had been snatched up. The food we'd found at Sav's had been divided up, a week's worth for each of us, ten days if we were careful. Wasting calories on fruitless searches was exactly that: a waste. But I had to find someone. Could I get a boat and make it to the Mainland on my own? With no backup to take Reya and Cora if anything happened to me? The state Tilly was in, she certainly wasn't going to be much help. Dying at sea with Reya in my arms wasn't worth thinking about. Frying in the desert so close yet so far from the shade of the Tunnels was a real possibility. But I would attempt it alone if I had to.

Walking with Reya strapped to me, hugging the walls for support if I needed it, I searched. Out of the apartment and alone, I felt the lure of the coast with every step. I could make the pain go away for a while and could relinquish myself of the sense of responsibility for a few moments, hours, days. I could find blissful ignorance in just a few rancid bites. Archie's arms reaching for me. Where in life he told me to run, in death I felt his need for me to join him. The cooling chill of death grasping for me. I had some fight, but how much?

I'll join you soon, my love.

I looked under the blanket at Reya, her eyes staring straight at me, seeing through the bravery I was trying to convey to her. But her delicate hand made a fist, like she was ready to fight. She'd be a bad-ass one day, for sure, but she was too tiny now. The precariousness of life was clear in her fragility. I stroked her soft head, ran my hand over her cheek, played with her tiny fingers. She looked so breakable to me, but when her hand gripped my finger, it held on as I pulled away, sturdier than such a tiny thing should be. It was an old evolutionary reflex telling me she was going to hang in there with every bit of strength she had.

My head was heavy with a yearning I could not describe; my body weighed down with sorrow. The air was thick and oppressive, every muscle a brick. But Reya looked at me with eyes of hope, with his mouth, his pointy ears.

I'll be the bad-ass for now, little one. I'll get us off this hellhole.

Sticking to the shadows, I searched the walls for slogans and signs, the corners and alleyways for people, wanting to see them before they saw me. But I found no one.

No one left? That can't be.

I saw it, though. The symbol painted on the render, the leaf design of the Golden Fifty. How long had it been there? It wasn't coated in pollution yet, just a light smattering of soot, so maybe not that long. But there was no sign of life. The streets were as eerie and quiet as ever. Even with my months of wandering the edge, I'd seen no one for weeks, maybe months now, other than Tilly and Cora. Not that I could remember those times with any clarity. The smog was thick. Anyone could have been lurking in the shadows, especially with my vision and consciousness as clouded as they were. A fugue state of grief and fish had sent my heads into the clouds.

Reya whimpered, and I checked her eyes for alertness, her limbs for reflexes. Guilt ate away at me for so many things. Poisoning my daughter was just another to add to the list. She seemed healthy, though. Bright eyed and responsive.

I'm so sorry, little one.

I walked deserted street after deserted street, not concerned with staying hidden now. What was the point in a ghost town like this? Buildings that were once glassy and shining were now matted with pollution and weather-beaten. Smooth surfaces tarnished, polished streets dull. My shoes left footprints in the soot that coated the floor, but they were soon filled in or churned up by the wind, erasing all trace of me. Little eddies of particulate matter swirled around my ankles, my fancy pilfered socks and shoes blackened with grime. How fickle the Centre's finery was. How quickly the products of the Elite turned to dirt without the Perimeter for protection. We had been their shield, their veil. Cannon fodder, as Archie used to say. Now their world was as corroded as the rest of it.

My search continued until my legs were too weak to carry on and it became clear that if there was anyone still here, they weren't going to reveal themselves easily.

But suddenly I realised I wasn't alone. I heard no footsteps, saw no movement. The cool sharpness at my back came from nowhere. I froze. I felt their breath on my neck as they leant in close to my ear.

'Food. What you got?'

My breath came out in shudders. They're just desperate, I said to myself. Not evil, just desperate. 'None. Nothing. No food.'

'Yeah, well, what's that under the blanket, then?'

'My baby. Please, don't hurt her.'

'Baby! What are you, Centre? Only Centre have babies.'

'No, Perimeter.'

Reya started crying and the pressure from the knife disappeared. I slowly turned around, my heart thumping. He was trembling all over, red eyed, lip quivering. Terrified was how he looked. Hungry and scared. Not evil.

'You shouldn't be wandering around out here,' he said, the knife now at his side.

'I've been trying to find people. There's a way off the Raft. To safety.'

His face twitched like 'safety' was a dirty word. 'You're talking crap.'

'No, it's true. The Mainland. Europe.'

'I heard those rumours. Load of bullshit. Everyone's dead. They all fell into the sea.'

'I've been there. Really. There are great cities still. I'm taking my baby there.'

'Stop lying!' His knuckles went white as he held the knife tighter.

I raised my hands defensively. I had to make him understand. 'It's true. I know you're scared. It's okay, I'm scared, too.' I tried to talk softly but had to raise my voice to be heard over screaming Reya. 'I have an idea to get us to safety. Please, I have to save my baby. I'm telling the truth. Come with us. I want to help you.'

He backed away, shaking his head. 'Crazy bitch,' he said, then ran off.

Microbes!

My shoulders slumped, defeated. One more life I failed to save.

'There, there, baby girl.' Reya's cries made her sound as frightened as I was. 'It's going to be okay. We'll find someone who knows about boats. Some Golden Fifty are still around, I know it.'

I returned to the apartment on sluggish legs, eyes squinting from the artificial light, my head banging. Too tired. Too stressed. Reya had settled, and I put her down as I collected what I needed for my plan. I found some scissors and sheets of thin plastic, and set to work, carving out the symbol I knew so well. A symbol of hope, of remembrance. Of my people. Now I needed some paint.

The living room was painted a pale yellow, neutral, the sort of colour I imagined a nursery would be. I rummaged through the cupboards and found a paint pot, about a third full, and a brush. That would have to do. It wasn't exactly gold, but yellow enough. It would stand out on a blackened wall, anyway.

Reya woke from her nap. *Microbes*, I should have slept when she did. The nappy I had made from pillowcases needed changing. I tossed the dirty one into the bucket with the other dirty sheets. It felt obscene to ruin such fine fabrics and fancy attire, but I had no intention of washing any of it when there was so much in other apartments to use. Why waste the water? And yet, why did I feel like I had my priorities wrong? My mind was fixated on surviving and not giving a damn about the preservation of this place. The person who lived here before had the luxury of knowing they were safe. With certainty in their own survival, they afforded time and effort to preserve their fancy home, leaving it tidy and proud. This abandoned place was in a better state than any lived-in place in the Perimeter. And now I was trashing it, bit by bit. I shook the guilt from my head.

It doesn't matter. Sod this place.

Reya decided she wanted feeding again, reaching for me and sucking the air. She latched on and guzzled greedily. Painting would have to wait.

'Got a bit of spare food, dearie. How was your walk? No trouble?'

'It was fine, Danny. And thanks.' Best not to tell him about the man with a knife, I thought. No sense in worrying him over one hungry and scared person.

'Little one doing okay?'

'Yeah, she really is.'

'You look pale, love. You should rest a while.'

'I will, soon.'

'Been at the arts and crafts I see.' He glanced over at the mess I had made, the symbol I had made clearly lost on him. 'Cora is drawing with June. She's done a lovely one of you and the baby.'

'Can't wait to see it. Actually, Danny, can you do me a favour? Another one, I know you've done so much already. I don't think I've even said thank you.'

'It's quite all right. What do you need?'

'When you next go on a scout, can you take one of those stencils?' I pointed at what I had made. 'And some paint, and paint it on some walls? I'm trying to track down any Golden Fifties that are left. They might be able to help.'

'Golden Fifties?'

'Some old acquaintances, a group of like-minded people. Some of them are still here, I'm sure of it. There's no way they all went to the Mainland. We never got the word out like we planned. Plus, June said she's seen the symbol around here.'

Danny picked up the stencils and inspected them. They looked flimsy and roughly made; the symbol wilted and sad, but they'd have to do.

'That's a dangerous thing, dearie,' he said, 'drawing attention to yourself.'

'It's more dangerous to stay here and starve.' I lifted Reya to burp her, and she obliged instantly. 'I'm leaving for the Mainland. We're getting on a boat somehow, and I know some of the Fifty can use a boat. It'd be great if you and June came too. I'm not lying, Danny, I've been there. There are great cities underground.'

'I believe you. I do.'

I wiped Reya's mouth with some cloth. I knew she wasn't smiling. She was way too young for that, but her face screwed up and she winked at me. She looked so much like Archie. My eyes stung, but no tears would come. I had none left, no energy for such remorse. 'And look,' I pointed at the computer monitor, 'the satellite images. We're not that far from the Mainland. We could sail round the west coast here, and land the boat here, and walk to the tunnels from there. There was a city here, once. Bordeaux. If we could land the boat here, it's not that far to walk. The time of year is not too bad. It'll be hot, but it's a hot walk there or certain death here. If we can carry enough water, we could make it.' It was clear in my mind, the route the boat could take, docking close to where the city once was. A day's walk, maybe more. We could do it, we had to.

'That's a lot of "ifs," dearie. A lot of uncertainty.'

'The only certain thing is, if we stay on the Raft, we'll starve. I have to try. Reya deserves a chance at a life. There's nothing for her here.' She looked at me, slowly blinking, full of milk and so content.

'Danny!' June's voice cut through the air like a knife. 'Come get your dinner. It's naff all since you've given loads of food to the hussy next door.'

'You'd better go,' I said.

'She means well. Heart of gold.'

Chapter 15

The Tunnels

'Professor Selbourne.'

Giao's voice instantly made my neck itch. What the hell was he doing coming to the lab? He never came down here. I wanted to speak to him on my terms, not at any random time he decided. Even the sound of his footsteps annoyed me, moving too slowly, like every step was some ominous warning.

'What do you want, Giao? I'm busy.' I was doing my best to look busy, anyway.

'There's a lot of unrest among the Rafters,' he said, his left eye twitching with his tic.

'Well, some of the political campaigns are fairly divisive,' I said, looking back at my screen.

'My concern isn't the Rafter's animosity towards me and my colleagues, it's towards each other. Your people are a rabble.'

'What are you talking about, Giao? Seriously, I'm busy.'

'There was a fight in the mines this morning. Something about a Centre and a Perimeter not getting along.'

I sighed and looked up at him. 'And what does this have to do with me?'

'Our disciplinary methods seem ineffective. Especially against the bigger of your kind.'

'The *bigger?*' It took me a moment to realise what he was on about. 'You mean the Centres? Microbes, Giao, there's about ten of them here, not exactly an army. And they're hardly "my kind."'

'Well, as I understand it, you used to write news articles that helped keep the peace on the Raft.'

'No. I wrote articles that the Centre edited and twisted to suit their own agenda.'

'Well anyway, it seems your people at one time actually paid attention to what you had to say. Perhaps something along those lines would be a good idea. Remind your people that they need to behave, that they are all Rafters here.'

'We're all human here, equals, something like that?' I didn't hide my disdain.

He furrowed his brow, his twitch abating for a moment as he pondered. 'Peace in the Tunnels is imperative for our culture here.'

'What do you care, anyway? You'll be stepping down soon. Pretty soon it won't be your place to micromanage anymore.'

'I've been in charge here for eight months, and I do not want my legacy to be that of a mob. One of crammed in and hungry citizens is bad enough.'

I scowled. It still didn't fit. If Giao wanted to go down in the Tunnel's history books as a peacekeeper, he would stay impartial instead of having his picture printed on Isaac's leaflets. I eyeballed him, watching his twitching increase as I tried to figure him out.

'Let me translate,' I said. 'You don't want the Select to find out that the place turned to shit once they left, and you're worried that Blane won't come back.'

His eyes were so wide I thought for a moment they might pop out. Had I hit the nail on the head?

'Blane has nothing to do with this,' he said, but his tightening mouth made me believe otherwise. His eyes could have given me frostbite. 'We never had any trouble before the Rafters arrived.'

I stood up and pushed my screen away, leaning over the desk, my cold stare rivalling his. 'You have a short memory. Before the Rafters arrived, you had a dictatorship that ran this place like a prison. Now people have a bit of freedom and you and your media are playing on their fears and emotions. The Rafters, whether Centre or Perimeter, are not trouble. What caused animosity between them was the National Press on the Raft, and their hateful articles creating divisions. And now the Tunnels are using the same tactics to turn Sub against Rafter.' I turned back to my screen and logged onto TunNet, the Tunnels social media, then swivelled the screen round to face him. 'I've seen the latest articles and nonsense circulating here. This one, for example, depicting a Rafter as a thief, another as a beggar. Perhaps if you stopped your citizens from spreading hate and lies about us, they will stop hating each other?'

'Don't preach to me, Rafter,' his voice was loud and echoed in the lab. 'The issues with your kind were entrenched well before you arrived here. Just write something, anything, to make it clear that a Rafter is a Rafter. There's no need for you to see yourselves as two separate species, despite the obvious aesthetic differences.'

Prick.

I thought for a moment, trying to control my anger before I spoke. Giao had put it horribly, but some sort of written piece might do a world of good for the Rafters. Unity was in everyone's best interests. Every Rafter here hated the Centre Elite and the Blue Liberation party. We had all escaped an oppressive regime, and all wanted freedom to be ourselves and to live by our own volition. We had all understood that the National Press's propaganda was merely that, and had learned how to read between the lines. There was so much we had in common. It was only a fence that had divided us.

'I'll see what I can do,' I said. 'On one condition.'

'You're hardly in a position to dictate conditions,' Giao said, folding his arms.

I carried on regardless. 'I've made this nation a lot healthier with the vitamin injection I introduced here. How's your skin these days? It looks clear. Your energy levels? You must be buzzing from all those B vitamins.'

He rolled his eyes and exhaled, like the reminder of the good I had done was boring him. 'All right, Selbourne, what are you after?'

'Kevin. He does nothing but get in the way. I need to get rid of him and replace him with decent, able staff.'

'No can do. Kevin stays, his mum wants him to learn, well, something. But I'll see who else we can spare to help you out.'

I sighed. 'Fine.'

Giao left, and the air felt immediately lighter. *A Rafter is a Rafter.* What the hell was that even supposed to mean? What a prick.

Since I now knew how to make food but had to avoid doing so, writing an article was actually a welcome distraction. I got to work on it straight away, reminding all the Rafters how bad the Centre Elite had been, and what we had achieved by escaping. I was complimentary of the few Centre that were here, as they facilitated the escape of so many of us. Jerome and his colleagues arranged the flights for every single Perimeter who had escaped. They had rejected their luxuries for an honest life outside of Blue Liberation control. I commended the Perimeter on what they had endured, how hard life had been on our side of the fence. We all had our hardships, but the blame lay with the Blue Liberation and Centre Elite, not with each other. I also wrote how we were like the Subs, overcoming the tyranny of dictators. Labelling the Select as such would no doubt get Isaac's back up, but I didn't care. The Select were every bit as bad as the Centre. Uniting behind common enemies seemed to be our best chance of forming friendships and the Select were on another planet, so who cared? I wanted to help everyone find common ground, despite what Giao said.

I laughed when I read through the article, imagining Peter reading it. If he were still editor, he would twist this out of all recognition, making the Perimeter at fault and touting the deserving fortunes of the Centre. But he was not the editor. He was no longer in control. I remembered that tatty collectable poster from a hundred years ago that hung on his wall. *Whoever controls the media controls the mind.* Well, now he was just a miner, the same as everyone else.

I published it and left the lab, walking home through the crowds, listening to their e-pads ping. No doubt my article was being read and shared. It wasn't what Giao wanted; I was sure. He wanted something that pitted us against the Subs, something that made the Rafters their own genus that fulfilled some separate niche to the Subs. I just hoped it healed divides rather than widened them.

Among the clamour were two people I hadn't expected to see together. She was playing with her hair, stroking its waves and looking up at him through her eyelashes, standing straight as she could, up on her toes. He was leaning against the tunnel wall, covered in orange dust from a day at work, flashing those dazzling teeth. Jerome and Clementine. I hadn't envisioned such a match. Yet she had been going on about the 'Rafter influx.'

A high-profile relationship like that was sure to be a sign of a cohesive society. I walked quickly by, trying not to gawp. It was none of my business, I reminded myself.

Amalyn would say it was cute, and that I was being too mumsy, sitting with a cup of MimikTea. A Sub and a Golden Fifty, she'd say – how wonderful! In my article, I was sure to comment on the Golden Fifty as being an eye-opening enterprise. Amalyn would love that when she got here. I used to call her group a cesspit shitshow, but that bunch of creatives were almost all that was left of the Raft population now. And she was out there, somewhere, trying to get here.

Chapter 16

The Raft

Danny came home tired, loaded with food, his arms and hands smeared with paint. He had painted so many logos the flimsy stencils had worn out and torn, so I set about making new ones.

'Pretty picture,' said Cora when she saw the symbol.

'Look.' I showed her my tattoo. 'Tilly has it too, did you notice?'

She shook her head.

'Well, we might be lucky and find more people who have it. Careful with the scissors.' She cut around the design, sticking her tongue out in concentration.

'I saw this symbol painted on some walls,' Danny said. 'Didn't see anyone, though. You sure this is a good idea, dearie?'

I nodded as I helped Cora with her cutting. 'They're calling out to us.'

Tilly came out of the bedroom then. Her face had regained some colour, and she stared down at the floor where we were working.

'I'm going to find the others, Tilly,' I said. 'There are more of us out there, I know it.'

She didn't speak but showed some recognition with a slight nod, and she held her forearm to her chest, her tattoo pressed to her heart. I wondered how many people she had lost, how many she had seen perish as the Raft crumbled.

Danny explained to me where he had been, and as soon as I was rested and ready, I went out to cover more ground. Cora stayed with Tilly, sitting next to her on the sofa as I left. I heard her whispering, 'Amalyn's going to find people who can help us.'

I needed to learn not to make promises I couldn't keep.

The Autocar was still outside and working. I took it all the way to the fence, across roads that were buckling, past empty billboards and deserted Selfie Stations, their mirrors blackened and cracked. The Centre-model Autocar was as rickety as the Perimeter range, cascading over the bumps about as smoothly as a fall down the stairs. Every jolt sent pain tearing through me. I should have brought a pillow to sit on.

The eye-watering discomfort motivated me, reminding me of why I was doing this. Yet my thoughts rattled back and forth between the task and what I could catch at the edge. The rotten pain relief would be welcome. My mouth salivated at the thought. I glanced down at Reya, sleeping, content enough.

The guilt of eating the drug-laden fish during pregnancy gave me a headache, one that only more fish would cure. I tried to convince myself that starving would have been worse. But I knew it wasn't all about food, it was about the pain relief as well. My mind spiralled with the never-ending cycle of wanting to ease the pain. I shook the thought from my head and kissed Reya's hand. I could do this. I could be strong for her.

When I alighted, the smog had thinned slightly, the wind mercifully cooler. The loose-fitting skirt I had taken from the apartment whipped up almost joyfully in the breeze. A bit of colour among the grey.

I got my brush out and began looking for suitable walls, ignoring the whispers on the wind, the callings from the deep.

Not now, my love. Not yet.

I started painting the symbol occasionally, then more often as I got closer to our apartment, making a trail. I added arrows as well, pointing the way. If there were Golden Fifty here, they'd figure it out. I wouldn't tell Danny and June about the arrows, though. They'd only worry.

When I got back to the apartment building, I paused at the bottom of the stairs to remove my shoes. My feet ached from exertion, my legs cramped, and my back throbbed. Reya was fast asleep, nuzzled into my chest and sucking her thumb. The pain dissipated a little as I watched her contented little sighs.

Their voices filled the air as I approached our floor. Loud, angry, discontent.

'She's insane. Some wannabe Centre liability jacked up on fish. She's imagining everything.'

'But I read that book she found. From the journalist.'

'The Centre suck-up.'

'No, a food researcher. The book explains everything. Please, just read it.'

'How do we know she even found that book and didn't make it herself? She's a madwoman. Mad.'

'I believe her, June. I do. It makes sense. Where else did all those people go?'

'Into the sea. They all fell in the damned sea with the rest of the Perimeter.'

'But we heard the phone call, that person saying –'

'It's madness, Danny. There is nowhere else. Just listen to yourself.'

I crept back to my apartment, but Reya's waking protests ruined my stealth. *Microbes!* The last thing I wanted was to be the subject of a marital feud. Once inside the apartment, the thick walls shut out their continuing argument.

Tilly and Cora were snuggled up on the sofa. Cora looked at me with a worried face.

'It's all right,' I said. 'They're just having a row. Nothing to do with us. Shall I make some dinner?'

They both nodded, and Tilly got up to help, putting a pot on the stove.

'You feeling better?' I asked.

She made a sort of shrug–nod movement that I took to be a good sign.

'I painted the Golden Fifty symbol everywhere. We're going to find them, more of us, I know it.' She almost smiled, the corner of her mouth curling up just slightly. 'You want to come to the Mainland with me? I've been there, I promise. You believe me, don't you?'

Unexpectedly then, she reached out and hugged me, thin arms like wire around my neck, her ribcage against my side. I hugged her back, felt her body convulse as the tears began to flow.

'It's okay. You're okay. We're getting off this shitpile.'

She pulled away and there was no doubt she was smiling now. Her pink cheeks were wet with tears, bloodshot eyes lined with the hope of a promise I didn't know I could keep. Once, I'd said I'd save so many lives, now I only had to save three. Screw June. If she didn't believe me, that was up to her. I'd find a boat and get Reya, Cora, and Tilly to safety all by myself.

As the food was heating up, I pulled Reya in for a feed. I could do it. I could take a few supplies and make it without June and Danny if I had to. On the table was the e-pad, still with over seventy per cent battery, so I loaded up the satellite images. The time and date confirmed they were recent enough. I mentally drew the line a boat would take south from the dock, down the west coast of France, all the way to Bordeaux. We were in the perfect spot, the Raft just spinning around the northwest coast of France. Caught in some current, probably. Archie would know if he were here.

'How about it, little one?' I said, as Reya continued to feed. 'You inherit any of your father's genius? Can you tell us if the Raft is going to move much?'

She made little happy feeding noises but otherwise gave no insight. *Figures.* I smiled at her, then looked away with a crushing feeling in my chest. She looked so much like him.

I did not know how to model the trajectory. All I knew was we should leave soon. It was October and the summer storms had mostly passed, the winter ones not yet begun. It was hot, but not unbearably so. With shade, we could cope. Bordeaux, well, that would be hotter, but we'd have water, hats. We could make it. We'd have a chance, at least. I'd set myself on fire if it meant getting Reya to safety.

I walked to the bathroom and sat on the toilet, stifling a yelp as it stung. My eyes watering, I grabbed the towel rail for balance. Reya carried on feeding.

'It's okay, little one. Mummy will be fine.'

In the mirror, a stranger stared back at me. Frizzy hair tied up, the rest a soot-clogged mess. Skin lined with worry, eyes darker than night. I had a Russian doll as a child, one little person hidden inside another and another. I felt like that doll, new layers emerging as salt peeled away my youthful exterior. What layer would be revealed next? I saw myself being weathered away to nothing, just a hardened stone remaining.

There was a knock at the door, and June and Danny came in. Danny cleared his throat. 'June would like to apologise for anything you heard.'

'Would she now?'

'She didn't mean what she said, or anything nasty she has said at all, for that matter.'

'Is that right, June?'

June looked at her feet and fidgeted. 'I did not mean to cause offence to a new mother.'

'Apology accepted.'

'Did you find any food?' June asked.

'No. I'm sorry. I've made dinner though. It's on the stove, if you want to join us?'

June glared at me, my lack of foraging clearly making her regret her apology. Tilly came out of the kitchen with the pot and put it on the table. June looked at her, chewing her cheek with a mixture of distrust and surprise, but said nothing. I fetched bowls, and we all sat down. I ladled some stew into bowls and Tilly looked at hers with a keen longing, but waited for us to start eating before she did.

'It's all right,' I said. 'Eat up.'

She grabbed her spoon, and with delicate movements ate spoonful after spoonful. She winced through every swallow.

'Does it hurt, your throat?' I asked.

She nodded.

'There's some medicine in the bathroom cupboard. Let me find you something.'

As I stood, she grabbed my wrist and looked up at me, lips quivering, eyes telling me what her mouth could not. I leant down and kissed the top of her head.

'It's all right. You're all right.'

'This is yummy. Tilly is a good cook,' Cora said through slurps.

Before anyone had the chance to agree, the sound of the door downstairs swinging open came up the stairs. Caught on the wind, perhaps? We all froze and listened. It clicked shut again, gently. Then came the sound of soft footsteps on the stairs.

'The bloody idiot! She's led them straight to us!' June said. 'Close the apartment door! Danny, hide the food!'

My heart skipped a beat. Had someone seen the signs? Friend or foe? I quickly handed Reya to June, who held the baby like I'd handed her a bomb, and went to her apartment. Everyone stayed quiet, the only sound the slow climbing footsteps getting closer.

'Hello?' I called out.

The footsteps continued. Up to the first floor, then the second.

'Hello?' I called again as they approached our floor.

Rounding the corner, out of the darkness, a man came into view. Dishevelled clothes like rags, though a lot cleaner than Tilly when I found her. When he saw me, he stopped and slumped against the wall.

'Is this ...?' He trailed off, and instead of talking, pulled back his sleeve. The sight of his tattoo filled me with warmth, and I lifted my arm and showed him mine.

'Welcome,' I said, and held out my hand. 'I have so much to tell you.'

Chapter 17

The Tunnels

Ethan was crying when I got home, so loudly that I could hear him several doors away. I picked up my pace, slick with sweat, and rushed through our door to find him sitting on Grace's lap.

'What's wrong, big man?' I asked.

He didn't answer, and nuzzled closer into Grace.

'Don't you want to see mummy?' Grace asked.

His sobs and cries grew louder. 'I hate it here! I hate it, and everyone hates me.' He jumped off Grace's lap and ran to his bed, planting himself face down in his pillow.

Grace stood and pulled her hair back into a bun. Her eyes were almost as red as Ethan's. 'Pierre has gone round to Matteo's house for a playdate. They didn't want Ethan to come.'

'Why?'

'They told him, "No Rafters allowed."'

Her words sent a chill through my blood. 'That's awful. Have you spoken to the parents?'

'I didn't have the chance. They picked their kids up from school and left in a flash. I think this is coming from them, not the kids. The kids don't even know what a Rafter is.'

'That's just ridiculous. Ethan is a good boy!'

'Magda, one of the mums, she says that those parents are thinking about moving their kids to another school a few kilometres away. The teacher there is a Sub.'

I held my head in my hands. They couldn't be saying that, they just couldn't. We were here to help. We had already done so much good. Why couldn't they see that? 'But you're a good teacher. Your school is lovely.'

'Not good enough, apparently.'

I stroked her back. She turned away from me and stretched her neck, and I felt her shoulders slump. 'This is crazy, Grace. They'll see sense. I'll get the lab working soon, I promise, then they'll wonder what they ever did without us.'

'I know you will,' she shrugged me free. 'And I don't care, anyway. I don't want Ethan socialising with children from awful families like that. I mean, Pierre seems like a nice boy, but if his mother is some bigot, god knows what he'll grow into. A bad influence, I'm sure.'

'Pierre doesn't like me anymore,' Ethan wailed from his bed.

'Leave him be,' Grace said as I went to console him. 'He just needs some space to calm down.'

I sat at the table feeling like some inept piece of furniture. Unable to comfort my wife or my son. Grace watched me, then took hold of my arm and gave it a squeeze. 'You've gained a bit of weight. You've got some meat on your bones.'

My face grew hot. 'It's just from the samples. We're getting close now, I know it. And when Amalyn gets here, the lab will be fully functional.'

'I miss those roast potatoes.'

My face was ablaze. 'Soon, real soon. I can't risk bringing you samples, not after last time.'

'Don't you dare! I don't want those guards beating you again. Your bruising has only just gone.'

I smiled, and she went to take her frustrations out on the stove. Ethan's cries were dampening, his wails turning to trembling breaths. His toy trucks were scattered across the floor around his bed. He didn't have many, less than the other boys, no doubt. Some of his drawings were pinned to the wall, and his e-pad displayed the last game he'd played on it.

'Why don't we play with your trucks, big man?' I asked and sat on the floor next to him. I pushed some cars around and made some noises like I'd seen him do. Pointless little rituals, but they usually made him happy. He climbed down from his bed and sat on my lap instead, his little chest pressed into mine, sucking his thumb.

'You shouldn't let him do that,' Grace said. 'I'm always telling him it'll ruin his teeth.'

'It soothes him.'

'The Centre kids never have thumb-sucking teeth,' she said, so quietly I almost didn't hear it.

After a while, Ethan's breaths evened out, his chest moving up and down rhythmically. I remembered being a little girl, sitting on my father's lap in much the same way. I would try to time my breaths with his, slowing mine to match his pace. If only I could breathe in time with him, I would be more grown-up, I thought. Stronger, tougher, like him. He was the strongest man in the world to me back then.

What was I to my son now? A protector or a tyrant? The parent who had stolen him away from all he knew, leaving most of his toys behind and bringing him to a place where he was unpopular, picked on. Different.

His breathing turned into little sighs, and I knew he had cried himself to sleep. Grace served up his dinner and left it on the side as I stood and tucked him in to bed.

'He can eat later if he wakes,' I said.

'The children would never be so cruel on Mars,' she said, and sat with her own bowl of filth food, chewing the bitter slop, picking the lumps out of her teeth.

***

In the morning, I walked to work through the Rafter's wing, the sound of urgent conversations bouncing off tunnel walls, the air thick with disdain. Many people had read my article, it seemed. But the news on everyone's lips was not the peace I had tried to portray but the rumours of more Rafters arriving. The murmurs were rippling through every corner. My words had done nothing to avert the gossiping.

Through the dining room chamber where the Rafters had been eating, the chatter continued. Their plates were being cleared to make way for the Sub's shift. Here, excited mutters gave way to scoffs and tuts, eyeballs following me as I walked through. Arguments were erupting. Someone had sprayed a wall with the slogan: *Rafters should sink! Sub lives first!* Any Rafter I saw on their way to work kept their head down, huddling close to one another, skirting the shadows and edges. None would speak up for more of us coming over, too afraid of the repercussions. I continued walking to the lab, the voices quietening as I approached, then starting again behind my back, bouncing off the walls and following me.

That's her, bringing more of her kind here! Enough is enough!

When I arrived, I switched my computer on and realised the extent of the hate. TunNet was awash with arguments for and against more Rafters. There was fear of there being thousands or even millions more, and of equal numbers dying in the Tunnels. Not enough of this, too much of that, not enough of that, too much of this. No cohesive argument, just unfounded nonsense and overzealous statements. In the gossip about quantities of everything, no mention was made of the fact that they were talking about human lives. Instead, resources were gauged, prices depicted. Each life was portrayed in terms of currency.

Groundless fiction was being represented as fact, with outrageous exaggerations designed to make the divisions deeper. It reminded me of the National Press on the Raft. Such crap had been circulating on TunNet for a while, only now it had expanded. Reality was spun to suit the speaker, the same sort of twisting and exaggeration that Peter used to write. Only Peter didn't write this. He was on the receiving end of the malice now.

The reports spoke of an invasion and of widespread food shortages to cater for the influx, reminding everyone that the Raft had made off with their food stockpiles. I clicked and scrolled through post after post of nonsense. The lies and half-baked truths were insane, and the Council wanted *me* to keep quiet! Isaac had even shared some mocked-up picture of a Rafter stealing as a Sub looked pathetically on.

How could he?

Amalyn's name came up a few times, citing her as the leader of an invasion rather than the scientist who had made them all healthier. I kicked the table in frustration and started up some machinery just to drown out the echoes from outside. As the machines got going, there was a knock on the door. I looked up as they stepped into the lab and my chest tightened, their ashen faces streaked with tears, filled with hope and fear and denial. Amalyn's parents. I had been so caught up in my own problems, I had forgotten all about them. How cruel my negligence was!

'Lydia, Dennis, hello, come in. I'm so sorry.'

'Is it true? Amalyn is alive?'

'It is. I wanted to come to you with good news, with a plan to get her here.'

'But she's alive! Oh Dennis, she's alive.' Lydia collapsed into her husband's arms. Dennis held her, though he looked too weary to take her weight.

I pulled up chairs for them both. They sat down, and I took a breath. 'There's more. I've spoken to her twice now. She's had a baby, Archie's baby. A little girl.'

I told them everything, omitting the part about having the information I needed for the food production.

'She's actually going to get a boat?' Dennis said, eyes full of awe.

'So she says.'

'Well, if anyone can pull that off, it's Amalyn.'

They looked so frail; I worried they wouldn't be able to stand again without some sustenance. A box of substandard biscuits had come out of the factory machines, and I fed them both. With bellies less empty, they looked like they could take on the world again. I quizzed them but they assured me they had been eating the filth food, but like all Rafters, their rations were small. It looked like they had aged a lifetime since we'd arrived. Shadows framed their eyes and lines criss-crossed every bit of skin. The manual labour was hard for two people in their sixties and their grief robbed them of the motivation to go on. They'd believed their only daughter was dead. Now they knew different but, despite my assurances, they were riddled with disbelief.

How could she have survived? Where had she been all this time? They asked these questions again and again. I had no answers.

'You know Ams,' I said. 'She's bad-ass.'

As they left for their own work with many hugs and handshakes, I promised I'd keep them updated. Any news, good or bad.

Alone again, my joy left me and I grew angry once more. Angry at the hate that was spreading. Angry at the sort of welcome Amalyn and the others could expect when they arrived. They were just trying to survive, to secure a future for their children. And we had enough in the Tunnels. I *knew* we had enough. The Rafters were working so hard mining new tunnels, building new accommodation. I looked at my computer screen again. I shouldn't have, it did nothing but make my anger burn hotter. Isaac was spreading lies, as were Giao and Celia. Almost all the Council members had shared something, using hate to stoke the fire of Isaac's political campaign. I thumped my desk again and again until my knuckles bled, then loaded up a message thread to Isaac and Giao.

I typed: 'The fear across the Tunnels is getting ridiculous. One of the posts was from you and your secretary, Giao. Isaac, you shared it! Warning of an "invasion" of Rafters. You know that's not true. It's just fear-mongering.'

Isaac: 'Surely the whole country should fight this involuntary increase in our numbers? This dilution of our culture?'

'They're dying on the Raft!'

'Now who's fear mongering?'

'It's the truth. Remember that Amalyn has what we need to get the factory working, and she has a newborn.'

Giao had seen the messages but not commented, and I didn't wait for a reply. I exited the message thread and thumped my desk some more.

Bollocks to keeping quiet. I wrote another press release. The Council wanted me silent on the new Rafters coming so they had a blank canvas to spread their lies. So I typed, fingers bashing the keys as I ground my teeth. I would send out what I wrote word for word. Unedited truth. Informing people of the facts, not the trivial gossip they were being served up.

By the time my lunch ration arrived, I was famished. A meagre portion of minced muck. I could make more potatoes, I could make some IcyCrema, some Veg Chunks ... anything I used to make, I could make now. But then Amalyn would lose her advantage. I stared at the food, and then, for the first time since arriving, I ate it. I pinched my nose and gagged it down, feeling faint, but I managed to finish it. Afterwards I had to block the thought from my mind, shake my head to stop the mental images of the filth crawling down my throat. It wasn't that bad, not really. I could cope. For Amalyn, for the baby.

Chapter 18

The Raft

Jacob was just the first to come. Over the next few days, many more Golden Fifty arrived at the apartment, desperation ridding them of caution, the painted logos giving them some hope. Those who arrived with weapons soon dropped them when they saw welcoming faces and the hint of cooperation. Nearly all had the tattoo to show that we were friends rather than enemies, that we were all there to help each other. The fear that had plagued them for months was replaced with warmth and trust. We greeted empty arms and sallow faces, hungry and scared people. Every evening, new soft footsteps came plodding up the stairs, malnourished faces full of anguish and worry. Gaunt and thin. Full of loss and misery.

So many had perished, whole families, entire workforces. The ones left behind had mostly given up. They had waited for news, dutifully. Watching the strip billboards as the last rockets left for Mars, awaiting an update until they realised that none was coming, the screens were blank. News as absent as return flights.

Then the Internet disappeared, and reality hit. The new arrivals talked about the following weeks, the fear, the looting, the dead, the isolation. Abandoned, marooned. Their whole lives, the Centre had taken whatever it wanted, the Elite wiping their shoes on the Perimeter. We expected nothing better, no kindness or sympathy. But still it had hit everyone like a brick.

Talk of escaping was either nonsense, or an opportunity missed. Stories were told of whole families and groups jumping into the sea, or hanging themselves from whatever infrastructure was left. Pills were swallowed, arteries slashed. Others lost their minds from eating too many fish.

I should have been there to spread the news and facilitate their escape. I could have helped. Every story weighed on me. If I hadn't lingered in that bar, if I had run as soon as Archie said to run, if we had moved away from the edge as soon as he heaved me over, if I hadn't wallowed ...

As Danny said, 'that's a lot of "ifs," dearie.'

One night, as I sat waiting for the tears that wouldn't come, Archie's voice echoed over and over in my head.

Go, Ams, you have to live.

Wallowing was a luxury for the childless and the lost, for those without responsibilities. That was no longer me. Each of their faces was etched in my mind. I had seen their hopelessness turn hopeful, watched as their loneliness dissipated when they found us. This handful of people were worth saving. Reya needed saving. Those that were left, the last survivors, their dreams had turned to nightmares. A hint of a plan was a shining light in the darkness. They were out of other options, and they came, listening, wanting. Despite all the shit that life had thrown at them, they still wanted to live.

We shared food, nursed wounds, helped others clean themselves up. June's scorn was dwarfed by their gratitude. She and Danny had preached caution when dealing with other survivors. Yet in everyone that arrived, we experienced nothing but kindness and friendship. June's tuts and scoffs were inaudible against the volume of compassion and benevolence. When faced with the end of the world as they knew it, humanity was outshining hate. Where in the past, surplus had triggered animosity, now mercy was found in despair.

I told them everything. Shared Sav's book, her words. I showed them the details I had printed out, spoke about the Tunnels. I painted a picture of Toulouse, adding a vivacity to the Tunnels that I only half-remembered, a slight embellishment here and there. A touch of colour in the grey. The confirmation that other civilisations existed brought tears to some eyes, and doubt to others. I showed them food orders, Harold's video blog. They winced at the mention of the filth food and silkworms, and gasped in wonderment when I described the nuclear reactors, the grandiose scale, the ornate carvings in the rocks. When they learned about the trade with the Centre, they nodded. The Perimeter had been propping up their greed for decades. This came as no big surprise.

One evening I managed a conversation with Sav on the Satellite phone.

'How many?' she asked.

'Over sixty now. Can you believe it? There are still so many clinging on.'

'That's good, Ams. Really good. But there's still no way we can send a plane.' The signal was patchy and her voice echoed.

'We'll make it. I have a plan.'

The line went dead, but it didn't matter. I'd said enough. She knew we were coming. I looked at the satellite phone – sixty per cent battery and no way to charge it. I would have to use it sparingly from then on.

They had all heard of Sav. The Selbourne Range had been in everyone's shopping baskets at one stage, and her articles in the National Press were well known. A Centre pawn, they'd assumed. But her book confirmed otherwise. She was a woman trapped by the Centre, trying to survive, like all of us, I explained. They had to believe it.

I went back to the hub with June and Danny, leaving Cora with Tilly. Tilly was mooching around the apartment, rested yet restless. She was eating more, could rasp a few words. The medication I gave her helping her throat a little. She was alert, had some energy, and Cora made her smile. Tears still came freely, the previous months haunting her at night. Husky screams and croaky sobs filled the apartment after all else was still. But she was improving. Cora was sensible, mature for a seven-year-old.

She enjoyed Tilly's company. Their mutual survival had bonded them.

***

The wind was quiet, the smog thin. It was a rare day where being outside didn't feel like wading through gravel. Through the Autocar windows was the best view of the outside I'd had seen since being compos mentis enough to pay attention. Smashed windows were everywhere, render breaking off, tar-like smog dripping from every surface. When I spotted a Golden Fifty symbol I had painted, it stood out more than I had realised, a dash of colour against the gloom.

I wanted to see if Savannah had emailed, and to make sure that I hadn't missed anything at all about the Tunnel entrance, the information on the boats, the lab and factory instructions. I was still so tired all the time; I didn't trust my memory.

After June and Danny set up the computer again, I read and double-checked, mentally ticking off everything we needed. Then, when I was sure, I hovered over the computer, Archie's compiled proof at my fingertips. I could let Mars know. I could leak all the information about the Raft and the Centre. Let the Select know that they had been ripped off, their people left to starve, their protein sources poisoned by the Centre. It was Sav who'd promised she'd keep a lid on it, not me. Did the Centre Elite really have contacts in the Tunnels who would elicit revenge? I doubted it. The lab was important to the tunnels. They were hardly going to bump off their lead scientist.

My fingers twitched over the keys as June tapped her foot impatiently, waiting for me to finish. Sav would tell me not to, that it wasn't worth it. She was rational and obedient, always so quick to conform. I didn't begrudge her that. She had to prove herself, rid herself of her parent's reputation, and the Centre had blackmailed her. But the Centre had also blown up the Raft's edge and killed Archie, so screw them and their blackmailing. They were a world away. Sav would still say to be cautious, though. She had always been mumsy, even before she was a mum. Bollocks was I going to be that sort of mother.

Fuck it.

I sent the proof, exactly as Archie's instructions said, to every Martian email on file. Revealing what scum the Centre Elite really were. Revenge felt good. It was like my skin fitted me again, like I'd found my true self. I wished I could be there to see the fallout, to watch the reactions as the Blue Liberation party fell. I hoped they'd get stamped on in riots and beaten to death. They had taken Archie from me. They needed to suffer, to hurt, to lose. I wanted to hear their bones break.

There were plenty on Mars who would be appalled, I was sure. Not every Centre was as bad as the Elite. For us Perimeter, the salt and battering wind whipped our skin away, exposing our bones. Now the Centre's facade would be as eroded as their buildings. I set it to release twice, in case one got intercepted, on a delay to give us time to get off the Raft, in case, somehow, they could retaliate. That gave me two days.

There was no need for the computer now. I had everything I needed, and we had to save our energy and leave bag space for any food we could find on the way home. I turned and had one last look at the screensaver. The photo of us, Archie's face next to mine, kissing my cheek. He was smiling at me, urging me on.

I'm trying, my love. I'm trying.

As we were leaving the hub, we paused. A noise. We instantly froze, looking at each other for confirmation, and stood still a moment. I turned my head to where the sound had come from as Danny put his hands behind his ears. Had we really just heard that? Voices. Getting closer. Laughing, giggling. From the gloom they approached, slowly, tottering on platform shoes, pretty handbags dangling from their arms.

'And who are you? More invaders?' Their faces were so smooth they looked swollen. Too clean and made up as if they were expecting a night out.

'Excuse me?' I replied.

'You look like Perimeter. This is Centre ground. You're not supposed to be here. Get back over the fence.' She reached into her handbag and pulled out a knife, the metal blade catching the light.

'Woah,' said Danny as we backed away. 'I don't think the fence counts for much now.'

'This knife says otherwise.'

'We don't want any trouble,' said Danny.

'Seriously,' I said. 'We're unarmed. We're no threat to you.'

'That's what all Perimeter vermin say,' she said and slowly put her knife back in her handbag.

The man stepped forward, arms folded across his chest, sequinned top sparkling in the dim light. 'If you're here for the Selfie Stations, don't bother. We cleaned them out ages ago. Actually, it's about that time, isn't it Izzy?'

'It is, Pepi.' Izzy smiled with fat, lined lips, and got her phone out, holding it up for a photo.

'Mars!' they both said through their smiles, their inflated lips revealing their whiter-than-white teeth.

'What are you doing?' I said. 'There's no Internet out here.'

'We're still doing our selfies, though,' said Izzy, as if it was the most sensible thing in the world. 'Imagine how many we'll have to upload! We'll take the Internet by storm.'

'Shouldn't you be on Mars?' June asked, face filled with contempt.

They shuffled, scuffing their perfectly clean heeled shoes on the tarmac. 'We missed our flight. Partied so hard the night before we slept in. But they'll come back for us,' Izzy said, holding her chin high. 'My father owned the mining company that made the metal for the fence. He's very important in the Centre.'

'And my family were shareholders in RenterRafts,' said Pepi. 'We basically own this country.' He walked around purposefully, shoulders back to accentuate his height. 'That building there, that one, and that one,' he pointed his manicured finger. 'My family own them all.'

'Quite the legacy,' I said, not hiding my sarcasm. 'Anyway, if they were coming back for you, they'd be here by now. You might as well come with us to the Mainland.'

'With you? Don't be ridiculous,' Pepi said with a laugh.

'Yeah, don't be ridiculous,' June said to me.

'They'll die if they stay here.'

'Who gives a toss?' said June, and spat on the floor. 'Centre pricks.'

'Hey, we did everything we could to help the Perimeter,' said Izzy. 'I even signed a petition.'

Reya gave a little grizzle under the tent blanket.

'Oh, you have a baby!' Izzy squealed. 'Gosh, look at the state of you. You must be one of the better Perimeter to have a baby, and you've let yourself get like this.' She looked me up and down with disgust.

Pepi cleared his throat. 'How's your tomorrow?'

'Fucked,' I said. The usual formal greeting seemed ridiculous now. 'I really think you should come with us.'

'I think you're supposed to say, "uncertain,"' Pepi said. 'Perhaps you're not Perimeter? Your skin and hair look bad enough to be, though, although not as bad as theirs.' It was June and Danny's turn to receive the scrunched-nose look.

'She's not *that* Perimeter, to be fair,' June said.

'June!' Danny scoffed.

'For Raft's sake,' I said. 'What does it matter? If you stay on the Raft, you'll die. It's that simple. Come with us and you'll have a chance.'

'We're fine here,' said Pepi. 'We have beauty supplies, a wonderful apartment and stockpiles of food.'

Izzy elbowed him. 'Shut it! They'll rob us!' She took out the knife again, waving it around like she was cutting holes in the smog. 'And we are certainly not going anywhere with any Perimeter. I mean, look at you!' Izzy said as Pepi put his arm around her, shaking his head at us.

'Fuck these two,' said June. 'Let's just go.'

I sighed. 'Well, there's a working computer with Internet access in there.' I gestured at the hub building. 'You can contact Mars if you like. Let them know you're here waiting, in case they haven't noticed.'

'You have a computer?' Izzy said, cocking her head.

'Careful Izzy, it's probably a trick to lure us away so they can drink our blood. That's a thing the Perimeter do, you know. Drink the blood of someone younger, thinking it'll make them look youthful. I read it in *Centre Life* magazine.'

'Or maybe they want to steal our Selfie Station supplies? We're almost out of collagen injections as it is.' They both cried out and grabbed each other for support.

'Piss off, Perimeter,' Pepi said. 'We're not going anywhere with you.' He grabbed a lump of tarmac from the floor and threw it at us, though it came nowhere close and smashed on the ground.

I held up my hands. 'All right, just listen. The computer is in the hub right there. It has power. If you click the browser, it'll take you straight through to the Mars system. I'll leave you to it.'

'Do you think we can upload our selfies?' Izzy asked.

'Whatever. Just see if anyone is going to come and get you. I mean it, you'll die if you stay here.'

'Oh my, Pepi, social media! How do I look?' Izzy turned to the side and pouted.

'Gorgeous, how are my teeth?'

'Perfect!'

We walked away from them. Danny's eyebrows were as high as they could go. June looked like she'd eaten dirt.

We got back in the Autocar, and all three of us loudly exhaled.

'What the actual fuck?' said June, summing up my thoughts nicely. 'They pulled a knife on us. Centre pricks.'

It took me a while to find my voice. 'I'll come back in a day or two, try to convince them.'

'Why?' said June. 'Fuck 'em,'

'No one deserves to die here,' I said, and told them about the man who'd threatened me with the knife, his desperate and starving face. 'He was kind, really. He just needed help.'

'That's a Perimeter, though,' said June. 'Those idiots are Centre arseholes.'

'Desperation makes good people do bad things,' said Danny. 'Greed makes bad people do worse things.'

'You have to understand that I was meant to save people, to get them off the Raft and to the Mainland. And I didn't. They died because I didn't help them.'

'You can't save everyone,' Danny said.

I have to try.

Chapter 19

The Tunnels

Chris, Betsie, and Ester's motivation had been short-lived, my temper not tenacious enough to make them clean more regularly. But, for a moment, I was pleased with their nonchalance. They were idle enough not to notice me carefully calibrating the equipment, making it just a bit more efficient, upping the 4D printer speed, making the starch synthesis perfect. With my delicate tweaks, I increased our yield to thirty-five boxes. Kevin watched, his cluelessness no threat to my plan. I sent him away to deliver the boxes as I made a little extra to take to the miners. 'Substandard stock,' I labelled it. I made the shapes irregular, crushed bits to make it less aesthetically appealing, making sure it was no longer warm, so its scent was less strong. There was nothing wrong with it, but the Council guard accepted that I wasn't wasting prime food on the miners. Their vitamin count was fine, but they lacked calcium, had almost no fibre and their calories were in short supply. VitaBiscuits were rich in all three, so I broke up a couple of boxes, labelled them as imperfect, and delivered them to the hungry workers.

My arrival made them drop their tools instantly, their sallow faces gaining some colour just at the sight of me and the boxes. Grateful hands reached out and thankful faces smiled.

'Is it true that more of us are coming?' one asked as he shovelled broken VitaBiscuits into his mouth.

'It is. They're trying to, anyway.'

They nodded. No whoops or cheers or ecstatic smiles. The response was alarmingly lukewarm. Their worries about sharing what little they had, and about further prejudice towards them, outweighed the good news of more Rafters coming. I reminded them that Amalyn had the lab information, which meant more food, and that seemed to put them a little more at ease. Peter was among them. What little teeth he'd had previously were now gone. His mouth sagged, as did the skin under his eyes.

'Professor.' He attempted his usual sneer.

'Peter.'

'Any luck finding my family?'

I had forgotten about that. Did he seriously think I had nothing better to do? 'The Tunnels are huge, Peter. And it hasn't really been at the forefront of my mind.'

'Well, if you could just ask around –'

'This is Toulouse, one city of many. I have no way of contacting other cities. Have you put your name on the register?'

'No.' He ate his biscuits, looking at the floor. 'I was hoping you could test the water for me. They might not want to see me.'

'You've upset someone? That's so unlike you.' My sarcasm was unkind, but the articles stirring up hatred for us Rafters had brought back so many bad memories of him that I had even less patience than normal. 'Seriously, Peter. Just register. I've zero hope of finding them for you, and neither the will nor the time to try.'

I handed out the rest of the biscuits and made my way back to the lab. The sound of content chewing behind me was music to my ears. I wished I could feed them more, make the lab run at its full potential. I shook off the guilt and promised myself I'd mock up some more substandard stock to keep them going. Just for now, that would have to do. *Soon,* I reminded myself. It would all be fine soon.

I walked slowly along the mezzanine back to the lab. It was too noisy to relax, too quiet to motivate me to move quicker. Bicycles screeched past, their rusty components bringing my attention back to the Tunnels and away from my daydreams about Amalyn. Impatient Subs yelled at me to move as I meandered along. So much hostility, too much resentment. I heard my name against the din, echoing down the tunnel. I turned around as Sara came running after me.

'Sav!'

'More bad news from the Council?'

'What? No.' She caught her breath. 'I was just doing a stock take of pickaxes. That man you were talking to, the miner. He looked so familiar. Who is he?'

'Some dickhead I used to know on the Raft.'

'What's his name?'

'Peter Melrose.'

She stopped walking, and the colour drained from her face. 'That's my dad.'

'Seriously?' I almost laughed. So much for zero hope. 'No wonder you ran away.'

'Is he that bad?'

'Yes.'

Her forehead furrowed, her eyes went to the floor. I saw it then, the same facial expression that he had. Peter was a troll, though, whereas Sara was exquisite. Peter was malicious. Sara had a heart of gold. How could someone as malevolent as him create such a kind soul as her? I regretted my outburst and tried to choose my words more carefully.

'He's just not my favourite person. I was surprised he was here and not on Mars, to be honest. He was as Centre as a Perimeter gets.'

'My mum told me he'd meet us here. But he never came.'

'He was the editor of the National Press. His job was to brainwash people into doing the Centre's bidding.'

She looked crushed. My words were still too insensitive. Peter had trained me too well, it seemed.

'I don't remember him too much, to be honest,' she said. 'He wouldn't recognise me now. I was a little girl when we crossed the bridge. He was pretty upset about my sister dying and never seemed the same after that. He said I should change my name when I left.'

'Why did he say that?'

'Kids were being mean. My sister died of hay fever anaphylaxis before the Great Sterilisation Project.'

I was shocked. 'Well, that explains a lot, I guess. The Press really pushed the Great Sterilisation Project. What was your name before?'

'Lily. Like the flower.'

I couldn't hide my grimace. 'Sensible advice, I reckon.'

'I think he just wanted justice for Daisy.'

'Daisy?' I winced at hearing another filth word.

'My sister. That was her name.'

'Ah, I see.' *Daisy?* I swallowed back the bitter taste of bile and blinked hard. Peter having a family at all seemed ludicrous, let alone him calling his kids such names. He was the Poison Maker, but perhaps the Centre had poisoned his mind the most. 'I spoke to him the other day. He came here hoping to find you.'

'Is he a bad person? I'm not sure what to do.'

'He was a Centre fan, like plenty of others, I'm sure. He was pro the anchors being blown. Elitist, overly nationalist. That's how I'd describe him.'

Sara nodded and didn't look up from the floor. 'He loved my mum. I remember that much. She said he would meet us here. But mum died when the bridges collapsed. I only just made it.'

Her face was reddening, her eyes glazed with tears. She must have been a little girl, such a young thing to be running for her life, watching her mother fall into the sea. And now she had a father. Shame it was Peter, but finding any family in this world was a miracle.

'So, you want me to introduce you?' I asked.

'I'm not sure. I'll think about it, I guess. Maybe speak to some others, get some more information about him.'

We walked a little further together in silence. I could be honest and tell her what a prick her father was, what his headlines said after they blew up the anchors ahead of time. If they had stuck to the schedule, maybe her mum would have made it. The headline that had been on display back in Greg's BioLabs office flashed through my mind – *Deserters Deserve to Drown*. Her father had written that. About his own wife.

I said nothing more. Sara could discover this all by herself if she wanted. Maybe Peter had been reborn since arriving here? I almost laughed at the thought.

We walked a bit further until I stopped dead in my tracks. Plastered all through the tunnels were posters of Isaac that must have been put up only moments earlier. *Vote for Isaac! Keep the Rafters out!*

Seriously?

Sara shook her head. 'Your brother is like a dad to me. He and Sofia took me in when I arrived all alone. But I'm not sure where he's coming from with his campaign. He's been different the last year, since the Select left.'

'Since the Rafters arrived, you mean?'

'Maybe. Anyway, I've got a meeting with the accounts department this afternoon. I'll probably see him then. I'll try to talk to him. Pop by yours this evening?'

'Sounds good.'

'You should visit the solarium. It'll brighten your mood.'

'I'll think about it.'

***

I spent the afternoon wasting time at the lab, a half-hearted effort to design some new flavours and to up the vitamin D content in everything. Our fruit flavours could be expanded, too. Extra fibre was always needed, the filth food gave us so little.

I didn't go by the solarium. That was a Sub hobby. I never saw the appeal of sitting in a cave with bright lights mimicking sunshine blasting at you. We never had sun on the Raft, such were the smog and the storms, so I certainly didn't miss it. A MindSpa is what I really wanted. It had been rumoured that one may be in the design process. A hypno-medic had made it over and was labouring somewhere in the Tunnels. But such facilities for Rafters were way off, given the current mood. Grace had been encouraging me to visit the library. She had been on several occasions with the children, and said she'd found it therapeutic. Though she'd not braved the gallery yet. She read a fictional story about a princess and a love interest. I giggled when she told me.

'Sounds twee,' I said.

'It was like an old film written down.'

'I'll stick to the encyclopaedias,' I said with a laugh.

I avoided looking at TunNet, but it was hard to dodge the worst of the gossip. My article had been circulated, criticised, praised, and disregarded. People had chosen their side and there was little information now that could help. Lydia and Dennis were posting pictures of Amalyn, baby photos, too. Telling the world she had a newborn, making heart-breaking pleas. I longed to speak to her again, but I knew I just had to wait. She would get here somehow.

The echoes in the Tunnels grew louder throughout the afternoon. By the time I was due to go home, the unrest was reaching a crescendo. Chants and heckles from Harvey's and Isaac's followers were thrown across the corridors and chambers. It reminded me of the anchor riots all those years earlier. I saw Sara and Clementine in the crowd, trying to make their way to me, but unable to get through the masses. As I approached the Rafters' wing, an unfriendly hand grabbed my smock and held me back.

'All Rafters are under curfew,' the Council guard said, his other hand hovering over his baton. 'You're causing too much trouble.'

A flimsy thin wire fence was being put across our wing to keep us in, though it didn't look sturdy enough to hold back even a child. If we had been causing that much trouble, we could have knocked it down easily. By the time Clementine and Sara made it over, they were on the other side of the makeshift divide, several Council guards flanking it.

'What's going on?' I asked.

'They're trying to keep people apart to stop any unrest,' Sara said.

'It's getting a bit heated,' said Clementine. 'The Council thought this would be for the best. The easiest solution, anyway.'

'This is awful,' I said, 'locking us in like this. This fence doesn't even do anything. It's symbolic, that's all.'

'It's for your own good,' said Clementine. 'And it's just temporary. Nobody wants this. It's just for a short while.'

'It's like the Raft all over again. Whose idea was this?'

'The Council,' said Clementine.

'But not everyone on the Council,' Sara said, reaching across the fence for my hand.

I smiled, despite my sadness and anger. At least someone was on our side.

'We really are sorry,' said Clementine. 'I've been listening, really listening. I know how tough things were for you on the

Raft. But he's my dad. I can't go against him. He just wants everyone to be safe. And Giao wants peace, for everything to calm down. Though this does seem unfair. I'll see what I can do.'

Before she turned around, I saw a hint of sadness and regret in her eyes. That gave me some hope. If Clementine could find some sympathy for the Rafters, maybe others could, too.

Sara had something else to say, and I leant into the fence so I could hear her soft voice. 'I need to talk to you about the accounts meeting.'

The Council guard was standing close by, keeping a watchful eye.

'Probably best to visit me in the lab tomorrow,' I said.

I arrived home to the sound of a pot slamming on the stove and Grace cursing out loud, something she rarely did. The room was untidier than usual, sandals thrown against the wall, schoolwork scattered across the table. A trail of mess followed Grace. Her usually pale face was red with rage, her curls pinned back tightly.

'They're treating us like bloody vermin. Caging us in like this, like we're the filth in the larders instead of people. It's just making things worse for us.'

'Clementine says it's only temporary.'

'I don't trust her at all. I saw her standing shoulder to shoulder with Isaac yesterday. Your brother, Sav. How could he say such things?'

'I don't know what's gotten into him. It's like this election has totally gone to his head.'

'We never would have been treated this way on Mars. Don't they realise the contribution we're making here?'

The pot was boiling now, spilling over as she did nothing to calm it. I walked over and reduced it to a simmer, and she batted my hand away from the stove.

'It's worse than the bloody Raft. We came here to help these people and give our son a future, and they cage us in. Everywhere I go, people look at me like I'm trash. I don't look like them and they avoid me. Then they hear my accent and run away. They speak languages I don't understand but I can tell what sort of awful things they're saying. They look at Ethan the same way. He's a child, he shouldn't be treated like this.' She looked over at him sitting on the floor with his trucks, more quiet than usual. 'He's lonely,' Grace said. 'None of the children will talk to him. He's the only Rafter in his class. And he's the smartest. What are kids meant to think when the grownups behave so appallingly?'

It wasn't long before this that we had refused to even say the word 'Rafter.' Now it came out of her mouth so easily. Our vocabulary was changing to suit the Subs, demeaning ourselves in the same way they demeaned us. We'd be caging ourselves in next.

'Well, he's coming with me to work in a couple of days. First of the month. His tests are due.'

Grace looked slightly relieved. 'He hates the tests, but I suppose a day off school will do him some good.'

Chapter 20

The Raft

We'd thought we had so much time. Archie and I never spoke about the future, not really, not past what we were going to have for dinner and plans for the weekend. It was just supposed to be there for us. We took it for granted. We'd grow old together, compare aches and pains, and share reading glasses. Even with the age gap, I expected a few decades together, at least.

How long could we linger on the Raft? We had left it too late before. No chance was I going to make that error again. I'd lost that part of me – the part that made the same mistakes, over and over. Burying my head in the dirt as the world turned to shit around me. No. Not again. It was time to act.

After a couple of days passed with no more new arrivals, I figured that would be it. Once we got to the Tunnels, we'd persuade the Council to do food drops for the Raft, somehow. The lab would be up and running, there would be food to spare.

And then we'd figure out how to collect people. Or they could follow our route, if the Raft stayed in place for long enough. But until then, I had almost sixty people to convince. To explain that I had lured them here wanting their help, even though they had arrived needing mine.

Danny and June attended every evening, observing from the hallway outside my apartment door. June's arms stayed folded, her eyes looking away, foot tapping on the floor until Danny nudged her and told her to stop. Every evening they played out this drama. Danny, leaning in, angling his head towards the conversations, muttering in June's ear. I never begged them to come and meet the Fifties, only suggested it. Hope and reason would filter through. June could only resist reason for so long. Hope would displace anger and distrust, eventually. Once I had convinced enough of the Golden Fifty, anyway.

'You want to use boats?' Chrissy asked. A younger woman, she'd been surviving alone, and spoke rarely. 'As in, vessels that float on the sea?'

'There are still the old docks. I found them on the satellite images, and I went there and took photos. There are two boats there. Centre fishing boats.'

'At the edge?' Chrissy asked, hugging herself. It was her third evening attending, and however hot it was, she always shivered.

'Which is why we have to hurry. It's a four-hour walk to the docks from here. If anyone knows of a working Autocar, we could use it.'

'The one outside is the only one I've seen working in a while,' said an older man called Vern. 'I'll keep an eye out, though.'

'Okay, well, even if we just have the one, that helps. We can load that up with the water and whoever has difficulty walking,' I said. 'The weather is calm. I suggest we leave the day after tomorrow.'

'The day after tomorrow!' Obey said. He was someone I recognised from the bars. He used to drink a lot. There seemed to be no pattern in who had made it and who didn't.

'You don't have to come, any of you. But I'm going. I know there are great cities out there.'

'Because this rag says so, written by a Centre journalist.' Obey threw the copy of Sav's book on the floor.

'Hey! Savannah is Perimeter as much as any of us. You've read it, so you know she was manipulated by the Centre. She was just trying to survive and protect her family. That's all I'm trying to do.' I looked around at everyone. 'There's a better life out there for us. A place with opportunities and space and health. A community that will care for us. We are Golden Fifty. This is why the Fifty were formed. To travel, to see the world. It's what we've always longed for. Now you have that chance and you're too scared to take it?'

'Who even knows how to use a boat?' said a woman whose name I couldn't recall, a new visitor with a scar down her face. 'Are they automatic?'

'I can sail it.' Jacob stood up. The first of our recruits, he was tall for a Perimeter, his back straight. Despite the food shortages, he had maintained some muscle in his arms. 'I sailed boats years ago, before the Centre took the old docks down,' he said. 'Their boats are a lot more modern, but I'm sure I can do it.'

'I sailed boats too.' Vern stood tentatively, though his posture didn't inspire much faith in his abilities. 'Years ago, mind. And we never went far. But I'm happy to skipper.' The vibrato of his voice made 'years ago' sound like quite the understatement.

I smiled and nodded. The rest of the group started murmuring, chatting about possibilities, of a chance of a new life. A better life.

We can do this!

On these bleak wastelands that were all that was left of the Raft, where colour never shone and smog smothered all life, I was finding the dimmest glimmer of hope. The smallest spark in the darkness.

'I've found manuals for the boats in Centre files, if you want to read them? And I took photos of what I could,' I said.

'That would be handy,' said Jacob.

I handed him printouts and the e-pad with the photos. I showed the proof to the new attendees who hadn't seen it, the food orders to Toulouse, where the Tunnels were on satellite images, and retold the story of my visit. Again and again I said this, and every time I did, the shadow that enshrouded them grew fainter.

'The day after tomorrow,' I said. 'The weather looks to be clearer then. We can meet at the Centre fence nearest to here, at the gate, in the morning. Eight am. Anyone who wants to come is welcome. Bring food and as much water as you can carry.'

'I could bring my fishing rod,' James said. His worn-out face made him look like he'd consumed plenty of those.

'Probably best we keep a clear head for the journey,' I said.

'There might be a time where we don't want a clear head,' he replied.

I walked over and put my arm around him, though he was too thin for a comforting hug. 'We'll make it. I know we will.'

Some stayed with me in my apartment. One of them was Bex, a young computer engineer who'd lived with her parents until they jumped over the edge. 'To save me,' she said. 'There wasn't enough food, so they thought I'd have a better chance without them.' She was particularly small, her thick glasses making her eyes look even smaller. Her asthma inhaler was in her hand always. The thought of smog-free air in the Tunnels gave her the kind of colour in her cheeks I doubted she'd ever had before.

Shaif was a creative whose family had cast him aside years earlier, writing him off as an Alternate. His arms were inked not only with the Golden Fifty tattoo but other designs as well. His hair flopped in front of his eyes often, like a shield from the outside world. And there was Glin, who had a degree in biomedical sciences but had been a stay-at-home dad for his husband and the child they were raising. It was his sister's child, orphaned several years earlier. He didn't share how. Now the child and his husband had joined his sister when their home fell into the sea. 'Family is just a leap away,' he said, with a longing for the beyond. A longing I recognised. The sweet release.

All three were lonely and did not want to go back to their own quiet, empty places. All three had heard about the planes early on, and none of them had made it.

'I had no means of getting an Autocar,' Shaif said.

'I just didn't believe it was true,' said Bex.

'I didn't feel I deserved that chance, when Kai and Joey didn't get that chance,' said Glin, wiping his eyes.

My heart broke with his.

Cora beamed at the extra company and delighted in showing all of them her drawings. Tilly shared her room with Bex without complaint. She was getting more alert by the day. She could whisper now, though when she did, she expressed little more than single words for simple urges. 'Tired,' 'hungry,' 'hurts.' She'd stopped shivering, her body temperature regulated, and was eating more. She smiled sometimes, at Cora mostly.

I had managed some sleep here and there. Cora decided my bedroom was the best place for her too, and she slept through most of Reya's late-night feeds. She added a warmth to the place it had lacked before and kept my mind busy. I couldn't wallow and cry when she was there, when she was counting on me. Her trust made me strong.

The next day, I got up and left early, wanting to do one more search. I had to speak to anyone I could find. If there was anyone left, they deserved to know the truth and have the opportunity to come with us.

'What's the point?' said June when I popped round theirs. 'How you going to feel when the first one dies at sea? And the next one and the next?'

'Dying at sea isn't part of the plan.'

'You should rest, dearie,' Danny said, brow creased with worry, as always. 'You look pale.'

'I know, Danny. I'll rest on the boat.'

'Well, I might as well come with you and watch you waste your time,' said June, grabbing a jacket, labouring over it as if it required every ounce of strength she had.

I left the others in the apartment, Bex minding Reya. She didn't object. Bex cooed every time she saw her and had a natural way with babies that was far superior to mine. We wouldn't all fit in an Autocar, anyway. I had most of the copies of Sav's book with me. As the Autocar drove around, I got out and placed them under doorways here and there, so they were protected from the worst of the elements. On the front I'd written: *We leave for the Mainland October 2nd, sunrise,* and drew a little map to the Centre gate and the dock. Just in case. After two drop offs, Danny took over the job, noticing my discomfort most likely.

After an hour of circling the most central streets, we saw the smooth and collagen-filled faces of Pepi and Izzy.

'Forget about those two, screw them,' June said and spat out of the Autocar door.

'No one deserves to die here,' I said as I got out. 'Hey!' I shouted at them, then louder as the wind howled and carried my voice away.

'Well, if it isn't the little not-quite-Perimeter hag,' Izzy said with a smirk.

'We're leaving tomorrow. There's quite a lot of us now.'

'Mars?' asked Pepi, his face lighting up.

'No, the Mainland. Did you hear from Mars? Are they coming to get you?'

'Well, we got loads of likes on our selfies.'

The ground dipped a little then, just a few degrees, loose bits of brick scattering down the side of the buildings.

'Come with us,' I said. 'Please. It's your best chance of surviving.'

Izzy grimaced and lifted her chin higher. 'Best chance of catching whatever it is that's made your skin so bad, more like.'

'Please,' I said again. 'They're not coming for you. Where would they even land a rocket? If you stay here, you'll be fish food.' Did they not feel the movement, hear the buildings crumbling?

'I'd rather die here, glamorous, then go and live like vermin,' said Pepi.

My shoulders sagged. Danny and June got out of the Autocar and stood next to me.

'You can't save everyone, dearie,' Danny said again.

'But they're right here. Why don't they see?'

'Leave us alone, Perimeter scum!' said Izzy, wielding her blade. Her smile was wide, manic. 'I've killed one of your kind before. Don't think I won't do it again.'

I gasped, and Danny put a protective arm in front of me.

'What does it matter what side of the fence we grew up on?' I said. 'We're all human.'

'Enough,' Danny said. 'Let's go.'

A groan then, from a building masked by smog, the creak of brick on brick.

'Do not compare me to a filthy Perimeter,' Pepi said, and picked up some loose bits of tarmac. 'This is Centre turf. Go live like the vermin you are.' He threw the tarmac, and it smashed at my feet.

We stepped backwards as they came closer. I almost lost my footing from vibrations coming up from the ground. Pepi grabbed some more tarmac, and Izzy bent double from laughing.

'Please,' I said again. 'We don't want you to die.'

'Speak for yourself,' said June.

'We need to get out of here,' said Danny, as a shower of loose render from the buildings behind landed next to us. 'I don't think it's safe to stay here.'

'Just one more minute,' I said, then faced Pepi and Izzy again. 'It's a nice life in the Tunnels. You'll have a chance of surviving.'

The next piece of thrown tarmac grazed my leg, and I stepped back further. Another bit hit June on the side of the head and sent her stumbling backwards.

Izzy and Pepi laughed. 'Vermin! Go away!'

'We need to go. Now!' Danny grabbed my arm, pulled me back, his fingers digging into the skin.

I wriggled free from him. 'Just wait –'

My voice disappeared, hidden under the crack that screeched from behind. We all felt it then. The sway of the Raft was unmistakable. The wind howled, the smog lashing all around us, and punctuating it was the creaking of the buildings, struggling against gravity. We all froze, just for a second, but that second was too long. The land groaned, toppling me over as dust stung my eyes. I got up and had just found my balance when the floor dipped again and sent me falling onto my knees as a terrible rumbling, splitting sound filled the air. Danny's arms were around me, lifting and dragging me to my feet, pulling me forward. The air was thick with dust. I couldn't see. It was all sound, noises, grinding and creaking, and my heart thumping in my chest. I didn't know what was happening until I turned and, in the sliver of air where the dust was thinner, saw the building behind us collapsing, rubble and filth tumbling towards us. Then I heard it, over the wind and the creaks – the thundering roar of a building turning to gravel.

For a moment, everything was still. There was no sound except my heart thumping against my ribcage. Then the grey air cleared as the ash flittered to the ground, settling as the wind died down.

There was a wheezing breath behind me, my own coming out in shudders. I rubbed my stinging eyes. It was all so grey still. Just piles and piles of grey.

'June?' Danny said. 'Where's June?' His eyes were wide, wild, streaming in the smog and salt. 'June! June!'

Over the debris, a limping figure appeared, a blood-soaked dress, one arm supporting the other.

'June!' Danny ran to hug her.

She struggled to form words, just a sound came out, a whine. One hand was almost completely crushed, fingers and hand mangled together.

'Ew. That's gonna need more than a collagen booster,' said Pepi.

I turned, scowling, as he and Izzy cleaned the dust off each other's faces. 'Don't you see?' I shouted. 'If you stay here, you'll die. It's all collapsing.'

'Leave it, dearie,' said Danny, anger in his voice.

Izzy threw her hair over her shoulder. 'Serves you right, Perimeter. Some people are meant to live under the rubble, some of us on top of it.' And then she and Pepi strutted off, their laughter howling with the wind.

Danny grabbed June as her knees started to buckle. I realised then that the Autocar had been buried. The last working Autocar, crushed.

'M-m-microbes,' said June.

Danny ripped his T-shirt to fashion a bandage and sling for June's mangled arm, wrapping her hand in layers of grubby cloth. And we walked. Danny supported the two of us, though June mostly. For once, I wasn't the weakest. I rummaged in my bag and found some ImmunoJuice and tried to make June drink. 'For the shock,' I said.

She winced through mouthfuls of the stuff. It was way past its use-by date, but I figured sugar is still sugar. She burped and sicked a little up.

Neither of them spoke to me. Flushes of guilt crept up through my veins. New guilt on top of the old. I bit my lip as my vision blurred with tears.

Reya. Thank god she hadn't been there. She must have been getting hungry. I had no way to check the time, but the heat of the day was diminishing when we got to our building. I crawled up the stairs and found some fresh, clean sheets and blankets to use as bandages, plus a bottle of spirit alcohol I had found. 'To clean it,' I said, when June paled at the sight of it. 'They have proper doctors in the Tunnels. They can help there.'

'W-waste of f-f-fucking t-time.'

'I'm sorry. I just wanted to help them. I'm really sorry.'

Danny took the supplies without saying a word, and they went to their apartment. I left them to it, June making it clear she didn't want me anywhere near her, and went to find Reya.

'I'm sorry we were so long,' I said to Bex as I picked Reya up. 'We had a bit of trouble.'

'It's fine,' said Bex. 'She only just started crying.' From Reya's red cheeks and Bex's tired face, I assumed she was just saying that to be kind. I fed her and she looked up at me, as if she was looking inside of me, to some deeper part, seeing the doubts I was trying to hide from everyone else. I kissed her forehead and put her to sleep, making promises of safety and a future I knew I couldn't keep.

I listened at June and Danny's apartment door for a while, wanting to go in and see if June was okay, to apologise. But I didn't. No doubt the sight of me would have made things worse. The crushing responsibility I felt towards every life left on the Raft was inexplainable, and trying to express it would not have made June's arm better. So instead, I went back to mine and dug out some alcohol, finding bottles of synth grape powder wine I'd forgotten about. I grabbed some glasses and laid them out on the table, to take the pain away. *Any excuse,* Sav would say. But I didn't drink. My head hurt anyway. I felt flushed and tired, and the thought of the next day made me queasy. The walk from the accident had left me exhausted; I couldn't think about the mammoth journey. I let my mind fixate on the destination only. A safe place. A home.

As Glin poured drinks, Tilly helped me rummage in the cupboards for better-fitting shoes and, finding only high heels and impractical sandals, I opted to stick with my current ones and soak my feet a while instead.

Cora gave us each a hug and said goodnight as she took herself off to bed. 'One more sleep,' she said.

Shaif, Glin and Bex drank, toasting their last night on the Raft, telling stories of happier times, of scandalous times. 'Oh, why didn't we keep the anchors?' they said over and over again.

'No point in remorse,' I said. Logic and reason had no place in the minds of the powerful who made the decision to blow up the bridges. Decades on, and so many of us still couldn't fathom it. The future of us Perimeter was not even considered. We were vermin in their great experiment, minions to do their bidding and propel them to higher highs, fatter wallets, and cleaner planets. We were just the dirt they left behind.

Reya was a gem. She was crying so little I worried she was sick. But her body felt warm, and she looked at me so intently, like she was trying to tell me she was fine. The company didn't faze her, the voices of strangers soothing her to sleep. I put her down in her drawer after the others had gone to bed and went to the kitchen, standing at the counter. I imagined Archie and me making house, Reya asleep, sharing a joke in the kitchen. Him grabbing my waist; me teasing him, pulling him in close. Our life that would never be. Still alive in my mind.

I swallowed some painkillers with a drink of water and sat in the bathroom. The pain was getting worse with every toilet visit. Finding a compact mirror in the cabinet, I inspected the source properly for the first time since the birth. I wished I hadn't. A deep gash ran the length of me, black and purple, lined with ooze, hot to the touch. I found antiseptic cream and slathered it on, my eyes watering from even the slightest contact. I packed the creams in with the rest of the stuff I was taking and went to bed. My last night in that bed, my last night on the Raft. My wounds could wait for now.

Go Ams. Save yourself, and the baby.

I will, my love. I will.

Chapter 21

The Tunnels

'Up on the counter, big man.' I lifted Ethan up and sat him on the tabletop. It was too easy. He wasn't as heavy as he should be.

'I hate it here.' His little legs kicked the cupboard underneath.

'Well, you'll be back in school tomorrow.'

'Not here. *Here!* I want to go back to the Raft.'

'That's really not possible. The Raft is all gone.'

'I don't want it to be gone.'

'I know, darling. Now open wide and say, "ah!"'

He opened his mouth, and I took several swabs as he made little protests after each one. It didn't hurt. He just wanted to let me know how inconvenienced he was. After a minute, he spat and pushed me away. 'Why do I have to do this?'

'Because of how special you are. Because of how you were made.'

'How was I made? Where do new people come from?'

'They come from labs, made from people who are very much in love.'

'Why does love matter?' He made a face like he'd eaten some bad filth food.

'That's definitely a question for another time.' Grace could answer that one. I handed him a little pot. 'Think you can go put some pee in here?'

'Gross.'

'Go on, the toilet is that way.'

Every month I had dutifully done the tests the Centre required. My son, their little experiment, needed prodding and validating, letting them know that their ideal of Grace's looks and my brains had paid off. The first child born of two mothers, no male involved, was their latest boast of progress. But our bond had tightened since I knew the innate pull of motherhood was not just Grace's joy. I felt like less of an outsider, that I had contributed something. Why the regular monitoring was required, I didn't know and didn't care. Stem-cell treatments were not my domain, and certainly no one in the Tunnels knew about Ethan's origins. He was a bright boy, but wholly unremarkable. Healthy, cheeky, too much energy. As far as anyone else was concerned, he was just an ordinary kid.

I set the machines to make some roast potatoes. That was sure to cheer him up a bit. I'd promised him a fresh start here, a life of adventures and space to run around. What had started out so promising was now getting harder and harder. All we could do was hope that the unrest would blow over. Once everyone was well fed with delicious synth food, they'd welcome us again.

I was regretting lying about the factory. Perhaps if I were proving my worth now, there wouldn't be anything for the Isaac camp to moan about. Was he anti-Rafter, or just pro power? Drumming up hate to rally supporters around a common, ill-conceived cause. I wasn't sure, but I decided to find out.

As the potato mix made its way to the 4D printer, I reset the machines for another batch. Taking some of this to the Council was bound to help my case.

'Here you go,' Ethan said, and handed me a full pot.

'Well done. Now, here are your cognitive tests. Go sit at that desk and try to complete them.'

He sighed, slumped his shoulders and plodded off, dragging his feet the whole way. Grace's looks and my brains, the Prime Minister had said. I had no idea what my cognitive abilities were at his age. I was hungrier, probably. The famines were just beginning then. How was I meant to know if he was exceptional? He was almost six years old. Kids aren't meant to be protégés, they're meant to be kids. Grace had so many dreams for his future when we were on the Raft. She'd seen a life mapped out for him. No wonder she was angry and regretful. He had a future here, sure, but one of aspirations and greatness? Probably not. The factory had some of the ProLabs and BioLabs staff, the data centres and nuclear power stations had some great names in engineering from the Raft. But here, our previous lives counted for nothing. Our qualifications weren't recognised, and we'd had to start from scratch. At least Ethan was young enough to do that. Being at the bottom of the ladder again at my age was exhausting.

Sara arrived, her bicycle screeching to a halt outside the lab.

'Hi Ethan,' she said. 'What are you doing here?'

'Peeing in a pot.'

'Right.'

'I'm just checking his nutrition,' I said. 'Call me overprotective.'

She smiled. 'I need to speak to you. I tried to get to you yesterday, but to be honest, it's probably best if Clem isn't here. Better to keep this between us two.'

'She's in a tricky position, with Isaac's stance on the Rafters.'

'Well, that position may about to be tested, since she did the end-of-month accounts. That's what I want to talk to you about. The amount of money the Rafters are using up is really high. Crazy high. The tunnelling, the food, the clothing. And the lab equipment here isn't producing much, as you know. It's a lot of money for little result. It all adds up to huge sums of martas. Another batch of Rafters arriving is going to hit everyone hard. Couple that with the stock the Centre made away with to Mars, it means that the funds for everyone's projects are being curtailed.'

'That makes no sense. There's hardly any of us here, really. And we're all working so hard for minimal pay and rations.'

'It adds up. I've seen the numbers. They do seem high, but they all add up. The Tunnels are simply going to struggle to finance more Rafters. I'm not saying they shouldn't come, just that it's the argument Isaac is using.'

'Thanks for the heads-up.' At least Sara understood that it was the Centre that had made off with the stockpiles of food, not the Perimeter. 'It feels so wrong. How can we counter that? When some people quantify human life in such a way.'

The machine behind me pinged, and some steam ejected from the top. I walked over to put the extractor fan on.

'What's that amazing smell?' asked Sara.

'Oh, I worked out a niggle in a recipe. Roast potatoes. They're just about ready. Want some?'

Her face lit up. 'The famous roast potatoes? I would love some!'

'I want some too.' Ethan called from his desk.

'Finish those tests first.'

'I was thinking about my dad,' Sara said. 'Maybe I do want to meet him. I'd regret it if I didn't. He's made mistakes, but losing Daisy was difficult.'

I still found it hard to believe Peter was her father. Her striking face next to his saggy one just didn't match up. His wife must have been a stunner. 'I'll let him know. He'll be delighted.' The alarm pinged again. 'Potatoes are ready.'

I plated them up. I could never get sick of that smell. The wholesome, nourishing scent, the texture a perfect mix of fluffy and crispy. And high in fibre to boot.

Ethan came running over, tripping over his sandals. I suspected he'd rushed his tests. *Sod it.* Mars could have substandard results and doubt his genius. I didn't care. He made agreeable mmm sounds as he ate a portion of potatoes the size of his head.

'Oh my god, Sav!' Sara said. 'These are amazing! This is what all food should taste like.'

'Save some,' I said, as Ethan reached for more. 'I need to take them to the Council.'

He would have eaten the lot if I'd let him. Sara probably would, too, judging by how happy she seemed.

'Well, I see why you don't like our food now,' she laughed.

'Imagine how many delicious things I can make when Amalyn gets here. Wait till you try IcyCrema.'

'Have you heard from her?'

'Not in a couple of days.'

'You know, so many of us are rooting for her. And once people taste this food, they'll see how important you are here.'

'Thanks, Sara.'

She got on her rusty bicycle and cycled away. Food was the best way to win anyone over, I knew that. Especially people who were not used to such deliciousness. I left a few portions for the lab staff, and Betsie agreed to watch Ethan for me while I took a plateful over to the Council offices. I made sure the plate was well covered, as letting the scent waft down the Tunnels would be more than a little unfair. Perhaps I could claim that roast potatoes were now on the menu, that Amalyn had given me some information over the phone, just to whet their appetites a little.

By the time I got to the Council offices, I had decided that was exactly what I would do. The blinds were shut, which was unusual. They generally seemed to want us all to gaze in and see how important they were. On the door hung a sign: *Meeting in progress, keep out*. Well, hot roast potatoes would surely be the best addition to any meeting, I thought. I opened the door quietly, respectfully. I was trying to learn a lesson and not just barge in. Perhaps if I made myself more amenable, these little meetings would be more productive, I thought.

I saw Giao and Isaac sat in the room, and no one else. The TV was on, and they were watching what appeared to be a video message. I recognised the caller immediately. The long auburn hair, shining in the Martian glow, layers of fabrics wrapped around her, each costing a year's salary for us here, skin as smooth as glass. It was one of the Select, a Monet. And besides her was Greg.

'Ten per cent GDP is simply not enough. We'll need to up that to twenty.' Her voice flowed like syrup. 'Your campaign is going well; I see from the Tunnels socials. Well done, Isaac, you are going to be exactly the sort of leader I always knew you would be.'

'Find Peter Melrose,' said Greg, as loud as ever. I could hear the spittle being ejected with each consonant. 'If you're struggling for a spin, he'll sort it. That little shit is there somewhere. He can make any news work in your favour. He's a dick, but he has a gift. And who the fuck leaked all that information? Making us, the Centre Elite, look like common criminals when all we did was look after ourselves. I want their fucking head on a spike, whoever it was. Do you know how embarrassing that was for me? Which reprobate there leaked it? And now you want more Perimeter scum there?' He pulled his head in incredulity, creating at least seven chins. 'We've contained things, but there's a fucking uprising on the brink here. Uprisings are expensive to quash.'

'Calm down, Greg. The Council are there to help us.'

'Oh, let them fucking starve,' Greg spat. 'And stop moaning about our interference with your "natural protein", as you call it. It's disgusting. We did you a favour.'

'Greg, please calm down. Now, Isaac, Giao. This is just a polite notification to let you know we'll be doubling our withdrawals from the Tunnels accounts, starting immediately. Costs are high here on Mars, and we have every faith that you'll sort out your niggles there soon. You don't need all that money in your bank. You have such wholesome, simple lives down there on earth. I'm sure you appreciate the needs of us, your Select.'

'We can't really let Blane leave until it's all stable and peaceful here, can we, Giao?' Greg was leaning towards the camera. 'Be awful if that sweetheart of yours was caught up in the conflict. Such a handsome face.'

'Oh, Greg,' the Monet laughed. 'You have such a silly way with words. Anyway, I hope this message finds you well. Wait until you see the photos of what we've done with the place! You'll be delighted at how luxurious it is.'

The door creaked behind me. They both span round at the noise and saw me standing there, watching them.

'Mars? The Select? The Centre! Of all the Centre pricks, Greg?'

'Savannah, what the hell are you doing here?' Giao said as he turned the video message off. 'How much of that did you see? Isaac, we should have her locked up.'

I walked to the table, trying my best to appear confident, despite my trembling. I put the plate down and unwrapped it. 'Roast potatoes, delicious and perfectly nutritious. Lock me up and they're the last of these you'll get.'

The anger in their eyes gave way to temptation.

'You got the factory working, then?' Isaac said.

'Just these. Amalyn managed to give me the small bit of information I needed on the phone.'

Lying was too easy for me, and any hint of dishonesty was unnoticed since they were salivating so much. They couldn't hide it. Poker faces weren't possible with that level of deliciousness. They each picked up a potato and took a bite. I saw their pupils dilate, their chests rise and fall slowly, as if they were hypnotised with pleasure.

'Why are you giving money to Mars? Tell me.'

'The Select are our landlords,' Isaac said as he took another bite. 'They still own the Tunnels.'

'They're on another bloody planet! They knew about the food, didn't they? They took all the synth food stock to Mars. You paid for it, and they took it.'

'It wasn't supposed to matter. The lab was supposed to be up and running,' Isaac said, reaching for more.

'You're going to have to enlighten me a little. You're still paying them, that's why the Tunnels are short on money. It's got nothing to do with the refugees.' I spoke through my teeth, my whole body tense.

'More tunnels means more rent. It's as simple as that.'

'They don't own the damned rocks, Isaac. Why pay rent to someone on another planet? They're filthy rich. Plus, their business caused the climate chaos that forced the cities to move underground in the first place. And you're paying them for that privilege?'

'It's a lot more complicated than that,' Isaac said. 'They are the *Select*. That's not a title we can just dismiss.'

'You elitist bastards. If it wasn't for the Select, the planet wouldn't be in this mess. Their businesses caused the majority of greenhouse gases. They traded carbon credits to make things even worse. They burned the planet to a crisp, then charged everyone rent to survive.' Archie had told me that. 'Nasty bunch,' he'd called them. He never knew quite what an understatement that was.

'Watch it, Sav,' Isaac said, wiping a crumb from his mouth. 'You don't know what you're talking about. Everyone caused the problems, and only the Select had the foresight to do anything about it. Their Excellencies –'

'Don't call them that. They are people.'

'They are the *Sel-e-ct.*' He emphasised every syllable, like he was spelling it out phonetically. 'They are still much loved here, and their influence remains. We will continue to provide for them. It's audacious to even consider otherwise.'

'Some filthy rich people a million kilometres away are taking all the money from hardworking people here, and you're blaming the poorest of the poor for the country being skint.' I grabbed the plate of potatoes and pulled it out of their reach. They could beg if they wanted more. 'And what about the Select's quarters in the Tunnels? Those are habitable tunnels that are now unlived in, and you're saying there's no room for the Raft's refugees. Why don't we house people there?'

'You must be joking,' Isaac laughed. 'Those quarters are the Select's. They are at a level of luxury for Their Excellencies only, not for common Rafters.'

'Listen to yourself, Isaac. The Select have more wealth than you could ever imagine and are literally on another planet.'

'A planet that's in a state of unrest because of leaked information. Who did that? Why would they do such a thing?'

'I have no idea. It wasn't me.' I knew it was Amalyn. It must have been. All the information we put together to blackmail the Centre Elite into letting us leave was on Archie's computer. One look at that and she wouldn't have been able to resist. I tried to stifle a smile at that thought. 'But I doubt any of the information is a lie. Why is it that rich people have such an aversion to the truth?'

Giao hadn't been involved in our debate, being engrossed in his computer. Now he spoke. 'Well,' he said, pursed lips and red faced. 'Security is picking up your wife and child as we speak. They'll be held in the prison. If you leak a word of what's been said here, they'll be sent outside. We may not be able to lock you up, but that pretty little family of yours can be held accountable.'

'You shit. Isaac, they're your family too. Stop this!'

'I'm sorry, Sav. This is out of my hands. There is too much at stake here to risk this leaking.'

'So the rest of the Tunnels don't know, I assume? They have no idea their money is being thrown away like this.'

Giao stood up, reached over to take another potato, and leant in close. 'And they never will know. Remember what I said, Savannah. Whatever the cost to make the Tunnels a success. Whatever the cost.'

I picked up the plate and ran out of the door.

Chapter 22

The Raft

The sun wasn't up over the buildings yet. The light smog and dawn glow trickling over the Raft made the streets away from the fence look more welcoming as they bleached out the grey.

We walked with a mixture of eagerness and nerves, each stride taken with stiff postures and fast steps. Shaif and Glin stood close together, brushing hands sometimes. They spoke very little, mouths shut and eyes wide, taking in their last views of the Raft. Tilly followed, slower, holding Cora's hand, whose long hair was tied in a ponytail and flowing behind. I'd found her a pink spotted dress in a downstairs apartment and she was delighting in swirling it around. Bex and me were the stragglers at the back. I was grateful for her company. She could easily walk faster, but she seized any opportunity to peek at Reya, lifting her protective blanket to make faces and cooing noises at her. All of them were still only half believing. The questions and gasps of disbelief had gone on long into the night. I guessed they were mostly thinking, what the hell, why not?

Cora's morning energy was enviable. She skipped alongside us, despite my protests for her to walk slowly and conserve her energy. She had no concept of savouring anything for later. All she could understand was the present moment, and right then, she was excited.

'How do boats work?' Cora asked.

'I don't know. Why don't you sit down a while?'

'What makes them float?'

'I don't know. Stop jumping up and down at least.'

'How long will it take to get to France?'

'I don't know. Maybe just stay in one spot. We've a long walk ahead of us.'

'Where's the Autocar?'

'Broken. Why don't you sit for a while?'

'Where is everyone else?'

'I don't know.'

'Will they be here soon?'

'I hope so.'

We were early. I had a newborn, I'd been up for hours. The others still had time. There were no sounds from Danny and June's place when we left that morning. Perhaps June had refused or was too weak to travel. I wanted to nag them to come, to convince them, or at least say goodbye. I opted to leave noisily instead. They knew where we were going and there was nothing more I could say to convince them. I really hoped they'd come.

We arrived at the meeting point, everyone huddling close like they were expecting a predator, except Cora, who continued to skip around. I lifted the blanket tent that was covering Reya, just a little, to watch her soft face dozy with sleep after her morning feed. *We're doing it, little one. We're getting off this shitpile.*

Shaif and Glin both had the tattoo of the Golden Fifty. Bex was too young and had only recently heard that such a collective existed. Raised by parents who read the National Press and nothing else, she had only just begun to discover that she could think for herself. Then the Raft broke up and all she had were her own thoughts. She was too young to be so alone. I wanted to mother her as well as Reya and Cora. I handed her some food and checked she was drinking. She didn't seem to mind.

We carried bottles of water and all the food we had in bags and boxes. The food would last if we were careful. The water, though, I had no idea, but it was all we could carry. I had some first-aid supplies, sanitary stuff, sheets and blankets for shelter, torches, the e-pad and satellite phone. As well as some formula for Reya, in case I starved and my milk ran dry. In case anything happened to me. In case I didn't make it.

I looked back at the Centre buildings, at what was once gleaming and grandiose. I'd never seen them up close in their glory days, only flown over them when I went to visit the Tunnels. Pictures of the Centre were everywhere before. Billboards, posters, and TV screens throughout the Perimeter reminded us of our honour to support such a city. We were meant to feel inspired by it. *Meh.* Their once shiny exterior was now blackened and rough. How fickle finery is when it can be tarnished so easily. It was hard to distinguish which side of the fence I was looking at. Without the showy exterior, it all blended into one. Windswept and pelted with pollution, it was all the same.

Through the haze, two figures approached slowly, one supporting the other. I smiled when I saw it was June and Danny, and felt remorse when I saw the state of June. Her arm was bandaged, her face pallid, wincing in pain with every step.

'Couldn't very well miss seeing these little ones grow up,' Danny said, as Cora came over to greet him. 'Careful, sweetie, June's not really up for hugging.'

'June can speak for herself, thank you very much.' She found her balance and bent down to stroke Cora's hair. 'Couldn't miss the opportunity to see what a waste of time this trip will be. Hope you've got enough supplies for the return trip.'

Danny added his bag to the pile. More food, water, and first-aid supplies. 'Cleaned out the cupboards,' as he put it. We now had the most food I'd seen since the BioLabs days. Maybe it would be enough.

Maybe.

'I'm so glad you came,' I said to Danny and June.

'Got nothing else to do,' said June.

Danny returned my smile, and June didn't scowl as much as I thought she would.

'Anyway,' June said, still breathing heavily. 'It's not like there's anything left here.' She almost smiled when she saw

Reya's head poking out of the blanket, a knuckle in her mouth. Almost.

I checked the time on the e-pad. Seven-thirty. No one else here yet. More would come, though, I was sure.

We had a lot of walking ahead, and I knew I should save my feet, so I sat on the ground, but the tarmac was cold and hard against my wound. It was too much to bear, so I stood again.

'You okay, dearie?' asked Danny.

'Fine, just impatient.'

My body was tired. Anaemic, most likely. My post-birth bleeding was profuse, and I had little strength. Reya seemed to sense my discomfort and began to make soft cries.

I'm fine, little one. It's all fine. We're all going to make it.

Seven forty. As the sun beamed through a gap in the high-rises, some more people appeared. Janu, Adrian, Bray, Jacob and Adisa, arms loaded with food and water, faces a mixture of apprehension and adventure.

'The Golden Fifty finally fulfilling their dreams,' said Janu. 'Finally getting off this fucking Raft.'

He got a slap on the back from Adrian, his arm around Adisa. 'We're actually doing this,' Adisa said.

Then more, Allison, Emily, Danica. Others whose names I couldn't remember. Obey came along, grunted, and spat on the asphalt as he arrived.

'Screw the Raft.'

Some of them high-fived him and added their own spit to the grey. Old Vern walked over, alone, with slow, rigid strides like he was disguising a limp. Chrissy came from another direction and linked arms with him as they met.

'Lovely to see you, sweetheart,' Vern said to her with a toothless smile.

The sun was cutting through the thin smog, higher now, dazzling against the concrete. Some final stragglers approached, silhouetted, and I raised my hand to shield my eyes against the glare. Just behind Chrissy was one person I had not expected to see, her frizzy hair smoothed back. She still wore lipstick, and her floral perfume overpowered the smell of damp concrete.

'Penny?'

'Oh, Amalyn, how wonderful to see you.' She shook my hand, cordial, professional.

'How?' I asked, words lost in shock. 'Are you Golden Fifty?'

'No, no, of course not. I'm just a good listener, and I read that book the professor wrote, *The Poison Maker*, and was simply appalled at the Centre. What a nasty bunch. I certainly don't want to live here anymore. Then I met this lovely lady Chrissy who told me all about this little trip, and I thought, why the hell not!' Her broad smile revealed more gum than teeth.

I smiled back. She looked only mildly more dishevelled than she had done at BioLabs. Thinner, of course, the lines in her face deeper.

'Savannah will be delighted to see you.'

'The Professor is really there? Oh, well, I suppose that's as expected. This treasure is your little one?'

'Yes, she's a week old.'

'How are you feeling? Any sadness? Postnatal emotions can be a lot to cope with. Are you getting enough sleep?'

'I'm fine, Penny. I'll catch up on sleep when we get to the Mainland.'

'It's important to talk about any negative feelings. It's quite normal –'

'Really, I'm doing fine,' I said, cutting her short, before I spotted the welcome distraction of Ollie and Flick arriving. 'Oh look, some more people.' As nice as it was to see a familiar face, Penny's concerns could wait until we were on the boat. Ollie and Flick added their supplies to the pile, and our food and water haul looked even more significant. I checked the time. Ten past eight.

The group looked at each other, nerves and excitement making them shift from one foot to another, twitching hands and loud exhalations. However anxious they felt, the fact that we were all here, that this many people had come together to try, gave me more hope than I had felt since I had Archie to prop me up. We were doing this. Together. We were getting off the Raft and leaving all this sadness and concrete behind.

'Not everyone is here,' I said to Danny.

'People can make their own choices. Free will, dearie. It's about all they have left. Look how many have come, though. You'll just have to let the others go.'

He was right, of course. I couldn't drag people to the boats. But the thought of leaving anyone behind on the Raft to perish made my blood run cold. No one should have to die there.

I cleared my throat. 'Well, that's as late as we can leave it. I guess this is everybody. I'm sorry but there's no Autocar. Carry what you can. We're all walking from here.'

I did a quick head count. Fifty-two. Fifty-three if you counted Reya. I hoped the boats were big enough.

'This way, then,' said Jacob. 'Not a moment to waste now.'

We walked away from the fence, past the finer Perimeter buildings into the low-rise blocks now covered in soot. After half an hour we were in my and Archie's old neighbourhood, but not close to our old place, thankfully. I needed to stay focussed on what was coming instead of dwelling on what lay behind. I could feel it, though. Maybe it was still standing, if the sea hadn't smashed it to bits. The home that never quite became our home. The spare room that would never be Reya's nursery. As much as I tried to keep focussed on this hour and the next, something tugged at me to run over there, to sit among his clothes and spend the few days or weeks I would have left there. Alone with the last essences of him. To inhale any of his scent that remained. To kiss his fingerprints on the glasses and teacups. If it wasn't for Reya, I probably would have done just that. She had given me strength. I set my resolve to continue. There was no opportunity to wallow. My baby needed me.

After another three hours, we were at the dock, or what was left of it. The sea had claimed more land since I was last there. A thin sliver of concrete remained that led to the wall, an old Centre truck still clinging to the edge. They'd obviously fortified that bit to safeguard their catch and vehicles. The Centre's precious cargo was more important than the homes and lives that perished. I thought back to Sav's book, to the Centre blowing up the edge. The fucking Centre who had taken Archie from me. Were they still watching, their hand over the button? If there had been fallout from my email, perhaps they were.

No time to worry about that now.

We stepped along the concrete path, just a few of us at a time. It didn't bow or buckle, but the scraping sound of the edge being eaten away made us move with more haste than caution. I looked down at the iron lintels sticking out into the sea, keeping our little walkway together. The water was a metre or so below, splashing up and licking the edges. Its slimy texture had made the short walkway slippery. Every step sent my heart to my throat. I arrived at the wall and climbed up the rickety ladder. A few metres up to the concrete bank, Reya tied to my front.

From the top, I waited as the rest of the group took their turn. It was a crush up on the wall. There wasn't quite enough room for so many of us. Jacob and a couple of others went on ahead to check out the boats, which freed up a little more space. Vern was the last to climb the ladder. His aged arms were stronger than they looked, and he heaved himself up the first few loops with a loud grunt, then froze and held tight as a wave crashed into the path. I held my breath, thanking our lucky stars that we'd already crossed. The sea gurgled as chunks of concrete were smashed and sucked away. My breath caught in my throat as the water receded and we all stared at the path, at what used to be the path, with hands over our mouths in disbelief. It was now just a gaping hole, rough vertical edges leading to the sloshing sea below.

After a moment, I dared to breathe, and utterances of alarm sounded from behind me. We had all made it. Just in time.

Still holding tight, Vern looked over his shoulder. 'No going back now,' he said, the most unruffled of all of us, and heaved himself up the final rungs.

The wall felt strong and was over a metre thick. We stood in single file as Jacob, Obey and Glin fiddled with the equipment on one of the boats. Every time a wave crashed into the ledge, we fell to our knees and held on. Bex was to one side of me and she grabbed my arm when we crouched, keeping me secure. Cora laughed every time. If there was fear among us, she didn't notice. It was just an adventure to her. The day was calm, my weather forecasting proving to be accurate. Perhaps some of Archie's abilities had rubbed off on me.

'This one won't work,' Jacob called out. 'The cables are fried and there's a hole in the side. Only a small one, but too big to fix than we have time for. The other one looks okay.'

'We can salvage some of its electrics,' said Obey. 'The batteries are worth taking. The other boat is fully charged. We can connect these batteries to its solar, and it'll give us a bit more power to work with.'

'I can help,' Vern called from the back end of the wall, but there wasn't room for him to get past everyone else.

'How long?' I asked.

'An hour, maybe two,' said Jacob.

Two hours standing on a thin ledge with no space to move an inch. It was already getting hot from being so close. The sun was piercing through the smog. Good for the solar, less good for us.

'Let's get some people onto the boat,' I said. 'As many as it can take without them being in the way. It'll give us a bit more room.'

'If we seat half on the boat, we should be able to work around you,' Jacob said.

Obey walked to the side of the working boat where the ladder was and reached out, hauling people over, one at a time. There was a half-metre gap between the wall and the boat, but there seemed no easier way to do it. Just over half got on the boat, huddling at one end away from the electrics, before it was clear that any more would make the process longer. The rest of us spread out a little, with not enough room to get past each other, but enough to sit on the ledge and put our feet up for a while.

For almost two hours, we waited. I lay on my back, Reya nestled into my chest. Even though it was calm, the sea still hit the concrete, sloshed up and sprayed the ledge, leaving greasy dollops behind. The stench of rotten fish. The heat as the sun bore through the smog. I sat up occasionally, shifted my weight, looked at those on the boat. Obey and Jacob, red-faced and dripping with sweat, didn't stop working. They scavenged all the electrics they could from the broken boat and connected them up on the good boat. Cora sat still, playing with her hair. June leant against Danny on the ledge next to Bex, and whimpered every time the sea splashed up, blood-soaked bandages staining her shirt.

'Is she okay?' I mouthed to Danny.

He nodded back, gave me a thumbs up and a smile. A lie born from kindness, I was sure.

As Obey and the others continued to salvage the useful parts of the boat, part of me wondered if it was worth the time we were losing. Then I imagined us out at sea, with not enough sun to charge the batteries, no liquid fuel to power the boat, and knew that we needed every bit of power we could get.

'All done. Ready to climb aboard?' Jacob's voice was like music to my ears, and the twenty-seven of us on the ledge got up and edged closer to the boat. June reached out her good arm for Obey, while Danny supported her from behind and she made it on, crying in pain with every movement. Danny stepped to the side to help Bex over next. When it was my turn, I first untied Reya from me and Danny passed her over, his arms a few inches longer than mine. I was torn between not being able to look and not taking my eyes off her as she was passed above the sludgy soup below. The moment she was aboard, I knew that whatever happened to me no longer mattered. They would all look after her. She would get to the Tunnels somehow.

I took one last look at the Raft. The smog was thin and the wind mild. From that vantage point, what was left of the high-rises were like ghosts, grey boxes in the grey air. I whispered goodbye, a silent farewell to everything I had ever known.

Everyone was aboard except me, Danny, and Vern.

'After you,' I said.

'I insist. You first,' Danny smiled.

Obey reached out for me and I lunged to grab his hand, but as I did, an excruciating burning pain shot up from between my legs. I yelped and lost my footing, slipping into the gap between the boat and the dock. I crashed against the concrete, then the boat, then the concrete again, and finally hit the water. The syrupy blackness washing over me, dragging me under.

There was no pain then, only fear. I was there again, at the crumbled edge, choking, debris falling all around me. My heart louder than the rocks. I saw them fall, so many people disappearing into the darkness. Then an eternity of silence before Archie screamed my name, his voice penetrating the din.

Amalyn!

I came up, gasped for air. 'Archie!'

'Grab this!' Not Archie, not this time. A lifebuoy hung in front of me. The boat smashed against me and wedged me against the wall before forcing me under again. Then the pain arrived, all over me now. When I couldn't breathe, it went away for a moment, like I was high. Asphyxiation bringing numbness. There was peace in the dark. The deep was calling me. Was this the moment I'd been waiting for, longing for?

It didn't last. The tranquillity of the deep ejected me and I was up for air again. Voices I couldn't understand. A hand this time. 'I've got you!'

Danny lifted me clear of the water, just like Archie had done, just before he died saving me. 'No, Danny. Let go, get back.'

My voice was a gurgle, my mouth filled with filth. He didn't understand. *Let me go. Let me go. You're not going to die for me, too.*

But he didn't let go. His grip was firm. Then there were more arms lifting, hoisting me up and passing me onto the boat where the others were waiting with towels and kindness. 'You're okay,' someone said. 'We've got you.'

'That cut looks bad.'

'Grab the first-aid supplies.'

I saw stars, the pain overwhelming. Then my vision went cloudy and dark.

Chapter 23

The Tunnels

The Council guards hadn't found Ethan. They knew nothing of his tests and there was no way Grace would have told them his whereabouts. There was no alert on TunNet to find him so I could be sure there was no significant manhunt going on. Betsie at the lab agreed to watch Ethan for a while longer, to his groans and her eye rolling. But at least he was safe for now.

I made it to the prison by hitching a ride on a trailer. I still hadn't learned to ride a bike, but other Rafters had, and one took pity on me. The extra kilo or two I had gained over recent days made me blush, and I tried to hide my guilt as I watched him grit his teeth with each pedal stroke. The Rafter taking me was thin, their scrawny arms pulling against the handlebars. I consoled my remorse by reminding myself he'd get decent synth food soon.

Charlie, the head Council guard, was sitting at a desk at the entranceway. I walked over, taking the wrapping off the roast potatoes, their delicious smell rising into the air. 'I made these for the Council, but with all this drama, I didn't get a chance to give them to them. Perhaps you'd like some?'

He eyed me, lips twisting with suspicion.

'I've worked out some of the kinks in the factory and can make small batches of potatoes now. These were famous on the Raft.' I placed them on the table close to him.

He picked one up, hesitated for a moment, then took a bite. I saw the delight on his face. His eyes widened with pure shock at such pleasure.

'Grace has done nothing wrong. Nothing at all,' I said as he licked grease off his fingers. 'Please let her go. I can make sure you get some of these every day, as a thank you. She won't be any trouble. She's a good person, never put a foot wrong. This is just Giao and Isaac being manipulative.'

He looked at me for a moment, then took another potato and savoured it again.

'First dibs on all lab food. I promise,' I said. 'Please, just let Grace go. She's done nothing wrong. She's a teacher, she looks after little children, she has a heart of gold.'

He swallowed. 'If it was up to me, we wouldn't have arrested her in the first place.'

'Really?'

'Sure.' He sat back in his chair and shrugged. 'I have no idea why we had to take her. Waste of resources, if you ask me. It's not like anyone is actually in charge at the moment. The guards are all just plodding along, doing what we're told, waiting for someone to take control of this mess. For what it's worth, I think the Rafters make a great contribution here. Especially if you can make food like that. It's cruel, what the Council make us do, setting targets for beatings.'

That last remark hit me like a punch in the stomach. 'They set you targets?'

Charlie nodded. 'Every guard must beat the Rafters three times a week, to keep it on a level with what we had to put up with from the Select when we first arrived, although I personally don't remember it being anything like that. But that's what the Council say. Those were the rules drawn up when the Select were here, when they said they'd welcome more Rafters. It was fair, they said. And nothing has changed since.'

I nodded, too shocked to speak. Charlie carried on.

'If we don't keep up with targets, we lose our rations and funding. I had three guys laid off last month when they refused to meet their quota. They're in the mines now, and no one wants that job. We're all just waiting for these damned elections. Hoping things will improve a bit. I think most people have forgotten where they came from.'

'So, Grace …?'

Charlie's expression changed. 'Grace will have to stay here for now.'

'What? No! Please –'

He held a hand up to stop my protest. 'Juan is on later. If he spots she's missing, he'll go straight to Giao and then I'll be in for it. I'll be out of a job here and tossed in the mines. Unless Harvey wins, and I'm not banking on that.'

'Which one is Juan? I'll speak to him.'

'It won't work. He hates all Rafters. New ones, anyway. His wife came from the Raft, before it was the Raft, you know. Anyway, he's working here tomorrow and if Grace isn't here, I can't guarantee what course of action they'll take.'

'But aren't you the head guard? She's done nothing wrong. She's broken no law. If people heard about how the Council are locking up innocent people –'

Charlie held his finger up to silence me. 'You're right, I am the head guard. But without public support, there's not much I can do.'

I rubbed my forehead. He couldn't be saying this, he just couldn't.

'You see,' he continued, 'we're the Council guards, under the command of the Council. But with no elected leader, the Council rely on public support for authority. It seems to me that if people knew that the Council had ordered an innocent woman and child be locked up, there would be outrage. Riots, possibly. They'd demand an explanation. What explanation could we, the guards, give? That would put us in quite an awkward position.'

'Exactly!'

'If that were my wife, I wouldn't bother speaking to the guards directly, I'd be rallying supporters, posting pictures of the poor innocents on TunNet, creating an outcry.' He picked up another potato. 'Obviously, I'm a Council guard, so *I* wouldn't do such a thing. But if I wasn't, and if it were my wife, that's what I'd do.'

He raised his eyebrows at me as he chewed, and the penny dropped. Giao wanted me to keep quiet about the money going to the Select, but I'd be damned if I'd be quiet about them locking up my wife. If they could lock up an innocent like Grace, who knew what they would do next? That was the line I could use. They're coming for anyone. No one is safe. We'd survived riots on the Raft, and some of the Council had lived through the anchor riots. There was no way the Council would let it get that far. The threat of unrest had to work.

Charlie got up. 'In a country with no leader, I'd say whoever holds the food holds the power.' He walked to the door to the cells and opened it. 'You can visit, though. No one ever told me you couldn't do that. Take a few minutes.'

I ran through the door into the dank jail. It was cold and dimly lit, the cells carved into the rock, lined with metal bars. More like a dungeon than a jail. The other cells were all empty from what I could see, though I didn't linger. I ran towards Grace's sobs and found her sat on the floor, leaning against the bars, her flushed cheeks wet with tears.

'Grace!'

She stood to meet me, hands reaching for mine. A cold grip of desperation rather than love. A fence dividing us. 'Sav, what's going on?'

She looked broken. I yearned to hold her. How could it have come to this? She was hunched, turning in on herself, like she was the one who should feel guilty instead of me. With one hand, I held hers and gripped the bars so tightly with the other that my fingers cramped. How could they do this to her?

'I had a row with Giao and Isaac, and they're punishing me. This is ridiculous.'

'Is Ethan okay? They asked where he was. I said he was in the library to throw them off.'

'Well done. He's fine. He's safe.'

'I can't spend a night away from him. He needs me.'

'I'm getting you out, Grace. Soon. Really soon.'

'But Ethan –'

'You just have to trust me, Grace. Please. Now, I need to take your photo.' I held up my phone.

'What? No, I look awful.'

'Good. You need to look sad and mistreated. I'm going to expose the Council. Now look at the camera.'

Those big, sad dark eyes could melt stone. I took a few photos with Grace looking more desperate and destroyed than she ever had.

'I'll be back soon, Grace. I promise. I need to get the word out. Stay strong.'

I kissed her fingers through the bars and left.

'This would never have happened on Mars,' Grace said as I turned away. The comment was under her breath, barely a whisper, but it made me clench my teeth. How little she knew. Again.

I checked the time. We had a couple of hours until curfew. Outside the prison entrance, I leant against the wall and logged onto the TunNet and posted the photos of Grace looking terrified and pitiful, shaming the Council.

Locking up innocents, I typed. *No crime committed. They have locked up Grace without charge, and wanted to lock up my son. Just because they are power mad. Rafters have rights! Who will they come for next? No one is safe while the Council has this power.*

Word spread quickly. Most people were finishing work for the day, gathering in chambers and discussing what I'd said. This time of day was prime time for gossip and opinions, and it was only moments before the comments came flooding in:

Why would the guards do this? Many people tagged the guards and the Council, demanding: *Explain yourselves!*

Of course there were some, quite a few, who said *Well, it's just a Rafter*, and *No doubt she's been causing trouble, she's a Rafter after all*. But sympathy was there. Not everyone hated Rafters. The replies from them were tenacious, and the supporters were keen to defend Grace. Even some who were anti-Rafter had to question the Council and the guards as they were led to wonder: *Who's in charge of the guards, anyway?*

The speed at which this line of thought moved through the Tunnels blew me away. I was still writing my third post when

Subs and Rafters alike started to question the entire hierarchy of the Tunnels. Harvey weighed in, saying we needed answers, promising action, insisting on Grace's release.

Giao and Isaac had told me to keep quiet about the money going to the Select. I hadn't disobeyed them. I'd kept that information out of it. If they wanted to explain why Grace was locked up, it was up to them to reveal it.

Half an hour later, the arguments online were heating up, and still there was no word, no justification from the Council. Sounds of unrest came down the corridor, travelling up from the nearby chambers. It was impossible to hear the details from where I was sitting, but the voices sounded angry, worried, resentful. Echoing the distrust that was building online. The same message began to circulate, again and again: 'If they can arrest anyone for no reason, who's next?'

An hour remained until curfew. A bit of anger online wasn't enough. Rubbing my eyes, I thought about what to do. I could go to a chamber, stand on a table and incite a riot. I could storm the Council offices and spray-paint the walls, but that would only play into the hands of those who saw the Rafters as trouble. The disdain was still gaining momentum online, so I posted one more message: *I demand a statement from the guards. Under whose authority are you working? The unelected Council who dictates that you arrest innocents, or your own morals?*

I waited, biting my nails, pacing the corridor. It was a risky move, calling into question the guards' ethics when I needed them as friends. But I was broken, brittle as glass. Any hope I had for a future here was eroding by the minute. I felt like my optimism had sunk with the Perimeter. All I could do was try to salvage something from the pieces that were left. I'd bitten three nails down to the skin before the guard's statement came.

I can confirm that this afternoon we were told to arrest a woman and a child, to be held without charge. We still have not been given the reason why we are holding this woman. Since the Council has not been able to confirm any charges, we will release her immediately. She will be kept under house arrest for twenty-four hours as a precaution, in case the Council are concerned about her safety or any danger she poses. Let it be known that the guards do not hold people in prison without reason, and that we follow the proper protocols. The guards would like to remind everyone that these protocols will be adhered to, no matter who gives the orders.

My heart skipped a beat. Even underground, a ray of sunshine can glow and shimmer on shattered glass. Perhaps I had some optimism left, after all. I ran to the prison, past the unmanned desk and through the door to Grace's cell. Charlie was unlocking the cell door when I entered.

'Grace!'

The door swung open and Grace leapt into my arms, holding me closer than she had in months. Her limbs felt bony against mine, her tears soaking through my smock.

'Not all the guards agree with me, just so you know. You should get home as quickly as you can. Stay out of trouble. Some guards may come and check to see she's at home.' Charlie didn't have to say this twice. We made for the door as if the place were on fire. I thanked him over my shoulder as we bolted.

The corridors were getting louder, the unrest in the chambers increasing. I posted online to say that Grace was free, thanked the guards, and called for some regulation, for protocols to be maintained. I scrolled through the media feed as we walked and then a new post popped up from the Council: *To try to limit disruption from the Rafters, a new identification procedure will be put in place.*

That was it. No apology. Instead of an explanation, they were retaliating.

Chapter 24

The Tunnels

I put my e-pad away, and we picked up speed. It was not long to curfew. Charlie's words, 'Keep out of trouble,' played in my head. I looked at Grace, her eyes wide and darting, like anyone could steal her away at any moment.

'It's okay, Grace, it's going to be fine.'

She didn't respond. Her hand just gripped my arm tighter, and she tried to stay in my shadow. I couldn't flag down a lift. There were no bikes going towards the centre of the city. I really should have learned to ride one. We had to get through the middle chambers before we could reach the balconies that led to our tunnel. I barged my way through the crowds, dragging Grace along. Some people were idling, and we found ourselves in a queue to pass through one chamber, guards flanking the entrance. I craned my neck to look at the mezzanines above, but it seemed to be the same there. When we got to the front of the queue, one guard shone his torch straight in my face.

'Name and status.'

'Selbourne. What do you mean by status?'

'Rafter or Subterranean?' His abrupt tone got my back up, while Grace cowered behind me.

'Rafter.'

Another guard scanned through his e-pad, then gave his colleague a nod. He took my hand, fingertips so firm it felt like he was trying to bruise it, and he strapped a bright yellow band to my wrist, then did the same to Grace.

'Just making it clear who's who. New ID process, by order of the Council. You've twenty minutes till curfew.'

I gaped at my new wrist wear.

'But it's at least a half hour's walk to our place,' Grace said, leaning into my arm.

'Get a bike,' replied the guard.

'We can't cycle,' I said.

'Not my problem, miss.'

Grace exhaled a little whimper, noises of protest that were barely audible above the clamour.

'Come on, Grace. Let's hurry.'

'You should have said we were Subs.'

'We look and sound nothing like Subs and we'd have to give false names. Anyway, since when was lying the best answer?' I said, too curt in my tone, but I was too angry to be polite.

Grace made a disgruntled noise, and we jostled through the masses. Through the chamber the crowd became thicker, my elbow-barging more of a chore. So many people were on their way home, a few night workers in the power plants on the way to their shift, along with a small gathering looking up at Harvey, who was standing on a table. Those onlookers were standing still, not rushing for curfew, yellow wristbands dangling from their arms. They had as far to go as we did, but their resolute postures in the face of repression were inspiring. Yet I fretted for them. I worried what the repercussions of missing curfew would be. An excuse for the guards to make their beatings quota, most likely. Guards stood at every entrance to the chambers, some seeming relaxed and nonchalant, others had hands hovering over batons, keen to exert their authority, reminding me that not everyone was on our side, as Charlie had said, and the events of the evening would have only polarised them more.

As we left the chamber, Harvey's voice was lost in the racket, a distant protest against the rules and corporal punishments singling us out. We should have stayed, showed support, thanked everyone for helping get justice for Grace, but we were limited by the curfew and had so far to go. Harvey was just a murmur above the commotion. Impassioned yet for the most part unreciprocated, his 'Save the refugees' chant dissolved into the din.

In the furore of bikes and bodies, we managed to get a trailer.

'Hurry up,' the driver said. 'Hey, you're the woman they locked up.'

Grace blushed and nodded.

'Glad you got out. Don't worry, I'll get you home.'

The driver stood on the pedals and groaned as the bike and trailer moved away, picking up speed quickly as we gained momentum and swerved through the crowds, soggy perspiration staining the back of her smock.

'Ethan! Will he still be at the lab?' Grace asked as the trailer bumped its way down the tunnel, swinging into corners and skidding past people.

'Betsie won't stay out after curfew. I'm sure she would have taken him back to the Rafters' wing with her.'

The driver continued with her effort, standing up out of the saddle and hammering at the pedals. Her arms tensed as she pulled against the bike into the corners, wiping perspiration from her forehead. She wasn't a Rafter. No yellow band dangled from her wrist, yet she was exerting herself for us anyway. Not everyone hated Rafters. More and more, I was learning that. Grace and I clung to the sides of the trailer as we careered through the Tunnels, screeching to a halt by our wing. We got down, and the driver sped off before I even had the chance to thank her.

To my relief, Ethan was behind the fencing. Betsie was waiting in the Tunnel with him, tapping her foot, arms folded.

'Thanks, Betsie. I owe you one.'

'No problem,' she said, not smiling. 'Glad you got out, anyway.' And then she walked away.

'She's not very friendly,' said Ethan.

'Well, you're here and you're safe, so that makes her very nice indeed,' said Grace.

As soon as we got home, I regretted not making a larger batch of roast potatoes, or at least keeping some back for us, rather than giving them all to the guards. Ethan ate the filth food without too much complaint. It was Grace I felt sorry for. She washed, then served up the food, clean hands and cold eyes. She had likely smelled the potatoes I gave to Charlie and was now staring into a bowl of minced yuck.

'I'll bring some home tomorrow, Grace.'

'How's the lab on Mars going? I'll bet they've got loads of good stuff to eat there.' Her voice was as bitter as the food.

I didn't respond. What could I say? Nothing that would make her feel any better. Nothing that would make her regrets go away. She ate every spoonful with a scowl, chewing laboriously on every gritty mouthful.

She looked Ethan up and down and stroked his back. 'He hasn't grown much since we got here. He's never going to be tall enough now.'

'Tall enough for what, Grace?'

She didn't answer. Tall enough for a Centre, was what she meant. He had grown plenty since we'd arrived. Variations in growth spurts were normal. I'd been doing his stats monthly and his height had increased. Modestly, sure, but he was hardly stunted. Just not exceptionally tall like a Centre. Like she imagined the overindulgent diet of the Centre was the only reason for their height and it was not twinned with their genetics. Her dream of prestige was still alive. Nothing but the best of the best was ever going to be good enough for her.

After they ate, as Grace was battling to get Ethan to bed, there was a knock at the door.

'Sara? How'd you get past the fence?'

'The guards aren't being too strict. I just said I was visiting, and they let me through. I heard about Grace. Everyone has. Why the hell did they lock her up?'

'I found out something about the Council. They made me promise not to say and held Grace, thinking it would keep me quiet.'

Sara covered her ears. 'Don't say anymore. The less I know, the better. I'm just glad she's out.'

I put the kettle on and divided up some tea leaves for three small cups of weak tea.

Sara took hers and sat down, tall and elegant at the table. 'Giao and Isaac were so mad when I saw them just now. The guards disobeying them is huge. It shows what little power they have. No one really knows what to do. Giao's interim leadership means nothing now. I can't see that anyone will take his orders seriously. These elections can't come soon enough.'

'If Isaac wins, though, things could get a lot worse.' That thought scared me more than anything. I sat on my hands rather than reveal how much they were shaking. 'Did you know the guards have a beatings quota? And they lose their jobs if they refuse?'

Sara sipped her tea with wide eyes. 'I mean, I had my suspicions. It was something that was discussed when the Select were here. And I think I know what else has been going on, too. The money, the sums add up, but it's not right. Some of it is being syphoned off, I'm sure of it. My guess is you figured out where it's going.' Her astuteness was the only resemblance she had to Peter Melrose. That ability to find the truth. Only she had an integrity he lacked.

I mimed zipping my mouth shut, the same way I had seen Archie do so many times. Who knew what sort of trouble me or Sara would be in if I talked now?

'Okay, well, if what I think is going on is actually going on, I'll find a way to get it out of them. There's no way they should be secretive about that,' Sara said, and then left.

Grace had ignored Sara the whole time she was there. She stayed on Ethan's bed, humming gently to him as he nodded off. As soon as the front door closed, she got up and sat at the table.

'It's hardly right that her sort is coming round here.'

'Her sort?'

'A Sub.' There was venom in the way she said it, spitting out the 's.' 'In our house, after the way they've treated us.'

'Sara is as sweet and kind as a person can be. Not all Subs are the same.'

Grace narrowed her eyes at me and went to the bathroom.

That evening, there was a debate between Harvey and Isaac. A video link was sent out so we could all watch it live. The central chamber was bedecked with posters for each party, *Save the Refugees* dominating Harvey's, *Subs First* on Isaac's. The audience looked solemn, respectful, not like the anchor riots from the Raft years earlier. Of course, none of the people there were Rafters since we were under curfew. The Rafters I'd seen supporting Harvey earlier had been cleared somehow. I couldn't bring myself to imagine the tactics that may have been used. The camera swept over the crowd, and I was shocked to see how many supporters for Harvey there were. My heart warmed a little. Some Subs really did care about the Rafters.

The sound quality was poor, and the video glitched often. Policing was the first topic discussed, and the protocols for arrest. As much as Harvey tried to keep the debate there, the subject of financing kept resurfacing.

'We don't have the budget to stick to all the protocols,' Isaac said. 'Or for enough guards. The Rafters are too expensive.' Grace watched with folded arms and tight lips. Whatever Harvey said, Isaac responded to it by listing the costs of taking in more Rafters. I squeezed my fists so hard my knuckles cracked.

'We're a burden here,' said Grace. 'We should never have come. The resources are too tight. These people hate us and they're never going to accept us.'

'It's bullshit, Grace. They're lying. I can make more food now. There'll be plenty to go around.'

'But the cost. We're burdening poor people with the cost of us. We should have gone to Mars. They're rich there, they can afford to support us.'

I bit my lip. She looked so fragile and thin, slouched on the chair. I should have been trying harder to get food for her. With a full stomach, she would stop thinking about Mars. Her regrets would melt away with contentment. If Grace could ever truly be content.

'I can't even teach anymore now that I'm under house arrest,' she said. 'What good am I here? Ethan can't thrive when the other children don't even like him.'

'This will blow over, Grace. Once they start getting food –'

'And look at our tiny home,' she interrupted. 'It's half the size of our first Perimeter apartment. We don't even have our own bathroom.'

I looked around the room. To call it basic would be putting it mildly. I could appreciate Grace's dissatisfaction, but it was still a home. It was ours and not bribery from the Centre Elite. I sighed a little as I saw her mouth turn down, her eyes moisten.

'We could move into the Select's quarters,' I said, as casually as that. The idea had been turning over in my mind since I'd blurted it out in the Council offices. I'd been wondering why I hadn't thought of it before. It seemed too simple. Too obvious.

She looked at me, her mouth open. 'We certainly could not! That's for the *Select!* Not the likes of us.'

'The Select are a world away. Literally. There's so much space and luxury there lying wasted. Why not move there?'

'What if they want to move back?'

'Sod them. They left it. I say let's take it.'

Grace tutted and turned away from me. 'I don't know what's gotten into you. You never used to be so disrespectful.'

True. I used to put up and shut up. But hearing Isaac blame Rafters for the Tunnels' financial hardships had lit a little fire in me. Seeing Harvey's supporters ignoring curfew had stoked the flames. Put up and shut up was not an option anymore.

I lay down and stared up at the ceiling. Grace would see soon. Amalyn would make everyone understand. She had a way of making people listen. My eyes stung, and I blinked, but no tears came. We shouldn't have been rowing over what a burden we were. We should have been planning to meet Amalyn and the others, formulating a plan, doing all we could to ensure they got there alive and well. All the unrest and stupid politics were just some nightmarish distraction. I wondered where Amalyn was, if she was on a boat yet, if she was okay. In my mind, I was reaching for her, dragging her closer, her and her baby. I'd promised safety in the Tunnels, and she was damn well going to get it.

Chapter 25

I was lost in a daze. My mind still in the darkness, the world crumbling around me. Skin prickling against a shower of dust. The stench of the sea sloshing against the concrete, the warmth of his blood trickling through my fingers. He didn't want to go until he knew I'd climbed out to safety. I wouldn't go while he still had breath. I couldn't leave him until his grip on my hand slackened and went cold. He fought for so long, trying to convince me to leave him. He took so long to die.

I climbed out for her. I could have stayed with him, waited to join him, but I climbed out for her. Unknown yet loved already. Instinct propelled me. She deserved a chance. She was the essence of him, the last of him. Her cries pierced my dream, blowing away my mind fog.

'Reya!'

'Lay still, dearie. You banged your head and bashed yourself about a bit.'

Danny's voice sounded like I was still underwater. He pushed me back down to the floor, his touch gentle, but I buckled, pain making my muscles turn to mush. The metal deck was covered in bumpy grips that poked every bit of me, so uncomfortable now I was conscious. With every slight sway of the boat, I could feel my blood moving through my pounding head. My boobs throbbed like I'd been hit by an Autocar.

'Where is she?'

'She's fine. Bex found some formula.'

'No! I can feed her, give her to me.' I could barely sit up, but I could feed my baby. I needed to; my breasts were swollen to bursting. As I reached out for her, I noticed a towel was draped across my lap.

'You were bleeding. We covered you.'

I nodded. *Great.*

I ached from head to toe. Every bit of me hurt. Any post-birth healing had been ripped back open, but I would feed my baby. I cleaned myself with alcohol wipes so Reya didn't have to suckle on mucky sea tits, then used a sparing amount of water to rinse myself. Bex passed her to me, gingerly, as if she was putting the baby in danger and Reya latched on like she was starving.

'Thank you for looking after her,' I said, as I cradled Reya close.

'It's okay. She's a delight. I never really thought about having a baby before. Now I can't wait to have my own.'

I squinted up at her. 'You're a natural,' I said and tried to smile.

She sat next to me, in easy reach of Reya, letting her hang on to her finger, her protectiveness giving me some reassurance. A baby couldn't be loved and protected too much. If anything were to happen to me, someone had to look after Reya. And at that moment, anything happening to me seemed quite plausible.

Reya continued to guzzle hungrily, relieving some of my pain. 'How long have I been out?'

'A day.'

'A *day!*' I looked across at the sky. Blankets hanging over the entrance to the cabin offered shade, but the sun was piercing through. 'Where are we? Have we made progress?'

'We're just sailing down the Bay of Biscay. Pretty close to the land now,' said Danny. 'It's quite clear. When you're ready, come have a look.'

I stood. My knees wobbled, and Bex jumped up to support me, her hands ready to catch Reya.

'Careful now,' said June from her slouched position propped up against the side of the boat. She still looked washed out, green and grey. Her bandages had been changed, black and blue bruising spreading up as high as her neckline.

'How're you doing, June?' I asked.

She shrugged and winced, then stood and came to support me with her good arm, showing me more kindness than she ever had.

I clutched the towel and held it around my waist with my spare arm. It seemed pointless preserving my dignity now, but I tried nonetheless. I stood and walked out of the entranceway to the outside deck, up to the railing that surrounded the boat. I grabbed on as the boat rocked, the smell of the sea so different to before. No rotten fish smell. Just salt and a fresh breeze. I could see where the thick sea met rolling sand dunes. Land. Real land that wasn't the Raft. Land made from earth and not covered in concrete. Some greenery remained, patches of growth clinging on. Smoke billowed up in the distance.

Adisa came over and gave me a little nudge, a grin on his face. 'We did it. Whatever happens now, it was worth it. We're seeing other lands.'

'It's what the Golden Fifty always wanted,' Shaif said. His whole face was smiling.

'In all my days, I never imagined I'd actually get off that blasted Raft again,' said Vern. 'Dream come true, this is.' His eyes glistened with nostalgic tears, toothless mouth wide with a smile.

Ahead of us we saw possibilities. Opportunities. I remembered the old picture Archie had on his wall of the anchor bridges. Like a kite on a string, he'd said. Now we were flying.

I sat again, weak and woozy. Penny fussed around me with food and water. I wanted to refuse, to make sure everyone else had theirs, but I needed something. I swallowed down mouthfuls of dry VitaBiscuits, feeling queasy with every chew.

'We think you have a concussion,' said Penny.

'Yeah, maybe.'

She tried to keep me awake, talking to me about our old days at BioLabs, I think. It was hard to hear through the whooshing tinnitus that filled my ears. The sea was loud, too. The crashing echoed in my head.

Shaif and Glin came to join us. They sat close together, and I saw Shaif brush Glin's knee, the glint in Glin's eye. A joy they had both been without for so long resurfacing in each other. I smiled, yet sadness tore at my heart. I missed Archie more than I thought possible. If time was meant to help, it was being bloody slow. When I thought of him, I choked under the weight of it. Glin and Shaif's happiness was so enviable, alive with newness, and I knew, for me, it would never be so again.

'My mother told me that my grandmother went to France once. When she was a kid. I assumed she was making it up, it seemed that weird,' Shaif said.

'Kai suggested we go to France on honeymoon,' Glin said, laughing. 'I thought he was joking.'

They sat in silence for a moment, their fingers now intertwined. Bex came and sat with us and handed around some water, which we all sipped. She sat next to Glin, then noticed his affection towards Shaif. She smiled a knowing smile, raising her eyebrows at me.

'I wonder what the people are like in the Tunnels,' she said. 'I'd like to meet someone special.'

'They were all bald when I was there,' I said.

'Bald?'

'Yeah, they made everyone shave their heads.'

Bex stroked her hair, and a little colour drained from her.

'Sorry,' I tried to laugh, but it came out as a cough. 'I should have warned you.'

'Better bald than fish food,' Shaif said with a smirk.

'Let me take the baby,' Bex said. 'You need some rest.'

I had little strength to argue, and Reya didn't complain. Bex cooed as she cradled her, making faces as Reya lay still and silent, curious eyes staring back.

Shaif rummaged through his bag and took something out. A small, flat object, which was met with gasps.

Bex dared to lean in a little closer. 'Is that ...?'

'Yep,' he said as he held it up. 'It was my grandmother's. I took it when I left home.'

'I've never seen one,' Bex said. 'Is it safe?'

'I'm sure it is.'

'A real book from before the Great Sterilisation Project. Wow! What's it about?'

'Children with magical powers.'

Bex spat out some water as she laughed. 'No way! Why did people write such things?'

'Fucking Alternates,' June said under her breath. No one paid her any attention.

Vern shuffled closer, his eyes wide. 'I had the same one as a kid! May I?'

'Sure,' Shaif said, handing Vern the book.

Tears fell freely down Vern's cheeks, which he wiped on his sleeve. 'Beautiful. Just beautiful.'

'There's a room filled with books in the Tunnels,' I said. 'And a room of art.'

'A library?' Asked Vern, his voice breaking.

'That's it. One of those.'

'Seeing one book again is a dream come true. A library ... well, that would be something.'

'Can I see?' asked Bex as she reached forward, and Vern carefully handed it to her. When she touched it, she snapped her hand back, like it was burning hot, then took a breath and touched it again. She still had Reya in her other arm and I couldn't help but flinch as the book was close to her. *Stop it, Ams,* I chastised myself. I wanted Reya to see all the wonders of the world, not be scared like the Centre taught us.

'The tree carcass paper is so rough,' Bex said as she turned the page. 'I'd love to read it all when we get there.' She handed it back to Shaif as the boat rocked, seawater spraying onto the deck.

'Thank you for showing me that,' said Vern, as he swallowed back his emotions. 'You've made this old man so happy. You all have.'

We had shared something; I was sure. Contentment, even though we were so far from the end of our journey. A satisfaction the Raft was never able to deliver, like some dormant part of our brains had come alive. Away from the smog and the concrete, faced with the most arduous part of our journey, we felt alive.

The waves continued for a time and the boat swayed from side to side, up and down. My body throbbed with every movement as I tried to keep myself upright. In the end, I opted to lie flat, becoming one with the motion, the sun past its peak now, leaving me in a dusky shadow.

There were sounds of vomiting all over the boat, groaning and retching as the boat rocked and bobbed. The sour smell of rotten puke. It didn't last long. The boat stilled as the waves passed, and we were gliding serenely again once more. The grip of sleep pulled me under, and I gave in to it.

***

When I woke it was dark, and I was shivering with cold. There were piles of blankets on top of me, a cold sweat across my forehead. Even my bones were cold. There wasn't enough fabric in the world to warm me. No one spoke, not really. Just a few murmurings around me.

'Where's Reya?'

'Sleeping. She's fine. Just rest.' The voice came from the darkness. The outlines of people stood over me, merging into one another. I had no idea who was who. Shadows re-sculpted themselves in the dark, morphing and distorting. I was becoming smaller and smaller.

I slept some more, unable to fight it. When I woke, every pulse sent aching pain through my whole clammy body. I was too hot and suffocating under the blankets. Burning up like a star in the cold night sky. I tossed and turned as much as my pain would allow. My bones ached, cramps in places I didn't know could hurt. When I slept again, I dreamed of darkness, of being trapped, of sludge filling my lungs and fish guts covering me.

'Amalyn.' Danny shook me gently.

'What?'

'We're here.'

Here. His words took a while to digest. Where was 'here'? The hard floor beneath me dug in, I reached out for support and my hands found luggage and bottles. I squeezed my eyes shut. When I opened them, it was still dark, alien. The air smelled strange. Nothing was familiar.

Danny knelt next to me, took my hand. 'France, Amalyn. The boat, all of us, we made it to France. We're safe.'

Sweat stung my eyes as realisation washed over me. We had made it? Shit, we had made it. I tried to stand too quickly. The blackness became tinged with greeny yellow.

'Woah! Slow down. You've got a bit of a fever.'

Penny and Danny supported me, and I stood, found my balance, sort of, and saw it. The boat was still against a concrete platform. Only, it wasn't on the Raft. There were no endless rows of dilapidated high-rises. No grey street after grey street. In the torchlight, there were soft rolls of sandy hills, the orange piercing through the dark. The smog was gone. I looked up and saw a clear sky dotted with stars. Another land. We were on another land. And we had docked. They had done it. Jacob and

Vern came over, though their faces looked more worried than happy, with wide-eyes and tight-lips. Adrian and Ollie shook their hands. Everyone joined in with the thank yous. They had got us here. We were moored on foreign land.

'Did you check the e-pad GPS?' I asked.

'Yep,' Jacob said. 'There's enough battery for the walk, too. We're as close as we can be.'

I changed my underwear and sanitary protection as Bex held Reya, and Penny steadied me. I threw the rubbish into the sea and tried to douse my wound with antiseptic, but it was too bloody and sore to be effective, and the cream mostly dripped off. Three people lifted me over the boat's edge and onto the dock. No more accidents this time. My legs pounded with every step, blood throbbed in my head.

'Remind me, how long is the walk?' I asked.

'Thirty kilometres to the closest tunnel entrance,' said Jacob. 'We'll carry you if we have to.'

I laughed. He looked strong enough.

Thirty kilometres. I wasn't sure I could walk three, let alone thirty. I saw Bex holding Reya, and I knew then that I'd walk three hundred kilometres to get my baby to safety.

The day was mercifully calm. The sun was rising ahead of us, a blinding slither poking above the horizon. I dipped my head and pulled a thin scarf down over my face.

Sand dusted the tarmac, and with every step, our feet sunk a little, adding to the effort. Roads were only visible sporadically. Detritus of the old world poked above the dust, the charred remains of infrastructure and vegetation looming ahead of us. Any shade was sparse and dappled. The sun was still low, not yet at its most ferocious point, but the heat was brewing, making my head thump harder. The sand that kicked up over my shoes burned as it touched my ankles.

'Let's do a quick stock take of supplies. Water, mainly.' I struggled to speak, my tongue sticking to my dry mouth.

'About seven litres each,' Jacob said after a brief rummage. 'Maybe we should wait here a while, find shade, wait till night time to walk. We don't know if we'll find shade on the way.'

No one answered. We all looked for shade: a few buildings providing patchy shadows, their roofs spilling gravel in the wind.

'Amalyn?' Danny asked. 'What do you think?'

'I ... I don't know what's best.' My lower body pulsed with pain. I felt swollen, tired, uncoordinated. The orange sand looked like a migraine and I struggled to focus. 'Okay,' I eventually said. 'If everyone agrees, let's wait till sunset. Or at least close to sunset, so the sun is behind us and it'll be cooler sooner.'

'Good idea,' Danny said. 'I agree. Anyone disagree?'

Everyone looked at each other, clueless faces with scared eyes, shrugging shoulders and wheezy breaths.

'Okay,' Danny said, 'everyone, find some shade, get some sleep if you need it. Amalyn, time to call them and tell them we're coming.'

'What time is it?'

'Seven a.m.'

'Sav might not be up yet. I'll call when we head off. We need to conserve the battery as best we can.'

Danny nodded and tucked the phone back into one of the bags, and we made our way to an old building about a hundred metres away. Its ceiling had partially caved in, shattered glass hiding under the sand. At two storeys high, it cast several metres of shade. Another building across the street was similar, and between the two, we all managed to stay out of the sun. The shadows were long that early in the morning. We knew the shade would shrink as the day wore on.

'There are more buildings over that way,' said Bex. 'We should spread out.'

A few nodded and made their way over. Bex stayed with me, holding Reya nestled under a muslin, shading her from the sand blowing up. She had a maternal nature about her that I'd only ever witnessed before in Grace. A natural instinct when handling Reya, face melting with delight at the sight of her. She kissed Reya's head and passed her to me as I quickly covered her again with the muslin. We wriggled into seats in the sand, the soft ground sending shooting pain up my back. I fidgeted to find a comfortable position but, in the end, decided to just put up with it.

As I leant back, I took some deep breaths and allowed the moment of stillness and calm to find a place within me. I couldn't stop a smile forming. Somehow, we had made it to France. We were sitting in another country, had made it there on our own. We had done something no one else from the Raft had attempted, let alone succeeded in doing. We were on foreign land, with possibilities before us. Where I had failed before, I had succeeded now. Partly, anyway. We had walked across the Raft, commandeered a boat and sailed across the revolting sea. I looked across at the faces of the others. As tired and scared as they were, they were pinching themselves. They were off the Raft. Away from what the Centre and Blue Liberation had done to us, away from the eternal grey and futures ring-fenced by place of birth. We had escaped. I allowed my chest to swell with pride, just a little. I lifted the muslin to give Reya a kiss, and then my tears began to flow. All the sadness and joy and fear flowed out of me. I sobbed and sobbed. Penny put her arm around me, and I cried into her shoulder. I wasn't the only one. I heard others in the group crying as well.

It was too soon for tears of joy. I knew that. But still, we allowed ourselves that moment. The Golden Fifties achieving what they never thought they would – taking their first steps off the Raft.

The others all sat in their allocated shade, five groups in total. We seemed too far apart. I wanted everyone next to me so I could count them and make sure they were okay. Little Cora hung off my skirt. Tilly hugged her knees, shivering despite the increasing heat.

And like that, we waited.

Sitting, dreading the sun, fanning ourselves as the heat intensified, huddling closer to the buildings as the shadows shortened. Nobody said much. We all drank a little, rationing what we had. I shifted in my seat, sand getting in places it shouldn't, the pain now continual. As it got hotter, I drifted away from that place and to another where I could hear his laugh, see the twinkle in his eyes, feel his arms around me. His breath licking at my ear, his scent sweet and clean, familiar, mine. Was he watching me now? *Don't be stupid, Ams*, I chastised myself with a grin. However gone he was, his eyes were on me. Maybe that was just hope, but I want him to know what I had denied him in his final hours, to see that I was saving our baby.

I'll try, Archie, I promise.

Danny nudged me, his clammy hand snapping me back to the present. 'Probably a good time to call, dearie.'

I looked around. The view had changed. We'd moved around the buildings since we first arrived, following the shade. I hadn't even noticed. Had someone carried me? Didn't matter. The sun was behind us now, moving down towards the sea. We'd have to leave soon.

I took the satellite phone and dialled. She answered, saying my name, her voice a medley of relief and panic.

'Sav. We're here. At the coast. Just the walk to go.'

'You made it to France? Across the sea?'

'Yep. On board a beaten-up old Centre boat. We made it.'

'Oh my god, Ams, you're actually here!'

'Almost.'

'You sound rough. Are you okay?'

'Just tired.' The battery light on the phone started flashing. 'I need to save the phone battery. We're on our way to Bordeaux. The western entrance.'

'I'll see you there. I'll get help to you if I can. We'll see you soon.'

I switched the phone off. My burning fever gave way to a comforting warmth for a moment. My friend was close by. I'd see her soon. I missed her moaning and griping. Right then I'd give anything to hear her tut at me and tell me off for being too outspoken or drinking too much. Soon, though. I'd see her soon.

Chapter 26

They had made it. They'd actually made it! Amalyn sounded weak on the satellite phone, but she was on French land and they were on their way to Bordeaux. She had sailed across the sea on a commandeered boat, like some bad-ass superhero.

I ran from the lab when the line went dead and, without thinking about it, jumped on a bike. For a few metres, I managed it, cutting valuable seconds off my journey. Momentum. That was all I needed. Keep legs moving, don't look down, just keep pedalling. Almost as soon as I thought I'd got the hang of it, my stability went and I cycled into a wall. I ditched the bike and ran the last part of the journey, my crappy unsupportive sandals a trip hazard, so I took them off and ran holding them instead. Several curse words later, covered in perspiration, I arrived at the Council offices.

They were empty. No sign of Harvey. *Microbes!*

I jogged along the busy mezzanine, dodging Subs with scowling faces, leaving a trail of tuts and accusations of calorie wastage in my wake. By the time I arrived at the next chamber, the distant sound of Harvey's voice was louder than the indictments. He stood on a table giving a campaign speech, complete with animated gesticulations and damning reports of the Select. I ran straight up to him and shouted, jumping up and down, waving my arms, a sandal in each arm giving me some extra length.

'A boat of Rafters has arrived. Forty, fifty, maybe even sixty have sailed across the sea. They are weak, hungry, thirsty. They need our help. Amalyn is with them. She holds the information to getting the food production up and running.'

The crowd murmured little whispers of excitement and approval. I noticed smiles, some nudges, and they started to cheer: *Save the refugees! Save the refugees!*

'We need to send a rescue party,' I said. 'They'll need water and food for the rest of their journey. It's still a long walk from the coast.'

'We need to alert Giao,' said Harvey. 'He cannot refuse to help them now, after they have overcome such perils to get here. These are precious human beings. They deserve our help.'

The crowd became enthused, chanting louder, *Save the refugees! Send help!* Louder and louder until others came out to listen. The chamber filled from all entrances; the news reaching every corner. As new arrivals heard, they added to the mass of support and impassioned pleas. From an entranceway across from me, Giao emerged, Isaac in tow, their faces solemn.

'We must send rescue,' I shouted as I climbed up on the table next to Harvey. 'They need our help, and we need them here.'

Isaac and Giao stood quite still, talking to each other, and waiting for the crowd to quieten down. Harvey lowered his arms a few times, shushing the chanting for a moment.

'You heard the news,' he shouted at Giao. 'Amalyn, the one who can save the food labs. Her newborn baby and her friends have made it across the sea to France. They have braved the ocean and need our help.'

The chamber was silent, a stillness settling that I had not experienced here except in the dead of night.

Giao stepped forward towards the edge of the crowd. 'Sandstorms are brewing,' he said to the room. 'We cannot risk the lives of our people. It's too dangerous. The temperatures are still high for such a journey. Bear in mind that they will need to quarantine, since they have had no vaccinations or medical checks in almost a year, not to mention they've been at sea. Anyone who comes in contact with them will also need to be quarantined for two weeks. If anyone is willing, once the storms have passed, be my guest, I cannot stop you from being foolhardy. But my opinion is, they've made it this far. They can make it the rest of the way.'

Hushed gasps echoed through the room, but there were many nods of approval, many people muttering 'fair enough.'

I stared in dismay. 'But they're so weak. Amalyn has a baby. This is not about just fifty or so individuals. This is about our society, who we are becoming, what message we want to give our children. Surely we want them to show compassion and love. To help those in need.'

'"We" is a big word, Savannah,' Isaac said, contempt in his voice and disgust in his eyes. '*We* are Subs, remember? *You* are Rafters.'

My insides went hollow. My brother's words stung like gravel on skin.

'I will not risk the lives of our people,' Giao said, face as stern as his words. 'Maybe when they get closer, we can reconsider.'

No one stepped forward to argue otherwise. No one dared. There were a few gasps and hurt faces at Isaac's words, but no one countered. Giao's speech was met with silence. There was no dispute, no counter from the crowd, which remained an ambiguous mix of agreement and opposition, not a hero or a renegade among them. The gathering thinned, the corridors filling with acquiescence and cowardice. The echoes began again, undertones of agreement changing the subject. I deflated like a punctured tyre.

'He's right, Sav,' Harvey said, looking disappointed his campaign speech had come to an abrupt end. 'As much as I'd like to help, it would mean risking lives here.' His hand went to his scars as he spoke. He knew all too well the ferocity of the world outside.

As crushed as I was, I couldn't argue with Giao's logic. It could be a suicide mission. I was asking people to risk their lives for strangers. As cruel as it seemed, no one wanted to brave the open desert, and it was unfair to guilt them into doing so.

I walked back to the lab the long way, meandering down quieter tunnels and chambers, sandals back on now, dragging my feet, exhausted and holding back tears. I knew there was no way I could go alone. What use would I be? No one in the Tunnels was trained for such a rescue mission. No one had even been outside, except for punishments when the Select were here. Marco Paradiso had been campaigning for Council leader by stating more time outside was possible. But his campaign had died a death and, as I scanned TunNet, I found no endorsement from him. My breath shuddered. I was elated yet terrified. She was so close, yet a world of peril away.

When I arrived at the lab, Kevin was leaning against a desk, his normally confused, half-closed eyes now alive and laser-like. His mouth wore a smug grin. Behind him, my computer was on, displaying all my research, detailed spreadsheets and diagrams. In my excitement, I hadn't shut it down before I left.

'So you know how to make food. You've been denying the Tunnels all this time.'

'I can explain –'

'Making all of us fund this lab while you purposefully fail to deliver, denying the Subs the nutritious food that you promised.' He was shaking his head, yet his eyes had a malicious sparkle to them.

'Just let me explain. Let's discuss this over some VitaBiscuits, please.'

'Explain to the Council.'

With his shoulders back and head high, he walked out of the lab as I followed, begging, pleading for him to listen.

'I only just got the information. Amalyn told me some on the phone today, and I managed to figure the rest out.'

'Bullshit.'

'I just wanted everyone to know how important she is, how much she deserves a place here. Please, Kevin. Everyone will be fed now. Don't you see this is a good thing?'

He didn't answer. My legs were slow and heavy, drained from running. I hoped he'd at least get a bike with a trailer, but he stomped, loud and purposeful footsteps the whole way, a metronome to my pleading.

'Please, Kevin, you don't have to do this. Listen, please –'

'Save it.'

'They're not being truthful with you, Kevin. About the money, about the expenses. Please, just listen to me!' I'd promised not to say anything, but what would they do to me now for lying? Why were my lies worse than theirs?

Kevin marched all the way to the Council offices, and I crossed my fingers, hoping it was still empty. It wasn't. Of course it wasn't. As if I would be so lucky. Kevin didn't hesitate. He barged in, the same way I had done so many times. Determined, insistent, rude.

Isaac and Giao were there, Celia with her head in a notebook, red curls all over the place. With them, to my surprise, was Peter Melrose.

'Ah, Kevin,' Giao said, the sight of me and my panic making his face lift with delight.

Celia looked up and smiled at her son. It was clear where Kevin got his gormlessness from. 'Found something useful, I hope?'

'I have. And it didn't even take much digging since she left her computer on.'

'Good,' said Giao. 'Nice to know you have been useful to us in the lab.' The satisfaction on his face was making me feel sick.

Kevin cleared his throat. 'Professor Selbourne can make all the food she wants. She's been lying to us.'

Giao and Isaac stared at me, mouths agape, their faces reddening. Out of the corner of my eye, I saw Peter's saggy lips lift into a sneer.

'Just listen, please, you haven't given me a chance to explain.'

'What am I meant to tell the Subs? That the Rafter they were so looking forward to welcoming has been deliberately withholding food?' said Giao. 'I told you these Tunnels must be a success. Whatever the cost. And *this* is what you have done.'

Isaac was shaking his head slowly, teeth clenched. 'Savannah, my little sister, how could you? Taking to TunNet to make claims of injustice, accusing the Council of being immoral, when all the time you have been withholding food.'

'You don't understand. I only received the information recently. I haven't even tested it. You think I'm going to say I've sorted it when I'm not a hundred per cent sure? It's not easy, you know. If Amalyn were here –'

'Oh, enough about Amalyn already,' Isaac said with a theatrical sigh. 'Like she's going to arrive and all the problems of the Tunnels will be solved. She'll be just one more drain on our finances. You undermine this Council, cause unrest, and yet you do something like this.'

Anger fizzed like a nuclear reactor inside of me, about to explode. 'You steal the Tunnel's money and send it off to the Select without telling anyone, and you accuse the Rafters of being a financial drain!'

Kevin gasped. Peter's eyes were huge. He was enjoying this.

Isaac leant in close, his breath hot on my face. 'You know what happens if you talk about that.'

'People aren't stupid, they'll figure it out. Sara already has.' It was a knee-jerk reaction thing to say. I didn't mean to drag Sara into this. Sod it, I could apologise later. 'What sort of democratic country is so dishonest? Leadership should be transparent.'

'We're not a democratic country *yet*,' said Isaac. 'Once we have our elections, and I have won, I'll have the mandate to continue with whatever funding I see fit. Until then, we're still under the rule of the Select. They entrusted the running of the Tunnels to this Council, and we shall continue to do what is right by them, our founders, Their Excellencies. The ones we owe the very existence of these tunnels to. Our very survival.'

'If it's so justified, then why are you trying to keep this a secret? Why blame the lack of money on the Rafters?'

Kevin's bottom lip stuck out the way Ethan's did when he was sulking. 'What is she talking about?' He looked at his mum, who was shaking her head and holding her finger to her lips. 'Mum, explain. I don't understand.'

Kevin not understanding something was hardly the revelation he thought it was. I turned to him. 'It's exactly as I said, Kevin. Your Council here are syphoning off money to send to people on another planet and blaming Rafters for the financial hardships.'

'There's a lot you don't know, Savannah.' Giao now, his voice somewhat softer than Isaac's, his face less puckered. 'Mars is on the brink of turmoil. The Select need our support. They're building a new biodome, a safe haven for the Select and Centre Elite. They're too close to the Centre commoners at the moment and it's causing friction. This is for everyone's safety. There are weddings between Centre and Select to plan, to help bridge their differences and promote peace. A wedding venue needs to be built, the ceremonies paid for. These are all expensive.'

My stomach knitted with disgust. I tried to stop my body from trembling, but anger shook out of me. 'Don't tell me you're creating hate towards Rafters, denying people the right to survive, so that the richest in the solar system can have fancy parties?'

'It's in our national interest, for the common good,' Giao said, still calm, too calm. 'They are our representatives on Mars. Ambassadors for our planet. They are still our founders.'

'And if you don't pander to their wants and desires, they won't send Blane back.' It wasn't a question.

Giao's eyes widened with rage. 'Of course I worry about Blane, and he is a priority for me. One of many. Just like feeding people should be one of yours.'

'Our founders, our rulers, require a certain level of care, Savannah,' Isaac now, his voice etched with spite. 'Coming from the Raft, I am sure it is difficult for you to appreciate. These things are necessities.'

'No, they're luxuries.' *The patronising arsehole.*

Where Isaac was composed, I was a mess. Screw being professional and tranquil like some robot. They'd both rehearsed this, I could tell. Their voices were droll, evenly paced, unfazed by being put on the spot. They were giving me some practised speech to justify their actions, like nailing the grammar would make it okay.

'If all the Subs feel the same way, if they would all agree that this expense is necessary, why don't you want them to know? If it's such a good thing you are doing, shout it from the rooftops! Tell people the truth!'

'You're hardly in a position to preach about telling the truth,' Isaac said, on his moral fucking high ground. 'According to Kevin, you've been lying to us.'

'I told you,' I said through gritted teeth. 'I haven't tested it yet. I'm not ripping off the population. I'm being truthful.'

'The truth is as murky as the sea, Professor. You must remember that lesson.' Peter's breathy voice was unwelcome. It gave me chills, telling me that after everything we had been through, escaping the Raft, the Centre Elite, all the freedom I had hoped to find, we were back to square one.

I turned to face him. He was leaning back in his chair, scrawny chest puffed out with pride. 'What the hell are you here for, anyway?' I said, spit flying from my mouth.

He didn't answer. His thin smile widened, mocking me.

'We are following your old boss's advice,' Giao said, 'and offering Peter a position on Isaac's campaign. To help with our message.'

Our message. Giao's 'neutral' stance really was a load of bullshit, then. 'To spin fabrication into fact, you mean? That's all he ever did on the Raft.'

'A good wordsmith is all any politician needs,' Peter said, rubbing his hands together. 'Campaigns are won on little more than phrases and slogans. You know that, Professor.'

'I do. It's what I'm afraid of. The Tunnels are one slogan away from becoming the "us and them" of previous civilisations.'

'There will always be an "us and them," little sister,' said Isaac with a sneer like Peter's. 'Centre or Perimeter, Rafter or Sub, there are always differences, different levels of what is required and needed. Some require expenses, some don't. We are simply different.'

'You grew up in the same country as me, or have you forgotten? A few years separated us, not DNA, not requirements, not even the vastness of space. We have a lot more in common than you have with the Select.'

'I never lived on the Raft.'

'What does that even matter? It's a stone's throw away. We're starting anew here. Why not base a society on truth and fairness instead?'

Blank faces answered me, the idea of truthfulness more alien to them than a Rafter. I might as well have been speaking a forgotten language. The only words these people understood were those of deceit.

Life was a tease, a never-ending peek at what could be. Little glimpses of happiness that were visible for a moment before they slipped through the sieve of lies. When all that remained was truth, was there really very much left to salvage? I looked around at the walls carved from the earth, across the corridor, a seating area with benches made from rock. Each rock unique, yet the same. It was all dirt. The toxic truth was laid bare soon after we'd arrived. We were too different. We were never meant to fit in.

'You'll do well not to accuse Subs of being the same as Rafters,' Giao said, his tic intensifying. 'Subs never withheld food. It will not help your cause. We should lock you up for that.'

'I told you I never withheld food. And even with the email that Kevin has seen, you'll have no chance of getting the lab working. I mean, it's Kevin. He's hardly competent, and the rest of the staff have limited experience.' It wasn't true. Bestie and Chris were perfectly capable. I hoped they'd think my face was red from rage rather than dishonesty.

'Can someone please explain to me what's going on?' Kevin pleaded.

'Screw this,' I said as I walked out, quickly, before they had a chance to call any guards. 'They're all going to know the truth.'

Chapter 27

'I reckon it's about three hours till sunset,' Jacob said, shielding his eyes as he gazed at the horizon. 'If we wait and walk through the night, it would be cooler.'

Danny looked at our supplies and shook his head. 'I don't think we can wait another three hours.'

My head hurt so much it was hard to open my eyes. Pain coursed through every inch of me. *In three hours, I'll feel much worse than this.* 'If everyone is able, let's get moving.'

'I'll take Reya,' Bex said. 'You're very weak.'

'No, I'm strong enough.' I needed her with me, as much as I needed my strength. Her breath on my chest was what enabled me to stand, to walk. Her eyes looking up at me were what kept me going. She snuggled into me like she was part of me. Secured in place with her papoose made of luxury scarves, she looked like a lavishly cared-for baby instead of a homeless refugee. Such finery for somewhere so desolate.

Bex puffed on her inhaler, the dry air making her breath rasp and wheeze. She smiled when I looked at her with concern, sharing in the resilience and determination of all of us.

In the medical kit, we had some painkillers. I swallowed two without water, and we set off. Glin and Shaif stood on either side of me, steadying me if I needed it. I told them I was fine, but they saw through my lie as I staggered more than walked, hunched more than stood straight. I wasn't the only one. June leant on Danny. Tilly's strides were more wobbly than most. Vern dragged one leg behind him often, though made an effort to seem sturdier if he caught anyone looking his way. Chrissy kept in-step with him, rubbed his arm occasionally. We just needed to get moving properly, I told myself. Our muscles needed waking up. I squeezed my eyes shut and tried to shake the doubt from my head. Tried to ignore the niggling voice that whispered behind me with a chilling breath, telling me I was leading everyone to their deaths. That voice had cold arms fumbling for me, bony fingers trying to dig in and pull me to the sea. That voice had to go away. I shook my head. We would make it, all of us. Whatever it took, we had to get there. If I didn't make it, others would take Reya. But I'd hold her until then. I'd cherish every moment with my baby.

The sun beat down behind us, my back dripping with so much sweat I was worried the papoose scarves would slip. I paused to tighten them, and they rubbed and chafed my skin. Where was the air pollution when we needed it? A bit of smog protection would have been useful right then. The sky was clear, so clear. The odd orange wisp of dust and sand, but not a cloud in sight.

'Why is the sky that colour? There's no smoke,' said Cora, blinking and staring up. The only sky she'd ever known had been thick with smog, or tinted blue from the smoke engineered by factories.

'That's blue, kiddo,' Danny said. 'That's what it's meant to look like.'

'I've never seen a colour like that before,' she said, mouth hanging open, so in awe, her young eyes keen to learn.

The others agreed. That natural blue was more beautiful than the blue smoke the factory chimneys ejected, and there was no smog to overpower it, no particulate matter to choke on. The sun was behind us, yet we squinted from the colour. It was flamboyant, visual gluttony.

Still, there were murmurs of disbelief that we were treading on foreign lands, that we were on our way to a civilisation most of us hadn't even known existed. It felt like a lifetime ago since I had discovered the truth and I was taking that knowledge for granted. I tried to remember my giddiness and frivolity on that first journey. How Sav chastised me for being too indiscreet, how worried Archie was.

Archie.

Cora's hand found mine, and in its soft touch, I felt him. A slight pull. With his guidance, it almost made the pain go away.

Almost.

The backs of my ankles burned as the wind blew my skirt to the sides. My neck, too, was raw. My headache centred on the back of my skull, a dull throb that beat with every step.

Cora dragged her feet, tired little legs struggling already. She went to Danny, who smiled at her but couldn't help, as he needed all his extra strength to assist June. Obey called her, his naturally chilly demeanour thawing at the sight of a little girl in need. His big hands grabbed her wrists and hoisted her onto his shoulders, meaning he now sunk lower into the sand with each step. The sand almost always obscured the road, so it was impossible to stick to the hidden tarmac. If we strayed even slightly off the road, we sunk deeper into the sand. When the sand eclipsed our shoes, each step became a soul-sucking effort. The wind was light, and our groans were easily audible.

The sun was dipping lower, but its heat was tenacious. My lips split and the pounding at the back of my head didn't ease. If I moved my head, it felt like a heavy ball was bouncing around in my skull. Conversation dwindled, mouths ran dry. Bottles of water were handed out like sacred chalices. VitaBiscuits with the texture of ash were spat on the ground. Obey grew tired and put Cora down, his face redder than anyone's, his eyebrows white with desiccated salt. Cora didn't complain, but thanked him and hugged his leg as he righted himself. I knelt down and checked her. Her skin was pink, too pink. Her eyes bloodshot and heavy.

I put a thin blanket over her head and told her to keep herself covered. 'You're doing so well, young lady. So well.'

She smiled and nodded. Looking proud of herself. Her desire for adventure was still there.

I paused a moment to allow Reya to latch on. Somehow, my milk was lasting. Danny insisted I drink more water. 'Drink for two,' he said. I sipped cautiously, thirsty faces all around me. None begrudged me extra. Yet.

I turned and watched the last of the sun dip below the horizon, the blue sky turning peach before darkness came. There was nothing ahead but blackness and sand.

Jacob looked at the e-pad. 'Twenty-two kilometres to go.'

Chapter 28

Harvey was on a mezzanine when I found him, a couple of other Council members with him. One was flustered with paperwork, the other had her head buried in e-pads, quoting TunNet posts. He strolled between them, his head high, seemingly victorious already. If elections could be won on confidence alone, it'd be a landslide.

'Harvey!' Despite my cramping legs, I ran the last few metres when I saw him, grabbing his attention.

'Savannah, I'm sorry but unfortunately Giao is right. It would be a suicide mission.'

The Council members didn't look up. The one to his right nudged him away from me.

'That's not what I want to talk to you about,' I said, and stepped closer. 'It's about the accounts. First, I have to get Grace and Ethan somewhere safe. Is there anywhere you can suggest?

Giao is threatening their safety to stop me telling everyone what I know.'

'What?' He stopped in his tracks. 'Are you serious?' He pushed away the e-pad one of his staff was holding under his nose.

'That's why he told the guards to keep her in prison yesterday. They let her out, but I can't be sure they will again. They might come to our house to check she's there. She needs to be somewhere safe, and quickly.'

'Well, there's one place they'll never think to look. But I'll need to get a key. Clementine has it, I believe.'

'Clem can't know. It would put her in a difficult position.'

'Let's go. I've got an idea.'

Harvey grabbed a bike with a trailer, and I sat in the back. He left his staff putting up posters, showing the sort of initiative I wished my own had. After we'd cycled across a chamber and entered a tunnel, we found Sara cycling the other way. *Microbes!* I'd forgotten all about her, and I may have dropped her in it with the Council. Harvey stopped the bike next to her.

'Sara, I need a favour,' Harvey said.

'In a minute. Sav, I was just coming to see you.'

'I'm so sorry,' I said. 'I had an argument with Giao and Isaac, I confronted them about the accounts, I may have said you know –'

'That explains the emails telling me to meet with him. I've just seen one of your lab guys. Kevin, is that his name? The guard Juan had him handcuffed.'

I held my head in my hands. 'They're trying to bury this. Kevin knows too, they're locking him up to keep him quiet. Where are the other guards? Charlie?'

'Another unjust arrest?' said Harvey and took out his e-pad. 'I'll inform the public. They simply can't keep doing this.'

'The guards seem divided,' said Sara. 'Which means they could be going back for Grace. I guess some are still doing what the Council say.'

'No regard for protocol, at all,' said Harvey, as he slammed his fingers into his e-pad. 'No regard whatsoever.'

'We need to tell everyone the truth before they get to Grace. And, Sara, I'm so sorry, they might do the same to you too,' I said.

She didn't respond, just nodded slowly.

'We're going to get Grace somewhere safe,' I said. 'You should join us. Have you seen Clem? Harvey says she has a key we need.'

Her eyes widened, and she looked at Harvey.

'She's in charge of maintenance for those quarters. That's what I wanted to talk to you about,' he said. 'We can't ask Clem, obviously.'

'The key for the Select's wing?'

It was my jaw's turn to drop. *That* was Harvey's safe place? Isaac and Giao would go nuts, a thought that made me smile.

Harvey saw my face and shrugged. 'Seems like a good place to hide.'

Sara thought a moment. 'I know where it is. We used to live together so I know where she keeps them. You go get your family and I'll meet you there to take them to the Select's.'

Harvey fell in behind Sara's bike for a few metres before we forked off towards the Rafter's wing. The corridors narrowing, the detailing becoming less ornate.

'The Select's wing, Harvey, really?' I shouted over the screeching bike. 'This sounds like trouble.'

'It's empty. Why not?'

Grace's disapproval when I had joked about it rang in my ears. But Harvey was right. Why not?

'There's so much space there we should be using.' His tone was casual, matter of fact, like it was such an obvious solution. Because it was. I knew it was.

'Watch out for Giao and Isaac,' Harvey said. 'Keep your eyes peeled. Duck if you see them. We don't want to give the game away.'

I stared, not daring to blink, searching faces for the ones I dreaded. The guards appeared unengaged, their usual patrols doing nothing noteworthy. I checked TunNet on my e-pad. There was nothing about a search. Harvey's phone was pinging, but he ignored it.

When we arrived at the Rafter's wing, a Council guard was at the fence, not paying attention to anything. I walked past without him even glancing at us, and I ran to our apartment.

'Grace?'

She was sitting on the floor with Ethan. 'You're home early.'

'Grab some essentials, we need to go. Now.'

'What? Where?'

'I'm worried they'll come for you here. I'm taking you somewhere safe for now.'

'What the hell, Sav?'

'Please, just pack a bag. Or don't, it doesn't matter. Just come with me. Ethan, big man. Put some of your favourite things in here. Some underwear, your toothbrush –'

'They're not my favourite things.'

'A couple of trucks as well, then. Come on, quickly now.'

'Sav,' Grace hadn't moved. 'You're scaring me.'

'Sara will be here in a moment. She has a bike with a trailer outside the fence, go with her.'

'She's a Sub,' she replied through her teeth.

'She's coming to help, Grace,' I said.

I escorted Ethan down the tunnel just as Sara was arriving. She gave me a thumbs up as I loaded him onto the trailer, giving him a kiss on the cheek. 'Little adventure today. How's that sound?'

He smiled half-heartedly as he saw Grace's less-enthusiastic face. She huffed as she sat next to him and turned away from me.

Harvey and I rode alongside them. It took over half an hour to reach the Select's quarters, through several chambers, and across exposed mezzanines. I was sure we'd be stopped by guards, that an alert would come across TunNet at any moment. But I checked my e-pad and still there was no search party.

They wanted to bury this; I reminded myself, and took comfort in that. Creating headlines was not on their agenda right now. They wanted silence.

I had never been to the Select's quarters before, but it was obvious where we were as soon as we arrived. Thick curtains lined the walls on the approach, softening the echo of the bikes. They flapped slowly in the gentle breeze, their colours and patterns dancing. We stopped cycling and walked the final few metres, muted footsteps in the soft light. The engraved tree design was here as it was everywhere, embroidered in the fabric as well as carved into the walls, only here its eye was absent. No one kept their eye on the Select. No one peered in to scrutinise their every move.

Sara took out a large brass key with the tree design carved into the end. The lock released with a clunk, and she pushed the heavy door open. It creaked on its hinges. What was inside stunned me more than I thought was possible. The luxury reminded me of that in the Centre, only where the Centre gleamed, the Select's quarters were invitingly tactile, every surface soft, decorated, tantalisingly comfortable. Padded seats and benches, walls and floors decorated with colour and texture. I remembered the factory in the Tunnels where they made fabrics from worms. *Actual worms.* As alluring as it all looked, I shuddered. I didn't tell Grace. No sense in grossing her out with stories of worm shit.

Where we had seats carved into rock, the odd cushion to make it bearable, here every surface was squashy and relaxing.

Fabrics were woven with exhaustive designs, the tree image repeating. Worshipping such a relic among the splendour seemed a strange juxtaposition. Huge, beckoning sofas were nestled into corners, plush rugs surrounding them. All this had been left empty, reserved for people living on another planet.

I walked down a hallway and found bedrooms, bathrooms, entertaining rooms, study rooms, more bedrooms. All lavish, all ready to live in. All empty.

'There's enough room for all the new arrivals in here,' I said as I struggled to take it all in.

'Lock yourselves in,' Harvey said to Sara, who nodded and made her way to the front door. Grace wasn't listening, she was staring wide-eyed at the luxury. 'Sav and I are going to have a chat about what's been going on.'

'I'll bring you some food later, Grace. I promise,' I said. 'You'll be safe here.'

She didn't look angry anymore. She looked at home, stretching out across an oversized sofa, not even looking at Sara with disgust, too captivated by the beauty of the place.

'Sure, sure, we'll be good here,' she said dismissively, stroking the fabric and sinking into the cushions.

We left them to it, and I heard the door lock behind me. Harvey and I jumped back onto his bike and rode off away from them. The last thing we wanted was to give their location away. After twenty minutes or so, we came to one of the acoustic dead zones where there were no echoes, and we could speak freely. Now we were stationary in the quiet, it was all starting to sink in.

Amalyn was close, yet so far. Peter was working as a spin doctor *again*. I was turning in circles and landing right back where I'd started. Unbalanced, falling, weighed down.

I told Harvey what I knew. About the money, the Select, their new biodome on Mars, their weddings of luxury, a possible uprising all eating into the Tunnels finances, and Rafters getting the blame. Harvey listened, nodding, contemplatively chewing the inside of his cheek.

'This is all just so wrong,' he said when I had finished. 'The Select being gone was supposed to rid us of their tyranny, but we're still their puppets.'

'And the Centre's'

'Ambassadors.' Harvey scoffed at the word. 'What the hell are they playing at? As if that was ever going to stay secret, anyway. These tunnels whisper, you know. That tree and eye design is a warning. You can't have secrets here. The Select are the ones who killed this planet. You know they used to deal in carbon trading? Literally buying up the rights to pump as much carbon into the atmosphere as they liked. That's how they grew their business and made their money.'

'I heard. My friend Archie told me.' Warned me, I should have said. Archie knew exactly how evil the Select were. No big surprise. No one becomes a billionaire by maintaining their morals.

'Well, your family are safe,' Harvey said. 'No one can use the lab but you, so they need you, especially now that it's functioning. You've nothing to fear. Your contribution will be legendary. Come on, let's rally some support.'

There was a warmth about him then, a substance to his claims. Genuity replacing pomposity. Perhaps I had judged him too harshly before. Wanting to win did not make him Centre. He had a purpose, that was all. Maybe not every politician was evil.

It was getting towards evening rush hour. We arrived at the central chamber just before most people would be passing through and bumped into Harvey's Council supporters on the way. They'd worked hard. His posters were everywhere and his leaflets were in the hands of many people. They looked exhausted but ran around checking the speakers were on before joining us, standing on the table. The sound system around the chamber was ready to go, and Harvey took the microphone.

'Attention Subs and Rafters alike. Every Tunnel resident. It is time for you to hear the truth.'

Chapter 29

Our pace was slow, and as the sun set, our backs grew cooler, an icy chill blowing over me. Sweat still poured from my forehead and trickled down my neck as I shivered. I wiped it away with my stone-cold hand, salt stinging my eyes, and I rummaged for extra blankets in the bags to keep Reya warm. Her breath felt hot on my chest, her little snores reassuring me she was okay.

Around me, dry mouths made smacking sounds, teeth chattered, breathing came in wheezes. Bex used her inhaler, the small puffs reminding me that I was with friends, that we were all together. Occasionally someone asked the group if everyone was all right. We all replied yes, and sometimes someone cheered in an expression of comradery and morale that made me smile, but it was infrequent and energy was waning. In between, there was almost silence, the thoughts loud in my isolated mind.

The darkness was the blackest black. A never-ending pit which extinguished all light. We used torches from time to time, keeping them set to their dimmest settings, saving the batteries. In the nothingness, I saw shapes, clear as day, which faded and disappeared. As we walked, I heard voices calling for me in the night. Laughs, whispers, beckoning me into nowhere. A feverish spectacle of illusion, reminding me I had so far to go. As if the pain ripping through me wasn't enough of a reminder. Stars shone above like we'd never seen before. They were real; I was sure. Everyone else could see them too, and talked about them in hushed voices, Cora gasping 'wow' as she looked up.

Vern shone the torch towards Jacob as he checked the e-pad to see where we were. Somehow, we were staying on course.

'The stars above will guide us,' Vern said, though I suspected that his cloudy eyes had more ambition than sight.

As I looked up, the bright twinkles were eclipsed as a gust of sand blocked my view. The blackness turned hazy. Then the sand hit us. It came from nowhere, unstoppable, like razor blades carried on the wind. A great cloud engulfed us in an instant, worse than the smog on the Raft. Tiny particles stabbed like needles at our burned skin. I turned my back to the wind to shield Reya, arching over her, but it whipped up and pummelled every inch of me.

'Make shelter!' someone screamed over the roar, and we huddled together. Torch beams were obscured, the haze masking everything. We grappled for each other, relying on touch and screams alone. In the dark, we fumbled for blankets, for limbs, for anything to grab onto, anything that felt like safety. Every grain of sand felt like a blow, a smack on a bruise. I heard voices and stumbling footsteps. Shrieks. What was that? Help? Was someone shouting for help? I couldn't tell, my ears clogged with sand, my eyes jammed shut. Reya cried. Thank god, she cried! Her cries let me know she was alive, that the sand hadn't suffocated her.

We shouted for each other over the din, calling out names and directions, sobs and howls, our ears filling with sand as quickly as we could empty them. The scant blankets we had brought were not enough to protect us. Why hadn't we thought to bring more?

Keep crying, Reya, keep crying!

Her tiny hand gripped my finger. I screamed for Cora and heard her crying, too.

'Keep talking to me, Cora!' I yelled as loud as I could, spitting out sand with every syllable. 'Hum, Cora, with your mouth closed, like this.'

I hummed like my mother used to when I was a girl, but it wasn't loud enough, so I screamed, my dry throat burning, finding a forgotten song in my fear. In response, I heard Cora whimper, the smallest sound that let me know she was alive. I thought so, anyway; it was impossible to be sure. Then a tiny hand grabbed my waist. Cora was with me. I grabbed hold and held her tight, tucking her under me, under all the people around me, whoever they were. She was so small and easy to shield. Another hand grabbed my arm, thin and bony. That must have been Tilly. I heard her cough through the wind. I kept humming, my chin on Cora's head, Reya crying beneath us. A trembling pile of fear. In the blackness, the sand grazed my skin, cutting me like I was falling down a cliff and hitting rocks on the way. Trapped, awaiting the end.

After an eternity of shaking in the darkness, the wind calmed. Reya stopped crying and sucked my finger instead. A tinnitus remained in my ears, a screeching in the new silence out there. After a while, no one knew how long, we dared to step away, to let go of each other's limbs. I fumbled in the dark and found Cora's face.

'You okay?'

I felt her nod. Wet tears rolling down her cheeks.

Torches were retrieved, those that hadn't been lost, and switched on, useful now that the sand wasn't blinding us completely. As we all stepped away, Adisa fell, tripping over a mound of sand. But it wasn't sand, it was too solid.

No! No, no!

We dug. On our hands and knees, we brushed the sand away, throwing it into each other's faces. Then we stopped and instinctively snapped our hands back as the sandy surface gave way to something softer. Velvety soft. Skin. It was too late.

The torchlight caught her lifeless face, skin bloodied and pale grey. Ghostly grey. One hand still reaching for someone that never came, the other grasping her inhaler. Mouth open, mid-scream, silenced by sand. A call that was never answered. Bex's lungs were too weak to survive, the sand too smothering. Her eyes bulging and open as she'd gasped for air that wouldn't come. She was not even thirty years old.

Glin wailed, a guttural cry from a pain he knew too well. He buried his head in her hair. Shaif knelt next to him, arm around him, trying to be strong. Failing. We all failed then. Our cries were loud. I grabbed Bex's delicate hand and sobbed into it as her warmth disappeared. The life sucked from her too quickly.

'She was going to read the books, all the stories about children with magic,' I said through my sobs. 'She was going to be a mum one day. She wanted to meet someone special.'

Vern knelt next to me, his hand also reaching for hers, talking into her cold palm. 'I'm so sorry, miss. I should have found you, should have heard you.'

'Oh Vern,' I cried and clutched his arm. 'We couldn't have done any more.' My words were to comfort him, but they did not soothe my own remorse. I was the one to blame. This journey was my idea. I was accountable. Cool moisture trickled down my neck as I looked around in the torchlight. Innocent, expectant faces, lost in grief, all of whom were in my charge. None of whom I had any power to save. My sobs came from within, from a deep place inside me, a pit where only sadness could survive.

Cora tugged at my skirt, looking to me for answers, for reassurances I could not give.

'Is she with my mummy now?'

I pulled her into my embrace, kissing her head. 'Yes, sweetie. She's with her mummy, too.'

She understood that eternity, that desolate goodbye, and she gave a little sniff, wiped her eye. 'Tilly said it's peaceful where mummy went. More peaceful than here.'

My heart ripped, another rip, another of the million pieces it had been shattered in to. Even young Cora was broken into bits. How much loss was it possible to experience and still feel human? How could it be that we had to live like this? As mere fragments of our former selves, a jigsaw puzzle with pieces missing.

'That's right, sweetie,' I said. 'She's at peace.'

We all pressed our forearms into our chests. The Golden Fifty tattoo, the one that Bex didn't have because she was too young. She was only just beginning to learn about the world. Our hearts felt the loss of one of our own.

I had persuaded Bex and all these people to come to this hellhole. My idea of salvation had led us here, to a sandstorm, so far from home, to her death. My actions had cost yet another life.

Save yourself, Ams.

But at what cost, Archie?

Jacob checked the e-pad. 'We need to keep going,' he said. 'Eighteen kilometres to go.'

Chapter 30

The crowd around Harvey grew, everyone listening in stupefied silence. He told them where their money was going, that the Rafters were not the financial drain the Council claimed, and that Amalyn had made it to France. He also reassured them that my lab would be functional within days, so what did they have to complain about? The truth bounced off the walls, going from ear to ear, trying to make its way through to the listeners. Some vague enthusiasm sounded as reality ripped through the fabrication. Then Isaac and his entourage approached. The chants from their supporters proceeded them, alerting us, taking the attention away from Harvey.

'Fund glory, not grime!'

'Sub supremacy!'

The chants were loud, louder than Harvey, and his voice faded into the background. My skin crawled. The slogans had the mark of Peter Melrose all over them.

Riders twisted their way through the people, handing out leaflets, thrusting them into hands and throwing them into the air. I grabbed one and had to blink a few times to take it in. Across the front were pictures of the Select, looking majestic, shining, glossy, enviable. Draped in fine fabrics with both authoritative and benevolent expressions. Hands to their chests, raised chins, sympathetic eyes with stern mouths. The text glorified the Select and what they had done for the Tunnels, obviously omitting the part about how they'd caused the mess in the first place. Next to them was a picture of some Rafters looking dirty, villainous, deceitful and odious.

'Where should your hard-earned money go? What sort of person should your taxes support?' Isaac said now, arms open, as if trying to embrace the whole population. 'Our ambassadors are representing us across the solar system. What impression of the Tunnels do we want to give? That we are cheap, discourteous, that we do not look after our own? That we spend our taxes on dead-end charities? Or that we support our glorious leaders, respect them for all they have given us, and are proud for them to showcase all we have achieved, the best of us.'

The mutters of support grew louder, statements like 'The Select are Subs like us' and 'Rafters are nothing like us' rippling through the crowd.

'You can cast your vote as you wish. But remember, the deep stinking pit that is the plight of the Rafters will continue to degrade our society. It will make us forget our values and dilute the very essence of what we call the Tunnels.'

My breath came out in shudders, my fists clenched.

'Fund glory, not grime!'

'Sub supremacy!'

The chants grew louder, hateful words papering over the reality that Harvey had only just revealed. Every Council lie was being concealed under a fresh layer of lies. So many people were falling for unfounded crap. At the far end of the chamber, I saw Peter and his toothless grin, rubbing his hands together.

Not all of Harvey's supporters were fooled. Some scowled and stamped their feet. Their voices were smaller, drowned out by Isaac's slogans, but they were there.

A divide had opened up, the slightest crack in the crowd. 'Save the refugees! Save the refugees!' was shouted from the hearts of a few. They grouped together at one side, their collective voice more than the sum of its parts. Yet such a philanthropic statement did not rally the same level of enthusiasm, and their voices were dwarfed by the glory chasers.

'We were all Rafters once!' I shouted, again and again, until a few joined in, but not enough. Not enough by far. It was like the crowd didn't want to be reminded of our similarities, only our differences. Giao had warned me about that.

'I'm not some grubby Rafter!' someone on Harvey's side shouted at me, and then pushed his way over to Isaac's supporters. I couldn't believe what I had seen. He'd rather turn his back on the refugees than be likened to one.

'Save the refugees' continued, gaining a little heartfelt volume, but still not enough. The chant of kindness seemed meek against the din of hate. We needed something punchier, something that spoke of anger instead of compassion. I looked at Peter's smug face once more.

Two can play at this game.

'The Select are stealing!' I shouted. 'The Select are stealing!' Harvey's supporters heard me and became angry, their faces growing redder. The voice of rage is louder than love, so if rage was what I needed, I'd find a way. I shouted it again, 'The Select are stealing!' Knuckles cracked, big hearts withered and gave way to hatred and wrath. Fists became tighter. Kind faces distorted to frowns.

'The Select are stealing!' they started to chant. 'The Select are STEALING!'

Council guards stepped in, batons in hand, pushing the two sides apart. Within moments, a chasm had opened up between Select and Rafter sympathisers. Isaac supporters all on one side, Harvey's on the other, the space between a fence of reason. No one even wanted to breathe the same air as one another, and the gap widened. By now it was hard to tell which crowd was larger, only that everyone was shouting as loud as they could, the sound of hate, slander and lies louder than ever. I heard my words resonate across the chamber, enraged voices ripping the space in half.

'You support thieves!' one man on Harvey's side shouted, and threw a plastic bottle.

'We support glory, not scum!'

'Fucking elitists!'

'Scavenging scum!'

Fights started to break out, rough smocks and soft knees scraping against the rock floor. A guard was knocked to the ground. More arrived, batons up and hitting anyone close. Blood sprayed from a broken nose.

I shook my head from my vantage point on the table with Harvey, watching the surrounding chaos grow. I held my hands to my ears, my insides aching with regret. No! This wasn't supposed to be the way! What had I done? Wanting to help the refugees and hating the Select were not the same thing. I had stoked the fire of hate, and now it was an inferno. We were supposed to be a peaceful society, welcoming Amalyn and her baby. In the divide I saw the Centre fence, the strip billboards, propaganda, the denial of healthcare to anyone who didn't conform. In the background, the Poison Maker smiled his menacing smile and nodded at me, like I was his apprentice, his protégé come to form. Below me was everything I hated about the Raft except for the smog.

The guards threw smoke grenades into the crowds to make them disperse, and all of a sudden I was back on the Raft. In polluted air and hearing polluted words. In a country riddled with hate and lies. I had gone full circle, back to the riots of years earlier. All of that unrest had followed us here, to this place that was meant to be peaceful and welcoming. Now it was as dirty as the Raft.

After some time, the coughs and whines of discomfort became louder than the chanting, and the crowd made their way home. A few more scuffles broke out, but nothing serious. Weary from impassioned ignorance, most of them just gossiped rather than resorting to physical disdain.

When the chamber was near empty, I stepped off the table along with Harvey. His face didn't bear the expression of someone who had almost witnessed a full-blown riot. Instead, he looked victorious, bubbling with excitement.

'Well,' he said, 'that was quite something, wasn't it?'

I realised then that my first instincts about Harvey had been right. He wanted to win, wanted drama. The wellbeing of refugees was not on his radar. He had merely chosen an angle for his own gain. We didn't matter to him.

I said nothing, too distraught to speak. Instead, I left and wandered down the newly quiet corridors to the lab. I set the machines, plugged in the coding, and did the one thing I knew how to do.

I made food.

Chapter 31

'Her parents died to give her a chance. They jumped in the sea to save her,' Glin said, as we walked through the night. 'Their sacrifice was for nothing.'

'She had a chance, a moment of hope. That's more than most get.' Shaif was holding back tears by the sounds of it, his voice softer and unsteady.

'What's the point in trying? What's the point of hope?' Glin cried. 'Where are we going, anyway? We're going to die in this fucking desert.'

'Hey!' It sounded like Obey, a gruff and stern voice. His torch beam shone over the crowd until it found Glin's tear-stricken face. 'Shut it, will you? There's a kid here. She doesn't need to listen to your crap.'

'She should know. We all need to know the truth of it. We've still got miles to go and we might as well curl up and die right here.'

The bright torch made him look washed out, transparent. His face was devoid of fear, of hope, of anything. The husk of the man I had met just a few days earlier. He was what defeat looked like. Crushed, overwhelmed by grief.

The torchlight jerked around as we heard Obey grab Glin by his shirt and lift him; the light catching his skinny ankles dangling above the dust. 'You can quit if you like, but there're cities out there, and this kid and that baby deserve to live a whole lot longer than they have already. And it ain't going to be as bad as the Raft there, because nowhere is as bad as the fucking Raft, not even this damned desert. So shut it, before I make you shut up.' Then he dropped Glin, whose ankles gave way, and he crumpled to the ground.

I squeezed my eyes shut, tears falling and soaking through Reya's blanket. She moaned a little. Her sleep had been disturbed, but perhaps the sense of loss was getting to her as well.

I felt a hand at my shoulder, urging me on with the lightest of shoves. 'We need to keep going,' said Jacob.

Obey had seemed like a thug from the beginning. I knew he'd be trouble, but he was the right sort of trouble. Bex had been nervous of him, and Chrissy always kept her distance, not daring to look straight at him. Such timid young women, so unworldly. My heart ached for Bex, for her kindness, her maternal instinct with Reya. She would have been a wonderful mum one day. Her warmth knew no limits. I wish I'd known her for longer. I said her name in my head, over and over.

Bex. Bex. Bex.

My attention kept drifting off, away from that place, to the past, to dreams. Bex needed to be remembered when we got there, her name repeated and told to others. Her body would rest forever in the desert, but that didn't mean her memory had to stay there with her.

I could hear Glin and Shaif behind me. They were still with us. Cora sobbed a little, her whistling sniffs distinctive in the dark, Tilly's scratchy cries just next to her. Such misery all around, such tiredness. Our sense of adventure had long gone and instead we were faced with the impossible, our prospects giving way to reality. My feet throbbed worse than my head. I couldn't tell where the pain was coming from anymore, it just enveloped me. I allowed my mind to wander, to take me away, out of this body, to leave the pain and gloom behind. I wanted to fly away with the stars or sink beneath the sea. Either was fine with me.

We walked the rest of the night with barely a break. Icy perspiration poured down my face, and I winced from its sting. Occasionally, someone close to me tipped water down my throat. Voices asked if I was okay. They sounded like they were underwater, like I was in the sea again.

My throat stung with bile. Everything smelled rotten. Where were we? I couldn't recall. Somewhere strange. The Raft looked odd. Footsteps and luggage sounded like the clinks from the lab. Where was my workstation? Had I left a burner on?

'Keep going, not far now.'

Hands were on me, arms holding me up, dragging me forward, taking my weight.

'The smog is bad, it's so dark,' I said.

'It's okay, we'll get you there.'

There was kindness in the voices, a trust in those arms that held me. In the blackness I saw Archie smiling, that face I knew so well, full of love and desire. I reached out for him. He was so close I could almost touch him.

I'll see you soon, my love.

Pain split my body into bits and dragged me out of my daydream. My blood was made of broken glass, my body hot coals. Reya's hands tangled in my hair, tugging at it, reminding me she was there, of what we were doing and why. She gave me lucidity in the obscurity. She wouldn't let me rest. I felt her breath on my hand, her hands beating my chest as she dreamed.

'Let's rest awhile,' I said. 'A little sleep.'

Did I say that out loud? Nothing changed, we kept moving. Except the black sky started to lighten. Was I there? At the end of the tunnel? Was he waiting for me?

Archie.

He wasn't there. We were nowhere.

Chapter 32

I shut and locked the lab doors. The other staff had gone home, and it was just me in my sanctuary. I woke up the machines, set the computers, typed in the coding and waited for the smells to fill the place. Delicious, homely, warming smells that made my mouth salivate and my tummy rumble. I didn't stop with roast potatoes. SynthoSpaghetti and RealioVeg chunks, so aromatic and flavoursome. I made IsoJuice and ImmunoJuice, their fruity flavours adding some zest to the savoury. IcyCrema. How long had it been since I'd had that? Not since the Raft, not since the day before we left. I made green fruits flavour and remembered the tangy sharpness mixing with the smooth, velvety cream. I closed my eyes and savoured it. Every pleasing clunk of the machinery, every fresh and comforting smell, the sight of trays and trays of real synth food rolling down the conveyor belt. It was like the old days, in that lab I knew so well, where I had achieved so much.

As soon as I'd made a few batches, I went to drop some over to Grace at the Select's quarters, flagging down a ride with a Sub who was more than happy to oblige when I handed him some freshly made IsoJuice and IcyCrema. Astonishment crept over his face with every swallow, eyes lighting up, groans of pleasure. I'd missed that. I felt worthwhile again.

We cycled past guards, and I handed them some sweet treats. They snatched them out of my hand like it was the only food they'd eaten in weeks.

'More to come tomorrow,' I said as we cycled away, leaving satisfied murmurs behind us.

The demonstration from Isaac's supporters earlier had not been as one-sided as I'd thought. So many were angry about the Select, and my food only served to reiterate the Rafter's value. And now I was adding to that value, creating ripples of delight and happiness, spreading joy and taste sensations. As I alighted, I gave the Sub a portion of roast potatoes in exchange for waiting and giving me a lift back. With the joy he was tasting, he asked no questions, and just nodded and revelled in the flavour.

I knocked on the door and called their names, and heard Ethan's cries of 'mummy!' as he ran towards me. It was way past his bedtime, but he sounded lively and excited. Grace opened the door, peering past me, wide-eyed with worry. Sara had gone. There seemed little point in her hiding now that the truth was out.

Grace had seen the news and was, of course, sympathetic to the Select. As much as she was enjoying the luxury – lounging on their great sofas, stroking their fine fabrics – she still expressed her view that such finery had a purpose. That it was not suited to the likes of her. I had no time to explain, to make her see. I left the food and returned to the lab.

I worked all night. Filling the lab with more delicious smells and piles of produce. With the right coding, I was on autopilot. The muscle memory in my arms sprung back to life. It was as if Amalyn was there, by my side, Mabel in the corner, Marcus cleaning up after me, Archie doing whatever Archie did. If I closed my eyes, I could see them all, feel their presence, the entire team creating delicacies once again.

At five a.m. I turned the extractor fans off, opened all the lab and factory doors, and allowed the smell of food to fill the Tunnels. I watched the steam escape, taking with it my promises and potential. The scent of the food would show all the possibilities that Rafters had brought with them. Boxes and boxes of food were piled up. I sat down, resting my tired legs and tasted a bit, letting the flavour mingle with my memories. As the machines whirred and clunked, I rested my head on the desk and dozed, remembering my friends. Remembering all we had achieved in that lab. Remembering the world we left behind, just the good parts. At that moment, the crappy bits of the Raft could be forgotten.

By the time the staff arrived, there was no room for them. Boxes of newly created food covered every available inch. I rubbed the sleep from my eyes as they stood in the doorway, dumbstruck and in awe.

'Grab bikes and trailers, plus anyone who wants to help,' I said in my bossiest voice. 'Let's show people what us Rafters are capable of. Let's get these people fed.'

They jumped into action, excitement making them move with an efficiency like I hadn't seen before. Kevin hadn't arrived. I couldn't imagine the guards were still bothering to hold him since the truth was out, anyway. He likely just didn't want to show his face. In any case, he wasn't missed. Within minutes, trailers had been loaded up and more bikes summoned. We didn't discriminate. Rafter or Sub – whoever wanted food could have it. We went to the mines first, where skeletal Rafters shed tears of joy as they ate properly for the first time in months. Their shaky limbs steadied, they stood straighter, and they smiled more than they had since they had arrived. Their emaciated arms reached for seconds before they'd even finished their firsts. The guard monitoring them didn't deny them those moments. She stood with them, enjoying the food while they all ate, chatted, laughed, enjoyed. The same people enjoying the same food.

I'd left the lab machines running, so when we ran out of food, we returned to more waiting to be boxed up. We sorted it all and left on bikes again to deliver it.

We went to the school, handing out sweet IcyCrema to the children. The elation on their faces brought a lump to my throat. Never had they tasted such a treat. They were all Sub children, born and bred in the Tunnels. They'd only ever known filth food. The children thanked me, and one ran to give me a hug. It was Pierre, Ethan's friend. I hugged him back and said Ethan would be back at school soon, which made his smile even wider. By lunchtime, people were content with full stomachs. Their rage and hate had completely dissipated. The atmosphere around the Tunnels was one of contentment.

Our last stop was the Council offices. The already well-fed Council members were bottom of our list. The regular people came first. Armed with a selection of everything, enough for several portions each, I entered the offices, pulling a loaded cart behind me.

The entire staff were there sat around the table. A video message from Mars was playing.

'Savannah,' Giao said, elongating my name like it was an arduous thing to say. He gestured to the video screen. 'What good timing. It seems divulging top-secret information is a common trait of the Rafters.'

On the screen was the eerie red sky of Mars, alive with spotlights and brightly lit billboards. The riotous noise of protests came through the speakers. Angry people, irate calls demanding freedom, an alternative to the Blue Liberation, insisting on a general election. The leak had clearly not been contained. People wielding banners demanded the truth, political freedom, a real democracy. They wanted change, saying that Blue Liberation were immoral: thieves, murderers, dictators, liars. All words us Perimeter had used many times, but seeing them come from Centre people made me fizz with glee. Perhaps the Blue Liberation's reign was finally coming to an end. I hoped.

I said nothing in response. There was no point letting the Council see my joy. I bit my cheek and stifled my smile, keeping my head low as I placed piles of food on the table. 'The Tunnel residents of Toulouse have been fed. I thought you might like some food, too.'

'Leftovers? That's all you bring to the Council? Leftovers?' cried Isaac. He clearly did not like being bottom of the list.

'The people needed feeding more than the Council,' I said, as I handed out plates and cutlery.

'Even the Rafters have been fed before us?'

'Leave it out, Isaac,' Giao said, his mouth already full. 'The miners need calories.'

When they all had platefuls in front of them, I turned to the video message. After a few minutes of footage from the biodome, the camera panned round to Greg's massive face.

'You see what we are dealing with here? We need the funds to build ourselves a new biodome, a better one, more fitting for the most important people here. Away from these scoundrels. All that bollocks about the destruction of the Raft, what happened when we changed currency, even stuff about the Monets' carbon trading. It's no one's business what the Select and Centre Elite get up to. That was private information. Whoever leaked it is going to be sorry, I promise you that. If you think you can act like a bunch of smug little bastards, you've got another thing coming. Look behind me. See? Behind me are all my friends, the entire Blue Liberation and their most loyal supporters. We've not been able to leave over fears for our safety. We've been stuck here for hours.'

The camera showed a group of Centre Elite, many I recognised from the Raft, the Prime Minister, the Minister of Impartiality included. They were huddled in a large room, looking pathetically enraged and sorry for themselves, still with their chins held high.

'Nothing leaked was untrue, was it?' Harvey asked.

'That's not really the point,' Giao said.

'They should just call an election. That's all that's being demanded.'

'And what about the Select?' asked Isaac. 'Our excellencies are not *elected*. They are *selected*. Chosen by some higher power, fate, destiny, genetics. They should not be subjected to something so common and trivial as an election.'

'Why not?' I asked.

'Be quiet, little sister.'

'If they did a good job, they'd be well loved and would win an election.' The argument was so evidently sensible to me, it felt like I was explaining to Ethan why he should wash his hands.

'Elections are a farce, and you know it,' Isaac said, waving me away. 'Good candidates don't win, slogans do.'

'Yet you base your own campaign on such a tactic.'

'I said be quiet. Leave your food and go back to your lab like a good little rat.'

Rat! He was calling me filth!

'Dad,' Clementine said, her plate now holding only crumbs. 'This has gone far enough. Don't you think Sav and Harvey have a point? I mean, you hate the Blue Liberation, everyone does. The Select made their alliances, it was their choice. An election seems like the fairest way forward.'

Lady Monet was in front of the camera now. She looked tired, her normally sleek hair sticking out in all directions, her perfect complexion paler. 'We've been trying to access funds all day. We're being blocked. What the hell is going on down there?'

Clementine answered. 'The codes have been changed. They don't have access,' she said, her lips curling up into a smile, arms folded across her chest.

'Clem!' Isaac almost choked on his IsoJuice.

'I'm sorry, dad. I had to. This is all so wrong. The Select took billions with them, the Centre trillions. If they can't make that much money work for them, I don't see why we should give them more.'

To hear my family, my niece, speak up for my cause made my heart sing. She was still wearing her altered clothing with padded shoulders and holding her chin high, but with her on my side, I felt less alone. Sara was sitting next to her, quiet, smiling.

Greg came on the screen again. I had synthesised an old vegetable once, a beetroot. It never went into production because it was disgusting. His face looked just like it. 'I read that email you sent to the Select, saying how we had enough money. You idiots! It's a matter of fucking perspective. It was easy being rich when we were surrounded by poor scum, now it's only rich people, the balance is off. We need more to correct it, don't you see that?'

'Now Greg, calm down. That's not entirely true.' Lady Monet stroked his arm, which did little to quell his rage. She seemed overly familiar with him. Were they an item? I shuddered at the thought, her pinned underneath him while he heaved and grunted.

'My son's wedding will not be a fucking shambles,' Greg ranted. 'The first Select–Elite marriage is going to go down in history as the biggest party in the fucking solar system, got that? Stupid earthling scum. Give the Select the money they are owed. They deserve every penny you fools are hoarding. We should go back and live on earth. Let's go be lords of the Tunnels. I'd be like a fucking god to those worms. A fucking god!'

Lady Monet held her hands to her chest. 'He's rather ineloquent, but really it might come to that. If we are not treated nobly here, returning to the Tunnels might be the best option for us.'

'My son's wedding will be paid for, you cheap scum! The new biodome will be paid for. Do you hear me down there? Fucking earthlings. It's that idiot of a food scientist Selbourne behind this, isn't it? I know it is! Her kid's research information was incomplete this month. She's holding out on her end of the deal. You hear me, those who didn't know? That kid of hers is nothing more than a science experiment. And now she's having some hissy fit because she hates the thought that men can exist just for pleasure. Fucking dyke. We are *men*. Procreation is women's work. Let the stupid women deal with the brats. We exist for pleasure. You hear me? Fucking pleasure!'

Greg continued his bombardment of expletives as Clementine and Sara stifled laughs, delighting in the man's panic.

'What is he talking about?' Giao asked me.

I couldn't open my clenched jaw to speak. I was ready to punch Greg. How dare he mention my son! 'Ethan, my son, was conceived from Grace and I. Part of the "deal" for them not dragging us to Mars was that I update them with his progress. I did his tests this month. He just got distracted for some of them, that's all.'

'Conceived from two mothers?'

'Stem-cell progress. I had no idea it was to take men out of the equation. That's the Centre and their agenda. I mean, who looks at Greg and thinks he's a man built for pleasure?'

Clementine's laugh came with a snort as Sara chuckled next to her.

'More importantly,' Isaac cleared his throat. 'The finances. I suppose it was you who sent that email?' Isaac glared at Clementine, who shrugged in response. 'What a stupid thing to do. Is this because of what I said about that Rafter I saw you with?'

'No, this has nothing to do with Jerome. It was the right thing to do. They've had so much money, they're going to need to make do. I'm head treasurer. I look after the finances of the Tunnels so I made the call. The citizens are largely unhappy with funding the Select, despite dad's campaign. We risk serious unrest by continuing to fund them.'

'Nonsense. The citizens want to fund glory, not grime. Tell me the new codes. Now!'

'Hang on,' Giao now, calm. 'Clementine makes good points.'

'You're happy with Mars descending into anarchy, are you?' Isaac said, as if he were addressing an insolent child.

'It won't come to that,' Giao said. 'They just need to establish a fair system. The Select and Elite being inconvenienced is hardly anarchy.'

'You want a ship returning to earth, I suppose? This is your plan? For the Select to return and to bring Blane with them?'

Giao didn't respond. His lips twitched, but no words came.

'We should prepare the Select's quarters, just in case,' said Isaac.

'They're occupied,' I said, the words coming out of my mouth before I'd had time to think.

Isaac glared at me, eyes cutting through me like lasers. 'Excuse me?'

'Some Rafters live there, and the ones that are soon to arrive also will. There is easily room for sixty. They're to be converted. Seemed like a waste of space. So you see, there is plenty of food, plenty of space, minimal cost. The new arrivals will be no trouble at all.'

'So that's where my keys went,' Clementine said and gave Sara a side-eye.

Isaac's face was almost as red as Greg's. His eyes bulged. 'You had no right! I'm head tunnel planner. That was my call to make.'

Giao cleared his throat. 'If we are to welcome refugees, we should welcome refugees from any country or planet. But of course, they will all be treated as equals.'

Isaac slammed his fist on the table. 'You can't be serious! The Select, living like commoners!'

'That is my view. I imagine it's that of Harvey, too, and the rest of the Council.'

My jaw relaxed, my fists uncurled. Had I heard that right? All refugees are equals? The Select's quarters did not belong to the Select alone? Sounds of agreement came from around the table, though in truth it seemed like many hadn't paid the argument the least bit of attention, as they were too busy gorging themselves on sweet treats.

Isaac stepped away and folded his arms. 'Well, when I win the election, my view will be the one that counts.'

***

I returned to the lab to find it full of food boxes again. We must have made thousands in a day. I called for more help and people got to work loading them onto trailers and taking them to the deeper tunnels. AutoKarts linked Toulouse to other cities, and Bordeaux was about to get its first delivery. Sara cycled over to take stock, stopping in her tracks and almost dropping her e-pad when she saw how many boxes there were.

'This is amazing, Sav, really amazing,' she said as she pulled up a stool to stand on to count the higher boxes. 'Have you got the numbers from earlier?'

I handed her an e-pad with the spreadsheets on. 'I couldn't have done it if it wasn't for Amalyn.'

'I'm sure she'll make it. She must be close now.'

I didn't hear his footsteps approaching over the humming of the lab equipment. He crept up stealthily like some sneaky creature. A snake, they were called. Slithering instead of walking. As soon as he came in Sara ducked behind the pile of boxes.

'Savannah,' he hissed my name.

I groaned and turned around. Peter's usually smug face looked needy, somehow. His conceited grin had fallen. 'You've got a cheek showing your face here. Come to do some more of Isaac's dirty work?'

'No.' his head hung low, so different to his posture in the Council offices. His sneer was gone, too. 'I was wondering if you had located my wife and daughter?'

'I'm very busy, Peter, and I'm not your errand runner. Go through the normal channels.'

'I told you it's delicate. I'd prefer a more subtle introduction.'

'Seriously, Peter. Piss off.' I could see Sara out of the corner of my eye.

'You're the campaign writer? For Isaac?' she asked as she turned to face him. Even side by side, I couldn't believe they were related. There was almost no similarity at all. 'You're the one spreading slander about the Rafters?'

'What do you care? You're clearly not one of them.' He looked her up and down, scrunching his nose like she smelled as bad as he did when he was mining.

'But you're a Rafter.'

'It's a job. Better than mining.'

'Better for you.'

'Are all your staff this preachy?' He asked me, turning away from Sara.

I looked her way, and she gave me a nod. 'Actually Peter,' I said. 'I did find your daughter. This is her. Sara. Previously known as Lily, I believe.'

He turned to look at Sara again, a moment of stillness as he took in her face properly. 'Lily?'

'I remember. Before we left. You were obsessed with blowing up the anchors. I've seen the headlines you wrote. "Deserters Deserve to Drown." That was you, wasn't it?' Her usual soft voice was loud and shaky.

'I wrote that before I knew you and your mother –'

'She died on the bridge. When it blew up ahead of schedule. That was you, too, wasn't it? Your idea. To drum the message home.'

'Julia? She died?' Peter's voice was small.

'And now you're at it again. Working for those who only give a damn about power. Not giving a toss about the regular, hard-working people. Out for yourself, that's all.'

'Lily –'

'You should have stayed on the Raft.'

Peter swallowed and stepped towards Sara as she backed away. 'You have your mother's fiery temper. Her eyes, too. I can see it now.'

'Shame she's not here for a comparison.'

'Your sister, what happened to her – I just didn't want to see that repeated.'

'So you killed thousands and divided a country. Spread hate and lies. Don't tell me it was all because of Daisy. That was just the catalyst. You were power-mad already.'

'Lily, my girl. Please, I'm your father. I love you. I've always loved you.'

'If you loved me, you wouldn't be Isaac's spin doctor, spreading hate like you do. If you loved me, you would care about the people I care about.'

'It's just a job, Lily.'

'It seems you even believe your own lies. Go away, back to the Council offices, back to your computer to make up your lies. I wish you'd never come here.'

He left, dragging his feet, head down.

Sara, her adrenalin drained, broke down, tears flowing freely, sadness buckling her, and she slumped into a chair.

'I'm sorry to talk that way in your lab. That wasn't very professional.' She sounded so quiet again.

'You have nothing to apologise for.'

'He's a monster, isn't he?'

'"Poison" was the term the Raft had for him.'

'Sounds about right. Must have been awful for you working with him, making your words sound like his.'

'Come on, I'll make some MimikTea.'

My laptop was beeping with emails from Marcus and Mabel. Video messages showed their bruised faces, trembling, voices quivering.

'They're accusing us of leaking information, Professor. We didn't say anything, we promise. We never would,' Marcus said with bruised and swollen lips. His blind eye weeping, the skin around blotted black and purple.

'We don't even have access to that information here. They keep us separate from everyone. We don't have access to anything.' Mabel's long neck wilted lower than ever.

I messaged them back to say I believed them, and I'd tell everyone I could that they were innocent. Not that my words would make a difference. They had enough trained staff on Mars now. If there was a ship bound for earth, they should get on it, I said. The Elite didn't want them there in the first place. Surely they'd be happy to be rid of them. They'd come to work in my lab, I supposed. That thought did not fill me with glee, but they were both competent, at least. A massive improvement on Kevin. I'd promised myself that I'd save them once before. I would try to make good on that now.

It didn't take a genius to figure out who had leaked the information. Amalyn, for sure. She had access to Archie's computer, she'd said. I smiled. Of course, she would have spread the word.

She was always fighting for truth, for justice, with an integrity so rare. I wondered where she was. It felt like forever since I'd heard from her. I hoped she didn't have far left to go.

Chapter 33

When the sun rose, we kept going. It was blinding as it came up over the horizon; the heat hitting us instantly. My sunglasses weren't enough, even with a blanket over my head. I felt the rays scorch every bit of me. I adjusted the papoose and tied Reya to my back instead, to keep her in my shade. Glin and Danny both helped to secure her, but having her out of my sight made me prickle with nerves. Was her head supported? Could she breathe? But the sun was so fierce, I had no choice. They said they'd walk behind and watch, but no one could look at anything but the ground with the sun up ahead, blinding us.

Every movement of the scarves over my skin felt like a rash on a bruise. The dust moved endlessly underneath my feet, making it look like I was walking on water. The pain still ricocheted through my body with every step. Every inch of me throbbed, the blood in my veins burning. People put painkillers in my mouth. I swallowed water contaminated with sand, gritty like wet dust. I coughed. Reya cried.

I looked at the crowd. There were too many to count. Was everyone with us? Had anyone been keeping track? Danny had his arm around June. She looked like she was asleep. With every step, she groaned a little. Glin and Shaif kept their eyes on the ground, like shells of people, really. Cora was on Obey's back, one hand supporting her legs, the other dragging Tilly. How he was still so strong I couldn't fathom. Tilly sounded like she was crying, but no tears came. Even Jacob looked as though he was struggling, a slight limp, a grimace on his face, shoulders low as he tugged me forwards. How was I still walking? Reya tapped at my back to remind me: I was walking for her.

There were no landmarks ahead, and we hadn't seen any for a long time. Yet across the desert I saw images of people waving, of buildings, green plants that looked like trees, ripples of water, not like the sea but inviting, cooling. Distorting the monstrous world ahead into something better. Anything would be better. I laughed, then cried. Dry tears and stinging eyes.

The inferno went on for infinity. People stretched out blankets for shade, taking it in turns to be at the front. Such coordination despite their exhaustion was incomprehensible. Had they discussed such tactics? I didn't know.

I saw false shade in imaginary shadows, and my pain dissipated. I felt light, like I was floating away. My feet were gone, I was drifting, like the Raft. Then the heaviness hit me again, and I sunk to my knees.

Those hands again, picking me up. Voices telling me we were almost there. I was on all fours in the sand. I thought I felt Reya grabbing me, the little fighter thumping me, telling me to keep going.

'Please,' I held an arm, I didn't know whose. 'Promise me you'll get Reya there. Someone has to get her to safety.'

I was lifted up, all three tons of me hoisted up and off the ground. 'We'll get you both there,' someone said.

False promises were what we were used to. Us Perimeter. My promise of a better land was like the propaganda they'd heard again and again. *Everyone is safe now.* I laughed at the thought. They couldn't hate me for it, surely? Sav's book played in my head, the poison, the lies. We didn't get our hopes up. We were Perimeter after all. I saw her face ahead of me, smiling, scowling, laughing, tutting. Her hair looked a mess, it always looked a mess. The warping air made it look like she had a cup of MimikTea close by. I reached for her and found only emptiness.

As the temperature escalated over the next hour, we faltered, all of us. Our pace slowed. It was like walking through an oven. My lungs shrivelled, desiccated. The breathing all round me was noisy. Those supporting arms began to buckle, the weight of my body too much for them. I tried to walk straighter, to be less of a burden. The pain from my wound and fever took my mind out of my body, then the pain from the sun snapped me back.

I listened for Reya's grizzles. The sun was high, too high for me to shade her. Her grizzles were quieter, her little kicks softer.

Not long, little one. Hang in there.

When the sun reached its highest point, we paused, made a shelter with blankets, and took stock. Their faces were scorched, burned, red streaked with grey. In their eyes, I saw death.

We sipped some water, then counted what was left. A litre each.

'Six kilometres to go,' Jacob said. 'So close.'

'Take mine,' Vern said and handed me a bottle. 'I won't need any more. For the baby. Keep her cool.'

'No chance, Vern,' I said, my voice sounding less determined than I intended it to be. 'We all need our share.'

'Please. I'm so old. All my dreams have already come true.'

'Don't talk like that. Drink now, please.'

He shook his head, his frail arm pushing me away, yet I couldn't match even his strength. We saved his share, Jacob put it back in a bag. 'Say when you want it, Vern.'

Vern waved Jacob away and shook his head. He was smiling still.

We took the shade down after an hour's rest and kept walking. Minutes later, Vern collapsed. We went to him as quickly as we could. I fell to my knees as others opened bottles, ready to pour. Vern used the last of his strength to push us away and roll on to his front. Refusing even a drop. By the time we could roll him over, the life had left him. His face frozen in its smile.

'No.' Someone gasped. Chrissy, I think.

We stood around silently, disbelieving, breaths stuttering from the tears that wouldn't come.

'He was going to see the library,' I said. 'We're so close. We wouldn't have made it this far if it wasn't for him.'

'It's all he ever wanted, to walk again on the Mainland,' said Chrissy, kneeling beside him. Her skin was as red as skin could get, as burned as the ground. 'He told me. He died so happy.'

Sand blew over his body, covering him in foreign soil. Immersing him.

Dry cries choked my lungs. Parched sobs came out as coughs. He would have lived if he'd drunk his share. He forwent that for me. For Reya. My fault.

I'd ended another life.

We were all so close to death. The sniffles and sobs from others were quiet, like they were listening for him, expecting to hear his voice. We waited by him, kneeling in the sand, as if we too were awaiting the end. Surely death was coming for us too. A knock on the shoulder maybe, or a hand reaching up from below. Melting into the ground, too exhausted to cry, too hot to move. Vern's lifeless body disappeared under the sand, out of the sun.

'We need to keep going,' Jacob said as he pulled me up. 'We'll mourn later.'

Vern. Bex. Archie. Names that would be remembered. I repeated them over and over. They should be with us, they should have made it.

Vern. Bex. Archie. Vern. Bex. Archie.

After another few minutes, Jacob checked the e-pad. 'Five kilometres to go. Maybe a good time to call?'

Obey rummaged and took out the satellite phone. It was hard to dial. Everything looked hazy, like a cloud had covered us, the numbers blurred, my fingers too weak to press the buttons. Then I heard her.

'Hello? Ams?'

It took me a while to answer. The sound of her voice was all I wanted to hear. 'Sav. We're close. Just five kilometres away. Please, we need water, desperately.' I had no idea if she could understand me. Speaking was like rubbing stones on concrete.

'I'll see you there, Ams. Just keep going. I'll be waiting for you.'

The line went dead. A red light flashed a few times, then went out. The battery had finally gone.

Chapter 34

My heart almost burst when I heard her voice. Five kilometres away. They had made it so far. But she sounded so awful, beyond tired. Was the baby all right? *She must be, she must be.*

Any exhaustion dissipated as my body buzzed with adrenalin, and I ran from the lab, feet chafing in my shitty sandals. I'd had only a few moments of sleep in the last day and a half, but my body sprung to life as if it were well-rested and full of sugar. I had to get to Bordeaux and assemble a rescue team. There must have been someone who could meet them.

I ran past guards who all smiled at me rather than tell me off for wasting calories with their hands hovering over their batons. Some even waved.

'Good afternoon, Professor,' said one as she eyed my hands, her expectation of food clear.

'The other Rafters, the refugees, they're so close now, just a few kilometres away,' I said, panting. 'I need to get to Bordeaux.'

'Bordeaux,' she sucked her teeth and leant back, too casual. Had she not heard me? 'It's a long AutoKart ride to Bordeaux. Couple of hours.'

A couple of hours! How had I not known that? Why had I not been more prepared? I should have left the previous night, days before, even. *They might not have a couple of hours!*

She nodded, slowly. 'I saw some Council members a few minutes ago. Let's go speak to them. Maybe they'll have an idea.'

We grabbed a bike with a trailer and cycled off down the corridor. I looked at my e-pad. Five minutes since she had called. Five more minutes she'd been in the open desert without water. Could the guard not pedal any faster? She was going at a leisurely pace, relaxed, like this was a social ride.

'I must say how much I enjoyed your food.' She took one hand off the handlebars to speak to me and slowed down as she turned around.

'Yeah, thanks.' *Hurry up!*

'Really great stuff. Is that sort of food going to be available every day now? That IcyCrema was to die for.'

'Yes, thanks, and I'm very worried about the Rafters. Could you possibly pedal any faster? I don't know how much longer Amalyn can hold on for.'

'Amalyn? I know that name. Is that the Rafter that helped you fix the food factory?'

'Yes. That's her. She sounds desperate. They need water. They're so close.'

'Well, why didn't you say?' She faced forward again, lifted herself up out of the saddle and heaved her slight bodyweight into each pedal stroke, propelling us forward. 'Anything to save Amalyn. After all she's done for us.'

I crossed my fingers and allowed the slightest bit of hope to wash over me as the orange tunnels blurred past us. It was only a minute before we found Clementine and Jerome, arm in arm. Walking the opposite way were Harvey and his campaign staff. The guard screeched her bike to a halt in the middle of them, the metal-on-metal grind making my teeth itch.

'Five kilometres, they're just five kilometres away, and need water, desperately!'

'Seriously?' said Jerome. 'Amalyn's made it all the way here?' He held his tattooed arm to his chest.

'She's not here yet, and they need help. Please, what can we do?' I looked at my e-pad. Seven minutes now.

Harvey rubbed his face as he thought. Charlie and a couple of other guards were within earshot and came over.

'It's nearly two hours to Bordeaux via the AutoKarts,' said Harvey, shaking his head. 'They'll need help sooner than that. I have friends in Bordeaux. Charlie, call the Bordeaux guards. The rest of you get ready to handle any unrest here at the news.'

'I'll go to Bordeaux,' said Jerome. 'I want to help. I'm sure some other miners will also volunteer for a rescue party.'

'It's too far from here, you'll be no help,' said Harvey. 'The best thing you can do is keep mining, keep showing all of Toulouse how valuable Rafters are. Savannah.' He looked straight at me. 'We'll get her. I promise.'

A little warm bubble formed inside me at the sound of an assured promise, of people willing to help. They scattered in all directions, grabbing bikes and trailers, and disappearing down the Tunnels before I even had a moment to thank them. I was left alone, useless, standing in the dim light, counting the seconds.

'Come on!' A voice came from behind me. It was Clementine, with a trailer. 'Jump in.'

I climbed up, and she pedalled away. I cursed every kilo of me, my weight making the journey slower. Why hadn't I learned to ride a bike? That would have been quicker than sitting in a trailer. At least I'd be doing something, pushing myself forward instead of relying on someone else. I felt sick; bile burning the back of my throat. However much I swallowed, lumps tried to inch their way upwards. It was all out of my control. I was no help, totally inept. It's not like I even knew anyone in Bordeaux. I had no contact to nag or persuade. It was too far away to get there quickly enough.

I checked my e-pad again. Ten minutes. I was at the mercy of a country that largely didn't want her here, anyway. I tapped my foot. Memories of that Autocar ride to the edge with Archie came to my mind. His last moments, panic, fear. I couldn't let him down again. Yet I had no power to assist and make good with any rescue.

But they'd help, they had to help.

Bordeaux had tasted Raft food for the first time. With satisfied stomachs, surely they'd see the benefit of the Rafters. Giao and Isaac would probably resist any rescue, but they had no jurisdiction over another city. Then again, nor did Harvey.

Clementine pedalled as fast as she could while I sat uselessly in the back, hands tapping my legs like old-world drums, watching the minutes tick away.

'I'll get word to the rest of the Council and tell Grace where you are. She's in the Select quarters still, I assume?' she said as she wiped moisture from the back of her neck.

'She is.' My face flushed as I remembered mine and Sara's theft. 'And sorry about the key.'

Clem shook her head. 'It's fine, really. I'm glad she's okay.'

She pedalled, standing up for a while, leaning from side to side to gain momentum. I wanted to help, to jump out and push, to pedal too, anything to get us there faster. But all I could do was sit. Useless.

'I'm just sorry about dad,' she said. 'You know, since mum died, he's been determined to climb to the top. To be in power, for the protection that brings. For me, I assume. I've been trying to explain things to him, but I think he's lost his way.'

She spoke in short bursts between panting breaths. I could hardly hear her over the grinding sound of the bike.

'The AutoKart entrance to the deeper tunnels is a little way away,' she said. 'I'll get you there as quickly as I can.'

While Clementine pedalled, her smock soaked with sweat, I bit my lip, twiddled my fingers, checked the time.

'Harvey and Charlie are right,' she said. 'There are a lot more sympathisers in Bordeaux, more than Toulouse. Now they're so close, a rescue crew won't be an issue. Check the news site, but for Bordeaux instead of Toulouse, see what they're saying.'

I took out my e-pad and tapped on the news screen, scrolling past the election gossip and slanderous slogans to find the Bordeaux icon. As soon as the news screen came up, a fresh headline lit up the page. *Rafter heroes have made it to Bordeaux! Rescue team on their way!*

I shouted out the headline to Clementine, who gave a cheer and punched the air. 'Rafter heroes are here!' She shouted. 'Rafter heroes are here!'

Chapter 35

Jacob heaved me forwards. We'd mourn later, he said, his voice now as gruff as Vern's. We had no time to grieve. I said their names again in my mind, one with each footstep.

Bex. Vern. Archie. Bex. Vern. Archie.

With every step, my limbs grew denser. I got heavier, hotter, swollen, like gravity had selected only me to act on. Arms supported me, lifting me when all I could do was fall. I was weighing them down.

'Someone take Reya and go on without me. I'll catch up.' My voice grated, incoherent. A pathetic plea.

No one did as I asked. Arms switched with other arms, new people dragging me, firm fingers digging into my broken skin.

'Please, don't let me weigh you down. Take Reya and go.'

'No chance,' someone said. 'We're not leaving you. We've got you.'

They hauled me on when my legs no longer worked at all, the tops of my feet scraping against the rough sand. They shifted my weight among them, my arms slippery, their fingers weakening.

Bex. Vern. Archie. Don't add more to the list, please. No more.

'Please, take the baby. She has to make it.' Don't die for me, no one else. Please.

A moment later, we all stopped, resting once more in the desert. So close, but so far. I couldn't sit, it hurt too much. Instead, I lay on my front on the charred sand, my upper body in the dappled shade of the blankets, my legs in the sun, exposed, burning. I didn't care. It was pain on pain.

'Just a minute to rest,' I said.

'As long as you need,' said one of them.

I looked at them, impressions of faces, flushed, blurry. An outline, some shadows and indentations, their features like soup.

'Maybe we should rest till dark,' one face said.

'No, we're so close.' Had they heard me? I couldn't tell.

Shards of light came through the blankets, each one like a hot knife. I wiped my brow. My hand came away sodden with sweat. Or maybe blood. I wasn't sure. My eyes smarted, gritty and singed.

'Please go, take her,' I knelt, wobbling so much it took a while, and pulled Reya round to my front. The scarves dragged across my skin like they were ripping right through to my bones. I tried to pass someone Reya. She was crying now, soft cries, not the great lungfuls I was used to hearing. Maybe my ears weren't working, and she was actually really loud. I hoped so.

I held her away and looked at her, looked at my baby. My scalded eyes distorted everything. The world was mush. She didn't look like my baby. It was a rock, a potato, a cushion. I laughed a raspy laugh.

What the fuck are we doing?

'Come on,' a voice said. 'Mind over matter.'

My raspy laugh sounded again. How did mind over matter work when my mind was fried?

My groans weren't the only ones. June, I think, her pitiful cries into Danny's shoulder. Cora, where was Cora? I hadn't seen her in ages. I tried to call her name but only a cough came out.

Reya was tied to my front now. I didn't do that. Someone else did. They tied the scarves roughly as Reya's cries protested, muffled only slightly by the thin blanket covering her.

They hoisted me up, strong hands under soggy armpits. Fingers digging into my swollen limbs, I thought I might burst, pop like a balloon. My feet struggled to find the ground. The wind whipped up, but there was no sound. All I could hear were my thoughts and the whispers telling me to give up, to sit down and not move again. Telling me there was an easier path. That the struggle was over.

We drank the last drops of water. Our arms were empty now, lighter yet heavier than ever. Wind kicked up sand, but I barely noticed. My vision clouded. The world looked as grey as the

Raft. However hot it was, cool arms reached for me, tempting me. The chilling embrace of the man I loved was only a rest away.

Amalyn, I love you, Amalyn.

I'm here, Archie, I'm so close to you now.

In my blindness, I saw buildings that weren't there. Felt the sea lick my ankles. The sun was high, yet the bright sky was turning dark, the blue misting over. In the heat, I felt the cold reach of death. I had no desire to resist.

Before the world went completely black, voices grew louder. Unfamiliar. Everything was unfamiliar. New arms grabbed me, cooler, stronger, liquid pouring over me.

'We've got you,' the voices said, clear as day. 'Drink. We'll get you home.'

Chapter 36

Clementine dropped me at a rickety cage lift that led to the deeper tunnels. With a 'Good luck, give Amalyn my best,' she rode off to go and speak to Grace and the Council. The lift delivered me to the dimly lit corridors. There were no engraved walls that deep, just chilly, damp air and a thin layer of dust. No echoes from the rest of the Tunnels either. Just my footsteps flapping until I arrived at the AutoKarts, boxy things with high sides and just a loose stool for a seat. They were meant for supplies rather than people, so no thought had been given to comfort. They ran on tracks, unimpeded by traffic and pedestrians. The coolness in the deeper tunnels meant that the breeze coming over the top was relentless and chilled me to my bones. I hunkered down and checked the time again. Thirty-eight minutes now.

The AutoKarts were fast, but the journey was still frustratingly long. I squeezed my eyes shut, willing with everything I had that she was okay, that the baby was okay, that they'd arrive safely, the rescue team would find them in time. I couldn't lose her again, not now, not after she'd made it so far.

Don't give up, Amalyn!

I reminisced about fun times in the lab, her achievements with the injectable, going out for drinks, when she was entertaining Ethan while Archie fitted the Interactive Cupboard, her Golden Fifty friends, when we first came to the Tunnels, everything I knew about her. She was alive and well in my mind. Her never-ending care for everyone but herself, her bad-ass attitude, her longing for adventure. If anyone could survive, Amalyn could.

It was about two hours of near darkness in the deeper tunnels before I arrived at the city. I didn't know where I was going, but found a cage lift that took me to the level above. It was even less comfortable than the AutoKart. Its poorly constructed floor dug in through my sandals and it stuttered all the way up. I held my breath as I imagined getting stuck mid-way, but it made it. Above, in the habitation Tunnels, it all looked the same as Toulouse in aesthetics, but the layout was different. Tunnels wound round different chambers that had different numbers of entrances and fewer mezzanine floors. The same tree and eye design was everywhere, the same smell from the dining chambers of minced filth, fooling me into thinking I knew where I was going. I grabbed people's attention and asked where the quarantine cells were, but no one knew, and many didn't speak English. All Subs, from what I could tell. The same long physique as those in Toulouse, but no yellow bands dangling from their wrists. Eventually I found Council guards who agreed to cycle me there.

'You're the food scientist,' they said. 'You sent us all that amazing food.'

'Yes, that was me, please, my friend –'

'Sure, we can help. Anything for you.'

It was another long ride. I looked at my e-pad. Three hours since Amalyn had called, but no update on the news site yet. The headline was the same. She must have arrived. They must have found her. She must have had water, food, rest. The baby would be sleeping, comfortable in the Tunnels. I imagined her surrounded by Golden Fifty, tears of joy, laughing and rejoicing as Reya slept in a cot.

They must be here by now, they must!

I refreshed the page but my battery died. *Microbes!* I called out to the guard, who was pedalling too slowly. Why wasn't he going faster? I asked if he'd had any updates, but he hadn't. 'Thanks for the food though. It was amazing,' he said nonchalantly, leaning back in the saddle and having a stretch. 'Is that going to be the norm now? Food like that?'

'Yes, as long as my friend is okay!'

Still, we weren't there. I squeezed my hands together as if in prayer. I tried to count my breaths, but it just reminded me of the passing seconds, each one telling me that I didn't know if she was okay, if the rescue team had found them.

She must be here by now, she must!

We arrived at a red 'do not pass' warning plastered over the walls leading to the quarantine cells and the guard braked, jolting me forwards.

'This is as far as I go,' he said. 'Good luck.'

I shouted a 'thank you' over my shoulder as I alighted and ran past the signs until I came to a wall with a single small window. A woman in a white coat stood outside on a phone, giving instructions to someone on the other side of the window. Supplies were being passed in via a small hatch near the ground. I grabbed the woman's shoulder.

'Excuse me, please, my friend. How is she? Amalyn? The baby?'

She held her hand up to silence me and continued her phone conversation for another frustrating minute. 'Yes, I see. Keep her on painkillers ... I'll get more bandages ... What's her temperature? IV fluids for all of them ... I'll find more supplies.'

She eventually hung up. 'The baby is alive. We need to run some more tests to make sure she's healthy, given what the pregnancy was like.'

Relief swept over me. My knees almost gave way, tears coming as I caught my breath. 'And my friend, her mother? Amalyn.'

The woman's eyes went to the floor. She didn't answer for a moment. A painful pause came and went as my heart dropped to my stomach.

'It sounds like she has an infection from an old-world bacteria called Strep B,' she said. 'We have given her all the treatment we have. It'll keep the infection at bay for a while. We have controlled her fever and given her painkillers, so she is comfortable. That's all we can do.'

'Okay, so she's sick. But she'll be better soon? She can fight this.'

'I'm sorry, I'm not being clear. The infection is serious. She has sepsis. She won't survive.'

I stumbled back. No! 'I'm sorry, I don't understand.' She was talking too much, her words a blur, clogging my ears. I hadn't heard right. Surely I hadn't heard right. 'She's alive, though. She made it?'

'She's comfortable and mostly lucid at the moment. But there's nothing we can do. I really am very sorry. You can go in, if you don't mind being quarantined. If you want to say goodbye.'

'Say goodbye? But she made it here. She made it all the way here!'

'I'm so sorry. It's a wonder she made it this far. A miracle she saved her baby and the others. She's an inspiration.'

I leant against the wall, the room spinning. It couldn't be. She'd made it so far. She couldn't be dying now. How was that possible? I'd lost her once, I couldn't lose her again. The baby, what about the baby? My breathing was shallow. Oxygen couldn't find its way in. I held my chest. 'You must be wrong. There must be something you can do.'

The doctor put her hand on my shoulder and shook her head. 'Is there anyone I can call?'

Her words seemed so far away. Her voice was coming through fog. My friend was here, and she was dying.

I swallowed back tears. 'Lydia and Dennis Blake, from Toulouse. Her parents.'

'I'll get a message to them.'

'How long? How long before ...'

'A day, maybe.'

A day?

'She's coherent at the moment. She's on a lot of painkillers. Best make the most of this time. She may only be able to talk for a few hours.'

My lungs managed to find some air. I stood straighter. Now was not the time for despair. I had a few hours with my friend. That was all. Just a few hours.

I wiped my eyes, and I went in.

Chapter 37

'Ams?'

She lay on the bed, hair messier than ever, encrusted with sand and black sludge like the sea, all strewn across her blotchy face, burned yet pale. She opened her eyes slowly.

'Sav?'

I ran to her, hugged her like I'd never hugged anyone before. 'Oh my god, Ams, you made it here, I can't believe it. Your parents are on their way. We've all been so worried.'

She coughed through sobs. 'I'm so sorry.'

'What for?'

'It's my fault he died. I shouldn't have let him die. I should have run faster. We should have run when he pulled me over. It's my fault. All my fault.' Her words came out in a torrent, a river of despair, useless, pent-up guilt that she didn't need to hold on to.

'Stop it! You're not to blame for anything. I should have waited. I should have been there to get you to safety.'

She held my hands with all the strength she had, red eyes wet with tears, burned face mottled with sadness. She looked so different to the Amalyn I remembered. A shell, really. Like she'd surrendered already.

'I was under the rubble for days. He kept telling me to go, to save myself. He threw himself under it to save me. I didn't want to leave him. He died thinking I'd die, too. I'm so sorry. I should have told him I'd try. I should have given him that much hope. It's my fault he died.'

I stroked her hair and tried to soothe her. 'Shh. Nothing is your fault. He loved you so much.' My tears were falling freely. Speaking in the past tense about my dearest friend still ripped my insides into pieces. *Loved* instead of love. How could it be that such emotion could ever be a thing of the past?

She looked up at me, and her cracked lips smiled. There was Amalyn, hiding beneath the sunburn and windburn and infection. That smile was all her.

'I know you thought we were dead, so don't feel bad. I read your book.'

'Book?'

'*The Poison Maker*. I found it in your apartment.'

'Oh ...'

'And don't apologise for anything. You did what you had to do to save your family. I might not have understood that once. But now I do.'

It was only then that I noticed the cot by the bed. There she was, a little sleeping baby, cleaned up and brand new. I gasped when I saw her. 'Look at her! Oh Ams, she's just gorgeous.'

'She looks like him, doesn't she?'

I walked over, and all I saw was Archie. His ears, his mouth. Amalyn's eyes, for sure, but so much of my dear friend. 'She really does.' As she slept, she made little sucking noises. 'The doctor says she's okay?'

'A bit small. She said they need to do some tests. But she's here. She's alive. Such a miracle.'

'You did it, Ams. You got her here. You got everyone here. What a mum! You're such a bad-ass.'

She laughed a weak laugh before her face fell. 'Some didn't make it, and there are still people on the Raft.'

'We'll send food. We'll do what we can. You sent that information to Mars, didn't you?'

She nodded.

'The fallout is huge. The Blue Libs are falling apart.'

Her cracked lips stretched to make her smile wider. 'Fuck them,' she said with a cough. 'You'll never guess who's here! No, I'm not telling you, wait till you see.'

Reya gave a little cry, and I rubbed her tummy until she fell asleep again.

'You'll look after her for me?' Amalyn said, her voice stern now, using all the strength she had. 'Raise her with your family. Ethan will love having a little sister, I'm sure. My parents will be too old now, I can't ask them. You and Grace are such wonderful parents.'

Her words knocked the wind out of me. 'Don't say such things. You're going to raise her yourself.'

She grabbed my hands, and her hazy eyes bore into mine. 'I've read your book, so please, no more lies. I know I don't deserve reassurances. I gave Archie none. But please tell me you'll look after my daughter.'

My whole body shook with the weight of her words, my legs weakened and I knelt next to her, stroked her cheek, kissed her hands. Her voice was strong where mine was weak, her body accepting where I was unable to.

This can't be happening. I can't be losing her again.

'It's okay, Sav. I got her here. That's all I wanted. Please tell me you'll look after her.'

I squeezed her hands. 'I will. She'll know nothing but love. I promise.'

She smiled and looked over at the cot. 'Are you sure? Because I think she's going to be a troublemaker.'

I laughed through my tears. 'Oh Ams, I don't doubt it for a second.'

We laughed like we used to. Amalyn's honesty making my sadness give way to joy.

'Her middle name is Bex. Reya Bex Reynolds. I'd like her to see the room with all the books. What is it called again?'

'Library.'

'And all the paintings?'

'Gallery.'

'I want her to experience all the things we couldn't. Have all the things we were denied.'

I swallowed. 'I promise, Ams, I'll make sure she has it all.'

'Is it as wonderful here as I remember? All the friendly people, so welcoming and kind.'

'Exactly as you remember,' I said. One more lie, that was all.

She drifted off then and dozed for a while until a doctor came in and gave her some more painkillers, and then Lydia and Dennis arrived. Wails and cries filled the room as they reached for their daughter, believing yet disbelieving. Happiness fighting with sadness. I stepped out to give them some space and sat on the floor near the door. Waves of emotion hit me. I couldn't take it in. She couldn't be dying. She was here, alive, talking. I quizzed the doctor, who confirmed what I'd already been told. The medicine was keeping her comfortable, but she was riddled with infection. There was nothing more they could do.

I made myself into a small ball, hugging my knees, feeling so alone. How could I say goodbye? How could she die after making it all the way here? It wasn't fair. She'd fought so hard. I couldn't catch my breath. The usually cool tunnels were suffocating. I got up and paced in a circle, trying to find the sweet spot between activity and exhaustion. A dreamlike state where my friend was well, where she was going to battle through. She hadn't given up yet. There must be some hope.

I must have fallen asleep and after a few hours, Dennis came to get me. He'd aged a decade since I'd left the room, his face sunken, his eyes dark and raw. 'Come and join us. We think it won't be long now.'

Amalyn looked worse than before. Her body clammy, swollen, skin turning black. One glance and I knew the doctors hadn't been mistaken. Death had her in his grasp. She was slipping away.

I picked up Reya, sat at Amalyn's bedside, placing Amalyn's hands on the baby, her rough hand on Reya's soft cheek. Showing her what she'd achieved, that Reya was alive. That a piece of her and Archie will go on. The baby didn't stir. She stared up at her mum with wide, curious eyes, leaning in to Amalyn's touch. The only hands she'd ever known.

We sat vigil at Amalyn's bedside, stroking her hair, holding her hands. We said little, except to remind her we were there, she wasn't alone, that Reya would be fine and that she didn't have to suffer anymore. That she was a hero and had saved so many people. No use in telling her to fight now. Surrender was all she had left to do.

As the fever took over, her mind drifted in delusion. We weren't there anymore. She wasn't in the Tunnels anymore. All she saw was him.

'Archie,' she gasped, smiling. And with her final breath, she called for him again. 'Archie.'

Chapter 38

After they took Amalyn's body away, the room was the coldest I'd known. I was sure even a walk in the desert couldn't thaw my bones. We shivered in the vacuum. Such a small space, yet we were lost.

I spent quarantine tending to Reya. She cried for her mum, for the scent and voice that she missed, for all that was familiar to her. As I fed her, she sensed my anguish. My tears were contagious, mirrored in misery. Lydia and Dennis doted on their granddaughter, then cried for their loss. Grief reignited, no less painful the second time round. We were all broken.

We didn't leave that room, the four of us. We shared stories about Amalyn and Archie, remembered their voices, their laughs, their mannerisms. Organising practical things like childcare distracted us from the sadness for a few minutes. They were too frail to have Reya full time, but they would move in close to us. Reya would see her grandparents every day.

The doctor came and tested Reya daily. Listening to her heart, checking her eyes, weighing her. She was a little on the small side, she said. But by some miracle, she was healthy.

Grief hit us like the thick waves of the sea. When we spoke of mundane things, we held it together for a while. Then we would start choking, drowning in sorrow like there was no way out. When we tended to Reya, we were loving, attentive. Our love for her gave us strength. Where before I saw so much of Archie in her, now all I saw was Amalyn.

After a week she started settling easier, looking at us like she knew us, the longing for her mother abated. I kept telling her about Amalyn and Archie. I said their names, told her their stories. She would grow up knowing all about her wonderful parents.

I gave little thought to the Tunnels over those couple of weeks. The world kept spinning; the sun rose and set, but anything outside that room didn't occur to me. I heard nothing about campaigns or Mars or the lab. All that existed was that room.

When our quarantine was up, we had blood tests and the doctor told us we were free to leave. The forty-nine other Rafters were all healthy, too. There had been heatstroke, dehydration, sunburn, other minor ailments, but they were fine and recovered. Amalyn had saved them all. My chest swelled with pride for my friend. When I looked at Lydia and Dennis, I could see they felt the same. Amalyn's legacy was something to behold. She had rescued so many people.

I stepped out into the corridor, expectant faces looking at Reya, not recognising me.

'Amalyn?' One man said.

I shook my head, and their faces fell, before they all held their forearms to their hearts.

'She saved us all,' a woman said, thin, pale, with a small voice. 'She gave us a chance at life.'

I wondered then what sort of life they could expect.

We walked down the corridor, all of them smiling in turn at Reya, then a voice I never imagined hearing again said my name.

'Professor?' She was still so shrill.

I gasped. Surely not? I couldn't believe it. 'Penny?'

Her frizz was scraped back and her makeup had gone, and without it she looked younger, fresher, though she had lost some teeth. 'How wonderful to see you. This must be hard for you. Amalyn was a dear girl. If you need someone to talk to, I'm here to help.'

'Thanks, Penny. I'm glad you made it.' I meant it.

I looked around and all of them were holding hands. Nervous smiles, about to take their first steps into an unknown civilisation. The Golden Fifty, living their dreams. A little girl was among them, maybe about Ethan's age. She stared at Reya. 'She looks bigger,' she said.

I smiled back and bent down so she could see her. 'Is Amalyn with Bex and my mummy now?'

'She is, sweetie. What's your name?'

'Cora.'

'Well, I suspect you'll be in my little boy's class at school. He'll be excited to meet you.'

She grinned a wide grin, eyes filled with excitement. I'd be sure to tell Ethan to look after her.

The doors to the quarantine cells opened, and waiting outside was a crowd of people. At the front were Grace and Ethan, who ran to me.

'Mummy! I missed you!'

'I missed you too, big man.' I knelt down to hug him. He had meat on his bones. 'You've grown!'

'Sav,' Grace knelt beside me, kissed me. 'And I missed you too.' She smiled at me and her arm went around me. There was warmth in her embrace. Then she looked at the baby.

'Why have you got a baby, mummy?' Ethan's eyes were huge when he saw her.

'Ethan, this is your little sister, Reya.'

He gasped, his tender hand reaching out to touch her. 'She's so tiny!'

I looked at Grace, who had her hands to her mouth, dark eyes glistening with tears.

'Is this going to be okay?' I asked. It was a pointless question.

She held her arms out to take her. Cradling her, holding her close, tears tumbling down her cheeks, face alive with love. 'Hey, baby Reya. Welcome home.'

Lydia and Dennis were behind me, and I introduced them. 'Reya's grandparents,' I said, and Ethan's face lit up even more.

'Can you be my Granny, too? I don't have one anymore.'

Lydia smiled and stroked his head. 'I don't see why not,' she said, and gave him a hug.

'Is that where you've been, mum?' he asked me – 'mum,' not 'mummy' anymore. 'Is there a baby-making lab in there?'

'No,' I laughed.

'Well, where do babies come from then?'

Grace and I both smiled. 'Love, big man. They come from love.'

The rescuers from Bordeaux had been quarantining too, and they led us to the AutoKarts. A cage lift station was right by the quarantine cells that took us to the deeper tunnels. No trip through Bordeaux first. The refugees huddled together, linking arms, those that could. One woman had a bandaged arm and leant against a man next to her.

'Come on, June, let me help you,' the man said.

'We've come all this way for a bloody dungeon.'

I laughed to myself. *Just wait.*

The two hours from Bordeaux were spent mostly in silence, sitting uncomfortably, shielding under blankets that Grace and others had brought with them. The dimness of the deeper tunnels did nothing to reassure the refugees that they had come to a safe place. I looked around at their scared faces, cold, anxious. I snuggled into Grace, who could not take her eyes off the baby.

A few at a time, we got into the rickety lift that took us up to the levels above. They still all looked crestfallen, like they'd arrived at some dingy cave. At the top of the lift, bikes and trailers were waiting, dozens of them offering lifts to all the refugees. They got in, wobbling into the seats, still holding on to one another. As we cycled through the corridors to the first chamber, I saw the look of awe spread across their faces.

'Bugger me,' the woman with the bandaged arm said. 'The junkie was right.'

'Well, June. Would you look at that?'

More whispers of delighted shock from all of them, Amalyn's name on all of their tongues. She had delivered. She had kept her promise to these people.

'Wait till you see what we've done with the place,' said Grace, and she squeezed my knee. Affectionate and supportive. My Grace.

Welcome Rafters signs were plastered everywhere where campaign slogans had been before. People carrying trays of food were walking around. 'Help yourselves, there's plenty,' they said to anyone they passed. The smell of synth food wafted around the corridors like it was one big home.

We cycled across the mezzanines, not stopping at the chambers, but everywhere was lined with Subs waving, smiling, saying welcome. Tears filled my eyes and warmth filled my heart. I looked at Grace, my eyes asking the question my voice couldn't find.

'With all the food and Amalyn's heroism, everyone is inspired. It's a different world from the one you left.'

I swallowed. 'If only Amalyn were here ...' Little Reya looked at me with the eyes of my friend I missed so much, reminding me that she was with us.

We arrived at the Select's quarters, or what used to be the Select's quarters, anyway. Stepping off the trailer, I could see that the huge door was now a porch that led to a corridor and more doors.

'We've divided it up. There's thirty residences here now,' Sara said from the doorway, greeting all the refugees with smiles and bottles of IsoJuice and cups of MimikTea. 'And the new Tunnel wing is pretty much complete. There's plenty of room.'

We walked in, Grace holding Reya, me holding Ethan's hand. He wanted to run ahead, to push through the crowd, but I held him back. 'Patience, big man.'

'This is our place,' Grace said, as we arrived at a door that had *The Selbournes* engraved on the front in the same swirling font as the old residences.

I opened the door to a beautiful, homey and modest apartment. Three bedrooms, a cosy sitting room, its own bathroom. Ethan's toys littered the floor. It was a fraction of the size of the Select's quarters I'd left her in, and not nearly as grandiose, but it was ample, I thought, and all we needed.

'And this is okay for you?' I asked Grace.

She didn't look my way, but sat on the sofa, Ethan snuggling in next to her, both of them engrossed in the baby. 'It's perfect. All I could ever want in the whole world.'

***

We stayed at home for a couple of days. I was feeling agoraphobic. There was too much noise, too many happy faces, too many 'congratulations.' I needed more time in peace with my pain. And Grace and Ethan had a baby to get to know. Grace's instincts were as impeccable as ever, and I didn't know Ethan could be so quiet, so thoughtful, so tranquil with his excitement. We showed him how to hold Reya, to support her head. He chatted to her, stroked her cheek, sang along with Grace. Being a big brother was all he had ever wanted, we learned. He showed Reya his toys, drew pictures of her, wanted to get involved with every feed and change, even helped tend to her in the night. It killed me, his attentiveness, his nickname for her, ReRe, as if he were still a baby himself.

Grace had made our apartment into a real home, keeping her favourite items from the Select's collection. Silk fabrics and cushions in every corner they could fit. One day, I told her the truth about them.

'You know those materials are made from worm shit,' I said.

'Oh, I know. I've read about it in the library.'

'Really?'

'Yep. And I finally went to the gallery. There are pictures there of so much old-world filth. It was quite pretty once, you know. Seems a shame it's all gone. I figured nothing natural can be all that bad when it looks so lovely.'

She never stopped surprising me.

After a few days, I ventured to work, the lab and factory in full swing. I hadn't been missed at all. Kevin, freed from prison, was piling up boxes. I guess when I spilled the news they had no need to lock him up anymore. With a functioning workplace, he almost looked useful. Sure, the boxes were piled up wrong and the order sheets not filled in, but he was trying, at least.

Walking past the mines, I saw some people digging who I didn't recognise, tattoos adorning their forearms. The latest arrivals being put to work, and gladly, by the looks on their faces. The guards were chatting with them, batons no longer swinging from their belts. Food boxes were strewn across the floor, and there was a smell of contentment rather than blood and sweat. Among them was Peter, pickaxe in hand rather than a pen. His spin-doctor days were over, I hoped. He didn't look my way but carried on labouring, taking his anger out on the rock rather than a computer. In the wall by the mine, someone had etched some words into the stone. *Vern*, *Bex, Obey,* and *Amalyn.* I thought of Reya's middle name, Bex, and wondered who she had been. Amalyn had said some didn't make it. I was sure I'd hear the tales eventually. The words of those who'd made it about the ones who didn't. Amalyn had made it, though. She made it all the way here. That pit in my stomach would never go away.

She made it all the way here. She should be here.

I had ignored TunNet and news sites during my time in quarantine and isolation. I hadn't asked Grace for a catch up, and she was too involved with Reya to think about updating me. As I made my way to the Council offices, I struggled to even remember what day it was. Had the elections happened? Mars? What had happened on Mars?

As I entered the offices, the outcome became obvious. Harvey was sitting at the head table, his staff flanking him. He had won by a landslide. He was leaning back in his chair, hands behind his head, elbows spread wide like he was trying to look bigger, more formidable. I was still unsure if he would make a good leader. Surely no one that wants power is capable of using it wisely. Still, him winning was a better result than Isaac.

Giao and Isaac were nowhere in sight. I walked off down the corridors, not knowing where to go. The Tunnels felt alien to me now. Too peaceful, too accepting. A strangeness in the welcomeness.

I found a seating area and put the kettle on, smiling when I saw the packets of MimikTea lining the shelf. The factory must have started making it. I made a large, strong cup, no longer concerned about rationing it. The smooth maltiness made me warm inside as I remembered cups from a previous life, made by old friends.

The cushions were in disarray, so I organised them and tried to relax, to feel at home. The echoes of the Tunnels were absent. I remembered this seating area, the auditory dead zone, where life truly stood still. I reached for an e-pad that was on the counter and loaded up the news sites. The Rafters' arrival was still making headlines. They were running an interview a day with each of the arrivals. The story of their crossing, how bad the Raft had got, the boat, the desert, their bravery, Amalyn.

Amalyn.

They described the others. Bex, who had died in a sandstorm. Vern, who had refused to drink water. Obey, who had helped the rescuers distribute water, then carried the little girl and an adult the final few kilometres. He'd then gone back to drag and carry the final stragglers. He'd died right at the entrance, giving in to exhaustion as soon as everyone was through. Such courage and sadness made my hairs stand on end. Amalyn had found true kin. The Golden Fifty were brave in ways I couldn't imagine. There were so many new arrivals I would have to meet and thank. So many who would want to see how Reya was doing. But not yet. I wasn't ready yet.

'Sav?' Sara's voice broke the silence. Her soft footsteps had crept up on me. 'How are you?'

'Fine, I guess.'

'I figured you'd be here. In the quiet.'

Funny how she knew me better than I knew myself. 'Harvey won, I see.'

'Yeah. Isaac conceded before the vote had even been counted. It was obvious who was going to win.'

'I'm glad.'

'Me too.'

I sipped my tea, more comfortable in silence than in conversation,

'Your friends are on their way from Mars,' she said.

'My friends?'

'The ones from the lab.'

'Oh, Marcus and Mabel. Good. I'm pleased they got out.'

'There's a ship bringing about twenty people, I think. Giao's boyfriend, too. A few Select. They'll be treated the same as everyone else, Harvey says. No Centre, though. Well, no Elite, from what I understand.'

'Good to know.'

'And they're still cut off from the Tunnel's funds. That's not going to change.'

I smiled, relaxing into the gentle sound of her voice. 'Any more gossip?'

'Well,' she grinned. 'Clementine and Jerome seem to be getting on like a house on fire.'

I snorted a laugh.

'She was wondering when to come and see you. Maybe I'll let her know you're up to visitors?'

'Sure. It'll be nice to see her. And Jerome.'

'And Isaac misses you. I think he really is sorry.'

I paused. Isaac. I hadn't missed him. Well, not the latest version of him. 'Where is he?'

'He didn't want a Council position. Harvey offered him one, but I think he's just embarrassed about the whole thing. The power really went to his head, you know?'

'I do.'

'He's working at a nuclear reactor. The one on the east side of the city, if you want to see him. Day shifts. He's home in the evenings, just so you know.'

'Thanks.' I wasn't ready to talk to him. He knew where I was. Why should I make the first move? I had my family.

There was a clumsy silence between us, my mind unable to think of words. Sara knew all I had to say, my face a picture of sorrow.

'You seen your dad?' I eventually asked.

'Nah.' She shrugged. 'I've done okay without him all these years, don't you think?'

I nodded.

'How's Grace, and the baby?'

'They're all great. Really great. Grace always wanted more kids. Ethan loves being a big brother ...' my voice broke, but tears wouldn't come. I had none left. My throat was parched with sadness.

Sara took my hands. I couldn't meet her gaze. 'I'm so sorry, Sav. She really was an inspiration.'

I walked home, refusing the lift Sara had offered me. Solitude was more appealing. I found Reya awake after her nap, Grace still snoozing on the sofa. I picked up the baby, and she sucked her fist, looking at me with those eyes I missed so much. Tucked away, in a box I hadn't opened since we'd arrived, I found that too-tiny T-shirt Amalyn had made when she found out she was pregnant, and dressed Reya in it. It was hideous, an awful faded green colour with a bizarre logo in the corner. I had to laugh. Archie would have loved it.

Grief still came in waves, and at that moment I was floating above it. I couldn't wallow. I had a little girl to raise, a son to be strong for, and a promise to keep. 'Well, young lady, let's get this over with, shall we?'

I'd asked Grace to come with me, but she'd refused. She'd said I should go alone with Reya. To take my time and absorb it all. It was my promise to keep.

It wasn't too far from our place. The Select's quarters had been built close to all the finest things. The corridors were quiet, soft echoes like a gentle wind. Everyone was at work rather than relaxing. Electric bulbs buzzed on as I walked down the tunnel, Reya in my arms, until we came to the two big, ornate doors.

'Which one should we go in first, little Reya? Which one would mummy have liked best?'

She gurgled and followed my gaze.

We waited a while. I needed to find some courage. *Donna's Library* was engraved on one door. That was the one we'd go in first, the one my mum would have loved so much. The pointless works of fiction that nurtured her soul. Sara had said that it's good for the mind. Maybe in there I'd find something to take my pain away. Maybe some words in those pages could put me back together again. I waited so long the lights clicked off and we stood there in the dark.

'Well, Reya. No time like the present, I guess. Let's go see what all the fuss is about.'

I took a breath, found my courage and, in the dark, reached for the handle and went through the door.

A note from Emma

Thank you so much for reading The Final Fifty. I hope you enjoyed it and if you did, please leave a review on Amazon and Goodreads. Reviews are so important for authors, and they help other readers discover books they'll enjoy.

Writing this series has been such a huge part of my life for the past few years and I have been so delighted to share it with you. I hope you have loved these characters as much as I have. I am going to miss them all and the world I have been so immersed in, but it is time to move on. Keep an eye on my website for updates on my next series. www.emmaellisauthor.com. You can also find me on Facebook.

If you are in the mood for some more weird dystopian, check out my other series, the Eyes Forward. This series is set in a world where, thanks to a new drug that restores youth, the global population has skyrocketed and the government goes to increasingly extreme measures to reduce human numbers. This series is packed full of fun characters and some sinister twists!

Subscribers to my website receive a free e-book, Goodbye Flowers. A prequel to the Raft Series, it's set at the time the anchors are destroyed. It gives a little peak into the Raft before it started to drift, and delves deeper into the story of the Poison Maker himself, Peter Melrose.

The Raft is a crazy world I dreamed up whilst I was living among nature, as a full-time nomad exploring the great outdoors. I am originally from the UK but now live nowhere in particular, mostly around mountains and trees. How bland the world would be without nature. The endless grey of the Raft is my worst nightmare! Some readers of the first book in the series, The Poison Maker, have messaged me and told me what the Raft means to them, my own metaphors in these pages often being different to theirs. And that's okay. Our differences add colour to this world. If all our thoughts were the same, the Blue Liberation might as well be in power. What does the Raft mean to you? I'd love to know.

Acknowledgements

The Final Fifty would not be in print without the help of my wonderful betas and critique partners. Thank you to Ansumana, Danica, Emily and Allison. Their time and honest feedback made this book what it is today. Thank you also to my editor Graham Clarke, for being so incredibly thorough.

Thanks especially to my partner, John, for giving me the space and time I need to write, for his support, patience and encouragement.

And thank you, for reading it.

Printed in Great Britain
by Amazon